MW01031134

MY TEARS, MY ONLY BREAD

A Story of Extraordinary Love

The journey continues
Enjoy!
Mary Ellen Feron

MARY ELLEN FERON

MY TEARS, MY ONLY BREAD

SECOND EDITION

About the cover: Croagh Patrick (Saint Patrick's Mountain), County Mayo, Republic of Ireland. Photo ©Mary Zablocki

Publisher's Note: This is a partially fictionalized account of actual events involving historical characters from the author's descendants. A detailed explanation is found in the end pages under the heading, "Non-Fictional Characters Disclaimer."

Cover Design: Elizabeth E. Little, Hyliian Graphics
Interior Formatting: Ellen C. Maze, The Author's Mentor, www.theauthorsmentor.com
Author Website: www.maryferonzablocki.com

ISBN-13: 978-1484973752
ISBN-10: 1484973755
Also available in eBook publication

PRINTED IN THE UNITED STATES OF AMERICA

Note to the reader:

In *My Tears My Only Bread,* the second book in the *Extraordinary Love Trilogy,* the story of Tom and Meg Phalen continues as we encounter them ten years after escaping GlynMor Castle, Meg's family home. At the end of book one of the trilogy, *A Tent For The Sun,* Tom and Meg were beginning life on Achill Island by opening a dairy and had begun their family with the birth of a daughter, Rose.

Lord Jeffrey Wynn had violently imprisoned his daughter upon learning of her relationship with Tom Phalen, his head groom. Lord Wynn had been seriously injured in an accident the same night Tom and Meg escaped along with her maid, Maureen. They now rest in the uneasy security of knowing he would not be likely to hunt them down.

Book two opens with Tom and Meg well established in their trade. They have prospered on Achill Island and their family has grown to include several children. As the story opens, we meet a family living in comfort; secure in their station and seemingly typical in every way.

My Tears My Only Bread begins with Tom and Meg reaping the fruits of their hard work and perseverance. However, despite the Phalens' success, integration into the island culture has proven difficult. The townspeople of Doeega have never truly accepted Meg's aristocratic birth and Tom's marriage "above his station". They are often the topic of gossip especially among the women led by Lizzie Ballard. For friendship, Tom and Meg have relied on both Maureen and Duffy McGee, the proprietor of Browne's Inn on the mainland across Clew Bay.

The Phalen children enjoy the usual rivalries and affections as Meg awaits the imminent arrival of her seventh child. The most immediate crisis is one of schoolyard taunting and the stubborn rebelliousness of Tom and Meg's older son, Denny.

In *My Tears My Only Bread,* new characters and terms abound. The glossary found at the end of *A Tent For The Sun* is repeated at the end of *My Tears My Only Bread* to clarify some of the unfamiliar words.

Some of the characters we met in *A Tent For The Sun* return to us and some have gone to America. For those who remain, life moves on season to season, sowing and harvesting, in the ebb and flow of years, sustained by land and sea.

Things, however are about to change. In the early autumn of 1845, the potato crop fails to yield even one field of the life giving food of the peasantry. Tom and Meg's life will not go unscathed by this devastation.

My Tears My Only Bread is the story of how this little family, so normal and happy on the surface, find themselves embroiled in the agony of merely staying alive. They fare better than most, but not necessarily due to the selling of milk. Hidden beneath the bucolic image of cows in the byre and milk on the table is a deep undercurrent of anguish as Tom Phalen grapples with a compromise of his soul. Meg manages to keep her family intact until she faces a crisis of faith that could put all of their lives in jeopardy.

The love and devotion Meg and Tom hold for each other, so strengthened by the events of *A Tent For The Sun,* is as full and strong as ever and the challenges they are about to face during the lean years of the Great Irish Potato Famine will be met head on by this remarkable couple, the way they have done everything up until this point: together, with grace and faith in God and each other.

A Tent for the Sun (February 2013):
My Tears, My Only Bread (April 2013)
White Dawn Rising (expected May 2013)

Dedication

Helen Casey Zimmer, my Grammie;
from beginning to end, this is for you.

Acknowledgements:

I wish, with a full heart, to acknowledge all those who made this book possible.

First, and without a doubt, foremost, my beloved husband and long-standing supporter, Ed. Without you, I would never have been able to write a single word. Ever since you put my very first essay in the mail, when I was too shy to do so myself, I have trusted your advice and relied on your support. Thank you. I love you.

Secondly, my sons, Francis and Paul whose personalities and traits, experiences and journeys are infused into some of my characters in ways so intimate and complex that only I, as your mother, can tell. You both are so very precious to me.

I need to say thank you to many friends, who over the years of writing, listened and supported my work. Thank you to the first reader of my first chapter, Meg Stoll; my colleagues in the Labor and Delivery Unit at Sisters of Charity Hospital, who allowed me to read a chapter to them one slow evening and offered some of the most solid encouragement I ever received and didn't take: the suggestion that I quit nursing and just write. I cannot number the times I remembered that advice during the course of this creation. Even before that, I thank my fellow nursing students at Sisters of Charity School of Nursing for appointing me editor of our senior yearbook and giving me the opportunity to hone my skills. I want to thank Tim Denesha, dear Old Bud that he is, forever so gently nudging me throughout the years, sharing his own wonderful stories and poetry, always turning me forward; always believing.

I must credit the leaders of the many writers groups I worked with: Tom O'Malley of Canisius College in Buffalo, New

York; Kathryn Radeff of the Just Buffalo literary group; my dear friends and fellow writers, Dianne Riordan, Patty McClain and the late Grace McMeneme. I learned so much, writing with you. Dianne, you have been beyond supportive and I am so grateful.

I chose certain individuals to read my manuscript with the clear goal of editing and winnowing, correcting and critiquing. I thank my friend, Ann Szumski for starting me off on the right path; Karol Morton, a writer herself, who read the book with a red pen. I thank her for her honesty and holding me to the integrity of the story; Bev Malona and my mother, Joan Feron read the manuscript before it was finished and lovingly badgered me to keep writing once they had reached the end of the pages; my friends Lynne Dulak and Elise Seggau, former editor of "The Cord" at St. Bonaventure University; my sisters, especially Kate who many times kept me from burning my computer my nieces; my cousin Kathy and my daughters-in-law who read the first printed draft and offered such positive response that I persevered in the final push to publish. I particularly wish to thank my male readers, especially my uncle, David Zimmer, whose suggestion to publish the book as a trilogy was the advice that provided the missing piece to the publishing puzzle.

There are many others to thank. Many of these are people I know only slightly or have never met. Thanks go to Allen Abel for his wonderful article in Sports Illustrated which gave me Dan Donnelly's arm and Lane Stewart whose photographs for that article haunted my dreams. It was a high point in my research to speak with Irish writer and former editor at the Evening Herald in Dublin, Patrick Myler who was interviewed for the SI article. His article on Dan Donnelly (The Ring, May, 1998) was kindly sent to me by the author himself to help me include old Dan in my novel. Dan's arm can be found in the third book of the trilogy as a bit of comic distraction in the midst of the potato famine.

I have been writing since I was a child. There is one person without whom the dream would have died on the vine. She deserves a special acknowledgement. When I first began to test my wings and seriously put pen to paper, Sr. Mary Matthias SSJ, now known as Sr. Joan Wagner, believed in me when no one else did. She took a dejected Freshman and calmly, sweetly planted the seed of confidence that has finally bloomed in this work. Sr. Joan, I thank you from the bottom of my heart. You taught me to believe in myself and never let go of the dream. Rich lessons indeed.

My tears have become my bread,
By night, by day,
As I hear it said all the day long:
"Where is your God?"
Psalm 42:3

CUSHING FAMILY TREE

Lord Bentley Cushing b.1768 d. 1820
1787 m.
Lady Eleanor Mcintosh b. 1769 d. 1835

Beverly b. 1788
1806 m.
Jeffrey Wynn

Robert b. 1793
1815 m.
Adelaide Dubois b.1799, d.1820

Madellaine b. 1820, d.1820

WYNN FAMILY TREE

Lord Henry Wynn b. 1735, d.1820
1767 m.
Lady Rose Carver b. 1750, d. 1815

John b. 1768, Willard b. 1770, Gerald b. 1781 d.1781, Jeffrey b. 1784
1806 m.
Beverly Cushing

Margaret b.1808

MEAHRA FAMILY TREE

Seamus Meahra b. 1743 d.1808,
1765 m.
Monica Shea b.1748, d.1795

Sean b. 1767 d. 1808, Daniel b.1768 d.1809, Terrence b. 1772 d.1834

Clare b.1774 d.1808,
1792 m.
Thomas Phalen

PHALEN FAMILY TREE

Thomas Phalen b.1772
1792 m.
Clare Maehra

David b. 1794
1811m.
Molly Quinn

Paul b. 1796
1816 m.
Anna Dunleavy

Thomas b. 1796
1835 m.
Margaret Wynn

Francis b.1808, d.1808

Table of Contents

Chapter One

May, 1845

"Danny O'Dowda and Billy Feeney, ye're the meanest, filthiest, evilest blackguards on this island!" screamed ten year old Rose Phalen as she slammed the gate behind her house on the beach. She whipped a rock in the direction of the fleeing boys and stamped her foot as it plopped a full yard behind them.

"And I curse ye' t'the little people!" she cried at the two skinny backs as the boys scampered off toward the town of Doeega.

Meg and Tom both came running at the commotion.

"What d'ye think yer doin' with this shameful bellowin'?"

Tom dropped a pile of rocks he was using to mend the fence around the front yard. He grabbed his eldest daughter by the arm matching her fury with his own.

"Haven't ye been raised t'be a lady and here ye're hollerin' like a fishwife!"

Meg, panting, rounded the corner of the house. She was

weeks overdue for her seventh baby and moving quickly took its toll on her. Behind her toddled two little girls and three geese chased by two older boys waving sticks.

Standing at the gate, was a girl a few years younger than Rose. Her black curls hung across her face hiding a quivering chin and tear-stained cheeks. Meg looked from Rose to the younger child and back to Rose.

"What happened, Mary Clare?" she asked, unable to keep the weariness out of her voice.

Everything was a crisis with Mary Clare and Rose had made her sister's well-being a personal crusade. Tom and Meg had exhausted themselves trying to break the cycle of Mary Clare playing the victim and Rose rallying to her defense. Rose was a fierce defender, far more likely to blacken the eye of a village boy than either of her brothers.

"Da, they threw turds at us and called me a sassy fanny. And they called Mary Clare a dumb omethon."

Rose struggled against Tom's grip and when she realized he wasn't going to let go of her arm, stuck out her lip defiantly.

"They threw turds at ye? I don't think so Rosie!" piped up Denny from the yard as five year old Thomas mimed being pelted with imaginary turds.

"That they did, Denny Phalen, and some lazy brother ye are t'be home playin' instead of walkin' yer sisters home from the hedgerow. Ye should ha'been there t'belt that miserable Danny O'Dowda! A fine one ye are!"

Rose stuck her tongue out at her nine-year old brother.

"Now, Rose there will be none of that. Ye' can't be blamin' yer brother fer the likes of Danny O''Dowda. Yer mam told him to take charge of Thomas and that he did. Ye can't seem to walk outside this gate without running into a boyo willing to pick a fight with ye so yer goin' to have to learn t'defend yerself, girl."

Tom released her with a playful spank and went back to mending the fence.

Meg was consoling Mary Clare, wiping her tears with the corner of her apron as Rose came up behind her.

"Mam! What am I to do? Peaches is so skinny and small we have to walk like old ladies and then we git behind the others and th'mean boys jist wait fer us behind the hedgerow. And they did throw turds at us, stinkin' dried up goose turds!"

This brought a new flurry of feathers and honking as Denny and Thomas began chasing the geese around the yard pretending to pick up droppings as they ran.

"Boys! Go and see if Finn needs help with the chores and wash up for supper."

"Denny, you need to finish shoveling that compost," Meg scolded as she led Mary Clare to the wicker chair by the front door.

"Rose, go in and stir the soup. And check that bread pudding but don't try to handle it. Just call me if it's ready."

"Mam, I know how to take things out o'the tin oven. I do!"

She stamped her foot as her mother shook her head.

Meg straightened up wearily. This baby exhausted her like none of the others had and it wasn't even born yet. She was huge and by her figuring very late. The others, after the terrible ordeal of delivering Rose, had seemed easy. She didn't even make it indoors for Denny, having him in the yard with a gush of water and only one bad cramp. Oh how Maureen had shrieked when she saw the little head right there. Denny had come so fast that all her friend could do was catch him and wrap him in her apron until Tom came running. She shook her head as she turned to go in the house. How she missed Maureen. It had been six years since she left for America and Meg still missed her every day.

Denny had been a different kind of child right from the start. He was difficult about everything, contrary to the point of exasperation. She saw traits of her father in him, the only one of hers who seemed to carry them. She didn't like it but there it was. Sometimes a look of consummate selfishness would pass across his face and he had a mean streak in him that no amount of whipping would remove. But Tom was determined to break him of the taunting and slapping and bullying of his sisters and even the animals. Tom, usually so level-headed, would fly into a rage at his antics. Denny had been sent home from the hedge school many times with a note from Mr. Mulcahy that he had been impudent or brutish toward him or a visiting scholar. Tom, who had almost no book learning at all, revered Mr. Mulcahy and tolerated no nonsense in matters of scholarship. Tom could read and write when he married Meg but the old teacher had opened his mind to the classics and helped him immensely in managing the dairy. Why, if not for Mr. Mulcahy, Tom would never be able to keep his own books and figure his profits.

When Denny stepped over the line of Tom's strict discipline, there was a stark march to the stone shed where the strong birch switch hung over the door. Meg hated that form of discipline but Tom would hear none of her entreaties. He was the man of the house and Denny was not going to defy him. Almost weekly, Denny would return from the shed, holding his trousers up with one hand, hiding his face in shame. He would painfully climb to the loft where he would be banished in silence until morning when Tom would offer him another chance, a new day filled with opportunities to redeem himself.

Today was one of those days when Denny was walking the line very closely and Tom had had enough of his sassy gob. Tom was worried about Meg, and Denny had been tormenting his little sisters all week, dragging Thomas along as his accomplice. That, combined with the frustration of trying to fix the fence with stones too small for the job, had put him in a terrible temper. The chickens were all over him, wandering through the hole in the fence, pecking and dropping turds of their own all over his brogans and tools. Now, Danny O'Dowda had been after his girls again.

As he shooed yet another chicken back into the yard, Mary Grace came running around the corner of the house and tripped, landing in a pile of compost he had asked Denny to spread on his mother's vegetable garden. Of course, it was Denny who chased her, Denny who had left the shovel across the compost pile that should never have been in Mary Clare's path and Denny who now stood laughing at his sister covered in fish skins, old potato rinds and swill. Mary Grace ran bellowing to her mother and Tom seized Denny by the collar.

"Ye're comin' with me, ye spalpeen!"

Into the shed they went and out over the strand anyone listening knew that Denny Phalen was about to get his fanny properly stung by the big birch switch from over the door.

Thus it was that amidst the wails of protest offered by the boy and the stern threat of being "worn out so ye'll never sit again", proffered by the man, Rose interrupted the ritual with one long scream from the kitchen.

Tom dropped the switch and ran to the house leaving Denny to heist his pants up and make haste to start shoveling the compost. Tom almost collided with Meg in the doorway as she burst onto the stoop with Rose in tow. She plunged Rose's hand into the bucket of cool seawater she'd been rinsing mussels in. Rose's sobbing slowed down to an occasional gulp as Meg explained to Tom that there would be no bread pudding for their dessert tonight. He went into the house and cleaned up the overturned pan of his favorite dessert from the stone floor. He could hear Meg half scolding, half comforting Rose as he carried the sloppy mess to the pigpen.

Dinner that night was a quiet affair. Denny, his reprieve secured, offered to wash the dishes and pans for Rose now that her hand was too tender to do it. Rose, her burned hand smarting with every move, gratefully accepted the offer. Tom sulked over the loss of his pudding while the younger children ate quietly and obediently went to bed.

As he drifted off to sleep, Tom thought seven children was plenty and promised himself that after this baby he'd exercise more restraint and stop pestering his pretty wife. As the moon cast lacy shadows across their bedroom floor, both he and Meg fell into an exhausted and well-earned sleep.

The next day dawned gray and threatening. Francis Martin Phalen was born May 31, 1845, without complication, shortly after Meg finished the breakfast dishes. Her pains had started around dawn and she had woken Tom around seven to get the older children off to the hedge school and take the babies to a neighbor. By the time Tom had summoned Mary Feeney to help with the birth, Meg was minutes away from delivering her son.

Mary emerged from the bedroom carrying a bundle of soiled bedding. Tom poured her a cup of tea and offered her a buttered slice of yesterday's bread. Sipping her tea, Mary looked out toward the water. Tom watched as she nibbled the bread and set the empty cup on the table.

As he counted out three coins into her hand, he toyed with the thought of speaking to Mary about Billy's antics with the goose turds but the sight of her tired, sad face at the door left him unable to bring it up. Mary Feeney had lost her husband and her eldest son years ago in a freak storm not unlike the one that caught Tom at sea a decade ago. She had been drawn and distracted since but still acted as the village midwife to feed her four other children and her dead sister's son, Andrew when he drifted into town. The job was anything but steady and Mary barely made the rent and put food on the table. Her young sons ran amok in the village and caused trouble wherever they went. Cora Foy had taken Mary on as an assistant in her store, and when she died in her sleep last May, Mary had taken on the running of both the store and the post office.

The store now fed her children but the boys needed the strong hand of a father to keep them in line. Her nephew Andrew had been brought to Mary from around Castlebar as a young boy when her sister was dying of consumption. She had taken him in and her husband had been like a father to him until he died. Mike Feeney had insisted that Andrew take his name and had worked hard to make a man out of the rebellious youth. He had even inquired up at St. Dymphna's about Andrew training for the priesthood.

Now, the lad was beyond schooling and should have been a big help to Mary but Andrew went wild after Mike Feeney drowned, leaving Doeega for long stretches of time and returning with shady companions full of dark politics and rebellious ideas. Billy and his younger brother John couldn't wait to follow in his footsteps and practiced their own form of terrorism by bullying both the young and the old. If it weren't for Peter, Mary's second oldest, the store would have closed.

Mary, fun-loving and pretty when her husband was alive, now drifted through her days, vague and dreamy, relying entirely on her sixteen-year-old son to handle the hard work and the customers. When she was called upon to assist in deliveries, she fell back on her excellent training. Cora Foy had done her job well and despite her difficulties, Mary Feeney was still regarded as the best midwife from Doeega to Achill Sound.

As he watched the midwife trudge into the misty, grey morning, Tom shook his head and thought how lucky he was to have Meg as his children's mother. She was that rare combination of strength and tenderness he remembered of his own mam. Watching her corral her brood for meals or church was like witnessing a dance. There was a grace in her movement and a steady calmness in her voice that made him think of the sea lapping gently against the strand, forming and sculpting, ever faithful, always present.

He felt for Mary Feeney. Tom knew he would be lost without Meg just as he had been lost for so many years without his mam. Mary couldn't help herself. Mike had been her balance wheel and her eldest son, her heart's greatest joy. Now, turning away from the weary little figure ambling across the strand, Tom hastened to see his new son and hold in his arms another priceless gift from Meg.

The summer of 1845 brought a great deal of rain and the typical hunger of the season was punctuated by the dreary weather. The people of Achill needed good weather to find enough food to survive until the potatoes were ready for harvest. The barley and wheat crops were never for them and they were used to working up in the hills under the scorching sun to harvest the cash crops that paid their rent.

Most of the younger villagers lived, all summer, in the little stone boolies that dotted the foothills of Croaghaun Mountain. After the sowing came the fish harvest. The bursting nets and traps of the fishermen paid the rent with the bounty of the sea but often the day-to-day survival of the families who harvested the bulging nets and dripping eeltraps depended on life-threatening, late night poaching. Many a fishwife silently smoked or salted illegally speared salmon and cod to serve with tatties and bread for dinner. Salmon spearing had been illegal since the 18th. century but everyone knew at least one fisherman who defied the law.

The beaches and streams of Achill were even more remote than the mainland but there was always the danger that Lord Lucan's agents might be lurking around the next bluff. Tom Phalen was one of them. But not one Achill poacher had to worry about Tom Phalen. He had never counted the number of salmon in the sea and he had no intention of knowing if one was missing. However, despite his deep hatred for the system that had enslaved and murdered his forebears, Tom was now a member of the "other".

The sun finally came out one day in mid-August. Tom was in Newport delivering the rent, and Meg, eager to enjoy the weather, bundled up her babies and walked to the post office at Feeney's Mercantile. She needed a few things and was long overdue for a letter from Maureen. She had left Rose and Denny to mind Mary Clare and Thomas. Duffy had brought them all a lovely wooden puzzle the last time he had been over and they were head to head on the kitchen floor piecing it together when she left. Approaching the outskirts of the village, Meg thought of the changes she had witnessed since moving to Achill ten years ago. Her mind wandered all the way back to the beginning when they first pulled ashore and took their first steps across the strand to the bright green door of their new home.

In 1835 when they moved into the little stone house on the beach, the town was bustling. Seven new babies had been born to the village, two new families had moved in and a new priest had come to St. Dymphna's Catholic church. Fr. O'Boyle, a stout energetic Franciscan, had arrived from Newport that July, just in time to baptize little Rose Phalen.The first spring after Rose was born, the landlord, Lord Lucan, had sent his nephew, the Rev. Harold Chisholm, to congratulate the residents of Achill on their industrious hard work and the timely fulfillment of their rent payments. His visit to Dooega was big news and the residents held a town meeting to hear what he had to say. Meg had not attended but she still remembered Tom's flushed cheeks and bright eyes when he returned.

"Meg, I'm thinkin' we can make a life here," he had said. "From what the good reverend said, Lord Lucan is that pleased with Dooega. I spoke to Rev. Chisholm meself after the meetin' and he was that impressed with me. He's comin' out here tomorrow before he leaves for Dooagh."

The Rev. Chisholm had indeed come out to the Phalen house. He looked around at the tidy house, the budding flower garden and the delicate lace curtain in the kitchen window. Clearly, this was not a typical Achill house and clearly the aristocratic bearing of the lady of the house was the reason for the difference. Rev. Chisholm took notes on what he saw and enjoyed a fine cup of tea served by a handsome hired girl. The reverend left, apparently pleased and well impressed by the Phalens and their servant. Imagine, having a servant girl in a place like Dooega! He would have to remember this place for a special rcport to his uncle.

The following fall, Tom had been summoned to Newport to meet with Lord Lucan's undertaker, another nephew by marriage, Mr. Robert Gilchrist, of the Scottish Gilchrists. As undertaker, Mr. Gilchrist had been instructed by Lord Lucan to take seized lands from the Irish and install English or Scottish landowners in their place.

Lucan had for some time been badgering his nephew Harold to find someone on Achill to fill the role of rental agent. He was wary of the fishermen and felt they needed closer watching than he was able to give them from his estate outside of Castlebar. It was common knowledge that Lord Lucan was not fond of his other nephew but Robert Gilchrist resided in Newport and was in a better position to keep an eye on Lord Lucan's more far flung holdings.

Gilchrist was his wife's nephew by marriage and had been a nasty, sneaky little worm since he was a boy. He had however, seemed very impressed by his cousin Harold's report on Tom Phalen's prosperity. When Harold's duties to his parish made it impossible for him to spend sufficient time on the island Lord Lucan gave the job of undertaker over Achill to Robert. Harold Chisholm had strongly recommended after his visit to Dooega that his cousin reconsider displacing any of the villagers and give this Phalen a chance to manage his uncle's affairs.

Meg remembered well Tom's vivid descriptions of his experiences on that trip. Tom and Mr. Gilchrist were to meet in the drawing room of Mr. Gilchrist's own home on Dublin St. facing Newport Bay. The house itself was a grand Tudor on a corner lot with a high stone arch dominating the front entrance. There were extensive gardens wrapping around the entire property with low honeysuckle hedges on the Dublin Street side and more formal rose gardens within. As he approached the grand walkway, Tom imagined the view from the upper windows overlooking the sweet-scented pink honeysuckle with the vast blue of Newport Bay in the background. The long walk was brick, rare in Ireland, and intricately designed in a pattern of fleur de lis, of all things. This amazing path was edged in tidy boxwood squares filled with full, mounded blossoms of delicate pansies and petunias soaking up the warm afternoon sun. These were set off by tall, whimsically carved topiaries giving evidence of a woman's taste and direction.

Window boxes graced the casement windows and huge arrays of flowering herbs and tumbling sweet peas bobbed in the breeze as heavy stone urns filled with white geraniums stood like sentries on either side of the massive oak door. Tom noted a tall border of privet hedges along the side yard affording deep shaded privacy. Several small children romped and chased a ball around the grass while their nurses kept watchful eyes on them. Tom counted at least two gardeners trimming and fussing with the hedges and another three taking care of the roses and topiaries. The very rich could afford anything, he thought shaking his head. He knew better than to approach the house from the front door and shuddered as he remembered picking himself up off the ground outside the last oak door he had encountered. He did not look forward to this meeting and could not stop the trickles of sweat that crept across his scalp and threatened to soak his thick, black hair.

The walk from the pier was had been long and hot, Tom's good wool suit itching him like a pox. Meg had insisted he buy the suit for this interview and had made him a fine linen shirt to wear with it. Duffy had given him a handsome cravat that had been left behind by a wealthy patron of the inn and loaned him a pair of good shoes given to him as cast-offs of Lord Sligo's son. The shoes pinched mercilessly and Tom could not believe there really was a man born with feet so small. When he had arrived at the Newport pier Tom had felt refreshed by the sea breeze and despite his burning feet, thought he cut a solid figure in his finery. But after trudging a mile uptown through streets filled with animal droppings and the leavings of hucksters and hawkers, he not only knew he should use the servants entrance, he knew he must look the part.

He had told Meg how he had stood before this bastion of good taste and prosperity, and how he had felt like a schoolboy in his tweed and linen outfit. One of the gardeners approached with a quizzical look on his face.

"May, I 'elp ye, Gov?" he asked as he wiped the sweat from his own face.

"Aye," Tom answered taking off his hat. "I'd be needin' the back entrance if ye please."

The gardener looked him up and down and a smirk slowly crept across his face.

"Sooo, ye must be the bloke Miss Fanny Carlisle keeps

braggin' about, eh? Nice lookin' enough fer the likes o'er I'd say, but a bit stiff in yer duds fer courtin' the cook, ain't ye?"

Tom felt himself flush from his collar to his brow.

"If ye please, I'm here to see Mr. Gilchrist," Tom said, drawing himself up to his full height.

The smirk melted off the gardener's face, replaced immediately by a look both suspicious and wary.

"Beggin' yer pardon, Gov," he said bobbing a bit and removing his own tweed cap. "No offense meant, I'm sure, Gov, an honest mistake an'all."

"None taken. Now if ye'll just show me…"

"Not atall, not atall, Gov. If Mr. Gilchrist himself summoned ye, it's the front door fer ye it is!"

The man was at the door and had pulled the bell rope before Tom could utter another word. He was sweating in earnest now, both from the warm day and from the horrible feeling of being in a place so far above his station. The gardener was talking now to a butler who could have been Stiller's brother. All of a sudden Tom wanted to laugh. Were they all cut from the same cloth? How did they get those chins; that ramrod up their backsides? Were they born like that? He watched the interchange between the two men and imagined the butler as a baby, popping out of his mother in full livery, toddling across the floor to fix tea.

Tom fought to compose himself as the house servant dismissed the gardener with a wave and turned to him. The gardener tipped his cap in Tom's direction as he hastened back to his chores.

The grey, lashless eyes of the butler bore down on Tom as he stood like a large, upended fish waiting for Tom to enter the cavernous foyer. Without a word, Tom was ushered into a large drawing room. The butler nodded for him to wait and silently backed into the foyer, pulling the twin mahogany doors closed.

Tom could hardly bear being there, surrounded by richly carved paneling and huge gilt frames filled with Gilchrist ancestral portraits. He was made to stand alone for an hour, his cap in his hand, while scornful and pampered faces bore down on him. The last time he had been in a room like this was the night he was bodily forced to leave Meg, beaten and cowering, in the hands of her father.

At first the cool dark room was a relief after the warm trek from the pier but after shivering in the chilly vault for an hour, his knees were becoming stiff. Dainty, gilt chairs lined the long walls on either side of a huge, carved mantel housing a deep fireplace. The sooty black cavern lay silent and empty beyond two heavy, black andirons that stood like sentries on either side. He thought about sitting on one of the gilt chairs but he decided not to, afraid it would collapse beneath his weight. He wondered who sat in chairs like that. Ladies, he supposed, waiting for a gentleman to approach.

Rich oriental carpets of varying sizes and patterns lay scattered on a parquet floor shining gloriously in the sun. Several deep burgundy leather chairs were nestled in groups of three or four, positioned for private conversation. Tom noted the fine crystal glasses and full decanters set out on delicately crafted tables, awaiting the fine manicured hands of Mr. Gilchrist's guests.

Highly polished candelabra adorned two long mahogany sideboards ready for the next evening soiree. There was no mistaking the prominent place of the masculine furniture and the relegation of the ladies to the periphery of the room. The club chairs looked wonderfully comfortable. Tom had never sat in a chair so large with cushions so thick and plump. He walked over to the nearest grouping and ran his hand over the cool russet leather. He fingered the knobby hobnails and traced the outline of the fat sturdy arm beneath his hand.

Meg smiled as she recalled how Tom's whole body became animated when he told her what had happened next.

Before he could stop himself, he had eased himself into the depths of the chair. The comfort he felt as the smooth leather swallowed him whole was indescribable. Even his bed at home didn't caress his body like the fine supple contours of this throne. Oh, he could get used to this. Never mind parking his hind end in a wicker hearth chair or on one of those miserable creepies again.

Closing his eyes, he had imagined himself being carried through town in one of these, four strapping men bearing him like a king. He thought of the look on Lizzie Ballard's face and a chuckle had formed deep in his throat. Before it could take form, Tom heard the sound of the latch releasing on the heavy drawing room door. He bolted from the chair, almost upsetting a decanter full of sherry and a tray of fine cut crystal glasses. In a split second, he was standing a foot away from the scene of his crime and the stiff, anemic butler was summoning him into to Mr. Gilchrist's office. If the old servant was aware of Tom's transgression, he had never let on. As he followed doggedly behind the man, Tom hadn't known whether to laugh or cry. Instead, he simply let out a long sigh of relief and smiled to himself at the knowledge that his posterior had been where Lizzie Ballard's would never dream of perching.

The undertaker sat behind a huge mahogany desk with still more ancestors glaring down from the silk covered walls. At the sight of the imperious little man, Tom immediately sobered up. Mr. Gilchrist enquired about Tom's ownership of the house and ten acres of land around it. Tom showed Gilchrist the deed, which he gave a cursory glance. When the man failed to return the deed, Tom withdrew his outstretched hand. Mr. Gilchrist's message was clear. Tom Phalen could stay on the land. He could establish a dairy and even rent fishing rights to the locals but he would be acting as an agent of Lord Lucan, required to collect rents and oversee the well-being of Lord Lucan's holdings in the village of Doeega and the surrounding townlands. He would not be titled, of course, being from obvious low birth but Lord Lucan was willing to overlook that on a trial basis of three years. If at the end of three years, Thomas Phalen had demonstrated sound capability and loyal service to Lord Lucan, consideration would be made to establishing a land grant free and clear. Until then, Mr. Robert Gilchrist would accept retention of the deed as a sign of Mr. Phalen's good faith.

The interview had ended with Tom standing alone again in the middle of the cold drawing room with Mr. Robert Gilchrist's parting words drumming in his head.

"Of course, Mr. Phalen, if, in the event that you fail to demonstrate to my Lord, the Earl of Lucan, that you are both capable and loyal, you and your family will be expelled. Good day to you, sir."

Again, the fish-faced butler approached. As he glanced at the bloodless face this time, there was no amusement and not a thread of pride in Tom's heart. He simply passed the man and emerged into the sunlight, glad to be standing on the free side of the door. It wasn't until he had registered at the local inn, imbibed heartily of a fine trout stew and stout and fired up a pipe that Tom allowed himself to acknowledge the heartbreaking truth about his fine wool suit and his borrowed silk cravat. The bitterest gall was the lingering memory of his few seconds of comfort in the finest chair he had ever seen.

Despite the funny way Tom had told his story, Meg frowned at his clownish portrayal of his humiliation. She pensively walked along the side of the road steering the girls around puddles and mud while balancing Francis on her arm. Her thoughts were interrupted when Francis began to fuss. Meg stopped in the shade of a tall hedgerow and sat down with her little girls to rest and feed her son. The grass was soft and green after all the rain but the warm day had dried it enough to sit on. Three-year-old Gracie nibbled on a little piece of buttered soda bread while Meg cradled Ellen in front of her, wrapping her legs around the busy toddler. Hot and tired from their walk, Ellen was content to lean back against her mother and suck her thumb.

Meg inhaled the deep sweet fragrance of thousands of wild roses that hung in profusion as far as she could see along the road. The tiny pink blossoms filled the air with a heady perfume that was a welcome relief from the unpleasant road smells of manure and turf smoke. She leaned against the bristly twigs that entwined around each other forming a wall that had stood through great tempests and fine evenings for hundreds of years. Her thoughts drifted back to Tom and his position as rental agent in Doeega.

Since that first visit to Newport, Tom had returned every spring and fall with the rent money. Meg remembered how dark Tom's face was as he climbed out of Duffy McGee's curragh when he arrived home that first time. She also remembered how scarlet his cheeks became as he roared out his fury. He was simply livid, castigating himself, humiliated by his own good will. He had been a fool, a child, naïve and trusting to the extreme.

Of course the slimy bastard dismissed Tom's rightful ownership of this land! Why should he regard Tom Phalen as anything but a tattie hokin' boob when he was the biggest toad in his cool brick pond up on Dublin Street! How could Tom have forgotten the curdled milk that ran in the veins of men like Gilchrist? How had he dismissed Lord Jeffrey and his ilk from his memory? Living on this island, content and at peace, had lulled him into forgetting the evil that controlled all of his countrymen even to the far reaches of the strands and crags of the most remote western shores!

He raged on, pacing the beach, venting to Duffy McGee and the gannets circling overhead. Meg and Maureen had listened silently as they went about their chores. The children and the few villagers on the strand stood back as Tom shook his fist at heaven and cursed the likes of wealthy men everywhere.

In the end, he became the agent of Lord Lucan. Like his granda before him he knew the bitter price of a warm hearth and enough to eat. And, like his granda before him he knew how quickly it could be taken away, turned to rubble on a whim, the example to others of the fickle nature of a freedom based on lies.

In the public house and tannery, smithy and street sweeper alike hushed their talk when the big man from out Lough Cullin way stopped in for a pint or a bundle of scrap leather. The fishermen proved to be the most stubborn of the lot. By nature, men who enjoyed the freedom of the open sea, they resented this intruder from the mainland. They hadn't trusted him from the start, many of them believing he staged his dramatic emergence from the sea.

These were men who knew a man could not survive a storm like the one that had raged that night. Over many a pipe and pint, they shook their grizzled heads and voiced their doubts. But they could not deny his fairness and his willingness to employ everything from barter to services in kind to collect the rents and keep Lord Lucan happy.

They could not, would not accuse Tom Phalen of meanness or greed. To the contrary, he was the fairest and most generous of men. But still, he had married up and he was in with Lord Lucan and look how he lived way out on the strand and kept his distance from the clachan. Seldom joining in the nightly singing and dancing of the clan members of Doeega, the Phalens preferred to spend their evenings at home, quiet and studious. This earned them snorts of indignation from the likes of Lizzie Ballard, bringing reproach from Mary Feeney who seemed to have a thing for Meg Phalen.

The women of Doeega scoffed at Mary's loyalty and defense of Herself, the Grand Lady Meg. Tom Phalen was no different from all the rest of the Irish who took advantage of a good thing and thought their shite was sweeter than that of good hardworking members of the clachan. He and his high-born wife did join in the festivals and parish affairs at St. Dymphna's but they never quite crossed the invisible line that the natives had written in the sand. The bizarre and frightening specter of Tom washed up on the beach ten years ago still evoked awe in the hearts of children but more often brought howls of laughter as Charlie O'Malley imitated Tom dragging himself along the beach with a piece of curragh stuck to his arm.

Tom pretended he knew nothing of these goings on but he did and he was hurt by the snubs of men he considered just like him. He had never put on airs, though, thanks to Meg and

Mulcahy, the hedgemaster, he could read and write and do sums. He was trying to make a life for himself and his family and knew how much Meg had sacrificed to marry him and have his children. If he had to swallow his pride and endure the stony silence and thick white pipe smoke that greeted him at the pub, then, for her, he would. He missed Da fiercely. Their easy, relaxed evenings at McPhinney's seemed as though from another life. He had never been a very needy man and other than old Ben had had few comrades. But it still hurt to be so obviously ignored by the boyos when he had never forgotten what side of the bog he was from.

Despite the slights of the villagers, those first three years had served them all well and Tom's next meeting with Mr. Gilchrist had brought stiff, miserly compliments and an insincere vote of confidence in Tom's good work. There was, of course, no further mention of a land grant. To no one's surprise, Tom was simply returned to his home bearing the news that the rents, having been met, were now raised and the next three years would be critical to the future of Tom and his fellow island dwellers.

On this warm, breezy July morning, ten years later, Meg thought the village had declined. No one new had moved to Doeega and while many new babies had been born, many of the young had left for greener pastures and a more fulfilling life off the island. The population had actually declined due to a bad winter the previous year when several adults and children had died of the black diphtheria. She thought ruefully that she was doing all she could to populate her village. In fact, at that particular moment, she had no intention of doing anything further to help the cause.

Francis had fallen asleep and Ellen dreamily wound her hair around her fingers and dozed in Meg's lap. Gracie seemed content to putter around the hedgerow, gathering stones and twigs, pretending she was serving a meal on a large flat rock. Meg never worried about Gracie. She was a good little girl, temperamentally much like Mary Clare. There was no one she would rather be with than Meg and she rarely left her mother's side.

Meg herself sat in dreamy contentment. Somewhere in the background bees droned about their work and the scent of the roses worked like a sedative on her senses. Her heart, at the thought of Tom's many sacrifices, burned with ardor for him. Days like this made her remember why she loved him and brought a smile to her face.

Meg couldn't believe how the years had flown. She knew the terrible sacrifice Tom had made for her and their children when he agreed to become the very thing he hated most in an Irishman. For this, Meg had decided early on to deny him nothing. He would have all of her love, as many children as she could bear him and the best home she could make for him. He had run the gauntlet for her and she loved him more every day.

There were times when she felt she could not stew one more cabbage or wash one more child or lay beneath Tom one more time. It was then she would remember his first meeting with Mr. Gilchrist almost ten years ago, and his face as he climbed out of the curragh onto the sand on his return. Seeing the pain and anguish again in her mind's eye made anything he asked seem small by comparison. Francis stirred in the warm summer breeze and Meg remembered another baby on another warm breezy day.

It had been a hot Sunday almost four years ago in August, 1841 when Thomas was her baby and Meg's decision to deny Tom nothing was far from her mind as she herded her little brood around the far end of Chilldamhnait Cemetery to church. Tom had hurried on to speak with Fr. O'Boyle before Mass, leaving Meg and the children to follow. Without warning, she was swept with nausea and realized with bone-numbing fatigue that she was with child again. The realization hit her so hard she had had to sit down.

Meg had instructed five-year-old Rose to take Denny and Mary Clare on ahead and find their father. She would follow with Thomas once she'd had a chance to rest.

Denny ran on ahead and Rose corralled Mary Clare who began to howl as soon as she realized Meg was not coming along. As if on cue, Thomas too, began to cry and Meg felt the familiar tingling in her breasts as her milk let down.

Finding a tiny patch of soft green shamrocks between the church and the low stone wall behind it, Meg lowered herself to the ground. Shielded by the church on one side and a tall gravestone on the other, she unbuttoned her bodice. Thomas quickly found her breast and began to guzzle hungrily. He had just had his first birthday and she could not bear to wean him and endure the rigors of another pregnancy.

Feeling weary and ill, she gazed down at his head full of dark curls. Why did she love this baby more than the others? The thought made her feel guilty and somehow apprehensive but she couldn't help it. Thomas was a part of her like none of her other children had been. Even Rose, Tom's beloved Lovie, could not touch Meg where Thomas could.

There had been many a night when Meg was nursing him that he would lock his dark blue gaze on her and she felt he was reading her soul. Only Tom had ever looked at her that way. There had been nothing remarkable about her pregnancy with Thomas and his delivery had been about the same as the others. But there was something about him that made her want to keep him little as long as she could. Now she would have to welcome another baby to take his place.

She had wondered then how she would cope again with the sickness and the inevitable clumsiness and backache later on, she didn't know. She had just calculated the time when she might deliver when the bells began to toll announcing the beginning of Mass. Thomas had lost interest in eating and had begun to poke his fingers in Meg's nose and mouth.

"Time to go to church my little one."

Meg patted his bouncy hair and fastened her bodice. She and Thomas had just ducked into the pew when Fr. O'Boyle intoned the Introit and Mass began.

Just two weeks later, Tom had announced that Fr. O'Boyle

would be coming for dinner. The two men were spending the day in Westport once again lobbying the bishop for a church closer to Doeega than St. Dymphna's. Rev. Nangle and his mission at Slievemore had expanded to found St. Thomas Anglican Church in Doogort on the north shore of the island. There was talk of expanding in the south.

Duffy had complained all the time about the Rev. Mr. Gibbs at St. Ambrose in Westport and St. Mary's Church of Ireland here on Achill had the Rev. Trent and his lovely wife enticing Catholics and pagans alike to their doors. Many of the parishioners at St. Dymphna's saw this as a threat to the stability of Achill's Roman Catholic numbers. Indeed, some of their fellow parishioners had already started going to St. Mary's in the winter when the long trek to St. Dymphna's could be treacherous. Fr. O'Boyle had had many meetings with the men of St. Dymphna's and had already expressed their concerns to the bishop in a letter. The bishop had agreed to meet with him to discuss these concerns and Fr. O'Boyle had chosen Tom to go with him.

Meg leaned back against the hedgerow and remembered the day they went. It had started out cool and overcast. Tom had borrowed a curragh from Seamus Foy and he and the priest had started out early. Tom was still skittish about the sea but Fr. O'Boyle's father had been a fisherman and the priest had cut his teeth in a boat.

That long-ago afternoon, as soon as Thomas and Mary Clare had gone down for their naps, Meg sent Denny and Rose to the shore to dig for mussels and gather dulse. Keeping one eye on the two of them, she had dug new potatoes and carrots for her stew. Once they had gathered all the ingredients for dinner, the three then packed a picnic lunch of brown bread, cheese and jam. When the babies woke up they took a slow walk to the back of the potato field where the nut trees and hedgerows full of berries still grew along the fence. Meg had felt well and enjoyed the day with her little ones.

Denny and Thomas collected nuts from the ground and

placed them in the lid of an old milk can while she showed Rose and Mary Clare the fine points of berry picking. The little girls had eaten more than they put in their baskets smearing their faces with red juice. Denny raced around with Thomas squealing in pursuit. When they started pelting each other with nuts, Meg decided it was time to head back.

The afternoon had found them gathered around the hearth, Mary Clare and Thomas playing on the settle bed, Denny and Rose counting and ordering the nuts into rows and ring forts. Meg remembered making a delicious stew of the mussels and kelp adding the potatoes and carrots along with a big sweet onion and some early peas. For dessert she had tried to duplicate the raspberry tart Maureen had made so many times when she was still living with them. As she pulled the pie, fragrant and bubbling from the tin oven, she wished more than ever that she could pour her friend a cup of tea and dive into the delicate buttery crust and sweet red filling together.

By the time Tom and Fr. O'Boyle returned, Meg had the children freshened up and dinner on the table. The weather had changed from dreary and gray to windy and threatening and the two men were glad to be ashore. Meg had just cut into the tart when the thunder started and a storm blew in off the ocean. Fr. O'Boyle would not be making his way to St. Dymphna's that night.

When the last of the dessert and tea was finished, Tom had taken his fiddle out and begun to play. Tom and Meg both knew the words to many of the traditional songs and sang heartily much to the delight of the children. After a rousing rendition of "The Minstrel Boy", Fr. O'Boyle asked if he could take a turn. The children clapped their hands and Tom and Meg danced around the kitchen floor as the priest had entertained them with reels and airs. Breathless, Meg rested as he brought to life the haunting old ballads from the days of the druids. As the evening wound down the music became slow and plaintive. Meg had put the sleepy children to bed on the settle and tidied the loft for their guest. She remembered how, long after she retired to the bedroom she shared with Tom, she could hear the low rumble of the men's voices.

Meg had been too exhausted to stay up and she wasn't even Catholic but she couldn't help feeling left out as the men visited. She had thought of Fr. Finnigan and a pang of jealousy struck her breast. She remembered asking herself why she couldn't have a priest to talk to.

Still, after all the years on this island, she sometimes felt so lonely as she sat at Mass, so removed from the others that her heart ached. Tom had never pushed her to convert to his faith but she had wanted to for a long time. She had never acted on her desire and worried that it wasn't sincere. But Meg knew how much his faith meant to Tom and she wanted that for herself. Could a Protestant ever achieve the depth of piety and devotion she had seen in the Catholics of the village? Could she ever leave behind her old way of thinking and embrace the sacraments? Could she ever believe that Jesus was really there on the altar during Mass? As Meg fell asleep that night, she thought that tomorrow she would talk to Fr. O'Boyle about it; tomorrow she would take that first step.

Francis started at the sound of several crows cawing overhead. His little foot smacked Ellen softly on the head and the two babies woke up. Ellen stood up rubbing her eyes grumpily and Francis fretfully burrowed into Meg's bosom. Carefully avoiding the nasty thorns, Meg grabbed one of the heavy twisted stems and pulled herself up. Gracie fell into step behind her as she prodded Ellen to do the same.

Back on the road, Meg juggled her two toddlers and her sleepy new baby. How far her thoughts had drifted while they took their rest. She thought about the work she had done with Fr. O'Boyle over the last few years. He had taught her so much about the saints and the mystical body of Christ. She had learned to appreciate the scriptures, and the whole concept of Christianity building on the truths of the Old Testament was amazing to her. In fairness, Fr. O'Boyle pointed out to her the great similarities between the Roman Catholic and Anglican rituals. Meg was shocked at this. Her experience had been so different, so coldly dismissive of those who would worship a man in Rome over God himself. She realized that much of what she had learned was rooted in untruth but she still had some doubts. She struggled with the great role Catholics assigned to Mary the mother of Jesus and she could not get her mind around the real presence in the Eucharist. Fr. O'Boyle said that much of faith was grace and these things would come to her when God knew she was ready and when that happened she would know. Walking along now, Meg shrugged to herself. Nothing had happened yet so she would just wait until it did.

As Meg approached the village, she smelled the offal dung heaps that were piled at the entrance to every house. She marveled at this disgusting practice. She would never permit animals in her house and the dung heap was in the far corner of her yard. But her neighbors seemed to think nothing of having the stinking piles right at the entrances to their houses, whether stone or sod. It was a sign of pride to have a high stinking dung heap. The manure represented the livestock a man possessed and the higher the pile the richer he was. Men even traded services for dung so they could not only appear richer, but have more fertilizer to enrich the chronically poor soil on their meager plots. Of course, it made perfect sense to have it at the door where anyone passing or stopping to visit could see and take note of his prosperity.

Clearly the people of Dooega were not prosperous despite the presence of their front door monuments. Achill housed some of the poorest residents in County Mayo and County Mayo was one of the poorest of Ireland's counties. The first three years of Tom's role as agent to Lord Lucan had been stable but the years since had seen a steep decline in the annual income of the villagers.

The lace making, so popular early on had waned as some of the women had found hoeing potatoes more lucrative. When the linen industry in Ireland failed, the demand for lace had declined and the women had turned to the old reliable sources of income.

They planted in spring and while the crops ripened they headed for the hills to live in little stone boolies and tend the cattle and sheep grazing on the scruffy grass. Some traveled to other areas of Ireland to help with early harvests while others went to England or Scotland to find work. Many who had no choice turned to begging, especially in the summer when the potatoes from the year before became scarce and the new crop wasn't ripe yet.

The rents were high and barely met. The villagers had no idea that Tom subsidized the rent for his people. Indeed, Lizzie Ballard had circulated a rumor that Tom Phalen actually siphoned off a hefty percentage of the rent entrusted to him. Fortunately, a town meeting was all it took to squelch the rumor and turn the angry stares toward Lizzie herself.

At times Tom did feel like a traitor and was filled with self-loathing. He would talk to Meg late into the night, deploring his position and formulating plans to pull them out from under the yoke of the conniving Gilchrist. Often Meg would awaken to the strains of sad, old Irish airs carried on the sea breeze. Tom was out on the thinking rock, pouring out his wounded pride into the night, the strings of his fiddle crying for him in the dark.

Over the years, along with other fortunate villagers, Meg had kept her little kitchen garden to fill the lean summer months with a few fresh vegetables. Usually there was an abundance of wild berries along the hedgerows for the children of all families to pick. It was not unusual to see rows of children three deep hovering around the prickly bushes like bees, vying for the sweet sun ripened blackberries and tart currants and gooseberries. By the time the harvest festival rolled around, youngsters could be seen perched in the fruit trees tossing down the ripe orbs of peaches, plums and apples to each other, relieved to be out of their cramped huts, enjoying the fresh air.

But so far, this summer had been a deep disappointment to the residents of Doeega as the rain kept the plump berries from ripening. As August approached however, the sun had finally started to appear more regularly and combined with the rain of the last several weeks, gave a promise of extra-large and juicy berries for the picking. The potato fields around Doeega were nearing harvest and a green carpet of leaves flourished under the high clouds and warm sun. After weeks of rain, the village had suddenly come alive with children at work and at play.

The rainy weather had been hard on the fishermen. The fish, which paid the rent for so many residents, were plentiful but fishing in the rain, day after day had put the clachan men in a foul temper and some of them had taken ill with fever. Two men, a nephew of Seamus Foy and his son had died after being caught at sea and exposed to two days of cold rain before finally making shore down by Achill Sound. They had ridden out the storm only to be felled by weak lungs and continued wet weather.

In contrast to the hardships of the villagers, Tom's dairy business was thriving. From his humble beginnings in service to Lord Jeffrey Wynn, Tom Phalen had indeed prospered. He provided milk for islanders halfway to Keel in the west and as far as Klockmore to the east. He employed women to milk his cows and men as drivers to deliver to the far strewn customers. He had hired Finn Kelly to thatch his house and byres, and keep his outbuildings sound. Finn had stayed on as a hand and was able to support a family of six on the wages Tom paid him.

Meg had taken on a few village women to plant and harvest the acres of potatoes that grew so well in the sea air. She had even taught some of them tatting as she had learned it from Mme. Nina, her grandmother's Belgian friend. Several of the women did excellent work and sold the lace they made at fairs and festivals despite the waning linen business.

From their little plot on the strand, life for the Phalens was rich indeed. But Tom and his family were not typical of the Doeega villagers. Most of their neighbors lived in tiny airless cabins many of them with their livestock. The differences were undeniable and no one felt it more than Meg.

To assuage his guilt, Tom Phalen lived frugally, providing for his family what they needed but having few luxuries. They never wanted for good warm clothes or hearty food and for this Meg was grateful. Her life as Tom's wife was a hard life but she was content. She knew her house was nicer than her neighbors. She knew that most of her neighbors houses were better than most of the outlying huts and hovels of the poor laborers and tenants Tom collected from each month.

The townspeople had always remained cool toward Meg and Tom but he insisted on returning their mistrust with honesty and kindness. He had won the grudging acceptance, if not the friendship, of the men who shared the pub life, but Meg had never been able to win over the women who still saw her as one of the gentry, a rich girl playing peasant. Meg had given up trying to make them like her. Her friends were few: Leona Trent, Mary Feeney and more recently, Peg Sweeney were the ones with whom she could enjoy a cup of tea.

As she came around the bend leading down the slope into town, she suddenly saw in the bright sunlight the dramatic difference between her clean windswept life on the beach and the tumbledown array of tiny, smoky one-room stone huts that huddled in clusters throughout Dooega. The women she saw at church every Sunday lived in hovels, plain and simple. Most of them were very poor and many of their houses were as small and as inhospitable as the byres Tom had built for their milk cows. While Tom had been building new outbuildings and expanding their dairy over the last ten years, the fisherfolk of Dooega had slid, like most of Ireland, into a dangerous poverty that threatened to take them over the brink into destitution. The whole process had been very insidious but was most evident in the shabbiness of the village, so quaint from a distance yet so empty and lifeless up close.

Shifting Francis from one arm to the other, Meg turned to see where her two little girls had wandered. Gracie and Ellen straggled behind her, Gracie picking up tiny pebbles from the damp road and Ellen stopping to sit down every few feet.

"Come along, girls!" Meg called, "Let's see if Aunty Maureen has sent us anything from America!"

Gracie came running, leaving Ellen sitting on the side of the road. She began to wail and Meg sent Gracie back to prod her along. Gracie pulled her sister to her feet just as a jaunting cart carrying two well-dressed strangers came around the bend. The two little girls were just getting their balance when the driver sped by kicking up pebbles and dried mud, almost sending them toppling into a ditch. They were both wailing now and Meg hurried to help them up.

Setting Francis down she dusted them off and dried their tears. Gathering her children to her with a heavy heart, Meg continued on to the post office. She knew how close the girls had been to being hurt or even killed but what made her heart ache was the knowledge that had they been maimed for life, the wealthy visitors in the jaunting cart would never have looked back.

Chapter Two

"Whatever are you doing, you stupid dolt?" Lord Jeffrey Wynn, twisted around in his bed, bumping the wash basin and splashing soapy water on his valet's polished brogans.

"Simply as you asked, Your Lordship. I'm lotioning your back."

"But I'm not even dry yet, you fool! What good is that?"

George sighed, "Remember, sir, that Dr. Simmon's nurse recommended lotioning while still wet as the best way to ease the itchiness of dry skin."

"That whore wouldn't know dry skin if it crawled up her skirt! We're through here! The water's gone cold."

"Yes sir. Right away sir."

George set the lotion down and patted Lord Jeffrey's back with a dry towel, his own back crying out in protest. How he hated this part of his job! Ten years a nursemaid to His Lordship! What a turn his life took that fateful night of Lord Jeffrey's accident. Until then he had enjoyed the role of gentleman's gentleman. He lived well, ate and drank well; his work was not hard despite the long hours. Being so close to the master gave him rank and power greater even than Lady Beverly and certainly greater than any of the servants.

Since that terrible night everything had changed for him. Before the fall down the servant stairway, His Lordship had needed almost nothing in the way of personal care. Draw a bath once in awhile; clean up after a drinking bout; straighten up his room after a night of debauchery. None of that had ever bothered George. He had been with Lord Jeffrey so long and had grown so used to his habits that even the worst of them had become part of a comfortable routine. Most days he had his domestic work done by midday, leaving plenty of time in the village wiling away the afternoon with the lads. He still regarded this as work, of course. There was the post to pick up and His Lordship's legal papers and sundries from the store. There were always gentlemen to deliver messages to often with urgent replies to carry home. Any time Lord Jeffrey traveled George had to go along. This had opened up whole worlds for George. Lord Jeffrey spent weeks out of the year in London and Dublin.

There was one year when they traveled as far as Germany and another when His Lordship had visited a school chum in India. George felt a pang, thinking about India. That had been so many years ago he had almost forgotten the dark eyed beauty who had captivated him for the months they lived there. Too bad her father was a rajah and had whisked her off to the Kashmir mountains as soon as he discovered George's amorous intentions.

He remembered now, as he refolded the towel, how he and his master had argued over the beautiful Rani Vilkhu. Lord Jeffrey insisted that George should despoil her. Doing so, he had said would force her father, a devout Muslim, to exile her as one dead to the family. He could then have her and take her back to Ireland for himself.

George, always a modest and temperate man had never been as close to quitting his position as he had when His Lordship had threatened to set up some subterfuge to allow George a time and place for the seduction of that innocent, unsuspecting girl. In any event, her father found out and she was gone before George could even clear his name. He had always held that against his master. George would never have done what His Lordship suggested and somewhere in the Far East a man and his daughter would always think of George as an immoral scoundrel. To this day the thought of her soft brown eyes reflecting the pain she would have felt at his hands deeply grieved him. He never mentioned it to Lord Jeffrey and he never would. There were years of silences between them. Nothing could change that, especially over the last ten years since the terrible event that ruined both of their lives.

Lord Jeffrey was becoming agitated with his bath and splashed George again.

"Get on with it man, I have things to attend to! You are always so slow and tedious, George. Like an old woman! You know as well as I do, you could wash my skin off and I'd still stink like a sow in heat. Just let it go!"

Ignoring the caustic remarks, George lifted his master from the bed into his wheeled chair and carefully washed his feet. Drying them with the soft plump towel, he half-listened to Lord Jeffrey prattle on. That damned Gilchrist had just left and His Lordship was more animated than George had seen him since the smarmy little rat's last visit. Why he liked that weasel so much, George could never understand. He had set him on the trail of Tom Phalen and Lady Meg years ago and nothing much had come of it. George thought His Lordship was wasting his money.

George had no love for Tom Phalen but he had always liked Lady Meg. She had never caused a bit of problem for him personally and he had felt genuine disgust when he had seen the terrible whipping His Lordship had given her that day back in '35. Lord God, but that had been a terrible year!

Beginning with that ridiculously cold first day of June, life at GlynMor castle had been one episode after another each more hellish than the last. And that useless Lady Beverly! If that woman had taken her household into hand years ago and done her duty as a wife and mother in the first place none of this would have happened. George was convinced of it. His master's wretched liaisons, his sick sexual appetites and his excessive drinking and gambling would have never gone so far if she had not locked him out of her bedroom.

Of course, Lord Jeffrey was no angel. What man was? And why should a man be cuckolded by his wife? He should have used his crop on her early on and Lady Meg would have had the proper attitude set by her mother's example from the start. But his master had always been besotted by that stupid woman. How many times had he struggled to settle His Lordship down after one of his drunken confessions? How many times had he listened to Lord Jeffrey plot and scheme to make her jealous or to make her pay? He lavished her with all those clothes and trinkets and that stable full of horses and for what? Her bedroom door had been locked as soon as they came home from Japan and his master had never been able to buy, threaten or cajole his way past it.

Then, no sooner did he fall down the stairs and break his back than she was out the door and traipsing all over Ireland on his money. As George struggled to stuff his master's feet into the short boots recommended by his doctor, his master tried to kick him away.

Lord Jeffrey, knowing he was stretching his valet's temper beyond endurance, chuckled a low, nasty chortle and said sweetly, "Poor George. And to think you could be shooting grouse or riding the hunt if it weren't for your lack of a title. Why don't you borrow mine? I'm not using it for much these days anyway."

He snorted derisively and chuckled again as George fought to cram his numb, useless foot into the smooth leather.

George silently cursed both Lord Jeffrey and Lady Beverly. She should be doing this! She is his wife and she should be his nursemaid. This was no man's work! Even Mrs. Carrey, God rest her cranky old soul, had shaken her head at George's new duties after the accident. But His Lordship would have no other caretaker. They had tried both male and female help to lighten the load. Lord Jeffrey behaved so vilely toward the females and so violently toward the males that in the end, George had always come back.

Now, he was getting too old for this work. Almost sixty, he could no longer do the bending and lifting required of him. He couldn't even sacrifice his aches and pains for the sake of loyalty and dedication. His master was just a shadow of himself. His body had wasted away to the size and form of a mere schoolboy. George thought His Lordship couldn't weigh a hundred pounds. But that was still dead weight and too much for George to be lifting.

It seemed the only parts of Lord Jeffrey to have survived the fall were the worst elements of his personality. He hated far more deeply than he had even on his worst days as a healthy man. Instead of manipulating the affairs of his estate, he plotted sordid acts of revenge on Lady Beverly and Tom and Meg Phalen. He had lost his ability to perform sexually or to even enjoy the visual pleasures of the opposite sex though he still saw dimly if someone was close enough.

At first he had tried to employ George's assistance in forcing the housemaids to submit to his mauling and probing hands. But George couldn't be a party to that. He and his master had had a huge row about it and finally agreed that George would arrange for his master to have regular visits from women whose profession it was to satisfy men of peculiar habits. Even those talented women could not satisfy him and he finally stopped asking for them. Years had passed and nothing had changed. Every day George aroused his master from a drugged sleep. Breakfast, bathing, vain attempts to rid his chambers of the stench of stale urine.

George took the bowl and spilled the dirty water out the window into the yard. There was a time when he would have carried it down the stairs and properly spilled it out behind the stables. When his master found this out long ago, he had paved over the space beneath the window, installing a small sluice leading to the gravel entrance to the bridle path. Now, George was very grateful for that act which at the time had seemed merely practical.

"Take me out to the fields today, George. I want to see my holdings and smell the gardens," Lord Jeffrey said with insincere pleasantness.

"Sir, it's threatening rain and you know how the dampness gives you difficulty breathing."

His master grew petulant and pounded on the arms of his chair.

"I want to go out! You can't control me, you insolent bastard! I should sack you and then where would you be? No one is going to hire an old maid like you, you useless baggage!"

George turned Lord Jeffrey's chair to the wall and let him holler at the sconces, ignoring him as he tidied up the room and changed the bed. The idle threats and juvenile outbursts were so commonplace that no he had learned to tune them out. He almost felt bad forcing his master to face the wall but eventually the yelling would stop and he'd behave civilly again.

George had grown to hate spring and summer when His Lordship could hardly bear being indoors. Most of the time, he felt sorry for Lord Jeffrey and did take him out when the weather was good. But he never rewarded his master with a favor after being berated or insulted. He had his pride, after all.

The property of GlynMor Castle was still breathtakingly beautiful. Lord Jeffrey had kept most of his gardening staff, and despite his age and infirmity old Ben still lived above the stables. There was no reason to let the landscaping go to ruin. He had plenty of money to keep it up and he enjoyed the scent of roses in the house. He still barked orders at the gardeners and fumed about blight and imperfections as George wheeled him about the consistory and gardens during the good weather.

The master insisted on hearing detailed accounts of his wildflower garden with its banks of daisies and Queen Ann's lace. He made George wheel him through his rose garden, stopping at every bush to cut a bloom and revel in the aroma. His gardeners carefully tended the hundreds of bushes feeding and mulching, clipping and pruning. All summer the house was filled with bouquets of roses of every hue and fragrance. Huge vases filled with red and white varieties adorned the foyer and the corridors were lined with deep scented yellow and white blossoms. In his own rooms Jeffrey preferred the light scented tea roses and the soft fragrance of his pink and white climbers.

He usually directed George to wheel him through his sculpted green garden where sweet boxwood formed squares and diamonds filled with topiaries and wrought iron towers entwined with English Ivy. Here there was no flowery fragrance for him to enjoy but the fecund richness of freshly drenched greenery calmed him and he would sit for hours breathing deeply of the green smell. He often asked to be pushed around and around the walkway just leaning back in his chair and listening to the crunching of the crushed seashells beneath the wheels.

He only inspected his grain fields on May Morning when planting was begun and again in late July when the early harvest began. Never particularly interested in the agricultural end of growing things, he left it to his undertaker to bleed the rent out of the many tenant farmers who rented from him.

The townland of Clydagh Glyn was very large and brought in huge profits. He never cared whether his tenants ate enough or had a warm roof over their heads but he was never stingy with them either. This farm had been in Beverly's family since Cromwellian days and many of the families had been living in the houses and stone hovels for just as long. He let his undertaker handle all the business of the tenantry.

Right after he fell, his old undertaker, Richard Riordan had died and Beverly had appointed Riordan's son Paddy to take over. He hated to admit it but her choice had been a wise one. When other landlords were struggling with poor crops and miserable workers, young Riordan had kept things at Clydagh Glyn perking along very nicely. He had had healthy if not huge crops of rye and oats, corn and wheat as well as several seasons of bumper crops in barley and flax.

Lord Jeffrey contemplated his wallpaper and knew he had pushed his valet too far. He decided to ask his opinion and get himself out of the corner sooner.

"What do you think of young Riordan, George? He does nice work and I just keep getting richer, but he told me he's placed armed guards around my grain fields. Is that necessary?"

George decided not to bite the bait. He knew the tenants were as vulnerable to bad seasons as any other farmers and George thought Riordan was wise to employ armed guards to protect the fields with the rumors about a blighted potato crop spreading like wildfire in Europe. But George pretended not to hear him and his master stayed where he was.

Once a month Mr. Gregory Guttman, His Lordship's solicitor came to review the finances. There was really not much to report. He had changed his will to eliminate both Beverly and Meg but would not reveal to George just who was to get his money. Mr. Guttman was a sour old man forever shaking his big head over Lord Jeffrey's lifestyle. He felt that His Lordship was squandering his fortune on gambling and let his client know of his disapproval at every opportunity.

The older man was the son of a Scottish charwoman and a German butcher. He had been orphaned very young and had had to make his way in the world with no family and no inheritance. He believed in frugal spending and adhered to a strict Presbyterian work ethic. More than once he had left GlynMor in a huff as the ugly sound of Lord Jeffrey's laughter followed him out the door.

George wondered aloud one night why His Lordship kept Mr. Guttman on if he was so disagreeable.

Lord Jeffrey had simply shrugged and replied, "I know the old coot will never cheat me. That makes him worth all the aggravation. Meanwhile, he invests my money wisely and my holdings continued to increase."

The closest port to Clydagh Glyn was Westport but since his accident, the harvest from Clydagh Glyn had always been sold in Castlebar and what happened to it from there was of no interest to Jeffrey. As long as he got his money he cared little for the distribution of his grain. In the past he had enjoyed the trip to

Westport with the harvest, visiting the Marquis of Sligo and his wife while Beverly talked horses with the locals.

Lord Jeffrey cared little about the expense of running his house, a fact that made working for him much easier than any other master around. As long as he could eat well, and have his whores and his poker he was a happy man. And, of course, his roses. George thought this was the oddest trait of all.

George's ears ached with the weighty whining of his master's endless monologues. He still blamed Beverly for Meg's disgrace but admitted he probably should have paid more attention to the big groom in the corduroy livery. Thinking on those trips spending days on the road with only George and Tom Phalen and a couple of footmen to talk to, Jeffrey wondered how it had escaped him that Phalen was such a cur that he'd bed his own daughter someday?

It mattered not at all now. His last trip to Westport had been to see Dr. Browne and his specialist friends. They had been able to do nothing for him and he didn't care if he never returned to that place. What difference did it make when he could hardly see his hand in front of his face and the only thing to smell in Westport was the stink of fish? Even a good whore was hard to find unless he went to Marie's on the quay. Jeffrey didn't like her stable. The women were too simple for his taste and the madam had an ugly attitude.

George smoothed the counterpane across the bed and turned Lord Jeffrey to face the window. The sun hurt His Lordship's eyes but this was where he liked to sit on cloudy days.

His master had settled down and seemed to be lost in thought, his tirade forgotten.

"Do you remember, George, when we were in Westport last, how that big oaf at Browne's wouldn't give us a room? Claimed there was no way to get me up the stairs. Damn fool was as cold as a nun! And those idiot doctors, telling me there was no hope! What's to become of me, George?"

George never replied to these self-pitying ruminations. When his master had first been injured, he had found himself caught in that web and realized that no matter what he said, he would be blamed for his master's misery.

Browne's wouldn't have them, George remembered well, and that big good-looking chap behind the bar had treated them as coldly as a nun. George knew by the sulking silence all the way home there would be no more Westport for Lord Jeffrey. He had contented himself with listening to Guttman recite his profits and settled for the ministrations of the local whores. He had confined his travels to his own land and seemed happy with it.

Everything he could inspect was thriving. The many acres of sycamore, pine and yew trees took care of themselves and Paddy Riordan assured him the hedges and stone walls marking his boundaries were inspected regularly and in good repair. Beverly's paddocks and bridle paths were probably overgrown but he cared nothing for them. As long as Jeffrey received good reports from Riordan and the trusted Guttman verified the figures, Jeffrey was content to sit back and smell his roses.

His Lordship had hired Peter to take on Tom Phalen's duties and George knew that the younger man did everything now that Ben had had a stroke. Everyone loved Ben and had never revealed to Lord Jeffrey that he was no longer able to work. He continued to live on the estate and Peter considered him a mentor and friend. Lord Jeffrey cared little for the comings and goings of the stable as he never ventured out there and rarely required a trap to take him anywhere. Occasionally he asked after old Ben and was content to know that he was still doing well.

The hedgerows along the back of the property were impossible to reach by chair and George would hoist his master into the old phaeton to drive around the perimeter of the huge townland of Clydagh Glyn. Lord Jeffrey always knew when they approached his hedgerows. Since the accident, his sense of smell had become so keen he could differentiate between the honeysuckle at the eastern border of his property and the dense climbing hydrangia where east met north along the creek leading back across Phalen's farm to his stables. Once Lord Jeffrey had insisted on being driven to the old Phalen house. George had complied though the terrain was very difficult to drive. Just what His Lordship thought he'd find, George had no idea, but the place was empty and Lord Jeffrey had sulked like a child when his hollered commands to appear at once went unanswered.

George had told him the place was abandoned but he would not believe him. He ordered George to take him out of the carriage to see for himself but in a rare act of disobedience George had simply turned the phaeton around and driven home. His Lordship had bellowed and threatened all the way to the stable yard but George just ignored him.

The next week had been filled with episodes of fury and temper with Jeffrey scooping bathwater out of his basin, soaking George; tipping his dirty supper tray when George reached to take it and peeing on George's hand when he approached him with the pewter urinal.

After this had happened twice, George believed his master could control his urine far better than he chose to and his disgust with Lord Jeffrey and with his job leaped to a new level the first time the warm, smelly urine slid between his fingers and down the back of his hand. Lord Jeffrey had just laughed and threatened to aim for George's face the next time.

Now George had finished his tasks and wanted to be dismissed.

"Is there anything else, sir?" he asked, perishing for his mid-morning tea.

"Is there anything else?" Lord Jeffrey mimicked. "Of course there's anything else, you moron! Anything else indeed! Anything else would be better than this!"

But George was already half-way downstairs and could no longer hear the whining drivel of his master. He would let the upstairs maid know about His Lordship's foul mood so she could wait until he was napping to do her chores. She had only his rooms to tidy and preferred not to encounter her master awake.

Lord Jeffrey had closed the east and west wings of the mansion and expanded his rooms throughout the north wing that formed the ell jutting out toward the back of the property. Entertaining in his library or dining room was impractical and he failed to enjoy any of the décor anyway so he had simply brought some furniture upstairs and did his entertaining there.

As he sipped his tea, George marveled at this dramatic change in his master. Once a man who would sack any worker that slacked off for an instant, he now trusted them like a child. George knew that he was helpless, especially because he could not see anyone more than a few feet away from him. His staff could easily have victimized him much the way he had victimized others in his day. But for some unknown reason, no one seemed inclined to do that.

George knew it wasn't from fear that his colleagues continued to serve this nasty, filthy old man. He doubted there was any loyalty behind it either. Most of the remaining staff simply knew no other way to exist in the world. They worked hard, received their wages and kept their private lives to themselves.

When Mrs. Carrey had died of a heart seizure on Boxing Day two years ago, her niece Sharon had assumed the duties of cook. Lord Jeffrey was an invalid and the scars around his mouth caused him some trouble eating but his appetite and preferences had not changed. The duties of cook were essentially the same. Sharon still needed a full kitchen staff to feed His Lordship and the staff and the many men who visited frequently for his gambling soirees.

George looked up from the newspaper when he heard a tinker talking about the potato problem that George had heard rumored about a few months ago. He had heard there was a fungus that had taken the early crop in the middle counties.

Sharon shook her head when the man asked her if any of the tenants of Clydagh Glyn had mentioned it.

"The harvest usually starts a bit later here. We have a later arrival of warm weather," she said. "But Mr. Riordan said it's true and suren' the stink is on the wind."

The tinker handed Sharon a length of cheesecloth and a spool of white thread and took the few pennies she dug out of her apron pocket.

"Well, brace yerself, ma'am. 'Tis only days till ye'll be holdin' a nosegay t'yer lovely face just to peek into yer yard."

George hadn't noticed. He shook his head as he realized again how shut up and isolated he was and how his nose was filled daily with the stench of his master's rooms.

Potato failures over the years had affected GlynMor some but the farm had always been self-sufficient. They had not had to evict anyone in years though two families had left on their own, migrating to England in search of work. And of course, there was the Phalen farm. He often wondered that His Lordship never had rented that nice little property to anyone else. Maybe he was waiting for Tom Phalen to come back begging. Or perhaps he was lying in wait for old Thomas to return.

George wouldn't put it past his master to hold an old man hostage to exact revenge on his son. George felt sorry for the tattie hokers. Without the tatties they would starve. Tatties were the mainstay of the Irish diet and George knew that despite his English birth he would be just as hungry as any Irish servant or tenant farmer were he not Lord Jeffrey's manservant.

So he stayed, trapped in the dim red rooms with their heavy Italian walnut furniture and thick brocade drapes drawn against the painful sun. He stayed not out of loyalty but self-preservation. This was the real reason most house servants stayed with their masters. They ate well and slept indoors. They had their half-day off a week and kept their mouths shut doing what they were told and gratefully settling down at night full, warm and as satisfied as any illiterate, poor born man could expect to be.

George got up and took his tea out to the stoop behind the house. He could hear Sharon humming inside as he watched the tinker pull a tarp over his goods. The air was heavy with impending rain and as he watched the old tinker turn his wagon toward the drive, George thought of the people who were forced to be outdoors no matter the weather.

It was the farmer's life that was the real gamble. They had a freedom of movement and independence denied the house servants but their very life was dependent on the whims of the weather and the wealth of the harvest.

While George tucked himself into clean linen sheets the farmers flopped down on damp straw ticking. While George drank good scotch whiskey from a crystal glass, the farmers drank poteen from tin cups. He had fresh shirts and fine moleskin trousers to put on every day. They had old smelly corduroys and patched cast-offs from his own closet.

But they were free in a way he would never be. They felt the sun on their faces every day and the wind in their hair while he had to be satisfied to be outdoors on his free Sunday afternoons.

Lord Jeffrey had always made George use so much pomade on his hair he had forgotten how it felt to have the wind tousle his thin gray locks and he hadn't ventured away from the property since his master took ill. George's days were without end. He was always at his master's beck and call. It had always been thus. That was simply his life, the way of the manservant.

He had enjoyed great privileges as Lord Jeffrey's first servant. He had never been so proud as to lord it over the others but he had always held himself aloof and somewhat austere. He had kept his small luxuries to himself and prided himself in his self-restraint among the housemaids and farm girls of the townland. His interest in women had never waned but he still smarted after all these years from his sad experience in India.

It had always been enough to be a man's man, listening and silently reveling in Lord Jeffrey's exploits. He had inwardly shuddered at some of His Lordship's more tawdry stories and cleaning up his suite of rooms had often disgusted him. Lord Jeffrey had been a brute to more than one girl in his rooms and more than once the trail of violent evidence had made George queasy enough to open the windows for fresh air to settle his stomach.

It had never occurred to him to question his master's right to mistreat the maids of the house but he had thought long and hard about that now that his duties were so different. George was a decent man by his own estimation. He had attended the Anglican Church of Ireland with Lord and Lady Wynn for years and still did despite His Lordship's absence in the pew.

He had learned to read as a child and enjoyed the many excellent books in the GlynMor library. He asked for very little, eschewing fatty foods and rich desserts to avoid the gout that had plagued his father. He always kept his person clean, tidy and presentable for any and all visitors. His rooms, now adjacent to Lord Jeffrey's were spare and manly, with only the necessary pieces of furniture. His ewer and bowl were fine, yes, but those were provided by the house just as his linens and bedstead.

He had taken, at Lord Jeffrey's suggestion, whatever he needed to furnish his rooms. He had been given the freedom to select anything he wanted from Lady Meg's suite or Lady Beverly's. He had preferred the rich, dark mahogany pieces in Lady Meg's rooms to the fanciful ivory inlaid pieces in Lady Beverly's suite. Without fanfare or flourish he had simply had some of them moved into his bedroom, making for himself a comfortable den.

He had a small fireplace with a carved rosewood mantel where he kept his only portrait. He had placed the small oval likeness of his sister slightly off center and embellished the space with a Chinese vase and brass candelabra. The other end of the mantel was occupied by an ornate clock trimmed with brass and onyx, clearly the fanciest accessory George had in his room. This he had bought at a bazaar in Delhi as a gift for his sweet Rani. This he treasured though he would be the last to admit it.

Life for George was very comfortable. He was well established in the house and in the village. No one defied him, no one questioned him nor did anyone really care for him. He spent his Sunday afternoons seeking solace in the open air.

He would rise early to see to Lord Jeffrey's needs, attend

church at eleven and head for the bogs or the river or Derryhick Lough where he would eat sparingly from the hamper prepared for him by Sharon. His routine never varied. The meal was always simple, cold meat and cheeses and a few fresh biscuits, fruit and nutmeats. There was always a jug of cold cider or a tankard of stout in there but he was never tempted to over indulge. Sharon would sometimes put a sweet tart or a pudding in the basket with fresh cold buttermilk to wash it down and despite his penchant for austerity he always wolfed those treats down with gusto.

He believed himself to be a simple man with simple needs. He was not an introspective man and rarely did anything to make himself feel guilty. He was usually pleasant with the townspeople. He had no reason to be otherwise.

He did not permit himself the luxury of wishing or speculating on other possible lives he might have lived nor did he allow himself regrets. He believed regret was a wasted emotion and George wasted nothing. He spent his free afternoons reading, soaking up the sun and hiking as far as he could in the time available. On inclement days, he put on his Macintosh and boots and vigorously trudged into the wind and rain. He almost preferred the windy, wet blasts of winter to the lazy warm breeze of summer and spring.

Autumn was clearly his favorite season with its high blue sky and wispy clouds. He admired the fields and the natural wealth around him as he hiked the trails and bogs of Clydagh Glyn. The Clydagh River was especially beautiful in autumn when the birch trees along the bend at the southeast corner of the estate rose up like a golden corridor, the branches glistening with thousands of heart shaped leaves. When the breeze caught the leaves they shimmered and danced like so many coins waiting to be plucked. There, beneath the wavy gold mantle George would lean back against one of the slender white trunks and think of Rani and how the gold bangles of her silken veil shimmered and danced when she laughed.

It was there that George had had a most unusual encounter

one Sunday in July. He had just finished a meat pie and was resting in the steamy heat of high summer contemplating the cooler days to come. Just as he was about to tuck into a cherry tart, he saw a man walking purposefully along the riverbank. He had the stride of an outdoorsman and appeared to be on his way somewhere. George wrapped the tart in a cloth and closed the basket, embarrassed to be caught indulging in sweets by one so obviously fit and lean.

The man approached him cautiously, his hand resting defensively on his hip. Suddenly wary, George reached into the basket for the cheese knife. They eyed each other for a moment like two wolves. George had never felt fear of any man but he knew this boy outweighed him and had youth in his favor. The young man made the first move.

"Might ye' be Tom Phalen, then?"

He stood a foot away from George, feet spread apart, hand hovering over the knife in his belt.

George was taken aback by the question. Tom hadn't lived in Clydagh Glyn for ten years.

"No, I am not. Who wants to know?"

He breathed a sigh of relief that he was not the target of this ruffian's attention. Scrutinizing the boy, he sized him up as a thug, up to no good, but his curiosity had been stirred by the boy's question.

The young man relaxed slightly though his hand still hovered over the knife.

"I call meself Andrew Feeney. And who might ye be in yer fine leather vest and fancy Sunday trousers?"

George did not like the belligerent tone of the boy's question and straightened up though he would not rise for this insolent laborer.

"I am George Spiner of GlynMor Castle."

"Well now, Mr. George Spiner of GlynMor Castle, how is it yer so far from home?"

"I might ask the same of you, boy. I've lived in this townland almost thirty years and I've never seen you."

To his surprise, the boy laughed. Shaking his head derisively he leaned down and sneered at George.

"No, ye wouldn't have found yerself where I've been fer certain, Mr. George Spiner. Where I've been no one reads fine books and sips, what is that, buttermilk? No one does that fer sure, I guarantee ye that. No, where I come from, real men drink real brew and sittin' is fer women and babies. Where I've been Sundays are fer fightin' like any other day and there can be no sittin' beneath the birch trees playin' the fine gentleman. No, Mr. George Spiner of GlynMor Castle, not where I come from."

George was growing weary of this exchange and wished the boy would move on but he showed no sign of leaving.

"Can I offer you a cold drink?" he offered lamely, hoping the boy would refuse.

"Thank ye' kindly fer askin' but I'm after somethin' t'eat moren' drink. Ye can't spare me a bit of victuals?"

Careful to conceal the cherry tart, George pulled out a pear and the remaining cheese he was saving for his evening meal.

He extended the food to the young man and he took it, eating it standing. George didn't know whether he stood for self-protection, habit or deference to his station. He seriously doubted the latter and figured that the boy was simply used to eating on the run. He had a feral look about him, an aura of both hunter and prey. George watched him as he ate, his hunger clearly intense and from the look of his spare frame, longstanding. He was fit but not developed in the way of young athletes. No, his thin limbs and sinewy neck belied the rosy glow of his cheeks and the hard set of his jaw. He was handsome in a callow, careless way. His hair was fair and his skin tawny from days living outdoors. His hands were young looking, strong, well-formed but like the paws of a big puppy, too big for his arms. He looked out over the river as he wiped the juice from his thin golden beard, more evidence of his youth in its sparseness. The breeze blew his fine hair around in light caramel colored waves.. An unusual boy, George thought. Poor as a peasant with the face of an aristocrat, he lacked the high coloring of the Irish. His eyes were arresting and bothered George for some reason; familiar somehow though he was certain their paths had never crossed.

They looked almost silver-green when they caught the sun, reminding George of the leaves on the olive trees of India. He felt that he should know this boy but knew he did not.

"So, if ye aren't Tom Phalen, can ye tell me where t'find him?"

George hesitated. He really didn't like this young man.

"I haven't seen him these last ten years but it's been said he lives in Doeega, Achill Island with his wife and children. What's your business with him?"

By now, George was feeling impatient with this interruption of his precious free time.

"I have a message fer him is all. Nothin' t'trouble yerself about, old man. I'll be takin' me leave and lettin' ye get back t'yer readin'. I'm that grateful fer the food."

Bowing insincerely, Andrew Feeney looked directly at George's face.

"Give me best regards to Lord Wynn, now, if ye please."

George was again confronted by those cold green eyes and felt a chill pass through him. Before he could ask the boy how he knew Lord Jeffrey Wynn, he was gone through the birches. He could hear scornful laughter fading on the breeze but by the time he rose to his feet the boy was around the bend of the river and out of sight.

He stood for a long time watching the golden birches sweep the sky. Finally, he returned to his book and his cherry tart, shaking off the chill in the air from beneath the merino wool blanket Sharon had packed in the bottom of the hamper.

Meanwhile, Andrew Feeney had all the information he needed. He had succeeded in finding Lady Meg Wynn, now simply Meg Phalen. He thought it was about time to visit his Aunt Mary. It had been ten years since he had run away from her home on Achill Island and now he had even more reason to go back.

Chapter Three

Meg had indeed received two letters from Maureen and one letter from the same post office but in childish block printing. Tucking the three letters into her apron pocket, she thrilled to the prospect of a good long read with a cup of tea when she returned home. She bought some salt and a few sundries. Peter Feeney, Mary's second son, cut an apple into slices for Gracie and Ellen while Meg proudly showed Mary how much Francis had grown. Suddenly a shadow passed over Mary Feeney's face and Meg felt a chill. Meg caught her breath at the commanding presence of a strong, handsome young man who had just entered the store.

"Mary, Pete, how be 'ye?" he asked in a tight, controlled voice.

Mary's mouth simply opened soundlessly forming his name. Meg watched as Peter's hand silently slid around his mother's arm as her body swayed with shock.

Meg looked from mother and son to the intruder in the door. She could see the muscles of his forearms tense and relax as he opened and closed his fists. Taking her girls by the hand Meg wished she had been gone before this man arrived.

Finally, Mary found her voice.

"Andrew, dear, 'tis that good t'see ye. Ye've been gone so very long, we wondered after yer life, we did."

The sight of Mary Feeney's painful relief was hard enough to witness but the expression on Peter's face was unbearable. Peter looked as if his face would crumble as he worked through ferocious pride and anger to arrive at shame and pity. Finally, his expression slipped into the bland indifference he presented to his customers as he addressed his cousin.

"We be fine, Andrew, praise God and all the saints. And you?"

"I'm alive, no thanks t'the tyrants who own me soul."

Mary crossed herself at this.

"Andrew, no such talk in front of the wee ones."

"And a welcome home from ye too, Auntie. I see yer still chokin' on the grand slice a'life yer God has given ye."

Despite the surliness in his voice, Meg caught a deep longing in Andrew's stance. He seemed wont to plunge headlong into the room and bury himself in Mary's bosom. Suddenly looking like a very small boy in a grown man's body, Andrew stepped into the store and as the sunlight flooded the little room Meg could see the expression of deep, angry sorrow on his face.

So this was Andrew Feeney, Mary's dead sister's boy. Meg remembered the night Mary had sat with her and Maureen on the thinking rock and cried over him. Her sister had been dying from consumption when she brought him to her as a lad of three long before the Phalen's had moved to Achill. Mary had taken them in and cared for her sister until, days before Andrew's eighth birthday, she died. He had been troubled by deep melancholy since the day his mother died and Mary's husband Mike had tried everything to make his life good.

When he was almost eleven, Andrew had overheard Mike venting his frustrations to Mary one night and ran away from Dooega. Mike had been so exasperated with Andrew that he had decided to take him to the Benedictines in Puntoon and see if they couldn't straighten him out. The next morning, the boy was gone. People all over the island from Achill Sound to Granuaille's Tower searched for the missing boy. Shepherds scoured the Minaun Cliffs and men in trawlers scanned the shores. He seemed to have vanished and the people finally decided he had drowned. Mary had never believed that and prayed many an Ave for his return. He did return, just in time to bury his Uncle Mike. As soon as the funeral was over, Andrew had left again, despondent over the loss of the only man who had ever cared about him.

Now, grown into a young man, Andrew Feeney was lean and hard. He was not a tall man but still filled the doorway with his hot anger and his thick hate. His fine, handsome features were hard as he took in the humble racks of fabric and dry goods. He said nothing, standing in a shaft of sunlight.

Mary put her hand to her throat and gasped. It had been ten years since Andrew had been home and here he was returned as from the dead.

But he was very much alive; the very essence of young fury, darkening her door with his deep penetrating hate.

Mary gestured toward Meg and her children. In a voice that sounded odd in its normalcy, she spoke.

"Mrs. Phalen, I'd like you to meet my nephew, Andrew Feeney. He left Dooega right around the time you and Mr. Phalen moved to the house on the strand."

Andrew's jaw jutted out and his wide mouth turned down in a sneer of contempt. He shot Meg a look that made her gather her children into her skirt.

Pivoting on his heel, he turned to her and she thought he was going to touch her. Instead, he bowed in mock deference.

"Lady Wynn, I see yer lookin' well."

Straightening up, he glared at her with disgust, his green eyes meeting her own. Meg saw in his smirk that he held something precious to her and shuddered at his use of her maiden name. She backed away from him and gathered her packages. His eyes followed her every move as she herded her children toward the door. She tried to ease past him, her shoulder brushing against his leather vest. There was no mistaking the shrinking disgust that passed between them as he sharply pulled away from her.

Meg fairly ran home, dragging the girls across the strand, jostling Francis on her shoulder as he blubbered his protests. She was completely shaken by her encounter with Andrew Feeney. How much of her secret had he found out and how? Meg was suddenly very afraid for herself and her children. Tom was in Newport for his annual meeting with Gilchrist, Lord Lucan's undertaker. He planned to stay and travel to his brother Davey's to see his da. He had received word that his da was ill and wanted to see him. Tom wasn't due home for another week when he would be needed for the early potato harvest. Meg was afraid of Andrew but she needed to talk to him. She must know how much he knew about her. She thought of Tom on the mainland and felt her knees weaken. Was Tom in danger? Had Andrew seen him? She desperately needed to speak with him in private.

Meg remembered Peter saying that Andrew was involved with political rebels who hated the gentry both English and Irish. She had heard rumors of arrests and death threats that followed him and his band of troublemakers. But Mary had always scolded Peter when he relayed reports of someone sighting Andrew or hearing about him. Mary could only remember the angry, frightened little boy who ran off for fear of being sent to the priests. She had never forgiven herself or Mike for frightening him so.

Peter hadn't spoken of him since Charlie O'Malley had reportedly seen him in Louisburg one Reek Sunday about six or seven years ago. Meg had never asked about him because it seemed to cause Mary such sorrow and eventually Mary had stopped talking about him.

For her part, Meg had grown to understand why the Irish hated the English so much, having lived all these years as one of them. But despite the scorn she had endured from people she would have scorned herself had she not married Tom, English blood ran in her veins and she felt angry and hurt by the severe judgment heaped upon her by these ignorant peasants. These people hated her simply because she was born the daughter of an earl. She was no more the daughter of an earl now than she was Grace O'Malley! Most of them had benefited greatly from her kindness and generosity. The same women who had learned a gentlewoman's pastime in her kitchen, who enjoyed her tea and eaten her cakes, used her thread and made lovely delicate lace with it shunned her on the street and turned away from her in the shops. Now, she felt it from the next generation as well.

Andrew Feeney had no reason to hate her yet he had looked at her with venom in his eyes. He was a perfect stranger yet he could hate her so? Meg could hardly understand how these people, the only neighbors and friends she had or would ever have, could harbor such chilling hatred for her and her own. This was Meg's private sorrow. Much as Tom bore his shame in silence every time he counted out the rent money for Lord Lucan, Meg swallowed her sobs so he wouldn't hear as she soaked her pillow over some cruel slight endured during her day. But this was no slight. This was serious. Andrew Feeney was no truant schoolboy. He was a strong, powerful young man who could do great harm to her and Tom. And now he had come back to Achill Island and brought her secret with him! He had used her maiden name! What did he know? How could she find out?

The letters in her pocket were forgotten as she raced across the beach, her head pounding to match her thundering heart. Not until she reached the safety of her kitchen did Meg pull the letters out and set them on the table to read. She wanted badly to see the news from America but by the time she put the young ones down for their nap, the older ones had become bored with their puzzle and Mary Clare had slapped Thomas when he scattered all the pieces under the settle bed. Meg's letter reading time had passed until all the children were in bed.

Later that night, when Meg again sat down to read

Maureen's letters, she heard a commotion in the yard. The chickens were in a dither. Worried the foolish hens would wake Francis, she went to the kitchen door to see what the matter was. The top of the dutch style split door was open to let in the sea breeze and Meg leaned out to see better. She saw nothing but fog billowing in from the ocean wrapping the yard in a milky shroud. As she started to close the door, Meg heard the noise again. She wished she had the dog with her. Their old dog, Bailey, had just died and Tom planned to bring home a new one from a litter Duffy McGee's border collie had delivered.

Meg picked up the hearth shovel. There were few animals on the island that would disturb her chickens but once or twice a roamer or tinker would try to steal one. Maybe she could scare the intruder without hurting him too badly. She wasn't afraid until she came around the eastern corner of the house and was plunged into the dark, swirling mist. The evening was cool and after the unseasonably hot day the thick fog had settled across the strand and slowly crept across the yard obscuring the light from the kitchen window. She couldn't even see the outbuildings but knew by heart the way to the chicken house and the booley where she kept things cold. The byres where Tom kept their cows were on the far end of the stone fence and all was quiet in that part of the yard.

As she crept toward the chicken house, the commotion grew louder. Shaking, Meg held the unwieldy shovel before her, ready to strike out at the prowler. She had never hurt another human being and prayed that she could just scare him off. The fog billowed off the water in soft moist clouds as she picked her way toward the little stone booley. She felt her skirt brush the hedges that covered the stone fence behind the outbuildings and realized that she had gone too far. The squawking and fluttering seemed to be coming from her left but the fog confused her.

She tried to reorient herself to the sound but she could see nothing. She held the shovel out straight in front of her to feel for landmarks. Just as she thought she should be in front of the booley, the shovel was ripped from her hands and clattered against the fence. Meg staggered forward into the corner where the booley met the fence and was grabbed across the mouth by a hard, cold hand causing her to bite down hard on her tongue and lower lip. An arm of iron spun her around and held her from behind. Meg instinctively tried to pull away but the intruder had her in a grip that raised her off her feet. She could taste the iron in her blood mixed with the salt of dried sweat on his fingers. When he opened his mouth to speak she smelled the sour pungency of stout.

The man could hardly conceal his drunkenness as he slurred a cold greeting,

"Lady, Wynn. What a pleasure t'be meetin' agin. We have t'stop, or folks'll be talkin'."

He let out a low chuckle.

"We couldn't be havin' that now, could we?"

Andrew! She should have known! How stupid she was to come out here and walk right into his trap! He had her so tightly she could hardly breathe. She felt herself go limp and her feet still dangled inches off the ground.

"We need to 'chat' as you English call it. Now, ye know as well as I that no one will hear ye if ye scream, exceptin' yer precious brats, and ye know better than to bring them out here when we have serious business between us. So, I'm inclined t'take me hand off yer mouth but I'll be needin' some promise from ye that ye'll be keepin' yer screamin' t'yerself.

Let me see. If I uncover yer mouth it gives me a free hand t'put where I want. But then, yer a lady, now and that means I need to be behavin' like a gentleman. But now, what gentleman should I be? Hmm. Now there's a decision I'm not oft' te make. Should I be a Lord or a magistrate? English or turncoat Irish? Ye know, M'Lady, not all gentlemen are gentlemen if ye git me point. And on the same token, not all bastard sons are cowards and vermin. I think I could be either and still give ye what ye deserve."

Still covering her mouth, Andrew released her slightly letting her slide toward the ground. Her knees buckled and she sagged against his arm.

"Now that's a temptation," he said, his arm across her chest, his hand cupping her breast.

"What kind of a lady would let a stranger touch her like this?" He gripped her hard evoking a muffled yelp of pain. Slipping under her bodice he ran his cold hand across her warm skin, fondling and kneading her roughly. Meg was almost on the ground and he let her slide to her knees. Kneeling behind her he hissed into her ear, burning her neck with his hot, stinking breath.

"Ye tried t'scream there, M'Lady. I see ye can't be trusted."

Still pressing her mouth tightly closed with one hand, Andrew fumbled around behind Meg with the other and unfastened her apron. Her arms free, Meg pushed against him but he immediately took his hand off her mouth and seized her neck. Her breath suddenly cut off, she opened her mouth like a desperate baby bird.

Andrew clearly had the advantage now. No matter how Meg fought and flailed, she couldn't breathe and the more she struggled the tighter he pressed his thumb on her windpipe. Taking the apron, he stuffed as much of it as he could into her mouth until she began to gag. Only then did he pull his other hand away from her throat. He wound the apron strings around her face, tying them tightly at the back of her neck. Bringing her arms up he trussed her from behind binding her wrists tightly behind her head.

She felt herself slipping further to the ground and he grabbed her roughly and forced her to kneel.

"Now, I have ye the way the gentlemen do when they want t'chat with the likes o'me."

He leaned over her in the dark and she felt the cold steel of a knife against her collarbone.

"Only they prefer t'do their chattin' like this."

With lightning speed he took his knife and flicked the buttons off Meg's bodice sending them pinging against the stone wall of the booley.

"Why d'ye s'pose they like to chat bare-chested, M'Lady? At least the Irish are stripped, mind ye', a gentleman would never stoop t'show his skinny chest in a public square. Did ye know that when an English gentleman wants t'chat in the public square with an Irish woman he does it the same way? It appears, now, that gentlemen aren't a bit particular about the Irish: man, woman or child."

Again Meg felt the knife against her skin as Andrew sliced her bodice and chemise to shreds. She was horrified knowing he could see almost nothing in the swirling mist and yet brought his knife again and again to her chest and arms. The knife blade was cold and he moved it so quickly she was terrified he would cut her. Finally, her clothes hanging in strips around her waist, she heard him sheath his knife and she again sank to the ground. He kicked her hard and yanked her up by her hair until he had her standing. Her eyes teared with the searing pain as he twisted her long hair in his fingers.

He leaned into her face and growled.

"I said kneel, M'Lady. Like a Catholic. Like a nun! Ye'll not get away with less than me own mam did when she knelt begging in the street for mercy from the gentlemen of Castlebar."

His breath was moist and hot upon her face and the apron in her mouth tasted of fish and dulce as she slowly sank to her knees in the dirt. He struck a lucifer on the booley wall and lit a lantern he had set on the ground. Pulling up a three-legged creepie, he sat facing her in the small circle of light.

He began toying with her, pinching and circling her breasts with hard, cold fingers, trying to hurt her and succeeding. Fat tears escaped from her eyes as he ran his rough palms down the curve of her neck and over her smooth, slender shoulders. Reaching up he traced the outline of her jaw above the apron strings and pulled her closer to him by her arms, straining the ties where they held her wrists behind her head. This tightened the ties around her neck, choking her again and forcing her to trundle forward on her knees. Kneeling as she was on her skirt, she fell into his lap. He lifted her up to face him and began to laugh. She looked at him with terror as he laughed like a madman, running his hands all over her bare skin, tangling his fingers in her hair. He suddenly jerked her forward and yanked the apron out of her mouth grabbing her head and bringing her mouth up to his. He bent her head back as if to kiss her. The apron ties around her neck threatened to cut her breath off completely as she gagged on his hot, sour smell. Meg could only squirm away from his mouth while he pursed and smacked his lips in mock kisses.

"There ye go. Kisses fer yer children from Uncle Andrew."

He released her as forcefully as he had seized her, flinging her to the ground. Again he hauled her to her knees and raked his filthy hands over her tender skin. Grabbing her to him, he groped beneath her heavy homespun skirt still biting and probing her ears, her neck, pulling out her hairpins with his teeth and spitting them on the ground. He clamped her mouth again beneath his hand and bit her hard on the shoulder.

Meg cried out against his hand. No one heard her. No one would, she knew. She lived far from the village in her fine, little house and had her acres of potatoes between her and her closest neighbor. Andrew knew this too. He had her at his mercy and he showed her none as he furiously molested her. Meg was convinced he was going to rape her and she steeled herself for the pain.

With drunken madness he pulled her to her feet, devouring her like a starving child, biting and grasping until she could bear it no longer. His hands seemed like claws as they found her private places and pillaged her dignity. She silently prayed for him to take her and be done with it but still he only used his hands on her. Then, as harshly as he had clenched her to him, he released her into the mist. She staggered backward and landed hard on the ground. Meg lay there waiting for him to descend on her but he stood towering over her in the mist.

Andrew's face shimmered in the ring of lantern light like some mythical specter right out of a bard's verse. He reached down and shook her hands loose causing her to choke and sputter against the strings around her neck. Meg felt the tight strings burn her skin as he ripped the apron from her, tugging and yanking the strings until he had torn it from around her neck. Meg lay in the dirt searching Andrew's face for any sign of humanity, finding none. What she did see filled her with the icy chill of pure horror.

Still looming in the mist, he placed his boot on her belly, resting his foot firmly right above her waist.

He spoke in an ominous monotone, his face contorted in pain.

"I could take ye fer the weak, miserable daughter of an English swine right here in the dirt but I won't. I could take me knife and cut ye so ye'd never suckle another babe but I won't do that either. I want ye t' relive this night every time ye dress yerself, every time ye put a babe t'yer breast. I never tasted me own mam's milk, she was that weak after havin' me in an old stone hut like ye keep yer butter in. Sure'n it was the only house te' have her. Smaller'n the dung heap at yer door it was. Oh, beggin' yer pardon. M'Lady, ye don't have a dung heap at yer door, now, do ye?"

He pressed hard on Meg's belly with his boot and her tears began again. With a look of disgust he pulled his foot away. Sitting again on the creepie, he motioned impatiently for Meg to kneel again. She stirred in the dirt and struggled to her knees. Her arms hung limp at her sides and she was overcome by exhaustion. Her body throbbed everywhere from the bruising assault of his hands and mouth and she could not stop crying. Ashamed of her weakness she tried to cover her breasts with her hands.

He put out his foot and kicked her arms to her sides.

"Gentlemen like their women bare breasted from what I've seen. So far, I've treated ye the same way all the gentlemen who 'chatted' with me mam treated her. So, don't be tryin' t'cover yerself. Ye got no more right t'cover yer bosom than me mam and she spent most of her life barin' herself for th'gentlemen."

Andrew got up and began to circle around Meg, first bathing her in filmy lantern light and then walking behind her throwing her into black, murky shadow. This had the effect of disorienting her as though she were rocking aboard a ship at sea. She began to shiver in the billowing fog. If he noticed, Andrew made no sign. Around and around he circled, his low, menacing voice rambling on about his mother.

"First, a grand earl taught her the ropes. Then, after she got me by him and he threw her into the street, she fed herself on the scraps of gentlemen's breakfasts. This, of course, after pleasurin' em all night. Funny how gentlemen aren't put off by the belly of a pregnant twelve-year-old colleen. I guess gentlemen are just more manly than t'feel squeamish puttin' their filthy part into a child already defiled by one o'their own."

He spoke this directly into her face, his spit landing on her chin. Again he began to circle her and she reached up to wipe the spit off. Pouncing like an eagle, he raised her again by her hair.

"Don't touch it. I want ye t'feel it sittin' there on yer skin. I hope it burns ye."

Throwing her to the ground again, he came around to the creepie and sat down, bellowing,

"I said kneel. Like a Catholic nun!"

Meg scrambled to her knees and he kicked her, face down into the dirt this time. She felt the small pebbles grind into her bare skin as he crossed his legs and rested his heavy boots hard on her back.

"I like to think of the nuns humiliatin' themselves. Ye know, beatin' themselves with little whips and what d'they call it? Mortifyin', that's it. Do grand ladies mortify themselves? I don't suppose they do. But poor colleens, that's another story, fer sure. They don't have t'look far fer gettin' licked with little whips or layin' face down in the dirt. No, little Irish girls don't need to be nuns atall t'feel the humblin' of mortification. I suppose that's why they make such good nuns at that. They get all their lessons from generous gentlemen like the grand earl that mortified me mam."

With this he ground his heels into Meg's back and kicked her again.

"I said kneel like a Catholic nun! Now! On yer knees facin' me!"

By now Meg could stand his torment no longer. Her silent tears turned into loud, gulping sobs that seemed to please him. He held the lantern very close to her face and leaned forward smiling at her with cold venom in his eyes. Despite her tears, Meg saw his face clearly in the lantern light. What she beheld made her recoil and she almost fell in the dust again. Hot salty tears fell from her eyes washing her lips and burning where he had drawn blood.

Her whisper barely audible, she formed the words, "Uncle Andrew".

Andrew just smiled and nodded at her recognition. Never taking his eyes off her face, he took a flask from his back pocket, and treated himself to a long drought. Finding that he had drunk the last of it, he threw the whiskey bottle to the ground with a curse.

Again, he leaned into her face, and wound her hair in his fingers. He pulled her to him and kissed her neck. He pressed his hot, whiskey coated lips into the bite on her shoulder, sending burning needles through her. She thought he would begin assaulting her again and braced herself. Feeling her tense up, he let go.

"I gave ye me word as a gentleman that I was done with ye, so what're ye gettin' all stiff about? I was only expressin' me gratitude t'ye as is only fittin' when a lady such as yerself gives of her time t'the likes o'me."

Now, he smiled at her again, his goulish face unreadable in the lantern light. Her eyes never left his face as she knelt at his feet.

He motioned for her to fold her hands in prayer.

"Like a Catholic nun, remember?"

His voice was even more menacing in its sudden gentleness.

Together they stayed that way for several minutes just looking at each other. Finally he reached over and ran his hands across her breasts, cupping one and holding it for a long time. She watched his face change from strong and hateful to that of the lonely, frightened boy she'd seen at the mercantile. Holding her breast in his hand, running his thumb over a bruise beginning to purple, he seemed lost in reverie. Finally, he let her breast drop heavily and resumed his expression of contempt.

"All in all, I thank ye fer havin' me taste a bit o'yer own babe's breakfast. Me poor mam was already dyin' when she bore me and her with no milk to give. I suppose our father had sucked it all out o'her."

He searched Meg's face for some sign of surprise but found none. She had seen what he had come to show her. Looking at Andrew in the lantern light, Meg had beheld her father's face and Andrew was pleased. She knew now that he wouldn't rape her. She was his sister and he would not debase himself with incest! But he had hurt her and humiliated her as much as he could in the same way their father had hurt his mam. How tragic that the evil just kept going from father to son and on through the generations. Would her own children carry it on? Did she have it to give them?

The thought struck her a blow more painful than anything Andrew had done to her. She still feared him enough to stay on her knees with her hands folded but he was no longer interested in hurting her. He looked exhausted in the dimming light of the lantern. The fog was intense now and they could hardly see each other. Meg knelt in the damp dirt until Andrew, seeming himself to be coming out of a fog, wearily told her to stand up.

Since he had confessed their common father, Andrew looked as though all the steam and stuffing had been let out of him. Meg knew he was finished hurting her but still she was afraid to move toward the house. She didn't want him to follow her in but she needed to find out what he knew and how he knew it.

"Andrew, I'm very cold. I need to go inside. You have

behaved reprehensibly toward me tonight and I should have you arrested. But oddly enough, I feel that this is somehow a family matter of such shame to me and my household that I will never speak of it to anyone. You are my half-brother and you would torture and degrade me so!"

At this, Meg began to weep again. Hard gulping sobs threatened to bring her to her knees again and in a complete reversal, Andrew reached out to steady her. Where she found the strength to push him away from her she had no idea, but she sent him tumbling backward over the creepie and he now scrambled to raise himself from the dirt.

This gave her the advantage she needed. Seizing the lantern she held it in his face blinding him to her own. Her tears stopped as she took control over the situation placing her own foot squarely below his belt buckle.

"What makes you think you can touch me after what you have done? You are appalling in your effrontery! Do you not realize that with one word to Lord Lucan I could have you hanged? You think you hold me in the web of a great secret and among the Irish maybe you do. But I am still the daughter of an earl as you so vilely remind me. You must leave this island and never come back. If you try to return I guarantee I will have you hunted down and hanged. Do not misunderstand me. I have no delusions about our father nor do I doubt your ability to punish me further once you find your rage again. But you cannot be excused for the terrible things you did tonight. Be gone by morning or as God is my witness I'll have you dead."

With this Meg left him lying there in the fog.

Andrew lay in the dirt for a long time. He had nowhere to go and could see nothing in the dark swirling mist. He crawled along the wall of the booley and finding the stone fence, followed it around the yard till he felt the wall of the first byre. He ducked into the warm stall and inched his way into the corner. Years of stealthy subterfuge spent living underground had taught him how to move like a snake, silent and undetected. With his left hand he felt the heifer asleep on her feet. With his other hand he piled straw for a bed.

The events of the evening had completely drained him but he could not sleep. What had happened between him and his half-sister had shocked him. He did not even know he had such behavior in him. He had wanted to hurt and humiliate her. He had plotted for months how he would force from her an admission of her complicity in the death of his sweet mam. He hated her for her guilt and he had let his hate overtake him. That was the sure sign of a weak man. He sighed aloud at his own weakness.

The Brothers would never let him fight with them if they knew how easily he became undone by his hate. This was a good lesson to him. He had taken Meg and smeared her with her own blood and left her to beg in the dirt. Nothing more than he had witnessed many a man do to his mother. How could he feel so cold and detached about it while he planned it and then become so thrilled by it when he did it? He was afraid of the thrill he felt while hurting Meg. He had thought he had controlled his feelings since his mam died. He had never cried, not even when the keeners had thrown the clods of wet dirt on her as he stood in the rain watching her go deeper and deeper into the mud, away from him forever. He was only a boyeen when she left him with Aunt Mary and Uncle Mike. He would always smell fresh sod and taste the clean salty rain off the ocean when he remembered her.

The day he ran away, the rain had fallen in torrents and the strand smelled just like the day they had buried his mam. A man had been killed on the sea and another had washed up. Now he had taken that man's wife, his own sister, and made her pay a long standing debt. He had almost smelled the sod from his mother's grave again as he had ground her flesh into the same damp earth of this godforsaken island.

He had wanted to do it stoically. He had tried to be dispassionate, clear-headed like the Brothers had trained each other to be. Instead, he had dissolved at the sight of her nakedness. He knew it was because she was a woman. If he was ever going to be of any use to the Brotherhood they would have to assign him to men. It was clear he could not handle a woman. His cool contempt had been shoved aside by a passion for revenge so powerful he shamed himself with his own sister. He had felt no lust toward her. At least he could comfort himself in that, he thought, as he tossed on his bed of straw.

Never a man for introspection, Andrew found this thoughtfulness a trial. He was tired and the manger was warm. He had slept in many a less hospitable bed and he'd sleep well tonight. Now, he had only to rid himself of the memory of her warm skin and pleading eyes so like his own. He began to remember how cold her voice had been when she ordered him never to return. He felt the chill of pure anger creep into his limbs. Reassured that he had only had a lapse in judgment tonight, he welcomed the one feeling he enjoyed. The only feeling he'd had for ten years, for anyone, excluding his martyred mam, was anger. Comforted by the return of his old familiar friend, Andrew fell asleep in minutes. He slept hard until dawn. As the rooster crowed, Andrew helped himself to a few warm eggs and stole into the grey mist that still blanketed the strand. Stealing a curragh from the beach, he slid out to sea. The slapping of the oars was muffled within the web of fog as it enfolded him in its billows and sucked him out to sea as if he had never been there at all.

Meg collapsed as soon as she latched the kitchen door. She thought she could not get up again but she somehow dragged herself to bed. As she tenderly washed the blood from her lips fresh hot tears coursed down her cheeks. How could her own brother do this to her? Having his mouth and hands all over her like that? The thought made her nauseous and she vomited into her chamber pot.

What was he doing? Was he seducing her the way their father had seduced his mother? Was he like that with every woman or just her? She knew Lord Jeffrey was horrible to Maureen as she supposed he was to Andrew's mam but did that make Andrew the same way or was his humiliation and brutality with her more personal? Was she singled out as the enemy because she was her father's daughter or because she had crossed over into his culture? Or was it because his poor mother had died so young after being ruined by their father? And how did he even know about her? Had he seen Tom? Who had told him where she was?

Oh, dear God! Tom! How would she explain the bruises and bite marks to Tom? She knelt down by her bed and really prayed like a nun now. Dear Lord, please delay him. Please don't let him come back before the bruises fade. Please Lord, he'll track Andrew down and kill him and then he'll be hanged himself. Dear God, please don't let him see me like this. She sobbed into her pillow and prayed.

Dragging herself to her feet she finished dressing her wounds and fell into bed. She lay there thinking that nothing Andrew had done had aroused her nor did it seem to work that way on him. She lay awake, her tears soaking her hair. As she wiped her face in vain, Meg realized with astounding clarity that what Andrew did was not lustful at all. His behavior was simply mad. He wanted her to nurse him and for a few moments be his mother. This realization made her bolt from the bed and reach for her chamber pot again.

Lying back down she shuddered at the far reaching tentacles of evil that she thought she had left behind in the red-gold haze of her father's bedroom. She wept for his blood running in her veins. She wept for the likeness of her green eyes to Andrew's, for the way Denny's tawny hair fell across his brow like her father's, for Rose's impulsive temper and brawling nature. Would she have to see him in her children's faces? How many others were out there looking at the world like she and Andrew through green eyes fringed with blond lashes?

Since she left her father's house, Meg had never thought about the others until tonight. Ten years and all these miles and it took one deranged man dragging her into his personal torment, forcing her into his mother's skin, baring her to his disgusting mouth and fingers to bring it all back. She couldn't tell whether she throbbed from her new wounds or whether she was feeling the pain of her father's beating all over again.

What did it matter? The same dementia inflicted them both. The fury of the same madman, insane and sordid, burned her skin. Her pain was not just from without, either. She throbbed from within too. The shame of her father and her brother was her shame too. She was connected to them and to all the other bastard children Lord Jeffrey had sired, both living and dead.

She cried for her dead sister, Mary Ellen Dougherty, whom she had thought of all these years as simply Maureen's baby, never even acknowledging that they were related. How callous was she that she could have denied this?

While Jeffrey and Andrew had shown their cruelty by inflicting pain on her and stripping her of her dignity, how was her silence about Mary Ellen for all the years Maureen lived with her any different? She felt a grave fear for her own immortal soul as she realized how effectively she had banished the thought of this innocent babe from her mind. What manner of selfishness allowed her to let Maureen, the mother of her own dead flesh and blood deliver her children without even mentioning or expressing sorrow over Maureen's own loss?

Meg was indeed no better than her brother. She had never physically violated Maureen the way he did her but she had disregarded her grief so easily that she was sure she had assaulted Maureen's spirit with as much violence. How did Maureen never say anything? How did she rock and feed Meg's babies without being maddened with grief over her own? And how was Meg ever to make amends for the sin she knew she had committed by treating her friend's heart with such indifference?

But Maureen never let on! Meg tried to justify herself with the thought that if Maureen had only spoken up she would have taken pity on her and they could have cried together over the loss of Maureen's daughter and Meg's baby sister. She tried and tried to forgive herself and to feel God's mercy upon her. If only she could confess like Tom did that time to Fr. Finnegan. Meg wished now that she had converted to his faith. She knew with a keen awakening why Catholics enjoyed this confessing of their sins. How else could such a great sinner as she sleep at night? How could anyone who had done what she did and failed to do what she had failed to do ever rest without absolution?

No wonder Andrew had her kneeling like a Catholic nun! He demanded her contrition! He would have her grovel at his feet imploring mercy for sins he somehow knew she had committed. This boy who didn't even know her, knew that she had never repented of her noble birth. He needed to exact from her his pound of flesh for all she had done to him simply by being Lord Jeffrey's daughter. He let her kneel with her hands raised in supplication to show her what it felt like to beg, not for her life, but for her salvation. And he made her do it naked.

Her own brother cut her clothes off with a knife and watched her kneel, bare in the lamplight, humiliating her as thoroughly as he knew how. He brought her to her knees over and over again in the dirt of her own yard, grinding her face down with his boot in the stinking droppings of her own chickens because he needed her to see the world she and her nobility had forced him to inhabit. He needed to bring her to her knees to feel his mother's pain. And he assaulted the breasts that fed her children to assuage his own starvation. He gagged her, bruising her mouth and tongue, to silence the lies she told whenever she spoke of justice or truth. What did Meg know of justice or truth?

Truth was to be found in the chicken droppings and justice in the piercing stones against her forehead. She strained against the guilt that threatened to swallow her whole.

Where was God!? She heard her voice call out to him but no answer came. She tossed on the straw ticking that had now become a bed of nails.

"Holy Virgin, help me!" Meg sobbed into the dark. "Help me, help me, help me!"

When still no answer came, she rolled over and squeezed her eyes shut. It was no use praying. Her guilt was too great. She knew she had to talk to Andrew again but the thought of laying eyes on him again terrified her. She didn't fear him harming her. What frightened Meg to her bowels was his knowledge of her sin. She shuddered at the thought of facing him again.

Imagine what he must have thought after he tore up her soul like he shredded her dress and she still stood before him ordering him to leave or she'd have him hanged in the morning! Was there no end to her arrogance? With a last shuddering sob Meg slipped Tom's rosary off the bedpost. Clutching the cold beads as she would her mother's hem, she again called on her heavenly mother to help her. Like a mantra she whispered the name of Mary until she finally relaxed and gave herself over to sleep.

Chapter Four

The morning came too soon and too bright. Not a soft morning like most on the island, there was no misty gray awakening. Instead the sun rose brilliant in the sky and last night's fog dissipated before six. Meg was aroused by the squabbling of her daughters. Rose was trying to fry slices of cold boxty and left over champ while Grace and Ellen fretted over which bowl they would have and Mary Clare slammed out the kitchen door to gather eggs. Denny and Thomas were still in bed, the former because he was lazy and the latter because he slept in the spot near the wall and risked a pounding if he crawled over his brother. Francis, being the baby of a big family accustomed to sleeping through anything, never even stirred. Rose shushed the girls with a wave of the ladle and poured hot water into the teapot.

"Mam, breakfast is almost ready. The tea is on the boil and I've just hotted up the pot."

Rose grunted as she pushed Gracie away from the boiling water.

Meg rolled onto her side and sat up. She ached everywhere. Even the light brush of her nightgown hurt her sore skin and her head pounded from crying herself to sleep. She ran her tongue across her lips. There was no new blood to taste and she was grateful enough for that. She was also grateful that her assailant hadn't blackened her eyes or left any marks she couldn't cover. Buttoning her nightgown high on her neck she could conceal most of what he had done and the rest she could explain away. Her tongue felt tender where she had bitten it but she could stick to liquids and soft food today and no one would be the wiser.

She peered into the little looking glass Tom had bought her for their first Christmas. Her eyes were swollen from tears but fortunately her lip was only slightly so. She could see no bruises forming on her face. How interesting that Andrew seemed to know just where to hurt her so it wouldn't be evident. Just like her father had with Maureen. Never had she suspected what Maureen's nights had been like when she swept into Meg's room and pulled back the drapes. A fresh wave of guilt swept over Meg as she thought of how easily she ignored what was so obvious to her now.

Meg wrapped her shawl around her and went into the bright kitchen. Rose looked up from making the tea and shot Meg a second look filled with questions. She must look worse than she thought. Kissing Rose on top of her head, Meg muttered something about having a little cold and not sleeping well.

"I'm fine, Rose. Just tired is all."

Having no reason to believe otherwise, Rose accepted this explanation.

Meg took a sip of the hot black tea and winced as it passed over her sore tongue. She looked up as Mary Clare came in with a basket full of eggs and a slab of bacon from the booley.

"Took ye long enough," Rose grumbled as she cut off a thick slice of bacon and plopped it into the frying pan.

As the meat began to sizzle and pop, the little house filled with the wonderful aroma of an Irish country breakfast. Meg winced again as she imagined the thin, grey gruel most of her neighbors would be swilling down. No bacon and eggs for them.

Denny bounded down the ladder from the loft and out to the outhouse. Never one for mornings, he never even grunted at his family in the kitchen. Poor Thomas, clutching himself through his nightshirt to keep himself from peeing, stumbled down the ladder and tore out the door after his brother. When Denny returned, he grabbed a piece of the bacon from Mary Clare's plate and dodging her slap, scooted up the ladder to get dressed.

Thomas, thinking he had the news of the day, stood in the door with a whiskey bottle and announced solemnly,

"I found this in the dirt. Can I have two eggs with my bacon?"

Meg snatched the foul smelling flask from Thomas's hand. Taking the filthy bottle back outside, she called to Rose to feed the others and start getting ready for school.

For the first time Meg felt like a stranger in her own yard. She looked around and half expecting to see Satan himself crawl out of the hedges, scanned the fence for signs that Andrew still lurked in the shadows. She saw no one other than the hired men loading the milk cans into the wagons for their daily delivery. Self-conscious in her robe, Meg decided not to look in the outbuildings for Andrew and tossed the flask onto the ground behind a small outcrop of lavender. Sickened by the sight and smell of it, she broke a sprig off the bush and crushed it between her palms.

Inhaling deeply of the sweet fumes Meg kicked the ugly reminder of her encounter with Andrew up against the fence and went into the house. Certain that the milkmen would have reported a stranger loitering around the property, Meg put him out of her mind and started the process of shooing her children off to the hedge school.

As soon as she was sure the older ones were gone, Meg took her three babies down to the beach. Andrew was nowhere to be seen. She waited until noon, when even the cool, foamy waves held no more allure for the girls and Francis began fussing to be nursed.

Meg realized how ridiculous her threats of Lord Lucan had been last night and knew that Andrew could be anywhere in the village waiting to return. She spent the morning shivering inside despite the very warm sun and balmy breeze. Every wave sounded to her like the crashing of a curragh against the sand and every wisp of breeze felt like needles against her skin. Her children played with a bag of seashells and toddled around her but she hardly saw or heard them. Instead she sat, wooden and immobile, her back to the thinking rock, endlessly scanning the strand and seafor signs of his return. Meg was so wrapped up in fear of Andrew approaching she didn't even see Jamie Grady, the constable and one of their few good friends, come around the house from the road.

"Mrs. Phalen, a word with ye', if ye' don't mind."

He said this with a tip of his cap but Meg knew this was no social call.

She simply gaped at him convinced he was about to tell her everyone knew what had happened to her last night. She looked up from her spot in the sand and wrapped her arms around herself protectively.

Instead, he began politely, touching his cap again,

"Mrs. Phalen, Phineas McLean reported his curragh missin' from yer beach this mornin' and I wonder if ye know anythin' about it, atall?"

Meg continued to stare at him. She knew then that Andrew had left. For now she and her children were safe from his evil probing hands and his cold angry eyes. Reaching out her hand, she allowed Jamie to help her to her feet. Embarrassed to show her soreness, she stifled a groan.

"No, constable," she lied, "I heard nothing last night nor did I see anyone around this morning."

Jamie Grady looked hard at Meg Phalen. He was a solid man in his fifties who had been on the force in Newport in his younger years and had moved home to live near his brother when his sister-in-law died seven years ago. He was nobody's fool and when Charlie O'Malley left for America had been the unanimous choice to replace him. Unlike most of the native villagers, he and Tom had become fast friends over the years and many a night found Jamie at their hearth telling stories and singing the old songs in his sweet tenor voice accompanied by the poignant strains of Tom's fiddle.

He knew Meg well and found her behavior to be very strange this morning. She never called him constable and she looked so cowed had he not known better he'd think she stole the curragh herself.

"Meg, uh, Mrs. Phalen, are ye' unwell? Beggin' yer pardon. Ye look all pale and peaked."

Meg busied herself picking up the scattered seashells and calling her children to her side.

"I'm just fine, thank you Jamie. I think I've just had too much sun."

She forced a painful smile and picked up Francis.

"You know how rainy it's been. I'm just not used to sitting out on the beach this way. Thank you for asking."

She turned and began walking toward the house.

"Not atall, not atall," he replied, lifting Ellen while Gracie clung to his pant leg looking for treats.

"I just find it a bit of bother about that curragh. But ye know Phineas as well as I do and he's so in love with his bottle he could have left his boat on any beach along the strand. We'll keep lookin' and never you mind about it. I jist hope ye'll feel better out o'the sun a bit."

Once in the kitchen, he set Ellen on a creepie and dug in his pocket for a ha'penny treat for Grace. Again taking note of Meg's wan appearance, he spoke again.

"Tom due home soon?"

Meg, her back to her friend, winced as she tied her apron around her waist. Every muscle in her body ached and her dress felt like thatch against her tender skin.

"He had several errands on the mainland and I don't expect him until next week to start the potato harvest."

Meg turned to face Jamie Grady hoping he could not hear the false note of normalcy in her voice. She took a deep breath and silently praying that he would refuse, invited him to stay for some soup and soda bread.

"No, I must decline thank ye. I need t'track down that curragh or Phineas McLean will be callin' fer me resignation. If ye' hear anything, send Denny down after school t'let me know. He loves t'visit the jail. Who knows, maybe he'll be the next constable of Doeega. I'll just be havin' a look around yer yard fer any sign o'trespassin'."

He tipped his cap again and Meg saw that she wasn't fooling his keen eye in the least. Again he assumed his formal air as he prepared to leave.

"And if ye need anythin' atall ye know where t'find me, Mrs. Phalen. I know it's rough bein' all alone out here with Tom gone and all."

With that he went out through the dutch door. Meg could only stare after him and pray he wouldn't find the flask under the lavender over by the fence. She gasped when his trained eye saw it immediately and he picked it up. Heat rushed to her face when she saw that the constable had also spotted the hearth shovel lying next to the booley

He returned to the house by the kitchen door and leaned in.

"Mrs. Phalen I found this old bottle among the shrubs. I'll be takin' it down to the station, if ye please. T'isn't one o' Tom's is it?"

"No, constable, it's not. Thomas brought it in this morning and I threw it out there, filthy old thing."

"Well, 'tis not from the local package shop. Must have been a transient come through here last night after all. And I found yer hearth shovel out there too. Any reason that would be?"

Meg forced another smile that hurt her mouth and shook her head.

"I've been looking for that. Denny and Thomas took it to chase a field mouse yesterday."

Jamie peered at Meg with a peculiar expression filled with

both doubt and the desire to believe her.

"Can I send me nephew Gerry over t'stay with ye till Tom gets home? It's not likely this lad'll be back if he stole a curragh but jist t'be safe?"

"No, no," Meg protested a bit too forcefully. "Denny is here and Rose will put up her fists at anyone!"

Trying to make light of it, Meg smiled again.

"Thank you anyway."

"Well, then, I'll bid ye good day, Mrs. Phalen. But we'll be keepin' an eye on yer property fer ye, not t'worry."

After Jamie Grady was out of sight, Meg bedded the girls down for their naps. She sat down to nurse Francis and reached for Maureen's letters. Meg could hardly bear Francis suckling and she needed some diversion. She had waited until all her children had gone to bed last night to immerse herself in news from America when she had heard Andrew in the yard. Now it was a full day since she had received the letters and she still had not read them. After all that had happened, Meg now felt almost afraid to open them. In her mind, the integrity of her friendship with Maureen had been severely tested and found wanting.

Meg held the first letter unopened for a long time turning it over and over in her hand. Francis fussed at the breast somehow knowing things weren't right and Meg again postponed opening the letters until he fell asleep. While her baby worried himself into a comfortable rhythm she closed her eyes and images of Maureen filled her mind.

Feeling a flood of love and guilt, Meg thought of the last time she saw Maureen. How she missed her! The closest friend she had, the only sister she knew was gone for six years now. How hard it was to believe. She could still feel the rough homespun of Maureen's dress as she embraced her for the last time.

Maureen had finally married Charlie O'Malley after a four-year courtship that spanned the Atlantic and sent Charlie to the United States along with his mother to pursue her when she left. Charlie had wanted Maureen from the first time he laid eyes on her but when he found out she had a deed to property in America, he launched a full campaign for her affection. Maureen had never returned Charlie's ardor. Her heart had always belonged to Duffy McGee and to all who knew them both, it was clear he felt the same way. The only one who did not know how Duffy McGee felt about Maureen Dougherty was Duffy McGee. Even old Mrs. O'Malley could see how Duffy looked at Maureen and openly propagated the greater virtues of her Charlie to anyone who would listen.

The summer night in 1839 when Maureen had finally made up her mind to confront Duffy, he had been over to the island bringing Dr. Browne to see Reverend Trent in what turned out to be his last illness. Meg remembered how agitated Maureen had been that night. Maureen was on fire the moment she heard Duffy's voice outside the cottage.

The Phalen children had surrounded him hanging onto his knees and clamoring for the wooden yoyo he always had in his pocket. As he had set Rose on one knee and Denny on the other, Meg heard Maureen sigh. Looking at her friend she saw naked longing on her face and Meg's heart melted with pity.

Over the last few years, Maureen had calmed down a great deal and now that she didn't scare him so much, Duffy had taken to paying more attention to her. They had grown accustomed to each other and spent most of their time together when he was over for a visit. They had a relaxed and easy relationship filled with bantor and teasing and a deep appreciation for the beauty and wildness of Achill's sea and shoreline. Duffy had taught Maureen how to use a curragh and had taken her out at dawn to fish for the limpits she then fixed with dulse for his favorite supper of cruasach and oatcakes.

The only boundary that was never crossed, the only area of their friendship that was never broached was the realm of feelings and the possibility of being more than friends. Meg had listened patiently after every visit as Maureen talked out her dilemma, going back and forth about Duffy. Maureen knew Duffy well enough to know that he had no fear of Charlie and his amorous intentions. On the other hand, Duffy never discouraged Maureen from allowing the village matchmaker to arrange rides for her and Charlie in the jaunting cart nor did he try to outbid Charlie when St. Dymphna's held their box lunch auctions each spring.

He came and he went, never minding any inconvenience, never making any promises, never really leaving any of himself behind at all. Nothing except the ache in Maureen's heart that he left every time she watched him row away home. To be fair, she had never encouraged him, afraid to let down her guard, longing to be even a wee bit seductive as Meg had suggested. The most she ever did when Duffy came to the island was wear her hair loose and borrow a dab of Meg's perfume to lure him close. Meg watched visit after visit, afraid that Maureen's hard life as her father's mistress had spoiled her toward men. She couldn't figure Duffy out, though. He was every bit a man who enjoyed the company of women. Tall, attractive, virile, Meg just couldn't reason why he would not settle down. Especially with a woman so well-endowed and suited for marriage as Maureen.

That summer evening years ago, Meg had watched the two of them walk along the strand, each absorbed in thought. All evening there had been awkward electricity between them. Maureen had been tense and preoccupied since Duffy arrived and Meg watched with bemusement as Maureen fussed over the meal, dressed in her prettiest red skirt and royal blue blouse. When Meg found Maureen loosening the ribbon to let the blouse show a bit of her shoulders and bosom she had raised an eyebrow and Maureen shrugged, saying she had made up her mind she would know how he felt before he left for Westport in the morning. So, like any good girlfriend, as soon as the meal was over, before Tom could involve Duffy in a card game, Meg had shooed them out the door.

Later, Meg had listened still again, as Maureen spared no detail in her report. The sky had been cloudy and Maureen could taste a storm in the air. They had walked all the way past the village to where the shore began to curve gently out toward the sea before it curved back inland to form the breathtaking Minaun Cliffs. With the bluffs and dunes at their backs, they had stood for a long time watching the waves churning in the blustery wind.

Maureen had shivered and Duffy had thrown his jacket over her shoulders. Even as she had been pleased at how the cold wind had plastered her blouse against her chest, outlining the curve of her breasts and rippling across the creamy whiteness of her shoulders, she had silently cursed it for bringing the jacket to cover her up. Her hair had escaped from the black ribbon she had tied around it and flew wildly behind her like a cape of flame. The salty mist off the ocean stung her cheeks to a rosy glow and her lips tingled. Maureen couldn't remember when she had ever felt more alive.

Meg remembered how Maureen shared every detail, and how painful it had been to listen to the breaking of her heart at every word.

Maureen had described looking at Duffy, seeing the small muscles along his jaw working while his full parted lips seemed ready to burst with words too long unsaid. If Duffy was ever going to speak of love, that was the moment. If Duffy McGee was ever going to make love to Maureen, that was exactly the night to do it, right there in this place so wild and free. But sadly, as the setting sun snuck in and out of the clouds, Maureen had known the moment was passing. She felt the magic start to slip away as soon as the rough wool of Duffy's jacket settled on her bare shoulders. She knew he meant to protect her but she didn't want to be warm.

She wanted him to scoop her up in those massive, freckled arms of his and lay her gently on the cold sand. She was wild to be filled with shivers and chilled with expectation. Her body had trembled as she imagined Duffy covering her against the cold, not with his jacket but with the warmth of his own body. She could almost feel the cold hardness of his leather vest against her mingled with the steamy heat of his heaving chest beneath his shirt. Standing in the howling wind at the edge of Achill's wild reaches, Maureen could have been swept naked into the sea and never looked back if she could just feel him being swept away with her.

Instead, she had felt the itchy, damp wool of his jacket chafe her collarbone. A gesture so simple, so naturally kind and polite had taken her from the heady, orgasmic heights of her imagination and plunked her down so hard on the cold, unforgiving beach that she stumbled causing Duffy to reach out quickly and grab her.

The firm grasp of his hand on her arm had completely broken the spell of her wild imaginings. There was no tenderness in his grip, no tugging her into his arms. There was only the strength and steadying hand of a friend trying to keep her from falling. He had looked at her and she could see a mix of genuine concern and deep confusion in his eyes. He had looked like a man in pain who had just been walloped and didn't know why. The look was gone in a flash as he fussed with the jacket and steadied her on her feet.

Maureen had then done something she could never have imagined herself doing. Reaching up and touching his face, she had leaned into him and kissed him tenderly on the cheek. Inches from the lips that only seconds ago she had imagined searing her skin with passion, she bypassed touching them, willing her mouth instead to place a chaste peck on the bristly blond stubble along his jaw.

Without another glance at the man she loved with her very soul, Maureen had turned and walked away. She knew then her love was useless. The realization that Duffy was gone to her, indeed had never been hers to begin with, had crushed her in a way that no other sorrow had ever done. She knew in her gut that he had been as electrified as she had by the wind and the sheer physical draw of her standing there next to him. But even that had not turned him to her.

As she confessed to Meg that night, she had been ashamed of her fantasy, deeply embarrassed at her wee bit of seduction and wished with heart wrenching regret that she had never done the slightest thing to change what they had had. She had overplayed her hand and had ruined everything. She had made herself available in a way Charlie would have found irresistible and Duffy had still not even touched her. His rejection was so humiliating that she knew she could not bear to face him again. She told Meg she had heard him calling to her, but with his voice faint on the wind, Maureen had begun to run.

Maureen knew she was beautiful in a wild, unfettered way. Meg had told her many times over the years how attractive her strength and energy were and she herself knew not every woman was endowed with such glorious hair and bountiful breasts as she. Her face had matured into a softer, less angular version of itself as she had shed the years of suffering that she had carried with her to the island. Her smile had broadened and her brown eyes had taken on a rich depth that Meg had called 'alluring'.

Many of the young men admired her. This she knew from years of watching them at dances and social gatherings in the village. But Charlie had laid claim on her from the beginning and eventually, the young men of Doeega had backed away from the constable's girl.

But there had been only one man that ever stirred in her bosom the true feelings of a woman. It was only with Duffy that Maureen had felt whole. Meg and Tom had both seen it. When Duffy looked at Maureen, she swelled with her own worth. When he walked her to church or helped her harvest potatoes or clean a chicken she smiled and moved like a married woman.

Maureen had said often that Duffy was not only the biggest, handsomest man she had ever seen but he was kind and caring. She saw how he was with children and her sleep was filled with dreams of their own house and family. But the moments she had spent with him were always borrowed.

He had come often to visit Tom and Meg but Maureen had always questioned whether he would have come if it had been only her waiting on the shore.

Like the runner in last place, she had always felt like she was chasing him, so far behind the others that he couldn't see her in their dust. Not that he was ever rude or hurtful toward her. Rather, he had just sort of taken her along with the rest of the family as though she were some sort of trinket at the bottom of a box of bigger gifts.

To be fair, she had never let on to him how she felt and Charlie had always planted himself squarely between them at every opportunity. At first, she hadn't discouraged Charlie, hoping to make Duffy jealous. Instead, Duffy had looked upon the two of them with amusement and even warned her once not to let Charlie get too possessive.

That fateful night, Meg was waiting for Maureen at home as she sped along the sand. Meg had been so excited, hoping that this time Maureen would bring news of a friendship turned romantic, maybe even a wedding! She had poured out her heart countless times as Meg listened sympathetically and Meg had longed for her fortune to turn.

Maureen would not allow Meg or Tom to speak to Duffy on her behalf. She had always said she knew, deep in her heart that if Duffy was ever going to want her, he would have to come to that knowledge himself.

Meg had heard her calling into the wind and went out into the storm to meet her.

"And where is he?" Maureen had hollered into the wind. "He's a great big strappin' man and if he were about havin' me he'd be chasin' me down on this beach by now!"

She plowed through the rain like a wild woman and watching, Meg suddenly found herself on the banks of the Clydagh River the night of their escape. Meg could tell in the dark swirling rain that Maureen didn't even hear Duffy calling anymore and she didn't care, either.

As she careened across the strand with the storm at her back, as the rain began to pummel her head and send the rich pungent smell of beer and horses from the wool jacket wrapped around her, Maureen fell to her knees. She later told Meg that she had been struck by a sudden realization that sent heat roiling through her and caused her to shrug Duffy's jacket onto the sand.

This was not the first time she had had a wool jacket placed over her shoulders only to have her life take a turn so dramatic as to never be the same. Maureen had reminded Meg of the deed in the pocket of Lord Jeffrey's old jacket. How many times had Tom and Meg offered to give her that deed, offering her the opportunity to start a new life across the ocean? How many times had she declined the offer, waiting instead for Duffy to sweep her off her feet and give her reason to burn the one document that linked her to her past?

Before Meg could go to her and help her up, Maureen was again running with purpose. She had begun to feel the energy of the storm. Instead of setting her body to trembling with the desire for Duffy's embrace, the fierce wind and pounding rain now drove her to the cottage where her future awaited her.

As Meg watched, Maureen climbed over the boulders strewn across the familiar beach. She had a terrible sense of foreboding, somehow knowing that Maureen could feel her feet leaving this shore even as she put one in front of the other.

By the time she arrived at the gate, banging in the wind, Meg knew Maureen was halfway across the ocean. Spurned by the only man she had ever loved, her heart now turned toward freedom and her best chance at happiness. She refused to turn and see where he was. She could not bear it if he had not followed her and she could not face him if he had.

As she reached the front door, she stood for a moment looking at Meg before entering her first real home for the last time. Her tears tumbled down her cheeks and mingled with the raindrops dripping off her chin. To anyone watching there was no way to tell one from the other but both Meg and Maureen knew. The rain off the coast of home had turned to icy rivulets running down her face and neck. Maureen knew her tears by the heat of their sting.

Meg could see that Duffy's rejection was so humiliating that she knew Maureen could not stay on Achill even one more day. What she didn't know was that Maureen's tears were matched, drop for drop by those of the man she had left on the beach to pick up his jacket and once again let go of a beautiful girl.

When Maureen had blown in from the walk, wailing and hanging onto Meg, Tom had gone out to find Duffy. He had found him a quarter mile down the beach, standing like a fool in the rain just staring out to sea in the darkening twilight. He had taken Duffy to McCoy's for a pint and a good talk but came home waving his arms in frustration at Duffy's refusal to listen to reason or reveal his true feelings. Tom would never know how much Duffy's silence had cost his big friend. Duffy knew that Tom and Meg could persuade Maureen to stay if he would ask them but he couldn't ask them. He was too afraid of his long-standing feelings for Meg and too confused by the overpowering desire for Maureen that he had experienced for the first time on the beach, to know what to say or how to say it.

And how could he say anything to Tom, of all people? It was Tom's beautiful wife who had filled his dreams for years. Was he supposed to simply shrug and reassure Tom that he no longer lusted after his wife now that he'd started lusting after Maureen? After drinking hard and getting very drunk, Duffy had bedded down with the cows, regretting that even they were females bound to give him a headache when they began moaning to be milked.

That night, after Tom had gone to bed and Duffy had bunked with the cows, Maureen had wept in Meg's lap for the last time, spilling out in detail the events on the beach, everything she had said and done; everything Duffy hadn't said and had failed to do.

Finally Maureen had told Meg of her decision to go to America. Meg had known this day would eventually come but the sorrow of losing Maureen broke her heart so she could actually feel it cracking in her chest.

As the dawn light began casting its net across the strand, Meg had stood in silence as she watched her best friend being rowed out to sea. In the end it had been so sudden, so finite, Meg had felt the breath sucked right out of her as she stood on the shore dry-eyed and numb. Tom wasn't even awake yet and her babies slept soundly in their beds. Meg hadn't had the heart to tell Maureen that she carried another child that Maureen would now never know.

Maureen had hugged Rose and Denny to her breast till Meg thought her heart would break and then, without another word left the little house and walked down to the water. Meg had followed her down to the row of fishing boats, upturned along the shore, like so many lurking whales in a row, glistening from the rain of last night's storm.

Finally after waiting together in silence, Meg and Maureen had stirred at the sound of the men coming to turn over the curraghs and start their workday. Jerry Pidgeon had come over yesterday from Westport to bring the post and agreed to take Maureen on his return trip. Meg and Maureen had embraced briefly, self-conscious in front of the men, and took one last look at each other before Maureen flung her trunk and a sack of provisions into the boat.

Meg had tried to give her money along with the deed but Maureen had shown her a surprisingly large amount she had squirreled away over the years for the wedding that never took place. Meg had watched until Maureen was gone from sight. As the sun began to crack the horizon and the rooster crowed the break of day, she had turned to her home and pondered how her day would unfold without even a wink of sleep. She never saw the bedraggled, broken-hearted man leaning against the byre, watching Jerry Pidgeon's package boat head out to sea.

Meg had found herself unable to even think about sleep. Her heart broken, she had fixed herself a pot of tea and sat in Maureen's favorite straw chair, one she had made herself years ago. The chair was set up in the shade by the dutch door where the butter churn stood ready for the day's work.

Today was butter day and Meg would be churning alone. The thought had made her eyes fill as she realized with a profound sadness how lonely life on this island would be without Maureen. She owed Maureen so much. Not only had she been a dear friend and companion but she had taught Meg everything she knew about running a household.

Sitting in her kitchen, holding the smooth letter in her hands, Meg remembered running her hand up and down the long dash that the two women had taken turns plunging into the cream. It was very hard work and Meg knew Maureen had taken on most of it. But that wasn't what she missed the most about churning or any other chore. Meg was already missing Maureen's endless story telling. She would never hear her friend's voice again as it drifted off into a tale of fairies and leprechauns. In fact, it had only been the previous Wednesday when they were skimming the cream from the milk that Maureen had told her again about the hag who stole butter from the farmer's wife. Meg had never tired of hearing Maureen's stories and this was one of her favorites. Maureen would be so serious in the telling that Meg would have to turn away to hide a smile but Maureen would not be swayed from the warning she had heard from her childhood.

As the story went, the local hag, of which there were so many on Achill that Maureen had never even tried to identify her by name, would use her charms to destroy the butter of any farmer's wife. There were two versions of the story that Maureen had loved to tell. Both of them placed the hag on May Morning before the May festival of Beltane began. In one version, the hag disguised herself as a hare and suckled the cows thereby stealing the cream from their milk for the rest of the year. The other was Meg's favored version.

In this story, the hag swept the fields on May Morning with a tether made of cowhair stolen from the farmer's byre. This rope, called a spancel, was used to tie the cow's front legs during milking and any farmer would be likely to have one thus making any farmer subject to the hag's evil charms. Once she took the spancel, the hag would gather up all the dew from the fields with it, chanting "Come to me, come all to me." As she dragged the spancel through the dew and chanted her evil ditty, she placed a spell on the spancel.

When the unsuspecting farmer's wife used the spancel during milking, there was no cream for her butter. No matter how much she churned, she would have no butter while the sniggering hag dashed an abundance of butter in her churn.

Meg had smiled to herself as she glanced up at the thatch to be sure the St. Brigid's cross was hanging in its place. Maureen was adamant about placing the cross there and on the byre to ward off the hag. So many things Maureen had taught her had amused her and made her shake her head. Since Maureen had gone from her Meg had been faithful to the sprinkling of Holy Water and the blessing of salt.

Francis stirred and Meg stroked his hair. As he began suckling again, Meg's thoughts returned again to that sad morning. She remembered that Denny had started crying and knew that while sleep had escaped her, the duties of the day would not wait. The piseogs, the superstitions embedded in Irish country life, and the antidotes to the evil fairies' spells had become such a part of Meg's own life that when she went inside and plucked her baby from his cradle she had never even noticed the heavy fire tongs hung above his head to keep the fairies away from him as he slept.

Almost a year had passed before Meg heard from Maureen. As she waited for her baby to arrive, Meg would stand looking out to sea wondering if her friend had made it safely to America. Winter came and turned into spring. Mary Clare was born and Meg was just starting out with Thomas when she finally received her first letter from Maureen.

Charlie O'Malley had been frantic when he found Maureen gone. His panic soon turned to fury and his mother's constant haranguing had taken its toll on his nerves. He had had a tidy sum that he too had been saving for a wedding that never took place and had claimed almost daily that he planned to buy two tickets to America with it. Charlie, however, was no fool. He had known Maureen's deed was for land in the state of Pennsylvania though he had had no idea where in Pennsylvania Maureen had settled. Tom and Meg had refused to tell him, which had only fueled his intention to find out. Finally, one July day as Meg gathered kelp for supper, she caught sight of Charlie strutting down the strand as pleased as a peacock.

He had stood before her waving a letter and Meg felt her heart skip a beat.

"I have here, Mrs. Phalen, a bit'o correspondence I'm sure ye will be pleased t'receive."

With great flourish, he had held the letter away from her and read the return address.

"It says here it's from the grand state of Pennsylvania, in the great United States of America, post-marked June 3, 1840. And, ye'll be pleased t'know that I'll no longer be troublin' ye fer the exact place of Miss Maureen Dougherty's new domicile, no I won't at that."

He had handed it to Meg with a little bow and had turned to leave.

As he began to walk away, he had said over his shoulder,

"Ye'll be excusin' me now, I have to be about resignin' me post as constable. I believe I'll be lookin' fer work in Johnstown P-A. Yes, indeedy! That would be in the great land of USA!"

He had laughed then, a self-satisfied cackle that chilled Meg despite the warmth of the afternoon.

Within two weeks, Charlie and his mother were on a ship heading west for America. In the hold of that ship, packed deep in a sack of mail, was Meg's letter warning Maureen that they were on their way; a message that would be too late when it arrived.

Six years later, after countless letters back and forth, Meg had three letters to read at once. Two fat letters scented with the sweet lavender cologne Meg had sent with Maureen the day she had left. The third letter was very thin, only one page, perhaps.

As hard as it was, Meg had waited until the babies were fed and put to sleep before she even touched the letters again. They had burned through her apron pocket and her light summer skirt as she turned and shooed her girls through the gate. Francis had fallen asleep in her arms and Meg rose and put the sleeping baby down on her bed.

She still had over an hour before the older three arrived home. And with Tom gone, there was no one to interrupt her. As extra insurance, she had given Rose a few pennies to stop at Mary Feeney's for a treat after school. She knew the three older children would then take the long way home, giving her plenty of time for a pot of tea and a good read. She picked up her tea and settled down in the wicker chair by the hearth with her letters.

It was not unusual for the mail to get behind and for letters to double up or cross in the mail so Meg thought nothing of the fact that she had three at once. What surprised her was that only two of them had Maureen's handwriting and the other was in a childish cursive, hardly more than printed.

She saw that the two from Maureen were dated a week apart at the end of May and the third in June, right around the time she had Francis. How long it took for the mail to cross the ocean! She decided to read Maureen's first.

29 May, 1845

Dearest Meg,

I have so much to tell you I hardly know where to begin. I found out I was expecting again in March and again lost the baby by the end of April. My heart breaks with every loss. I fear I am never to be blessed with motherhood. Ever since Charlie and I have been married he has demanded a son and despite the never-ending burden of his attention I cannot seem to carry any child he places within me.

Needless to say, he pursues the goal of an heir with such brutish persistence that my life is a misery from dusk till dawn. I truly believe if his mother were not staying with us he would pester me all the day long as well.

We passed our fifth wedding anniversary last month and I fear Charlie's severe displeasure with me somehow contributed to the loss of our little one. He indeed, has a violent temper. Even his mother has scolded him for being a brute toward me. Of course, his drinking makes it worse.

His mother, the scourge that she is, actually protects me from his rages. He won't be quite so brutal when she is present as he is when she is off to church or with her ladies group. The nights she is out, I admit I suffer greatly at his hands. If only I could convince him to leave me alone once I am with child, I may be able to hang on to one of them. Truly, though I have conceived and lost with such regularity that I have actually lost count of how many little lives there have been. My heart grows more numb with each one gone from me.

I fear his mother is unwell. I have found her clutching her chest a few times and she sleeps a great deal. Charlie continues on the force and I manage the store. It's drudgery but it keeps us fed and I am so glad that Charlie no longer tries to run it with me. That is the only victory I can claim, convincing him to use his 'vast' experience as constable to apply for the lieutenant's position on the police force. I always felt that the deed and the store were mine from the day I arrived and have always been so grateful to you for giving it to me so many years ago when we first discovered it.

Oh, dear Meg, how I long for the days before Charlie landed on these shores and brought his miserable self to me. I know I was hungry and making so little of my opportunity but I was beginning to turn the store around and had actually started to see a young man from Johnstown. Oh, but you've read all this before. You know as well as I the sorry story of my "rescue" from a life of squalor and sin (as you know, Charlie has never believed that my young man's intentions were honorable and that I had never compromised myself with him). I fully believe that Charlie doubted my purity from the first day he met me and I suppose with good reason after Lord Jeffrey's doing, though, of course, he still knows nothing of that.

Anyway, that's history. I want to tell you about some interesting things. Despite Charlie's jealousy and his most undesirable attentions, my life does have some good things in it. As you can tell by my writing, my English is improving and I am losing some of the peasant Irish in my talk. Mrs. O'Malley, in her passion for female companionship, has introduced me to the life of our parish. I am now taking elocution and cursive lessons from Sr. Mary Agnes, the principal of the new parish school. I am ever grateful for her sweet temper and patience. Charlie knows nothing of my accomplishments as I practice when he is at work and his mother has promised to keep my secret. She is an old crab sometimes but she is my only ally in the house of O'Malley.

I am also taking in handwork, using the lace making skills you taught me. The order of sisters that teach at the school is Belgian (no, I do not speak English with a Flemish accent, though it's sometimes a struggle) and some of them are expert lace makers. We do lovely things for bridal trousseaus and I have even made a cloth for the altar at St. Columba's. It thrills me to see my work gracing the altar at Sunday mass. So, despite Charlie, I have some life of my own.

How are you my dearest? I never pass a day that I do not miss you and long for a good oyster shucking or kelp harvesting with you. Johnstown is a growing town but the industry is heavy and the beautiful mountains surrounding us only keep the stench of the distillery in the valley and make me long for the open vista of the sea. If Charlie misses the sea, he'll never admit it and he sniggers every time I suggest that we close up the store for a few days and go where there is water.

Of course, life here in America is so different from back home. Time is money here and if you close your store you risk losing your customers to the store down the street. God forbid Charlie should ever sacrifice a nickel to a moment's idle pleasure. Gone is the Charlie of Doeega days who spent hours idling on the strand pretending to be protecting Doeega from mythical warriors. I haven't heard much about Grace O'Malley since he arrived here!

He works hard here and there are plenty of plant hands from Eastern Europe to keep his paddy wagon filled. I'm afraid though, that for Charlie, the greatest offense they can commit is to simply be other than Irish, the worst being Polish or Hungarian. I have to say though that any man who looks twice at me gets the same treatment, no matter where he was born. Charlie is fearfully jealous, though I am so weary from my wifely duties every night that there is absolutely no danger of my eye wandering in any direction.

As I mentioned before, his drinking has gotten worse and he goes after me something terrible when he drinks, Meg. Sometimes I am grateful we have no children. I couldn't bear it if he hurt them. He never raises his hand to his mam, thank God. She could never withstand it at her age.

Oh, I almost forgot to tell you my main news! You know that Tom's nephew, Philip and his wife Julie are here in the States. Well, guess who just moved to Johnstown? Philip has actually taken over the pharmacy and is doing very well. The town has just hired a physician and Philip's arrival could not have been more perfectly timed. The doctor is up on all the latest medicines and has even opened a surgery in his parlor. In fact, just yesterday he set the broken arm of Mrs. Gertrude Fleming, one of our oldest grande-dames and she paid him quite handsomely because he did it without pain. Thanks to Philip's apothecary, (and the quickness of his shoe-leather) Dr. Crawford had a hefty supply of chloroform to put the old lady out. Her praise for both doctor and druggist can only help Philip and Julie. She is by far the wealthiest American woman I know. I believe she is a sister by marriage to the long-haired Dutchman, Peter Levergood who bought the original village from Joseph Johns years ago. A good woman to impress!

I'm very glad that Philip and Julie have such a champion. They lease the building two doors down and I am just so glad to have them here! If you haven't heard from them yet, I will spill the beans and tell you that Julie is expecting again, due in December. They have three boys now, of course she's hoping for a girl. They live on the other side of town from us but I love seeing Julie every day and she too takes writing lessons from Sister.

Charlie seems to like Philip for some odd reason so I'm hoping he'll let me be friends with Julie. His temper has forced so many of our friends away. Speaking of friends, say hello for me to Duffy. Please tell him I think of him often and wish him well. You and you alone know what I am really saying with those simple words.

Well, I must go. Have a cup of tea for me, my love. Keep me in your prayers as I do you in mine. My love to Tom and big hugs to Rose, Denny, Mary Clare, Thomas and Gracie and a big squeeze for baby Ellen. If I guess right from your last letter, you should have had your baby by now.

Write as soon as you can and let me know whether I'm to send my kisses to a boy or a girl. I'll write as soon as I hear from you.

God bless,

Maureen

Meg held the letter for several minutes before she set it down and tore open the second one. This was written much more hastily and Meg could tell immediately that the news was bad.

June 7, 1845

Dear Meg,

How quickly fate can change a life! The very day after I wrote you my last letter, Mrs. O'Malley fell over in the vestibule of St. Columba's and died. We all knew she had a bad heart but it still came as a shock, especially to poor Charlie.

We had a wake and I was surprised at the number of people there. She had her ladies, of course, and several of the men from the force came with their wives. We saw a few of our old friends and Charlie acted like he was really glad to see them. Maybe he'll let me invite some of them over for an evening sometime.

Philip and Julie were there and she was just wonderful helping with the funeral breakfast and all. You would never know she was expecting. She says she's never had a sick day with any of her babies! And the food! This is a wonderful place to be. Americans are the warmest and most generous people in the world. And, I actually tried some of the dishes from an Italian lady whose husband supplies the produce for the store. Very interesting!

Things have been really bad though, between me and Charlie since we buried his mother last week. He hasn't been back to work and he hasn't stopped drinking either. I know he set such store by his mam but I've never seen him so desperate.

I went to Fr. Finn yesterday for advice and he came for supper and spent all evening trying to talk to Charlie. Fr. Finn, now there's a man who likes his bottle and even he was begging Charlie to ease up on the drink. You wouldn't believe it but Charlie actually raised his hand to a priest when he tried to take the whiskey away from him! To a priest! They'll never be able to close the casket on him! His arm will be stiff in the air. Fr. Finn said then that he'd not stay to be a temptation to Charlie to commit any more mortal sins against the cloth and he left me there alone to put him to bed.

Well, Meg I couldn't get him to go to bed and when he woke up on the parlor floor the next day, I had hell to pay. God forgive me for the use of the word but that man was devil-sent that morning.

My writing is a little shaky so I won't go on but I knew you'd want to know and the packet boat goes out day after tomorrow so I wanted to get this message to you. Pray for me Meg. Even if your God is a Protestant, he can't want me to suffer like I do with Charlie O'Malley. God help me, yours or mine, now that his mam isn't here to come between us.

I love you all and I wish I'd never left Achill, for sure.

Maureen

Meg's heart was leaden as she folded the letter and set it on the table. She picked up the third and latest letter and sat staring at it. Now she really was afraid to open it. This one she knew was not from Maureen and she feared the worst after reading how Charlie had snapped after his Mam died.

Finally she tore open the thin paper and began to read the scrawled words.

June 10,1845
Der Meg,

Hello its Julie. So sorry for my bad ritin. I am ritin about Maureen and Charlie. I know you can't do nuthin' way over ther on the other side o the world but I got to tell somebody befor I esplode. Charlie is a mad man. He's drunk all the time and beets Maureen. Since his mam died evry day she has a new broos. I think he's gonna kill her. I don't no what to do. Phil an me try to come betwen em but now Phil won't let me go there in case Charlie wood hurt me. He passes out at nit and Maureen coms over. Phil brings drugs an sav for the cuts but she wont let Doc see her. Rite to her so she wants to live. She cris all the tim and he just keps drinkin. How he stil works I dont know but he wont for long. I help her in the stor. Just pray and rit to her. Yor cuzzin, Julie

Meg sat like a stone as a buzzing sounded in her ears. What could she possibly do for Maureen from so far away? She knew no one in the United States on whom to call for help. Thank God for Philip and Julie! But even they couldn't do much for Maureen. This letter was proof of that. Meg knew it was useless to try to get the police to intervene especially with Charlie on the force. Maureen had already tried the priest. What could she do from Ireland?

Meg got up and paced around her little kitchen. When she heard her children calling to each other she went outside to greet them and their noisy return awakened the two girls and the baby. Meg knew she wouldn't rest until she responded to the letters. She wished with an ache in her heart that Tom were home but her life was what it was and she forced herself to carry on, vowing to write to Maureen as soon as she could.

It was evening when Meg finally sat down to answer the letters. She could not settle down and all the fear left by Andrew Feeney the night before swirled like a ghost around the little house. She missed Tom miserably tonight but thought again how glad she was he wouldn't be home until the worst of her bruises were gone. It was her fear that she'd have trouble hiding them from him. Andrew had burned his evil into her and she felt dirty and evil herself. Thank God she was so busy all day she had had no time to think about what he had done to her.

Now it was quiet. A crawly feeling came across her skin and she shivered in the damp night air. The hearth radiated the warmth of a low turf fire but Meg could not get warm. Rose looked up from her tatting and gave Meg a queer look when she threw not one but two new bricks on the fire.

Rose had not said much about her mother's haggard

appearance but Meg knew she suspected something was wrong. Rose was only ten but she missed nothing. Meg had felt her watchful eye upon her since the girl had arrived home from the hedge school that afternoon. Meg had been very careful to conceal her bruises with a high collared dress but Rose watched her eat supper and clearly noticed how Meg's mouth hurt her and how gingerly she chewed her food.

Before she could write to Maureen, Meg knew she had to reassure Rose that everything was all right.

"Come here, Lovie," Meg said, using Tom's special name for her daughter.

Rose came to her and nestled on her lap, her long legs hanging almost to the floor.

"You're so big I can hardly hold you anymore, sweet one."

When Rose tried to slide off, Meg held her tighter.

"No, we can still do this."

Meg smiled as the two of them tried to wriggle onto the warm stone seat jutting out from the hearth. They barely fit together under the deep canopy and had to be careful not to end up in the cinders.

Rose sat watching the low flames while Meg unwound her plaited hair. Taking a boar bristle brush from her apron pocket, Meg began to brush the long dark curls.

"You do have the most beautiful hair, Rose, just like silk. You were never bald like most babies. Ever since you came into the world you had thick black curls just like your da. And the sweetest little mouth all rosy and pink. Do you know that's how you got your name?"

Meg knew Tom had told her this many times but Rose loved to hear it and it usually brought a smile to her face. Tonight Meg had to settle for a shrug.

She continued to comb the silky mass of hair until it shone. Then she parted it from crown to nape and began to braid it again for the night.

"No, Mam, leave it loose. I don't want it braided tonight."

Meg wrapped her arms around her first born and together

they just sat and soaked in the radiant heat.

"Mam, do ye believe in fairies?"

"Well, I suppose I do. Why?"

"Just something Mr. Mulcahy said last week."

Meg wondered at Rose's curious question. This child was not one to believe in fanciful stories.

"What kind of story did Mr. Mulcahy tell?"

"Not really a story, just that sometimes the fairies can git into someone's soul when they're sleepin' and suck out their happiness."

Meg felt wariness creep over her and wondered what Rose was really getting at.

"Then what did he say?"

"Not much. Billy Feeney was bein' cross and nasty and Mr. Mulcahy said he thought that was what happened at night when Billy was sleepin'. Mam, do ye think the fairies could get all the way out the strand to our house?"

"Well, I don't suppose they would be bothered, with all the souls to suck in town."

"But I was thinkin' that maybe you see them sometimes."

"Now, Rose, do you think I'd let a fairy with such an evil plan anywhere near this house? And do you think Da wouldn't be out there waving them away with a torch should they ever show up?"

"If ye don't believe in fairies, why d'ye have the tongs over the baby cradle?"

"I never said I didn't believe in them. I just said your da and I would never let them hurt you. That's why we put the tongs there; to protect baby Francis. We did the same with all of you and no fairies ever bothered you. And we'll do the same with any new baby when it comes."

"What about mams and das? Can they get ye if ye don't have a tongs over yer bed?"

"No, I don't think they want mams and das much."

Meg lifted Rose's chin and looked into her sleepy blue eyes, so like Tom's.

"Are you afraid, Rose? Is that why you're asking about the fairies?"

The big cornflower blue eyes glistened with unshed tears but Rose shook her head.

"No, Mam," she lied.

"Rose?"

Meg could read her children like books and she knew Rose had a reason for her question.

"Well, maybe a wee bit," Rose confessed, a fat tear slipping over her long black lashes and down her chubby cheek.

"Why, Rose, you are afraid of fairies! No, no, sweetheart, Da and I will never let them hurt you!"

"But Mam, not me! The fairies never bother me."

"Then, who, Rose? Are you worried about Mary Clare, Denny, the younger ones?"

Rose started crying, pressing her face into Meg's shoulder.

Meg hardly heard her mumbled reply,

"You, Mam!"

"Me!? Rose, why would the fairies want me? I'm not even Irish!"

Rose giggled through her tears at the thought of the fairies wanting her English mam. She hadn't thought of that.

Out of the same apron pocket she drew the hairbrush, Meg brought out a clean hanky.

"Here, blow," she coaxed the sobbing child.

Rose blew her nose and looked at Meg with wide eyes framed by a fringe of damp lashcs.

"I was worried," she said, her little face crumpling again.

"This mornin' I thought maybe they sucked on yer soul durin' the night, ye were that sad when ye came out."

Rose tilted her head in the direction of Meg and Tom's bedroom.

"And tonight ye were eatin' funny. I thought they got yer tongue. Sometimes Mr. Mulcahy says the fairies got our tongues when we don't answer his questions."

Meg could hardly conceal a smile as she brushed a stray curl from Rose's forehead. She tried to look as serious as Rose did as she answered her fears.

"Well, Rose, I wasn't myself this morning. I am often lonesome when Da is away and I was very lonesome last night. Sometimes even mams get sad and cry, Rose. Da is my friend and I missed him very much last night. As for my chewing, you're right I have a sore mouth but it's almost better and I'm sure it will be fine by the time Da gets home. And so will you, my sweetie. But you need to go to bed."

"Oh, Mam, can't I do a little more on me doily before I go t'bed? That way ye won't be missin' Da so much."

Meg squeezed Rose and laughed.

"You are a conniver, missy. I suppose so, but I'm counting on you to be good and go as soon as you finish the row you're working on."

Rose slid off her lap with a sigh of relief and went back to her tatting.

Now it was Meg's turn to have moist eyes. She never had a mother who cared about her fears. In fact she knew without a doubt that she never sat on her mother's lap the way Rose had just done. Well, she thought as she rose from the stone seat that was certainly her mother's loss as much as it was hers.

When Meg finally sat down with her pen and paper, she thought she would not be able to write to Maureen after what she had been through the night before. Somehow the tender moments with Rose had dissipated much of her own pain and she had no trouble at all.

July 31, 1845
Dear Maureen,

I write to you this cool evening, chilly for the end of July. A fog has settled around the house and I can't even see the strand from the kitchen window. I suppose the cloud covers the whole strand, maybe even as far inland as the village. Remember how those clouds would come and sit like a hen brooding over the whole bay? Rose sits practicing her tatting and I can see the candle still lit in the loft where Denny reads.

I love this time of night. The babies are abed and I enjoy the presence of my older ones busy in their own solitude. Poor Mary Clare is never among them though. She is early to bed that one. Sometimes, especially when lessons at school are hard, she barely makes it through supper. Sometimes I think she is so frail but she has a subtle strength, more a strength of the spirit. Tom calls her his little nun!

Thank you for your letters. The first one was so filled with news. I am so proud of you for your beautiful penmanship. I'm glad too to read that you're still making lace. Never lose your tatting skills. The making of lace will always be a good industry for women. As long as fine ladies like frilly underthings and brides like lacy nightgowns, there will be a demand for your work. And of course, we can't overlook the altar cloths. I suppose, a much nobler enterprise than edging a chemise.

I was terribly sorry to read of your miscarriage. I know you think you will never be blessed with a full term baby. I wish I could promise you otherwise but only God knows that. Just know that my heart aches for you especially at this time of the year when Mary Ellen's birthday falls. You must believe your sufferings are etched on my heart and soul. I pray that you know how I love you as a sister. You are in my heart and your tears are my tears. I am so sorry, dear Maureen for any and all the moments when you did not know that of me. I fear I have been so absorbed in my own life that I have failed you as a friend. I beg you to forgive me.

I was sorry to read of Mrs. O'Malley's death. Please extend my sympathy to Charlie though he probably won't want it. He never had much time for me.

I am very distressed to hear of his heavy drinking and your suffering at his hands. Between your veiled references and a letter I received from Julie, I want to come over myself on the next boat and rescue you. I rue the day Duffy let you go. Tom and I should have nailed the two of you to your creepies until we could get Fr. O'Boyle to the house to marry you. But I carry on and that can only wound you more. Please forgive me dear one but you know how I feel about you and Duff.

He has not married, by the way. Still the same old Duff. I will *certainly give him your message.*

But getting back to you and Charlie. Maureen, dearest, you must find a way to protect yourself. When he hurts you please, please see the doctor! Perhaps he can intervene. If Charlie is unstable and the doctor can prove him a danger to others perhaps he can order him away from you. Oh, I know I'm thinking nonsense. No man would ever come between husband and wife. No man can legally do so. I just want you to know what I wish for you. Please keep me informed of developments in your life. Even the sad or terrible news. I cannot bear to be away from you when you need me. It is so small a comfort these words of mine but at least if I know, I can try. Stay close to Julie. If Philip can win Charlie's affection then you know he will try to intervene when he can. Maybe even protect you within the constraints of the law.

Enough advice. My sweetest hugs and kisses go out to you. If only I could take you in my arms and lead you to a fine cup of tea and fresh barm brack.

I will share my own news. Perhaps it will take your mind off your troubles for a few moments. Perhaps it will wound you more. Again, forgive me.

I had my third son in May, two days after you wrote your first letter which came together with your second. The delivery was my easiest, yet he seems to be my largest baby. We named him Francis John. It's still too soon to tell what color his hair will be but we think he may be a redhead. His eyes are very round and very blue. I think you would like him and I congratulate you on being Auntie Maureen again. Please forgive how hollow that must sound as you grieve your loss but if you were here you know I'd hand him right to you. I wonder, will Francis be my last? I don't know. I'm 37 years old but we'll see. When I think of Francis being my last babe, I'm not sure how to feel about it.

Of course, I write this letter at the old kitchen table, the one you and I fixed ten years ago. I still have the shells in a little basket near the window and a glass of fresh wildflowers on the sill. The kitchen looks much the same as when you left. What can one do with a kitchen? I have a new tin oven. The old one, so loyal and true has finally fallen apart. Tom brought me one from Newport when he last visited. He's there now. I expect him home within the fortnight.

The dresser is now painted green with yellow trim around the edge. I'm not sure what color we had it when you left. That is one thing I can really change and I enjoy freshening it up in the spring. We still have the same fence, boolies and hen house. The fruit trees are heavy laden this season and the peaches and plums are close to full size but ripening is slow due to a great deal of rain. The pears and apples are still tiny. The fish are plentiful for those who don't mind fishing in the rain.

My new oyster shucking partner is Rose. Oh, Maureen you would be so proud of our Lovie. She is strong and sturdy built more like you than me! It must be that good Irish stock. She is going to be very pretty when she comes into her own. Her hair as you remember is raven black and full of curl. She thinks it is a nuisance and wears it plaited most of the time but someday a young man will change her opinion of it, I'm sure. At ten she cares little for boys which bothers me none and truly pleases her father.

Denny at almost nine is nearly as tall as Rose and towers over Mary Clare who turns eight in January. My "Irish twins", as they say! I'm afraid she will always be petite. Again the little nun. Perhaps the very little nun! She is very pious and peace loving, fairer than Rose with auburn hair and Tom's deep blue eyes. Rose and Denny have almost aqua eyes because of the green in mine I guess. They change depending on the time of day or what they wear.

But getting back to Mary Clare, her poor sensitive heart is always being broken by everything from a trampled frog to a sad looking seascape. People are her passion though. She wants to save everybody and even tries to be nice to Lizzie Ballard earning her nothing from that old witch but sneers and scorn which of course breaks her heart. But there she is the very next day trying again. Why, one day I caught her slipping out the door with a loaf of hot soda bread. Going to Mrs. Ballard's, she said. She seemed cranky that morning and Mary Clare thought perhaps that would cheer her up. I'm afraid she didn't get past her father with that bread! I have to watch her or she'll be giving away the cows!

Thomas is doing well; my dreamer still looks exactly like his father.

He's beginning to lose that baby face and becoming a very handsome little boy with curls like Rose's and dark blue eyes. He has that same ruddy complexion Tom has. But then all of mine favor the Irish in their skin tone except Denny. He really has the more sallow coloring of the Wynns. I find Thomas much less a know-it-all than either Rose or Denny were at four. He chases around here mostly after Denny whom he adores but he is really the male counterpart to Mary Clare. Those two sit for hours together inspecting lichens or bugs. They both love the night sky and I have often found them asleep on the strand when I go out in the evening myself. Such rascals! But poor Mary Clare is going to lose her playmate soon I think. He wants so badly to be big he's started to walk, talk and even belch like Denny!

Ellen is finally weaned and walking as well, driving Gracie mad. I'm so glad she finally gave up nursing! I never was one to have a lot of milk and I need what I have for Francis. Ellen is very blond but like Denny, no curls. Fine straight hair like my father. Thank God she's not like him any other way though I sometimes fear Denny has a bit of his ugliness. She's by far my hungriest baby and Rose feeds her with two spoons. She sputters and spits her gruel all over just trying to demand the next spoonful. She is nowhere near the cuddler that Thomas was but then neither was Gracie. Gracie just wants to keep me nearby. Beyond that, she's very independent.

My girls do seem much more independent than the boys. Typical Irish sons! Little Gracie is coming into her own a bit. She's a sweet little thing and very quiet. I sometimes wondered if she'd ever talk. But then I worried that she'd never walk either and she's tearing around the place. She's finally getting hair. It took long enough! Ellen is chatty with a big mouth like her sister Rose and the hottest temper of all my children. She has quite the pout! Mrs. Trent says she that once she learns words, Gracie will have to talk just to keep up with her little sister. Another set of "Irish twins", they were born so close together. They could be twins. Both blond, green eyes just like mine. Little though. Both have short stumpy little legs and chubby little fingers! I'm not sure where they get the shortness from but Tom says his Da was never very big. Well, I suppose neither of my parents are either.

I wonder where Tom got to be so tall?

I am well. If I do have more children I think my body can handle it. I'm pretty strong. I can remember beating you in foot races along the strand though you could always out swim me. Remember the feel of the ocean against our bare skin on a moonlit night? I haven't done that since you left. It's no fun without you to sneak out with.

I always pray that you will have children and I feel awful prattling on about mine. I just know you'd be disappointed if I failed to give you a report on them. I know you love them so. Again, I will pray very hard for you that God will bless you with a healthy child or six! Why not? I know when you do have a child you will be a wonderful mother. I remember how you loved Rose and Denny from their birth.

Maureen, never lose heart. You are one of the most beautiful wild spirits I've ever known, and you have a strong heart. Not to mention your faith. I will pray to your God of mercy every day for you. You don't need me to pray to my God of harsh judgment. I'll pray to him for Charlie. He's a sad sack but he can't hurt you and get away with it. When I read about Charlie and his brutish ways, I wanted to slap him silly. He has no idea what a jewel you are.

I love you, I love you, I love you. Tom loves you and even silly old Duffy loves you though he's too dense to realize it. Give my best wishes to Philip and Julie and please don't be cross with Julie for telling me the truth about you and Charlie. Write to me soon and God bless you.

Your devoted friend, Meg

Chapter Five

While Tom Phalen did not lavish treats and luxuries on his family, he insisted on educating his children. Rose, Denny and Thomas attended the hedge school run by Mr. Mulcahy, the local ollav. He was a man gifted in the classics with a love for learning that reflected in his pupils' high performance. Mr. Mulcahy lived on the western edge of the Phalen land and ran a day school for the small children and a night school for older children and adults. He worked tirelessly to bring the classics of ancient Greece and Rome, reading and writing in both the Irish and English. He knew he could face death if he was caught but he fiercely drilled into their memories the history of battles and heroes from Chuchulainn to Brian Boru. He spoke to his students with hushed reverence of the druids and how, led by St. Patrick, they became the first bishops of the church in Ireland. He expounded with loyal intensity of the great Irish warrior clans of O'Neil and Fitzgerald who lived in the rustic claghans of old. He taught the children mathematics and history, rewarding their hard work with opportunities to perform the great works of the Irish bards and poets. No one would guess that Rose Phalen and Danny O'Dowda were fierce adversaries on the streets of Doeega when they saw the two of them performing the story of Grace O'Malley the Pirate Queen of ClareIsland. As often as possible, Fr. O'Boyle would come from St. Dymphna's to teach Latin and Greek to the older students and stir up any budding vocations to the priesthood. But it was the Ollav to whom the people owed their real debt of gratitude. Like hedge masters across Ireland, Mr. Mulcahy risked everything to bring the people their story, seized by the English and banned from their hearing. It was he and others like him who kept alive the culture, the language and the forbidden Irish history.

The hedge school had been situated for generations halfway along the road between O'Fearon's farm and the west border of the village. In the Cromwell years, before O'Fearon's moved to Achill from Donegal, when the farm was occupied by the Doogans, the illegal lessons had been taught only at night. The local families would send out one member into the dark countryside to creep along the hedgerow seeking the forbidden knowledge. The quest for the ancestral language and culture of the lost clans of history was such a driving force that tearful mams would sprinkle their elder sons with holy water and willingly send them out to risk their lives. They would stealthily venture out, glean the jewels of their history and sneak back to their hearths to share what they learned.

The visiting bards who had risked certain death for bringing the ancient stories to the people had been housed in booleys from one end of Ireland to the other. These descendents of the great bard caste of ancient times whispered late into the night, regaling their awestruck pupils by the shifting light of the moon. Deep in the shadows they had poured out their treasures. The ferocity of the great Clan U'Neill, the bravery of the legendary Brian Boru, the Clan Fitzgerald and the great saints: Patrick, Brigid, Dymphna. Night after night the seekers would wend their treacherous way to the little thicket of brambles and wild roses where the bard hid in the shadows. Those who had lived close to the Doogan farm met there and crossed the road and barley fields deep under the ground in a hand-dug tunnel that dropped down through a trap door in the floor of the chicken house. More than one student emerged from the earth covered in silt, shaken loose and sifted down as thundering hooves carried Cromwell's night patrol on the road above.

The little school was totally hidden by hedges, and a tiny booley that now stood in ruins, housed the students during bad weather. Mr. Mulcahy, himself a descendent of the bard caste, had been a boy when the laws had eased up a bit on hedge schools, but his grandfather had told him the story of the schoolmaster and the priest who had run for their lives after being turned in by an informer for teaching young Catholics how to read and write Latin and Greek. Though the patrols had ceased to terrorize, it was still forbidden to teach the old ways and the ollav still practiced his trade in secret.

The people of Ireland still regarded the ollav, or learned one, as one deserving the utmost respect and attention and in a place as isolated as Achill, not only was the teacher revered but the hedge school itself was far more common than the more modern farmhouse or town school on the mainland.

Three years ago the O'Fearons had packed their belongings and fled their little farm. Young Tommy O'Fearon had gotten into serious trouble in a drunken brawl outside Browne's inn in Westport. Tommy was a local member of the Blackthorn Brotherhood, a radical splinter group of the old Catholic Defenders that had started in Armagh two generations ago. When he had foolishly beaten to a bloody pulp the son of an English judge on holiday in Westport, Lord Sligo had had him deported to England where he was promptly hanged.

The O'Fearons had fled to Australia and the farm had been left to decay. Tom Phalen's potato fields were extended to include the old O'Fearon farm. The hedge master had taken up residence in the old farmhouse and his lessons now included Cromwellian history complete with demonstrations of the use of the old trap door and secret tunnel leading from the farmhouse directly to the overgrown spot where in fair weather, this generation of pupils learned in relative safety.

The weather had stayed fair in the week since Andrew had attacked Meg in her yard. The children had continued to attend the hedge school and were filled with Mr. Mulcahy's stories every afternoon when they tumbled in the door. Their lively chatter was a tonic for her and she threw herself into their midst. Those precious minutes when they filled her kitchen with noise and chaos were the only relief Meg had from the lingering effects of that horrible foggy night. The pain of her bruises was beginning to fade and she was anxious to have Tom home. Her eyes endlessly scanned the horizon for the curragh that would bring him. The warm weather had kept her outdoors where she had spent hours on the strand with the little ones, gathering dulse and mussels, building sand castles and wading at low tide. She could almost see Clare Island on the clear afternoons and any of the dozens of curraghs that came from that direction could be the one bringing Tom back to her. Her encounter with Andrew slowly became a memory as she began to feel more normal as her bruises turned from angry purple to faded green and yellow. She was hopeful that they would be gone by the time Tom had a chance to see her.

Inside, the healing was taking longer. Meg kept herself occupied with the usual chores but felt a cold fear seize her whenever she had to go out to the booley for butter or to the coop to feed the chickens. It was the inner effect of Andrew's brutality that worried Meg the most. Her bruises had faded but the fearful memories of Andrew's assault haunted her dreams and crept into her thoughts. She saw his evil face looking up from her wash water. She felt his icy hand on her wrist as she pulled the pins from her hair at night. She bolted the door at sundown and made Rose and Denny do the milking.

Even in daylight Meg found it hard to spend time in her yard. She had begun counting the minutes until she could sleep safely in her husband's arms and did her chores carelessly, her eyes ever turning to the sea. She was afraid Tom, like Rose, would sense a change in her and know something had happened while he was gone. Well, they would just have to deal with things as they came. Maybe he would never have to know. Her thoughts again drew her glance out to Clare Island but there were no vessels heading in and only Seamus Foy's hooker on the horizon.

Meg absently poured sand from a broken conch shell as Ellen let it sift through her chubby fingers. The heat made them all dreamy and she took the children in before they fell asleep on the beach.

This afternoon, Meg hoped she could finally answer Julie's letter. She had read and reread the three letters but could not find the words to respond. Twice she had attempted to write encouragement to Julie about Maureen but no matter what she put down, her words sounded hollow and fatalistic. Meg's own heart had been so singed by Andrew Feeney's accusations that she felt unworthy to even begin to advise Julie. When she put the babies down for their nap, Meg tried, again, to start.

The curragh that would bring Tom would take the mail back to Westport and she wanted to have her letter ready. But Ellen had a slight fever and would not settle down. Meg ended up sitting on the strand with her again, in the shadow of the thinking rock. Before she knew it, the afternoon was gone and she could see her older children strolling down the strand from school. When they saw her out on the beach, they ran along the shallows, kicking up the foamy spray, their soles slapping on the cool wet sand.

Today, the children had been given a demonstration as part of their lessons. Mr. Mulcahy had wanted to show his beloved charges the secret tunnel all summer but the wet weather had confined their lessons to the farmhouse kitchen. Now they greeted Meg with a cacophony of exclamations about the mysterious hiding place, the hated Cromwell, the trampled rights of the Catholics all jumbled into a history lesson she could hardly follow. Their noisy enthusiasm made Ellen fuss and Meg's head hurt trying to retain her thoughts for Julie. Finally, she gave up and lent her full attention to their report.

It was late when Meg finally sat down to pull her thoughts together again. She had just written Dear Julie, in her flowing script when she heard Denny get out of bed. He rarely sought her out and she was surprised to see him standing in his nightshirt at the foot of the ladder.

"Mam, is it true ye're English?" he asked, rubbing his eyes in the candlelight.

"Yes, I am. My mother, Lady Beverly, was the daughter of Lord Bentley Cushing, knighted by King George for bravery in the war with the colonies in America. My father is the son of Bertrand Wynn, Earl of Cantwell, who married the niece of Lord Amherst, another hero from the colonies. Why do you ask?"

Meg had not noticed the look of horror on Denny's face as she answered without looking up from her letter writing.

"Ye can't be English! Ye must niver be English!" Denny cried.

"Me da would niver marry ye if ye were! Mam, I can't be English! I'm a Phalen, I'm Irish! I'm Catholic!"

Suddenly he stopped and gave her a look filled with suspicion and fear.

"Yer not Catholic are ye Mam? I never see ye take Communion. Mam are ye not Catholic like me da?"

At this, Meg rose from her chair and tried to put her arms around Denny. He pulled away from her and threw off her embrace.

"Ye're Protestant, ain't ye Mam? I hate ye, I hate ye fer it and I'll not call ye me mam! I want me da!"

Meg saw a look of terror cross her son's round pink face.

"Mam, ye killed him didn't ye! He ain't gone t'see anybody is he? Ye've taken him out and done him in, haven't ye?"

Meg could not believe her ears. What had happened to her little boy that he could say these things to her? She took him firmly by the arm and swatted him hard on the bottom. She knew that her spank was nothing compared to Tom's switching but the effect it had was far more bruising. Denny brought himself up to his full height and looked at her with such pain and defiance that her heart melted. He was just a little lad and was fighting so hard to be a man! What had happened to him?

She shook him hard and spoke to him as firmly as she ever had.

"Now you listen to me, young man. I am your mother and you will not speak to me that way. You are a horrible boy to think I'd do anything to your father. You march yourself up that ladder this minute and expect a good switching when he gets home and hears what you have said. When you're ready to apologize for this scene and tell me how you came to say these terrible things to your mam, I will be ready to listen. Now, you'd best get out of my reach."

At this, he simply stuck out his chin and looking right into her eyes, he spoke in a voice she hardly recognized.

"Ye may be English but I will niver be. I hate the English."

Bursting into humiliated tears he pulled away from her and scrambled up the ladder to his bed.

Her letter forgotten, Meg sat heavily in her chair. Suddenly her healing bruises all began to throb. Denny's words hung like acid in the air. She could not believe what had happened to her just last week in her own yard. She could not believe what she had read in Maureen's letters and most of all, she could not believe what she had just heard from her son. There was no point in trying to think any more about any of it. She was exhausted and she burned everywhere Andrew had touched.

Meg went to bed but could not sleep. Lying awake in the dark she listened to the waves slapping against the shore. She couldn't wait for Tom to come home but she couldn't pray for him to come home until her bruises were gone. Again, she reached for Tom's rosary and held it tightly in her hand. She may be English and Protestant but she found comfort in the beads of the Virgin and comfort was what Meg needed right now.

The next morning Denny behaved as if nothing had happened between them. Meg wondered if he had been dreaming when he came down and spewed his hateful words. She made a mental note to speak with Fr. O'Boyle about it next time she saw him. And of course, she would have to tell Tom when he came home.

Three days later Meg looked out and saw Tom climbing out of Mr. Jerry Pidgeon's mail boat. He had expected to come on the mail boat and Meg was prepared for the surly old salt that grudgingly did the run between Westport and Achill. Instead, she was so thrilled to see Tom she hardly noticed the crabby old man in his rumpled uniform. As soon as Tom smiled at her, the specter of Andrew Feeney vaporized as well.

Denny had never mentioned the English again and Meg had put aside the incident. She had tried several times to speak to him about his outburst but the words would not come. She had been tremendously busy putting up fruit and vegetables for the winter. The potatoes were ready to harvest and she had told the women pickers to be ready as soon as Tom arrived.

Meg's heart sang as she watched him pick up each of his children and kiss them. Even the older ones got swung around in his strong arms. Their squeals of pleasure were compounded when Tom tossed each of them a new yoyo from Duffy McGee, carved and strung during the long, rainy summer when he thought he'd lose his mind with the boredom of his empty inn. Meg had just come in from the booley after churning and storing butter and her face was damp with the exertion of the task. She knew her hair had escaped its pins and damp curls clung to her neck but the day was warm and everyone's hair was damp.

Meg knew Tom caught sight of her by the way he set Gracie on the sand. She saw in his face the same longing she knew he saw on hers. Mr. Pidgeon had turned to unload provisions from the curragh and the children had scattered to play with their yoyos. Meg felt as if she and Tom were the only two people in the world and nothing that had or would happen to them mattered any more than this moment caught on one pulse of sun-drenched time.

She would always remember this moment as a golden hinge upon which their lives swung, as a door swinging gently closed, mysteriously pregnant with unspoken truth and graciousness. Neither had an inkling or care of what tomorrow would bring. They were so lost in the moment, so deeply embedded in this time and place that they would speak later of feeling a precise shift in the sand beneath their feet at the very second they beheld each other's face. Neither of them even thought it odd that it should be thus after thousands of such glances across the heads of their children, countless comings and goings into and out of each other's sight, the endless rhythm of days and nights, seasons and holidays, suns and moons rising and setting.

Neither of them thought about it at all. There was no thought between them, only a gentle rocking of time, an imaginary pendulum swinging between them catching them and drawing them each to the other across the sand. What was odd was that no one noticed but them. The postman moved in a sphere outside of their moment. Their children ran and called out but they neither saw nor heard them. Tom and Meg were simply one continuum, one single glance, one breath, one person in two spots along the same plane of the universe.

The magic lasted only a few seconds but touched them both so deeply and so truly that neither of them would ever have to explain it or describe it for the other. The straightening of hairpins, the setting down of Gracie, the gathering of Meg into Tom's arms were all part of this mysterious union but that is not what they remembered. Years later, when they would dare to return to that untouchable place, they would do it without words, often a simple touch of hands the only tangible acknowledgement of their return. And what they would find when they returned to that moment on the beach was the last complete vestige of who they really were.

The morning after Tom returned, the August breeze was warm and heavy. Meg fixed a huge country breakfast using the last remaining bacon from last year and giving everyone an extra egg to mop up with toast. She was dumping the dishwater out the kitchen door when the women arrived to start the potatoes. She waved to the familiar faces and returned to her morning tea.

She had scanned her letter to Julie one more time before sealing the envelope with sweet scented wax. Jerry Pidgeon had gone farther up to Dooagh and Keem right after supper last night to pick up the post there and had just passed by on his way to collect the post from Dooega before heading back to Westport. Meg had given him her letters and a cake of barm brack for his trouble. She had also tucked a fresh peach cobbler and a raspberry fool into a basket for Duffy. Jerry Pidgeon had assured her that he would deliver her basket to Mr. McGee without delay, though Meg had her doubts as she watched the postman sniffing around the linen towel covering the basket.

Once she had safely deposited her letters with the postman and straightened up the kitchen, Meg sat for a moment before heading for the potato fields. Sitting quietly, Meg knew she had only a moment to steal before she would be called upon to join the crew. Harvesting was such a huge undertaking yet she found it exhilarating. They hired on for the harvest but Meg enjoyed digging some of the potatoes herself. She never tired of finding the rough tubers beneath the bright green plants. They lay there underneath the soil like big nuggets waiting to be mined, their humble fate a simple pot of boiling water, their destiny to be the staple of an Irish farmer's diet.

Tom had been out checking the fields since breakfast. He had heard of some terrible blight that had infested the potato crops on the mainland and had been concerned enough to pick a few bushels himself last night before supper. They had boiled some up and they were sweet and fresh like new potatoes ought to be. With butter and salt, they tasted as warm and satisfying as ever.

Tom had been so relieved. After the children were in bed, he had turned to her like a schoolboy his eyes twinkling with mischief. He picked her up and carted her unceremoniously into the bedroom where he plopped her down on the ticking. She thought he'd break the bed when he toppled onto her but once he planted a big lusty kiss on her mouth she didn't care if he did break the bed.

They tumbled around like children, giggling and tickling, tearing each other's clothes off and gleefully coming together with shrieks of delight. She had never seen him so playful and he had never wanted her more. Together they made love in a wild tussle, abandoning all care, free from all worries. Finally after performing all the duties of responsible parents, they could return to the magic place on the strand. With a recklessness neither of them questioned, they held back nothing, refrained from nothing, abandoned all but what they could touch and feel until there was no space between them left to fill. In an explosion of love and the purest of joy they climaxed together, both of them somehow knowing they had made another child to witness their love.

Tom came to her again later, closer to dawn. This union was so different from the frolic last evening that they could not stop searching each other's face for the meaning of it. The light in their room was soft and gray, the bed was warm and they slipped together in their nakedness as gently and silently as one hand caressing the other in prayer. The tenderness between them almost made Meg cry and Tom groaned from deep in his center when he was finished. They held each other as if they feared being torn apart. When the cock crowed announcing the day they looked with one more longing glance at each other and the spell was broken forever.

"Meg! Meg, come now!" Tom's voice, filled with dread, tore Meg from her pleasant reverie. She leaped from her chair and bounded to the door. She saw him tearing across the yard with his arms full of spuds and cold panic filled her from head to toe. He burst into the kitchen letting the potatoes tumble onto the table.

"Look at these, Meg. Do they not look fine and healthy

t'ye?" he beseeched.

She picked up one of the firm tubers, crumbs of moist soil falling at her feet.

"Why, of course, Tom, what else? Aren't these the same ones you picked last night? We ate them. They were fine."

"That they were and they're not fine now. Look at this."

He cut into a firm, round potato with his pocketknife and she recoiled at the stench of its rotten core.

Meg took one piece of the rotten tuber from him and turned it over in her hand.

"They seem to have spoiled overnight, Tom. How can that be?" She looked at him questioningly and what she saw made her shiver.

Tom had true fear in his eyes. This was not the man who always had a solution for everything. Tom always found a way to adapt, mend, improvise or finagle. He treated the obstacles of life much like the horses he trained. He knew when to be patient and when to speak softly. He knew when to be stern and unyielding and when to be a hard disciplinarian. But now, as he held the stinking black potato in his hand, he was a man overcome. Sinking into a chair, he looked at Meg as if he would speak but no words came out.

Meg went out to the nearest plot to see for herself if the women in the field had found the same thing. They were still cutting back the green foliage and had not yet begun to pull the potatoes from the ground but the smell was there. Meg recognized the scent of decay before she was ten feet into the field. Approaching Katie Grady, daughter-in-law of their good friend Jamie, Meg asked her to bring her the first bushel before she went on to the next. Millie McCoy, Kate's sister and the wife of the pub keeper, was at the far end of the field while Maggie Creahan, eldest of Johnny Creahan's girls worked the middle section. Beyond the first field lay acres of little fenced in plots all filled with pretty green leaves and stalks waving in the breeze.

"Don't say anything to the others, Kate. Just bring me the first pickings, if you please."

Meg turned to go back to the house unable to shake the sense of dread that followed her on the foul smelling wind.

When she came into the kitchen, Tom had cut open all of the potatoes and every one of them was spoiled. Now he stood by the hearth staring without expression into the flames as he wiped his knife blade over and over. The stink of the rotten potatoes was overpowering and Meg gathered them up in a bucket and dumped the pile down on the strand. Taking a shovelful of embers from the hearth, she went down and began to burn them. The smoke from the burning potatoes smelled awful and Tom came out to stop her.

"Ye can't burn them all Meg," he said with dull resignation.

She straightened up and looked at him,

"Surely they can't all be bad Tom. We'll just get rid of these few."

Meg turned to see Kate approaching with her first bushel of tatties. Without a word she set them down and went back to the field. Meg knew that Kate and her partners were beginning to realize that the harvest below the ground was not going to be what it looked like from above.

Tom sliced open potato after potato and they were all rotten in the middle.

Meg took them and cut away the rotten core, peeling and boiling the rest. She put butter on them and they sat down to have them for lunch with a pot of tea. As soon as they put them to their lips, they had to spit them out. The blight had ruined the taste of the unspoiled parts as well.

Meg gave the girls a few coins for their half-day's work and she and Tom went out to the fields themselves. Tom tried samples of every row of the green leafy sprouts. Each row brought the hope of having been spared and every row disappointed. Finally after spending the rest of the day searching fruitlessly for a row of healthy potatoes, Tom put on his cap and walked into town. He had to find out how the others had fared.

Tom knew every man who turned to watch him stoop his big frame under the low doorway of McCoy's. He scanned the faces of farmers and fishermen alike, all grim, all wearing the somber news of the failed potato harvest. Some of the men nodded in acknowledgement of the big man from the mainland who lived in the fine house on the strand. Others, never able to accept Tom or his beautiful fine born wife, simply turned their backs to the door and busied themselves with their pints and pipes. Young Mark McCoy the Junior pulled him a draft and took Tom's yellowed clay pipe from its spot on the shelf. Tom sipped his drink and stood alone stoking his pipe.

He had no doubt about the widespread devastation throughout the village as he listened to the hushed conversations around him. Overnight, all of the fields around Doeega had been tested and most were infected. It seemed as if each field had a plot or two that was untouched but even the potatoes that had not rotted on the vine turned black in their creels. The people of Doeega would be hungry this winter and they argued over whether or not to harvest the rest of their vegetables or wait until the last days of the season. Leaving them in the ground after All Hallows Eve risked exposing them to a killing frost but even a couple of weeks would give the turnips and cabbages a chance to grow as plump as possible. They were all painfully aware of the need to stretch their meager meals until the next potato crop could be harvested.

This wasn't the first blight to infect the potatoes. In 1817 and again in 1819 the potato crop had failed and in the following years bad seasons seemed to cycle through the lives of the Irish farmers. The worst crop failures had been over one hundred years ago when the harvest had failed for three years beginning in 1739. Hundreds of thousands died in Connaught and Munster alone. Within the following fifteen years there had been further bad harvests and the laborers had turned to the growing linen industry for their sustenance. By the time the disastrous crop failure of 1782-1783, the farmers were well used to relying on the sale of fine Irish linen to pay the rent.

Tom knew all this from his own life with Da. They had paid their rent to Lord Cushing since his granda's time with the fruit of the land. It was after the bad season in 1819 that his da vowed to pick up and move to Castlebar. Tom knew that his da would never survive in a city. He had no skill but farming and was too old to learn. As Tom sipped his stout, he thought about the scene they had had about it and how relieved he had been to convince his da to try one more season of farming before leaving. The next year had been a good one for the Phalen's and Tom had breathed a sigh of relief. The following year Old Ben had come to them with the news that Lord Jeffrey Wynn was looking for an able bodied man to replace his stable hand who had fallen from a bucking stallion and quit. Tom had jumped at the chance to earn wages free and clear of the fickle harvest and during the next ten years while nature played havoc with the crops all over Ireland, Tom and his da were fine.

The bad seasons were always brutal for the poor Irish farmers who had very little to eat but the faithful potato. Aside from the little cottage gardens that provided turnips, parsnips, beans and carrots and the fruit and nut trees that dotted the small stone fenced yards, the other crops they grew were not food for them but rent for the land. They all lived with the constant fear of eviction if they could not meet the rent payment from their corn crops. The corn grown in Ireland was not the kind grown by the Indians in America or so Tom had heard from a puffed up lad from up on Croaghaun Mountain who had been there and returned. No sir, in the U.S.of A. the corn grows high as a house and the seeds are big and round and yellow, sometimes red and purple!

Tom had balked at this malarkey but the blatherskyte had insisted it was so. He had said that what the Irish called corn was called many things in America: barley, oats or wheat. It was the Irish who had it wrong. At this Tom had stopped listening to the fool altogether. To think that the Irish had been growing corn since the days of the druids and now some fast talking tweed suit from Indiana USA was spouting nonsense about giant purple seeds!

Musha! He could heist his kiester back to Indiana. What did

it matter if corn was the name they gave any grain in the field? The Indians could just call their fat kernels something else! And what did it matter what they called it if it paid the rent? A good harvest was a roof and hearth and a bad harvest meant the threat of the undertaker's wrecking ball. Plain and simple, whatever ye called it!

It was no different for the men of Doeega on this balmy September evening as Tom looked around the small, smoky pub. In solitude, he stood at the bar in the corner of McCoy's watching three of the fellows from town talking head to head at a table across the room. Dooley Creahan was gesturing emphatically and while Tom couldn't hear what he was saying he could tell Dooley was well on his way to one of his drunken orations. Occasionally young Peter Feeney would turn and look his way and Tom felt sure they were discussing him. He shook off this idea as nonsense until Finn Kelly got up to have his glass refilled and asked if they could have a word with him. Tom threw back the last of his pint and extended his own glass for a refill, admiring the shamrock that formed on top of the foam. Savoring a mouthful of the thick rich head, he joined the table with a nod to the three. Tom knew he had nothing to fear from any of these men. In fact just the opposite was true. They were beholden to him though they could never have known just how much they really owed.

The first to speak was Finn.

"Tell me Tom Phalen, how did the visit with His Lordship's man go?"

Tom told them about his latest conversation with Mr. Gilchrist, emphasizing the positive comments and leaving out anything that would set him apart further or cause them to worry needlessly. For the next two hours they pumped him for information and Tom answered all of their questions honestly. Soon Phineas McLean and Dan Ballard had joined them. They asked the same questions as the other three but Tom knew they were really asking if he thought His Lordship would be forgiving of the failed crop or would they need to listen to the weeping of their women that night. They answered their own question, reassuring themselves with every sip from their glasses that surely Lord Lucan would let them keep some of the corn crop seein' as how the tatties were bad.

Tom was much relieved when around ten o'clock Jamie Grady came in and brought his usual good humor to the table. The affable constable lightened the conversation so much that Tom found himself regaling the men with the old story about being mistaken for the cook's fellow by the Gilchrists' gardener. The howls of laughter and order of another round that followed that story made Tom feel more welcome in McCoy's than he had felt in the ten years he had been coming there.

Eventually, the conversation grew serious again and the men, mellow from their pints, fell into long pensive silences. They drew on their pipes and shook their heads at the bad luck of the failed crop. But Peter Feeney pointed out that their luck usually changed by the next year and Phineas agreed that they still had their fish to use toward the rent and their small plots of vegetables to sustain them. Not a one said it but they all knew that the occasional pilfered fish would find its way to each of their tables. Sure'n Tom Phalen had just been over to see that the rents were paid through year's end and before ye knew it spring would be upon them and there would be new potatoes to plant.

All in all, things could be worse. Despite the stinking, festering fields, the men around McCoy's still had a penny for a pint of stout. Tom Phalen lifted his glass with them in a toast to next spring's planting. The stroke of twelve from the clock tower of St. Mary's Church of Ireland found each of them wending their way home to sleep off the excesses of the evening. The sage words of Mark McCoy the Senior rang in their ears as they trundled up the cobblestone street toward home. As they weaved from one side of the narrow street to the other, he called out behind them.

"Sure'n none of ye'll be needin' te rise with the roosters fer any tattie hokin' this fine mornin'."

By the time Tom climbed over Meg and plopped his swimming head down, his laughing bag was empty and he quietly despaired over his next visit to Lord Lucan's nephew, Mr. Gilchrist of Dublin St., Newport, County Mayo.

Chapter Six

The Catholic population in the village had petitioned to the bishop for years for their own parish. But their appeals fell on deaf ears. St. Dymphna's was the ancient seat of the church on Achill. Her history was so rich and so entwined with the history of the island itself that the diocese would not even consider adding a parish along the coast. St. Dymphna's Parish, known locally as Chilldamhnait, was founded by a young woman in the seventh century. Dymphna's father, the king of Louth wanted to make her queen, a role the devout girl felt she could never play. After fleeing to Achill, Dymphna established her church and began to heal the sick. After her death, it became the center of the Catholic Church on Achill as it remained until this day. Fr. O'Boyle, still in good health, made the trek over the mountains regularly to visit his parishioners on the south shore. They in turn, faithfully crossed the same mountains every Sunday and Holyday to hear Mass and have their children baptized. The dead were carried by six strong men across the mountains to be buried in the ancient cemetery across the road from the church. Even in the worst weather, the villagers would traipse across the mountains resting the coffins on the leactai, the large stones along the way where one group of men would allow another group to pick up the burden exchanging places again at the next stop. The islanders believed that the longest trip to the cemetery meant the shortest trip to heaven. No one minded the hard walk and none would miss it, knowing that if they made the struggle for one of their own, someday, they too might have such a fine procession to go their last mile.

After the final prayers were said, and before the coffin was lowered, clay pipes were laid upon the lid. This was to offer the deceased a bit of pleasure on the last leg of the journey to his eternal reward. Many of the men would stop for a pint in Ailse, the stone village along the right side of the road across from the cemetery. Ailse was boasted to be the largest village in Achill, and sure didn't that make sense being only yards from the great church of St. Dymphna? The women and children of Dooega had little time for the pubs of Ailse, preferring in good weather to enjoy a cold lunch right in the cemetery among their ancestors and the ancient trees that sheltered them. During bad weather they took their children into St. Dymphna's to wait for the men to take the chill off with a wee tich o'the craither. As much a ritual as singing the dirges in church, the older women shook their heads and blessed themselves against the craither's demonic effect on their men. Every Irish woman knew that the divil himself inhabited the drink and the evil craither himself could make an otherwise good man into a demon.

At the end of the day, everyone began the long journey home. The men reprising the maudlin dirges and dancing their wives around in circles, the women steadying the men and trying to keep them from falling off the narrow paths across the foothills around Mt. Croghaun. Thus it was, just a week after All Hallows Eve 1845, that the cold November wind whipped around the long string of black shawled women and tweed jacketed men escorting one of their own to God.

Danny Kinneally had been the village mascot since he was born nearly twenty years ago. He had never grown taller than a child and his mind was like a child's as well. There were a few who taunted him and abused him as an idiot but his sunny smile and pleasant disposition had made him the favorite of the women. Most of the men had taken responsibility for protecting him from the ruffians and naughty children who occasionally pranked and teased him. Fr. O'Boyle had gone so far as threatening the fire of hell for anyone caught tormenting the tiny, sweet-tempered creature.

Danny had a short left arm with little blubbery lumps that should have been fingers. But despite his bad arm and diminutive stature he was very strong and his good arm could haul a net or sort a haul as well as any man. Once he had been taught what to look for in a good fish he could sort through a catch so fast that he never lacked for work and his days were filled with gleeful flipping as two silver piles rose like banks on either side of him on the strand. When he was through sorting the catch for one man he'd be off to the next curragh to fling the slippery harvest for the next.

There were only two things Danny Kinneally would not touch. He was afraid of shellfish with claws and would literally run from eels. The lads would tease him by chasing him with a wriggling eel or threatening to nip off his good fingers with a snapping lobster or crab. The haul at the end of any given day was regularly punctuated with Danny's shrieks of terror and the yelps of the village boys as they took their wallops from their das for bothering him.

Now, as the string of mourners crossed the mountains to put their little man to rest, not a word passed among them. The keeners wailed and the men took their turns bearing the little coffin. Even the young lads who had made Danny the butt of their endless jokes jockeyed for position at the head of the box. Despite their taunting, the Doeega boys had loved Danny Kinneally like a favorite pet and now that he was gone they knew they would miss him.

Danny's mother, the widow Kinneally was tall and gaunt, so unlike her tiny son that folks had long suspected that his deformity had to be the work of a fairy thief. After all, hadn't she herself been that frightened by a ghostly apparition on the night she delivered him? And hadn't she almost given birth on All

Hallows Eve when the little laddie refused to turn right in the womb begging to be kept safely inside till All Saints Day? Lizzie Ballard swore she saw the Pooka peering in the Kinneally's window waiting to take the wee Kinneally baby and leave behind his own fairy son in exchange. And sure enough, didn't it happen just like Lizzie said? There had been such an outcry among the women when they saw the babe! There were even those who said he should not be baptized atall, that he should have been allowed to die and his mam with him, that he was surely the changeling, son of the Pooka of November. Lizzie led the charge to Kinneally's door ranting that one should boil the water and another heat the tongs! They would boil the evil fairy child up the chimney back to the caves of Leinster, back to the land of the steed with the head of a man, surely the father of this monster-child. Then poor Marie Kinneally would have her own sweet boy returned to her and her sorrow lightened.

But the old pastor, Fr. Tierney, got there first. He and Cora Foy looked the child over and the good priest sprinkled the holy water over the house, especially the cradle and the hearth. Both the midwife and the priest decreed that little Danny Kinneally was not a changeling. He had a beautiful face and despite his deformed arm bore no resemblance to the Pooka. There were clearly not four legs nor were there cloven hooves on the two legs the child did have. Fr Tierney sent the women home and scolded them for their hasty judgment.

Once Marie Kinneally was on her feet she paraded her crippled baby around as though he were handsome as a prince and not one woman tried to stop her. Clearly the tallest woman in Doeega, the widow Kinneally possessed the fiercest of tempers. Not a woman in Doeega cared to cross her and so Danny was accepted and absorbed into the village like any other child. There were those however, who when they carried their own babies, would walk far off the path to avoid passing Kinneally's and risking the cursed limb and stunted height of Danny Kinneally, the fairy boy.

The widowed mother was led across the pass by her two

daughters, Dolores and Kitty. They led the procession in the traditional long red skirts and black shawls of the Aran Islands. Marie Kinneally and her husband Patrick had come from Aran to Achill as newlyweds and even these many years later, she still wore the same outfit to church. Dolores was a widow too, but Kitty had never married. Tall like their mam, they supported her under each bony arm, the three so skinny and black on the horizon that an observer from below might mistake them for the three crosses of Calvary. To be sure, their life had been a Calvary of sorts. Patrick had been taken by the fever right before Danny was born and Delores's husband murdered in a brawl outside a Newport pub the day after their wedding. The general opinion around the village had been that Delores was much better off without the brute and the thug who robbed him of her tiny dowry had actually done her a favor. In the end, the Newport police had recovered almost all of her paltry worth and she and her mother and sister lived for the next year on the money. Delores was the only one who grieved the loutish highlander, MacTavish, whose brief foray from Scotland had cost him his life.

Kitty Kinneally had had her fair share of suitors and rightly so with her beautiful heart-shaped face and wide gray eyes. The disposition of a holy saint; that's how people described Kitty Kinneally. The public opinion was that there wasn't a man born worthy of her. Privately, whispered wisdom about the Pooka prevailed. No man would risk marrying into a family that had seen a violent end to all of its males, including the normal boy snatched right out of his mother's womb on a cold October night. It was long whispered that Kitty had an urge to join the Mercy nuns but didn't have the heart to leave her brother. Even now, as she trundled behind the three women, Lizzie Ballard was canvassing opinions on whether she might join up now that he was gone. Suren' no one would grieve if the Kinneally family line ended right here on this hill.

After being buffeted by bone chilling winds and intermittent sleet blowing in off the ocean, the string of frozen villagers arrived at St. Dymphna's. Fr. O'Boyle looked out across the pass and leaned over to ask Maryellen McLean a question. She shrugged and looked panicked as the murmured question passed along the crowd. Finally, the answer came from the very end of the line that yes, indeed salt had been sprinkled along the pass over the mountains to keep the specter of death from snatching poor Danny from the gates of heaven. There had been enough snatching done in this family.

Poor Maryellen sagged with relief. Tom and Meg could see from where they stood in the piercing wind that Peter Feeney was quite put out that Fr. O'Boyle had singled out his betrothed to be responsible for the salt. Hadn't Fr. O'Boyle himself pointed out to him her nervous disposition?

Peter's pique was short-lived as he was called upon to take his turn carrying the coffin around the thorn tree in the center of St. Dymphna's yard. As she stood in the howling wind Meg wrapped her old seal coat around her. She tenderly touched her swelling belly where the new life, begun on the night before the potato crop failed, slept beneath the black serge of her skirt.

Meg always marveled at the rituals involved in burying the Irish dead. She had only been to a handful of funerals before moving to Achill and the only one she really remembered was her grandmother's in London. There was no keening and the trip to the cemetery was only a few yards instead of the long trek so favored by the Irish. The longer the route to the grave the quicker the arrival in heaven. She had heard it so many times it ran like a mantra through her head. After carrying Danny three times around the thorn tree, the little crowd packed into the stone church. It was a relief to be out of the wind and Fr. O'Boyle took advantage of the cold to give Danny and the assembled villagers a lengthy eulogy complete with a fierce, sputtering oration on the risk of temptation and the loss of their eternal reward.

The mourners bundled up against the wind and crossed the pebble-strewn road to the cemetery. As Danny was borne to the freshly dug hole, the rest of the mourners fanned out to pay a brief visit to their own dead. Meg thought this was an odd custom too. She and Tom had no one buried at St. Dymphna's so they stood with Marie Kinneally and her daughters trying not to stare at the gaping black hole waiting for Danny Kinneally to be dropped into it. The keeners drifted back to the gravesite and once the coffin was interred, began the caione. This hymn was much prettier than the wailing that had brought them across the mountain and Meg and Tom looked at each other with relief. In the time honored custom of the island residents, Kitty Kinneally gently set her breakfast plate with a small piece of toasted brown bread on it upon the coffin. She would never let Danny be hungry in this world or the next. The holy water was sprinkled on all present and the clods began to fall. No one seemed interested in starting a fight. It was simply too cold and blustery to keep to the tradition of spilling blood at this funeral. Besides, no one wanted to sully poor Danny Kinneally's big day. Suren' it was the only big day the little fellow ever had.

When it was over, the women and children started the long trek home. There was another funeral procession approaching from the north so they couldn't stay in the little church and wait while their men made the final toast like they usually did. Meg gathered her two older girls and Thomas under her coat for the trip back down the mountain. Tom took Denny and headed for the Ailse Inn for a pint in Danny's honor. Meg started to protest that Denny was too young but decided better of it. She knew she would have a time of it just getting the other children down the mountain without worrying about his shenanigans.

Meg shooed Rose ahead to relieve old Mrs. Trent. She had been kind enough to offer to take the three younger babies and Meg didn't want to take advantage of her. She watched as Rose scampered down the mountainside oblivious to the cold as her wool cape flapped behind her. She wondered how the time had passed so quickly. Rose was growing gangly and skinny as she headed into the awkward stage between girlhood and womanhood and Meg missed the plump child she had been. Mary Clare huddled under Meg's old beaver coat just peeking out enough to see where she headed. Thomas, on the other hand, kept shrugging it off and Meg had to hold his hand tight to keep him close to her warm side.

Thomas was miffed that Denny had been able to stay with Tom while he had to go home with the girls. When he caught sight of the house, he scooted away from Meg before she could grab him. Off he dashed into the icy wind tearing down the mountain toward the village.

Meg hollered for him to come back but her voice just floated back up the mountain on the wind. Thomas was dressed in a warm Irish sweater and woolen knickers but he had been nursing a cold and Meg was desperate to get him out of the frigid wind. She could do nothing but keep him in her sight and hurry to catch up to him.

The wind was coming off the Atlantic in wild gusts by the time Meg arrived at the strand. The more she progressed down the mountain the more the icy sleet blinded her. By the time Meg arrived on the strand, she could no longer see Thomas and the freak storm was bringing snow on the howling wind.

Frantic, Meg ran first to Mrs. Trent hoping to find him there with the other children. By the time she rounded the corner of the little stone vicarage of the Irish Church, her entire front was plastered with wet slushy snow and Mary Clare's howls from within the coat sounded worse than the wind. When Mrs. Trent opened the front door Meg literally blew into her tidy little kitchen.

"Is Thomas here?"

"Why no, was he not with you?"

The older woman put her hand to her throat.

Meg shoved Mary Clare toward the fire to warm her hands and face and turned to go back out into the storm.

"Mrs. Phalen, you mustn't! In your condition you could lose the baby if you try to navigate this storm!"

Meg looked at her, desperation on her face.

"If I don't, I'll lose one of the babies I've already had! I can't leave Thomas out there in this!"

With that, she forced the door open and plowed out into the vicious wind. The ice cut her like razors as she searched the churchyard and street where it led out to the strand. Where could he be? Could he have gone home? He was just a little boy! He could have been blown right into the sea this wind was so treacherous!

"Thomas! Thomas!"

Meg called till she was hoarse. She could hardly see in front of her and the further she slogged through the slush the more she slipped and stumbled. Meg fell more than once as her boot caught on a slick rock or tripped on a piece of snow-covered driftwood. Her face was so caked with wet snow she could hardly breathe and she became disoriented. Was she coming to her house or had she passed it? Was she even going in the right direction? Panic filled her with a rush of heat as she realized the wind was coming at her from the other side. Somehow she must have gotten turned around and she was going back toward the village. But she couldn't see the houses or the hedgerow or even the shore. What if she wandered into the raging sea? What if the sea had taken her little boy and was waiting to take her too?

"You cannot permit these thoughts," she scolded herself.

"You must think of Thomas. Where would he go? Where would he hide?"

There were no answers to her questions. Only the angry sea lapping and crashing so loudly she couldn't tell on which side it was. Hail the size of marbles pounded her head and bounced around her. It was almost impossible to walk on the little balls and she slid and skidded along. If only the wind were not so brutal and so biting! She was so confused and so very cold. With nothing left to do with her mind, Meg began to pray. After years of being immersed in the Roman Catholic culture of St. Dymphna's, Meg felt she knew the saints as well as any Catholic. She cried out to St. Anthony to find her son. Fr. O'Boyle had said once that he could help her find lost items. She called out to the Virgin who had lost her own little boy for three days. What if her baby was out here for three days? He would never survive this storm! He would freeze!

Who else could she pray to? St. Joseph, yes, yes, he was a father. Meg begged St. Joseph to find her baby and keep him warm. Thinking about him tenderly shielding little Thomas under his cloak made her cry and her tears froze on her cheeks. She was really lost now. There was no way at all for her to know where she was. The world was a swirl of silver sleet and pooling puddles of icy water and mushy gray snow mixed with sand. Her legs felt like lead and she was so very tired. Her sides stretched by her growing belly, burned like fire and her back felt like it would snap in two if she took another step. Finally, sinking to her knees under the weight of her slush soaked coat, Meg gave her soul to God. In a desperate bargain for the life of her son, Meg promised God she would take the final steps toward becoming Catholic, a desire that had flirted with her heart for years.

"Dear, Heavenly Father, I beg you for the life of my little boy. You can have me in your holy church if you just spare him from this storm. Help me O God! Help me find him and I promise I will join the Church of Rome."

Suddenly Meg felt herself being lifted and carried off. The wind blew in circles and she was awash in icy wetness. Was she on land or in the sea? She knew her feet were off the ground but she felt very safe. Someone had her in his arms and was carrying her away.

"No! I must find Thomas!"

Meg struggled against strong arms that clasped her to a broad chest. The face above her was that of a frozen snow creature. Ice hung from his heavy brows and coated his face like a thick beard. His wool cap was crusted with snow and looked like a crown of silver and white. Meg didn't recognize the man and had no idea where he was taking her. She screamed and punched his chest until she was exhausted but he never stopped trekking into the wind.

Finally she felt him push open a gate with her body and suddenly the wind was behind him. She felt a keen warmth once his body shielded her from the biting wind. Within a few paces he had her at the door to his house. The building was absolutely plastered with slush and sand that had blown up off the strand. He kicked open the door and Meg found herself surrounded by warmth. The man set her down by the hearth and began to wipe the caked ice from around her eyes and nose. Once Meg could see, she was startled to find herself in her own home! She was even more startled to see that as the warmth of the fire melted the snow from her face it also melted the caked ice from his. Once he had pulled off his frozen cap and swiped the layer of crusted slush that had bearded his chin, Meg gasped to see that it was Tom!

"Meg, Meg what were ye thinking, goin' out like that into a storm and here ye are carryin' a babe?"

"I have to find Thomas, Tom, he's out there and he's freezing!"

She tried to get back on her feet but he held her down on the hearthstone.

"No, Meg ye're not goin' anywhere. Thomas is fine. He's at Trent's. He caught his foot in a crevice and ye passed him on the way down the mountain. He said ye walked right by him but ye never heard him callin' fer the howling o'the wind and ye were lookin' so far ahead ye never saw him."

Meg began to weep.

"How could I have missed him? I was looking for him! How could I have walked right past my own child. Oh, Tom, he must have been terrified! How could I ever have missed him?"

"Meg, ye're that lucky ye even got off the mountain. There's those still huddled in boolies all along the side of it. This storm caught everyone out there. When Phineas turned to strike his lucifer on the hitching post outside the pub in Ailse and saw that sky over the ocean he had all of us on our feet and down the mountain in no time atall. Denny was the first one down calling for ye and Rose and Mary Clare. He himself was the one who found Thomas. Suren' the little laddie had no time atall t'be frightened. Just be glad old Phineas had trouble lightin' his pipe!"

He wrapped his big arms around her as she shivered by the fire. Meg heard his breath catch as he held her tight and stroked her wet hair. One by one he took the pins out of her matted and tangled curls. She reached up and ran her fingers through the snarls shaking and loosening them so her hair would dry.

"I almost died when Mrs.Trent told me you had gone back out into that raging wind, Meg. I no sooner had me family safe and sound than I found out I had no such thing atall. I can't believe I found ye. I couldn't have borne t'lose ye. Darlin', whatever were ye thinkin'?"

Meg was growing drowsy with the warm fire on her back. Her hair was almost dry and Tom had taken a towel to his when they realized that the storm had suddenly stopped. He lifted her and carried her into their bedroom. He helped her out of her wet clothes and she slipped a warm nightgown over her head. Sitting on the bed, he drew her into his lap. Picking up her hairbrush Tom began to separate the snarled blond curls. Tenderly he drew the brush through her long damp hair, raising each smoothened ringlet to his lips. He wrapped the ringlets around his hand and laid them gently in a row down her back. Leaning forward he buried his face in the sweet golden mass, breathing in the scent of lavender.

Neither spoke for several minutes when Tom realized by Meg's regular shallow breathing that she had fallen asleep. He laid her down and fanned her beautiful curls across the pillow to dry. Several minutes passed as Tom sat in silence just gazing at his wife. She slept as gently as a child and his heart swelled with a love deeper than any he had ever known. The knowledge that he could have lost her in a silly winter squall weighed upon him so heavily he found he could not move from her side.

Tom knew this pregnancy was proving to be hard for her. Between the threat of hunger and a houseful of children already, Meg was hard put to cope with it all. Thank God he had been able to add the extension. They had laughed then that they could have half a dozen more children before he'd need to add on again.

He had felt such mixed emotions when she told him she was expecting again. They both knew it happened the night he returned from Newport, the last night of their old life. The next several weeks had been so difficult neither of them marked the palor and fatigue on Meg's face. It wasn't until Michaelmas that they came together again and afterward Meg tearfully shared her news with him. He felt like a cad for wanting her so often but he loved her so much and she never acted like she felt burdened by his attentions. He had often asked her when he desired her if she would prefer not to come to him but she never turned him away. Her open heart and generous body only made him want her more and watching her with their children filled him with a pride and devotion he never thought himself capable of feeling. But now, as he watched her dozing on their bed, his heart was heavy and a prayer came to his lips.

"Heavenly Father, You made me a man of healthy appetites and I thank ye fer that. I thank ye too for this woman, yer daughter, who comes t'me whenever I ask fer her. She is a saintly woman, dear Lord. And I am so grateful ye gave her t'me. Not a day goes by that I don't realize how close I came t'losin' her."

"We have brought many children into the world fer ye O, Lord, as ye commanded in the beginnin' of time. And fine children they are. Have mercy on us now, Lord. We have many mouths t'feed and another on the way. If I am wrong to want her so, if I am sinful and selfish in me desire, Lord, show me. Lead me t'confess me sin, curb me appetites and leave me wife alone. But Lord, I will be less a man for it, and that's the all of it. Amen."

Tom slid off the bed, tucked Meg in and kissed her on the forehead. Meg stirred and opened her eyes.

"Ye need t'sleep. I'll fetch the children and Rosie can cook us an egg supper. Ye sleep now Meg and I'll send Thomas himself in t'wake ye when it's ready."

Chapter Seven

At the end of July, 1846, the situation took a profound turn for the worse. An eerie sound had carried across the bay causing men to look up from their nets and women to hurriedly gather their children to them. Those who had been to the Cliffs of Moher likened it to the groaning of the wind swooping through the curved cliff faces and back out to sea.

Some said it was the moaning of the pipes rising from the ring forts where the great warrior clans were being called from death to do battle for the lives of their daughters and sons. But soon the island of Achill began to reek under the hot sun and a cloud like a fog of death settled over the fields and the people knew it wasn't the wind they heard or the call of the pipes.

They knew the sound was the keening of starving women drifting up the coast from Galway and Dingle Bay. It was the wail of desperation wrenched from the empty guts of farmers carried west from Roscommon and Sligo, whose hands were again blackened by the stinking ooze of another rotten potato crop. Their brothers and sisters on Achill Island knew the sound because it began rising from their own throats at the sight of the first blighted leaf. How could this be when the crop had looked so good?

"Just yesterday didn't ye see the glorious blossoms like a wedding bouquet fer a queen?"

"Suren' the Virgin is smilin' just look at the size of these tatties, will ye?"

"Michael, will ye just marvel at it, so soon in the season fer such a grand crop!"

They watched it happen in front of them. Vast fields of lush green plants lay sprinkled with freckles like fairy dust that grew into sinister black ulcers before their very eyes. Some of them ran crazed into their fields gathering up the fresh green stalks, some with heavy tubers hanging off the ends. Dirt smeared in sweat, grins all around, they dumped the new tatties out by the apronful.

"See?"

"See?"

"Look here, now Michael, I think this field will be spared."

"Hurry Colleen, get them before it spreads!"

"Mary, quick, the creel! Let's load 'em up fer supper!"

And then it started. Even as the sound of wailing floated across Achill and out to sea, a second wave began. This time it was the hearts of Doeega that were heard breaking. There was no escaping the sound. It swept up the coastline all the way up Keem Bay, past Dooagh Village through to Achill Head and on across the ocean. It echoed off the Minaun Cliffs and climbed to the peak of Croaghaun Mountain. There the mournful keening joined the voices of Donegal and Aran and all the glens and riverbanks of Erin as it drifted across the cold Atlantic seeping down, down, down beneath the waves finally nudging the moruadh mermaids from their sleep.

Months ago, on Easter of 1846, after they had survived the first winter of the hunger, Meg had given Duffy a sack with the rest of her jewelry. She was confident that the worst was over but wanted the extra money as insurance. He took the baubles to Lord Sligo and laid out two necklaces of rubies and emeralds, sapphire earbobs and a 16th. century ivory brooch, Meg's only memento of her grandmother Cushing.

Lady Sligo was not impressed with the lot but Lord Sligo was willing to give her half of what he paid for the diamond necklace Meg had sold him last year, after the first crop failed. Duffy accepted the offer. They were again able to buy some staples and keep the dairy going. Tom knew he would not be able to help with the rents for the second half of the year.

On May Morning of the same year, as the dew burned off the new leaves of the spring potatoes, Martha Mary Phalen arrived, pink and wrinkled and howling. The smallest of Meg's babies, little Martha struggled for her first few weeks but by the end of June was suckling and thriving and gaining weight.

Now it was the end of August and Duffy had brought in his curragh, the few supplies he had brokered. He looked thin and drawn. Meg had noticed that even the folks from the city were feeling the pinch of hunger but the sight of her big handsome friend looking so wan, his coarse, homemade shirt baggy around his bony shoulders and his moleskin trousers cinched with a rope, shocked her. Her heart ached that she had so little to feed him. She had just boiled water and made tea from fresh mint leaves. A pot of dulse simmered on the fire but no one was peddling fish in the village. By law they had to take it to market in Westport and Newport as soon as they caught it to get the best price and offset their rent.

The temptation to eat the catch was horrific but they knew they couldn't spare even a limpet without risking eviction. Even the mussels from the strand and the cockles buried in the sand were sold to the brokers who exported them to London at huge profits. Sometimes, to avoid the pangs of an empty stomach a fisherman might poach a few small throwbacks but the patrols were strict and the risk of arrest was very real.

Just last week, down near Achill Sound a lad named Jimmy McNeal had impaled himself on his own eel spear as he tried to scramble behind some rocks after being caught illegally poaching an eel for dinner. The talk was that it was an accident but each man who heard the news wondered in his heart if poor Jimmy may have preferred to go by his own hand rather than face execution.

Up and down the strand fisher folk took note as the armed patrols warned that any illegal doings like that would be regarded as treason and the perpetrator would be hanged.

Duffy peeked under the white blanket to meet the latest Phalen and smiled his approval. He was so proud of Meg and still carried her in a special place in his heart. His physical feelings for her had never diminished. He still found her beauty arresting and her eyes so expressive he felt he could read her soul. He could only hope that she could not read his. Sometimes it was torment to be near her but their lives were so intertwined he couldn't avoid it. He had made a pact with himself that he would never act on his feelings as long as Tom was alive. Tom was such a good friend Duffy would never betray his trust and he meant to deserve it. Besides, Duffy wasn't foolish enough to think that Meg had the same feelings for him. He never doubted her devotion to Tom and wasn't this new baby proof of that?

Meg set Martha in her cradle and poured Duffy a cup of the sweet smelling tea. She couldn't remember the last time they had enjoyed the flavor of imported English tea. Duffy sipped the steaming brew and nibbled on a piece of bread and honey. Meg watched him savor every bite and marveled at how different he was about his food than the robust, hungry man she used to feed.

They were all different about their food now. They never knew when they would see another bite so they took each mouthful slowly, deliberately feeling the texture on their tongues. Even the blandest pablum or watery broth was treated like sweet nectar. Some days they were so far gone beyond hunger that to eat quickly would be to invite tossing back the very food they so badly needed. And so they nibbled what they wanted to bolt down and savored what they would have spewed out had they not been starving.

Meg brought up the story about the young fisherman who died.

"We are good and hardworking people. We deserve a bit of

food! Those patrollers ought to be the ones hanging!"

Duffy took another sip and shook his head.

"They're not all like that, Meg," he said, as he opened a copy of an old newspaper.

"My friend, Lord Sligo is a gentleman and a good God-fearing man fer a Protestant, that he is."

He searched Meg's face, hoping to earn a smile for his lighthearted poke at her church.

Finding none, he took Francis on his lap and spooned some of the tea into his mouth.

"Just listen t'this from *The Telegraph* last week. I was at Westport House sellin' yer jewels when this happened. I'm that impressed that the newspaper actually printed the story the way it truly happened. T'read the paper most days, ye'd think on Monday the rich were begot by the divil himself and on Tuesday he'd gone and possessed the poor. This at least is how I remember it happenin'. And a grand picture of Himself, the Marquis, at that."

Duffy could smell the crushed mint on Meg's fingers as she reached across to turn the picture to the light.

As he began to read, he sniffed the paper where the scent of mint remained on the page and he finally got his smile from Meg. Duffy really needed a wife to scent his newspapers for him she thought, shaking her head.

He cleared his voice and read:

"The Telegraph (26-8-1846)

On Saturday last, the inhabitants of Westport witnessed a novel, and at the same time a heart-rendering sight. About mid-day some thousands of the rural population marched into town to have an interview with Most Noble the Marquis of Sligo: they approached the grand entrance of the Noble Lord's residence, and having, after some little delay, obtained admittance, they proceeded, with the most becoming order to the Castle, none attempting to even walk off the road, lest their doing so might injure the grass of the demesne. Having arrived before the hall door the Noble Marquis (as was custom of his deceased father) instantly came forward to meet them: he talked with them: deplored the visitation with which God had affiliated the land: told them he would instantly state their condition to the government, in order to obtain them relief, and that as to himself, he would go as far as any landlord in the country to redress the grievances of his tenantry. He also told them that his intention was not to harass them with regard to his rents: that then it was almost useless to talk on that subject, as the time for collecting the rent had not yet arrived. Finally, the Noble Marquis assured them that no assertions of his should be spared to obtain for them, from Her Majesty's Government immediate employment. The people expressed themselves satisfied with the declarations of their Noble Landlord and returned to the town in the same orderly manner which characterized their march to the castle."

Duffy was shocked to look up from the paper and see Meg wiping a tear from her cheek.

"Meg, what is this, then? Why tears? In all th'years I've known ye I've never seen ye cry!"

He put Francis down and Meg picked him up. Seeing his mother cry made Francis's little lip quiver and he patted her cheek tenderly.

Meg shrugged and sniffed. She set Francis down with a salty kiss and sent him out to play with his sisters. Sitting down, she poured herself another cup of tea and warmed Duffy's cup.

Finally she spoke.

"Oh, Duffy, if only I could explain. Last year, before all this started, Denny told me that he hated the English and hated me for being English. He said he would never be English and was terribly angry that I'm not Roman Catholic. I intended to tell Tom when he came home but as soon as he got here our whole life fell apart. I put it out of my mind we were so busy just dealing with the crop failure but now he's started the talk again. He's been listening to the lads in the Blackthorn Brotherhood. They spew their hateful talk and their violent solutions and he just soaks it up."

"Tom just walks away when Denny gets going and for all I know he may agree with Denny! You know how he shuts up around me when the talk turns political. I fear he feels he has sold his soul to the devil ever since he became Lord Lucan's agent. And he did it for me! I'm the English one here! Even the children are only half. He's always hated the English, especially my family. If he had married an Irish woman he'd probably be in the Brotherhood himself! Now, ever since this hunger started, he's been brooding and pensive. I worry about him, Duffy, he seems all torn up inside but he won't talk to me. And Denny has always been able to get under his skin. I'm afraid for all of us. One minute Tom's himself, the next he's like a shadow man all darkness and gloom."

"Just last week while the Westport paper was printing that article about the virtues of Lord Sligo, Denny was storming around here, hungry, angry and ready to burn Buckingham Palace. Thank God Tom was in town. I know there is reason to hate. God knows I lived a life of luxury on the backs of the poor Irish. My own father is, if he's still alive, a monster! But I've tried very hard to be a good wife to Tom and rear my children with a just mind and a generous soul."

"Is that ever going to reconcile what my people have done to your people? Aren't my lullabies able to soothe my babies the way any Irish mam can? I believe more than ever that we're all the same under our skin. No one knows the torments I've suffered, the guilt, the shame and remorse just for being English! To hear the jibes and accusations from my own son is more than I can bear. And suspecting how Tom really feels is killing me! Every time he's tender or nice I wonder if that's the real Tom or whether the real man lies beneath, hating and seething against my people and merely tolerating me."

Meg wiped another tear from her face and turned to gaze

out the window at the sea. The temptation to spill the awful truth about her half-brother and the night of torture that haunted her every waking hour made her bite hard on her lip. No one could ever know what had happened with Andrew. Certainly not Duffy, as close as he was to Tom. No, what Meg really needed was a woman to talk to. Her heart longed for a good long afternoon with Maureen. She would set her straight. Maureen could be honest with Meg about being victimized by the aristocracy without being hateful and Meg could ask her anything and know she would answer as a friend.

Duffy sat silently, his big hands opening and closing, his blue eyes never leaving Meg's face.

She sat down again and began playing with the little pile of shells she kept in a bowl on the table.

"How silly these seem now."

Her voice was flat as the tears slid freely and she made no attempt to stop them.

"When Maureen and I gathered these so many years ago they seemed pretty. Now they're nothing more than empty vessels like I am. Now, none of the ones I love are full. When I hug my children they all feel hollow in my arms as if the solidity and substance of their bodies and the fullness of their souls have been poured out. When we had enough to eat my children were round and filled their little skins. Now they're like bony little birds, all skinny legs and spiny backsides."

Duffy began to rise from his seat at the catch in her voice. The sight of her tears made him queasy with anger and he longed to caress the fingers that rhythmically ran over the rough backs of the mussel shells. But he sat down again, choking back the desire to take her in his arms and kiss away her tears. His mouth went dry, the peppermint tea bitter on his tongue. His feet felt like anvils under the table. He longed to rise, to seize those fine, slender hands made only more beautiful and refined by their trembling thinness.

He crumpled the newspaper, his palms burning so hot he thought for sure they would set fire to the crushed words. God save him, but he loved her! God throw him in hell for coveting the wife of his best friend! What sort of man was he? Nailed down by divine forces, he was. If he weren't he'd be on his feet tearing at her clothes this very minute! He couldn't speak for the bile burning in his throat. He couldn't move for the wings of his angel pinning him to his chair. He couldn't let her see the sweat beading up on his brow or the twitch of his jaw as he fought for control.

What a fool he was! He was inches away from the woman he desired more than life itself and he couldn't even touch her. His love for Tom and his deep innate decency kept him in place, tortured by his own self-imposed restraint. Did she even know how he felt? Looking at her bowed head and soft, lank hair made dull by the terrible hunger, he knew she did not.

Oblivious to Duffy's private agony, Meg went on,

"Their eyes used to be lively and filled with hope. Now they gaze at some far-off vision and I have to call and call to get them to look at me. I know I am no different. If I didn't have their lives on my head, I would simply float away myself. Tom, too. He once seemed so massive to me, Duffy, so strong. I miss his heavy step thumping down from the loft and watching the little ones walk in his broad deep prints in the sand. His feet are so big!"

But now he just creeps around here like a specter leaving almost no trace of his presence. I miss him Duffy! I miss his songs about the druids and the saints that he used to sing as he went about his chores. It's been over a year since I've heard him sing and he never picks up his fiddle anymore!"

This last came out in a sob and Meg covered her face with her hands, ashamed to be crying in front of her old friend as Duffy averted his own stinging eyes.

Meg realized Duffy didn't know what to say or do. How could he? She thought for a moment then that he was going to touch her. Instead he sat staring at the sea turning his teacup around and around in his hands like a woman. He couldn't speak and was too embarrassed to look at her. She blushed with shame then, mistaking his silence for judgment and blaming his mortification on her blubbering display of weakness. She approached him, placing her hand on his arm and felt the hard muscles tense at her touch.

"I'm so sorry, Duffy. Forgive me breaking down like this in front of you. You must think me the worst of spoiled aristocratic brats! Here you are, a hungry man and all I have to offer you is thin mint tea and tears. I'm so ashamed!"

With this Meg went to the hearth to see if she could warm up a bit of soup to offer her guest. Francis and the girls came in and Meg was forced to calm down. When she turned away from the hearth with a small bowl of turnip soup, Duffy was gone.

She relieved when Tom came in the kitchen door and plopped a blood stained package on the table. Duffy was right behind him and seemed to have moved past the awkwardness of their conversation.

Tom was as proud as a savage returned from the hunt.

"That's it darlin'. Dooley Creahan had to sell his cow for slaughter and I bought a fine roast and some stew meat. It took all I had left from the milk money. We'll eat well for a while off another man's misfortune. I pray God we don't choke on it."

Meg was forced to smile in spite of her earlier tears. It was wonderful to see Tom so happy for a change. She wondered if Duffy had said anything to him about her concerns and prayed he hadn't.

Tom walked to the hearth and peered into the empty soup pot, looking for lunch. Meg offered to warm up the bowl she had ladled for Duffy but Tom shook his head. Instead he poured himself a cup of cold mint tea and toasted the little group.

"May we be half an hour in heaven afor' the divil knows we're dead. And pray God next year this is a tall, cold pint and not this woman's drink made out of weeds."

He swilled it down and clapped Duffy McGee on the back.

"Duff, ye'll be stayin' fer a nice stew I hope?"

Duffy shook his head.

"I need t'get back. I can't be so long from the inn. If I don't watch me stock, it'll grow legs fer sure. Besides, I'll not be takin' that rare bit o'meat from yer mouths. I eat like a lord at the inn."

He smiled and patted his flat stomach.

"Never mind I swill down the leavins' of the rich. The rich know how t'leave good table scraps, that they do."

Meg gasped when he said that and Duffy flushed deeply and could have bitten his tongue off as he realized again what a fool he was.

Picking up his cap, he kissed her chastely on the cheek and asked too loudly,

"Who thinks your fine mam is the very best cook in all Ireland?"

Her little ones screamed.

"We do!"

Duffy tipped his cap to them all and ducked jauntily through the door trying too hard to hide the effect Meg's tears had had on him. Before he started down the beach Tom stopped him.

Meg was probably not meant to hear what Tom said but she wanted to know the worst and knew Tom would withhold it from her. She had leaned into the doorway and eavesdropped.

"Duff, I'm thinkin' I'll be needin' t'sell some of me own cows. Keep yer eye open fer a buyer will ye? No one can afford me milk and I can't afford te be givin' it away."

Duffy lit his pipe, nodding in the billows of sweet sponc smoke.

"Sure, Tom, I'll be sure t'get ye the best price I can. How many cows are ye thinkin' of sellin'?"

"I need to get rid of at least three. I haven't the grain te'feed 'em. I keep the women milking but I'm not able t'pay 'em. At least they get free milk. Ye know, I'm sure, that the tatties are ruined again this year. Worse than last. At least we had a few barrels last year. Now they started rottin' back in July. We're goin' t'be a hungry bunch this winter fer sure."

They walked down to the water and Meg could hear no more. Duffy got into his curragh and rowed away. When Tom came back he had found Meg busy stirring some of the meat into the dulse for the stew he so anxiously awaited.

He stood in the doorway for a few seconds and caught her as she straightened up from the fire.

"Come here, Darlin'."

He took Meg in his arms and looked long into her eyes. She could not mask her sorrow and she knew her tears had made her face red and puffy. She tried to look away but he held her chin and made her look at him.

"I know 'tis a hard time Meg. God knows I'd sell me soul t'give ye and the wee ones enough to eat. But I know somehow we'll be all right. God has seen us through shipwreck and the likes of yer father and only He knows which was worse. We will be fine, I promise. We may come out of this as poor as the Creahans but we will come out of this. God loves us and we love each other and that, in the end, is all that matters."

Meg rested her head against Tom's chest and hardly noticed the thinness of his arms as they tenderly encircled her. This was where she was safe. Drawing strength from his embrace, Meg felt hopeful for the first time since she had heard about the tragic death of Jimmy McLean.

In spring of 1847, Lord Lucan's nephew, Mr. Gilchrist of Dublin Street, arrived to inspect the situation. Lord Lucan had earned a reputation for generosity early on but as the hunger continued into its second year, the grim-faced undertaker was not showing any sympathy regardless of his employer's reputation and rumors of the Crowbar Brigade crushing and burning the homes of Lucan's tenants at his orders, had spread all the way from Castlebar.

Gilchrist met with Tom for hours in the vicarage of the Church of Ireland. Tom relayed the story that night, his face pinched with anger at the temerity of the arrogant snake from Newport. Mrs. Trent, who had been allowed to remain as the cook for the new pastor and his wife and had been given generous rations as befitted the former wife of a Church of Ireland pastor, had hastened to take her barm brack out of the tin oven and back out the kitchen door when they arrived. Mr. Gilchrist, never a shy man, had helped himself to a steaming loaf and slathered a chunk with butter before addressing the issue of rent payments with Tom Phalen. Tom, whose hungry stomach could hardly bear the delicious aroma, had been hard put not to snatch the cake out of the undertaker's hand and take a bite.

When they emerged from the vicarage it was already noon. A town meeting was hastily called in the post office and Mr. Gilchrist addressed the townsfolk contemptuously, being most stern in his remarks. He had an article from the Achill Missionary Herald written that past January that described a most embarrassing episode of the most reprehensible behavior. He regretted to inform the citizens of Doeega that the crime outlined in the article was still under investigation and anyone harboring a criminal or withholding vital information would be summarily apprehended and severely punished.

Before a crowd of starved and half-starved men and women, Mr. Gilchrist, undertaker to his Lordship the earl of Lucan, read as follows:

"Achill Missionary Herald (January-1847)

We regret extremely to state that a hooker belonging to General Thompson, of Connamara, which put into Achill Sound, at the south of thc island, from stress of weather, was plundered by a party of the natives of this island. One person suspected of being concerned in this outrage has been apprehended, and there is reason to hope that others also will be brought to justice.

We tell the natives of Achill, and they know that the advice is given by a real friend, that any man among them who engages in such lawless proceedings is the enemy of the whole population. The general good conduct of our poor islanders under their distressing trial is deserving of the highest commendation; the lawless conduct of some to which we have alluded is the only exception.

We trust that there will be no repetition of it. Our appeals on their behalf have been enforced by reference to the exemplary patience with which they endured their trials, and if some evil-minded persons are permitted to pervert the general distress into an occasion for breaking the laws of God and man, we shall be deprived of the most powerful plea we had to advance in applying to those who have both the means and the inclination to relieve them."

Mr. Gilchrist removed his pince-nez and scanned the crowd. Many, being too weak to stand, had sat down as he read the news article. He surveyed them with particular scorn.

"Let it be understood, people, that my Lord Lucan is a most generous and compassionate man. There are those among his advisors, myself included, who have warned him about his extreme, dare I say even flagrant, disregard for his own financial security in dealing with his tenantry, being yourselves. It is not too much to expect therefore, a fair and honest pledge of loyalty to the very man who sees fit to sustain you."

"He is however, not a fool. He has the power, I remind you, to turn you out and burn your miserable abodes. He has commissioned me, in light of this travesty, most recently read to you, to secure the rents for the year 1847 in advance."

An audible groan of protest shivered across the crowd. Many of those sitting suddenly found the energy to stand up. As the volume increased, Mr. Gilchrist nodded to his deputies and they circled the group menacingly. The poor residents of Doeega who had already seen some of their best and brightest fall by the side of the road, were silenced at once by the threat of armed confrontation.

The weary sat down again and Mr. Gilchrist, secure in his unchallenged authority, described how the rent would be collected.

The first quarter would be due today. The chill that had passed through the crowd before returned, to set tongues to wagging again. No one had the rent. No one had any crops, no one had any fish to sell. No one had anything.

Mr. Gilchrist raised his hand and silenced the crowd again.

"You will be pleased to know that you have in your midst a man prepared to show his gratitude to Lord Lucan for his generosity in affording him the opportunity to become a successful businessman. You all know that Mr. Tom Phalen has been the rental agent for Lord Lucan for many years now. Mr. Phalen has been a very loyal servant to my Lord and to you as well. Mr. Phalen, as you know has a very lucrative dairy. He has provided milk, cream, butter and cheese for this entire area for many years. He has also subsidized the rent for this town for many years, has indeed sold three cows to keep a roof over your heads these last few months."

Mr. Gilchrist's mouth twitched with pleasure to see the shock sweep over the townspeople. Tom just hung his head. He had made Gilchrist promise not to say anything about that but the weasel couldn't keep quiet, could he?

"Oh yes, my good people, Mr. Phalen has kept many of you in your homes long after the battering ram should have been put to the wall and the torch to the roof. And now he has offered to pay your ransom again. His remaining cows will be removed from his farm this very day to pay for you to remain in your homes six more months. I will return in the summer to collect from you the rent you will earn fishing. Hopefully you will be able to remain unmolested by the necessity of eviction until next year at this time. Perhaps by then, providence will again smile upon you and there will be no need for any further drama."

At this, he swept through the stunned crowd and motioned his guards to escort Tom out to the street. Tom was so angry he could not speak. Mr. Gilchrist looked tremendously pleased with himself. He had finally put this Irish toad in his rightful place. How he had hated dealing with him over the years. For some reason, his uncle had seen great potential in the big Irishman.

The fact that he was right was brought home to Gilchrist every year when Tom produced the full rent and completely balanced books.

Any fool could see that the rents were not met by the tenants. But every year the money was placed on the undertaker's desk. When he asked Tom where the balance of the money came from, he would only say that God had been good to the people of Doeega. Gilchrist had brought it up every year to his uncle and he had dismissed it as unimportant. He had sent his spies into the town and never found any cheating or selling on the sly or any odd bit of dealing at all. It wasn't until the hunger came that Mr. Gilchrist had his answer. That first year the spring rents had already been met. Then in the fall, Tom Phalen had had to sell some of his cows. This sent up a warning to Gilchrist. If Tom Phalen was selling cows then evictions would have to follow. But the rents were met again in the fall.

So, Mr. Gilchrist came to Doeega to see for himself. After hours of reviewing the books and grilling Tom Phalen he finally got him to admit that he had been subsidizing the rents for years. There was nothing illegal about it. Gilchrist knew that. He was just astonished that a man as smart as Tom Phalen could be so stupid as to lose out on all that money for a bunch of dull-witted tattie hokers and stinking fishermen. So, he decided that if Tom was the angel of the Achill fishermen he could just as well be poor.

He had no instructions from Lord Lucan to collect the rent early. But as he sat buttering barm brack at the kitchen table in St. Mary's vicarage, he had thought of another conversation with another noble gentleman. An idea had come to him that could prove very beneficial to him and his secret friend. Now he'd see what this great benefactor of the citizens of Doeega was really made of. Now he'd satisfy himself with anticipating the pleasure of keeping his promise to evict the Phalens when this year's rents weren't met.

Meanwhile, the men of Doeega had been handed their shame in a public meeting before their friends and their women.

That was certainly going to make life miserable for Tom Phalen. Gilchrist couldn't decide which development made him happier.

He had taken the rest of Tom's cows to cover the rent for the whole village. As they watched the undertaker load the last three heifers into the hired curragh, Meg could feel Tom shrink into himself.

Later as they lay in bed, he confided in her that he had failed them all.

"Ah, Meg, the sight o'me prize red cow being dragged across the strand, her cryin', her calf cryin' and me own wee lassies cryin' shamed me t'death, it did. Didn't I wish the rocky beach would have opened up and swallowed me body and soul."

Meg said nothing. She simply held him in her arms and stroked his hair. They had been through worse than this and they would survive this too. How, she could not fathom but somehow they always came through.

He continued in the sleepy monotone she loved to hear but which now bore the weight of the world on every word.

"Now there's nothing when I look ahead, Meg. Just a black hole as deep as the ocean before us and me t'blame."

"Tom," Meg began to protest but he shrugged her off. He had failed to protect them. He had tried to be fair and just to all the men of Doeega, and had steadfastedly refused to accumulate wealth at their expense.

"All those years on me knees at St. Dymphna's, prayin' t'do the right thing, Meg. Sellin' me pride t' keep land that was mine t'begin with! But I never intended to sacrifice me manhood on a platter fer any amount Meg, now did I?"

He had hoped that he would have made better friends with the men of the village but they cared nothing of him or his past. They knew only that he was a man with a foot in both camps. He'd overheard plenty of their hushed conversations over the years to know what they thought of him. Even his friendships with Jamie Grady and of course, Duffy, couldn't remove the sting of it.

"T'the men of Doeega, Meg, Tom Phalen is a man who

hasn't quite sold his soul to th'landed class but walks mighty close to the edge of the abyss. I heard Rev. Trent himself say that not a week before he died. "

He caught himself before he said out loud some of the other hurtful things he had overheard after church one Sunday having a smoke outside the Ailse Inn.

It was Lizzie Ballard's oldest boy Liam and Tom would never forget his words.

"He has a wife from the other side, after all and don't he let her keep her airs and ways about her? Don't he push his sons and daughters t'learn th'classics and don't they spout th'Latin and Greek in Mr. Mulcahy's little skits and dramas? Suren' he's a grand lad at McCoy's when he's buyin' rounds but ye never can tell, don't ye know. If y'ask me he's no better than a traitor."

Lying with Meg in his arms he longed to share with her the pain remarks like this gave him but he knew that wouldn't be fair to her. He had never brought home these rude comments and wasn't about to start now. Besides, Meg's regular breathing and limp hand across his chest told him she was sleeping.

He got up and went to the hearth. He took his pipe off the mantel and scraped the last bit of sponc from the bottom of the can he kept on the windowsill next to the table. He'd be lucky if he could even beg some more from Duffy when he saw him next.

His heart filled with sorrow as he took in the pretty little kitchen. He had taken so much for granted over the years. Meg had made lace curtains for all the windows and every spring had freshened up the whitewash on the walls. The hearth was always welcoming for a sit or a smoke and she and Rose had knitted lovely shawls to throw over their shoulders of a winter's evening.

There were fresh flowers in the spring and dried ones in the winter, their fragrant bundles hanging from the rafters. He breathed deeply of brittle sprigs of lavender and thyme that still graced the lintel as he grabbed his box of lucifers off the table. There were only the two bundles left from last year's harvest and too early for the spring flowers yet.

Meg had actually fed the whole family one night on a nice pan of eggs and a bit of bacon she had bought with a few shillings she got for her dried flowers and herbs. A rich friend of Rev. Nangle, it was. Tom remembered her carriage pulling up to St. Mary's, her nose all wrinkled up at the smell of turnip soup and unwashed men. She was so grateful for the fragrant nosegays Meg was selling from her apron, she bought them all. He shook his head at the memory of her lace hanky waving dismissively in the April breeze as her driver hastened to get her away from all the unpleasantness.

He fingered the dried herbs and released their sweet pungency. The lingering scent on his fingertips brought back that day with a force that made him catch his breath. Unpleasantness, was it? God save them, it was a whole lot worse than that!

Grabbing his fiddle and bow, Tom went outside and stoked his pipe with the bit of sponc and some of the herbs from Meg's bundles. He lit up and inhaled the sweet smell of burning lavender and thyme. The night was cloudy and standing at his door, he could see nothing but he could hear the gentle lapping of the waves in their endless rhythm against the shore.

Tom enjoyed having a pipe out by the strand and he hadn't played his fiddle in awhile. Maybe a little music would soothe his soul. The moon peeked out from behind a cloud and lit his path to the gate. He could see the thinking rock shimmering in the moonlight as he walked toward the smooth damp sand. It was hard to believe this smooth glassy stretch was the scene of his total destruction just hours ago. The hoofprints and ruts caused by the dragging of his cows to the curragh had been washed away by the tide and the mute sand gave no testimony to the wreckage of his household.

He wanted to remember the day Duffy brought the cows in his curragh but he couldn't. He had been in his bed recovering from that awful shipwreck. He thought about the years since then and tried to piece together the events that marked their time in the pretty little house by the sea. His chest actually hurt at the thought of losing all of this. He had grown to love the sea and the fresh salt air and couldn't imagine being without it.

Tom sat on his favorite natural chair formed by a flat rock backed by another taller one. Tom enjoyed this perch for everything from reading the Good Book to contemplating the constellations over the ocean. He leaned back against the hard smoothness. The sweet smell of the herb scented smoke made him nostalgic and he wished his da were here to advise him. The little bit of sponc burned quickly and Tom set down the pipe. Picking up his fiddle he began to play a slow, sad air about a minstrel boy. Meg loved that one. The strains of the sweet notes drifted across the strand.

It would be twelve years in September that he was washed up on the strand and became a father the very same day. He thought about the last time he saw his da. How the time had fled them all, blowing on the wind across the sea.

Could they have ever known back in '35 how it would all end up with them all lookin' at starvation, now with his cows gone. Davey had promised him he'd write if Da needed him but that last time was two years ago before the crops failed. Since then, he hadn't heard from any of them, Davey, Da or Paulie. He didn't even know if any of them was still alive. He had left a whole life behind when he and Meg had run to the safe haven of this strand. His family was here now and the years were marked by the milestones of their lives.

He began the beautiful "Rose of Tralee" in honor of his Lovie. Rose was becoming a young colleen and soon the lads would be looking her way. Tom's first born had always held a special place in his heart. Meg had always favored their son Thomas because the boy reminded her of himself but Rose was in a class by herself. Full of beans she was, his Lovie. He knew he loved that the most about her. The world could be crashing around them and she'd still find a reason to argue the color of a bird on the fence. She always had a song in her heart too and a kind word for a stranger. None of his children loved to hear him play the fiddle as much as Rose and she, herself, showed a natural aptitude for it. He smiled to himself at her feistiness and her taste for speaking her mind. There was a real tender side of her for sure, that's why he called her his Lovie since she was a wee lass. She was marvelous with the children too but the man who got his Rosie would never lack for knowing where she stood.

She looked like Meg, all prettiness and fine bones but had Tom's ruddy coloring. Her eyes were exceptionally lovely. Clear and blue like the water of the brook at Clydagh Glyn with brown-flecked rings of green around the iris, they were big and round like Da's and set wide apart in her heart-shaped face. They could scarcely hide a secret and were a true mirror of her soul. Her thick black waves made her look like the miniature of his mam on the mantel, though Mary Clare looked more like her namesake with her auburn hair. Rose was a lithe, athletic girl whose body was still more like a lad than a lady but Tom knew this would soon change. He wondered had the hunger not happened if she might have started to flower sooner. As it was, there was nary a bit of roundness about her or any of the rest of them for that matter. Denny was even fuller in the chest than Rose and he was skinny from the day he was born.

Thinking of Denny weighed him down and he played the sad strains of "Macushla" to accompany his thoughts. That boy was trouble and no gettin' around it. Tom had been very strict with him, thinking he needed a strong arm to keep him in line but for some reason nothing he did ever phased Denny. He listened to no one except the lads in the Blackthorn Brotherhood causin' his mam tears and raisin' a ruckus at the dinner table. Tom didn't know how he kept growin' with so little to eat but Denny at eleven was a strappin' lad with thick sturdy legs and big feet.

His thoughts drifted back to his day. When Gilchrist revealed that Tom Phalen was subsidizing the rents for all those years, he knew that whatever friendship he had built over pints at McCoy's was gone. The men of Doeega, like so many of their brothers across the green hills of Ireland had nothing of their own to claim but their pride and their families. As long as Tom kept them from knowing that he was the one who had really put the food on their tables and the thatch over their beds, he could walk among them as one of their own. He knew he would never overcome the fact that he was a stranger among them, a fact made more sensitive by his marriage to an earl's daughter but he thought he could help them have the life they deserved.

He had often sat right here, mulling over his pipe, at war with himself over his right to oversee the lives of men with whom he shared neither blood nor history. Until that fateful day when he had stood at the top of Croagh Patrick and scanned the vast expanse of Clew Bay, he had never known a thing about Achill Island. Then, within a matter of months he was the local authority on the island, a position he had neither wanted nor deserved. For ten years he wondered almost daily if he had made the right choice in accepting the job of overseer for Lord Lucan. He had prayed a thousand Aves to clear his head of the haunting question of his true motive.

He was a stable hand who had risen to head groom in one of the hundreds of stables in Ireland and would have risen no higher if he lived to be a hundred. He would have lived and died in a rundown cottage on rented land had he not lusted after the warm flesh of a wealthy woman. The very basis for his prosperity was a falsehood. He didn't deserve to be married to Meg. He wasn't born to be comfortable and secure. He fell into bed with a woman born on a plane above him and had spent the last ten years of his life hanging on the edge of that plane, neither safely on top with her nor safely beneath with men he could honestly call brother. Then, as if it weren't enough to drag her into a poor man's bed, he had caused her to leave behind all she knew and held dear. Never mind that she was his very life and more precious to him than breathing.

He had owed it to Meg to take that position for Lord Lucan. He had been desperate to make up to her all that she had lost by marrying him. That's why he never pushed her to convert to Catholicism. To see Meg Catholic had been his heart's desire ever since that night in Newport when his own faith had been returned to him by the gracious ministering of Fr. Finnegan. And he would have waited until he died if it had taken that long. The fact that Meg had arrived at her own desire to convert should have brought him true joy and on some level it did. But the hunger had changed everything. Now, their life was in shambles and even Meg's completion of her studies hadn't brought him the joy he had anticipated. Now they would starve just like everyone else on this forgotten island.

Tired of playing sad songs and too weary to play anything fast, Tom set his fiddle down next to him. His mute instrument did nothing to keep him from thinking and his thoughts were deeply troubling.

Tom had taken his burning questions over and over to the kind ear of Fr. O'Boyle and received absolution from his blessed hand many times for the sins that haunted his soul. Fr. O'Boyle had told him each time that taking the position as Lord Lucan's agent was no sin; that he had his own family to think of, after all. The priest never chastised Tom for the lack of faith that brought him back again and again with the same sin on his heart. No matter how many times Tom confessed to the lack of integrity that allowed him to betray his father's name and the Irish blood in his veins, Fr. O'Boyle forgave him.

It was after a particularly long session in the confessional one cold, damp Saturday shortly after his dairy farm was established, that Fr. O'Boyle suggested to Tom that he might try giving some of his money to the poorest villagers if it troubled him so much to have it. The Franciscan priest had listened with indignation to the story of how Tom had purchased the land with the money from the sale of his own pig and yet still lived under the threat of eviction all these years.

Tom learned later from a giggling Biz Nealy that the faithful waiting in line outside the confessional witnessed with their own ears the dear priest's passionate diatribe against the unjust landlords and their lackeys. But by the time the story reached Biz's lying tongue, it was he, himself, who had received the stern lashing from the gentle Franciscan's tongue and well deserved at that, with his fancy wife and lace curtains in the kitchen window. That bit had tormented him all this time even though he knew better than to place any stock in Biz squealing like a porker to the likes of Maggie Ballard behind the Shannon Road wall.

Tom knew the men of Doeega would never accept his charity and that was why he decided to give it to them silently in the form of rent subsidies. How could he have known that he would someday be exposed and what he had seen as an act of justice would be twisted into public humiliation for the men he had only wanted to help? Meg had thought the idea a good one at the time but she wasn't of his blood and knew nothing of the Irishman's deep-seated need to be his own man and provide for his own.

Tom knew the only freedom an Irishman had was in his own home. There, behind his door, whether he lived in a tidy stone house or a turf sided booley, he assumed the role of lord and master over his wife and children. There his word was law and he prided himself on his strength and dominion over all he saw before him. Whatever went on the table was put there by his own hand and didn't the manure pile by his front door show the others the man he was?

It was the pride of a strutting boyeen that put the swagger in their walk and the fierce bellow in their belligerent pub talk. Tom also knew that the self-important boasting was often a brave and foolish lie that lived only in the minds of the men who believed it.

In many an Irish household the wife held the family together by her wits because the husband could provide so little from his meager scrap of land or shore. Many a struggling family lived from day to day on the barter a wife received for butter or eggs. It was a deep secret of Irish marriages that the women were not really ruled by the men but acted as willing partners in a fragile dance where the man protected the woman from want and she protected him from the truth that he was really powerless to do so. Tom had seen it time and time again among his old friends at

McPhinney's and at McCoy's. The louder the braggart the more likely it was his wife was the real man of the house.

Tom had always wanted something more than this for himself. That was why he had never married. Sure, as a lad he had had his share of women flapping their skirts and flashing their teeth at him. He had always thought he had a fairly nice face and being a big boyo hadn't hurt any either but whenever a lass put on the dog for him he backed right off. He never enjoyed the exchange of barbs and insults that seemed to be a requirement of courtship. Tom had never had any time for all that palaver tossed over a coy shoulder or shouted out from a group of lads walking past. He felt that if a man wanted to see a woman he ought to treat her like someone worth seeing. He could never understand why behaving like a couple of stray cats was supposed to be attractive.

And then there was the matchmaker. God forbid a man should approach a woman like he would any other animal, whether a man or a horse! As if women were somehow invisible growing up! As if a lad never laid eyes on a colleen until the matchmaker somehow knocked the scales from his lids! One day out of the blue, a girl's father calls the matchmaker and it starts.

Like two pigeons, the selected lad and lassie circle around each other, she in her red skirt and flowered shawl, he in a fine set of tweeds he borrowed from the last lad to walk down the aisle. Then they get to sit back to back in a jaunting cart while an old man makes smoke rings with his pipe, leaning into their conversation with a big ear to catch any juicy tidbit he can take back to the families.

Musha! What a tradition! No, this was not for Tom Phalen. But then, look what a huge bit o'bother he had started by doing his courting himself. Maybe there was some good to it.

His thoughts drifted back to the village men and their wives. He preferred to rest his mind by philosophizing tonight. He had enough time to ruminate on his own failings the rest of the day.

He thought about what love really was like in a good marriage. When the love between husband and wife was real and sustaining, the balance worked well and the couple lived in a mutual give and take that kept the relationship stable and the wolf away from the door. Tom had often thought his brother Paulie's marriage was like that. The land they lived on had been in her family, not his. Her father had lived with them for years until he was sure Paulie could take over the fishing and support his daughter fair and well. He was an old man when he finally died and Paulie had eight children before the old buzzard felt that it was safe to go to his eternal reward. As soon as the funeral was over, Paulie stepped up to be the man of the house, no hard feelings, no regrets.

As with Paulie and Anna, in many of these cases, a couple shared their love by giving life to children. Naturally, they protected and reared their children to believe, as they did, that the lot imposed on them as poor tenants was not of their making or fault. Their poor lot was simply the legacy of the landed class who had robbed their ancestors of their rightful place in history. Tom himself had been raised that way. His hate for Lord Jeffrey and his ilk was fed to him in his mother's milk. But he had crossed class lines when he married Meg and with his own children, he had to be very careful.

Tom knew a good marriage, like his own mam and da, Paulie and Anna or he and Meg had, was not nearly as common among the very poor as it was among people with enough to eat. In the worst of Irish poverty, the men abandoned any semblance of false pride and did little or nothing to provide for their wives and children, instead allowing them to beg in the streets. Somehow these men had sunk so deeply into the lie of their own victimization that they failed to hold themselves responsible for any of their family's suffering.

These were the men who drank pint after pint at McCoy's, blinding themselves to the sight of their ragged, starving children and deafening their ears to the wails of their wives. These were the men who beat the women who fed them and overpowered them in the night making one baby after another on them until aged and used up before their time, they died before their thirtieth year in the field or giving birth yet again in squalor. These men would then drink even more and beat their daughters and sons for looking like their mother.

These were the same men who bargained with men just like themselves for the hand of a daughter who foolishly thought she could do better with a home of her own. Whatever dowry came with her, the next wife found it squandered on drink and the taste of her freedom was tinged with beer and blood.

Tom knew too many men like this. Doeega was full of them. Men who lived on the sea and became hardened by the brutal salt air and cold winds off the Atlantic. He saw them in the village, their skinny, pregnant wives scurrying to keep up with them. He saw these men kick their wives and children away from the door of the public house as they plunked down the food money on the bar for another round of the blinding, deafening brew that poisoned their hearts. He knew he could change the lives of these women and children with the extra wages from his job as agent to their landlord. He talked at length to Meg about it and had asked Duffy his thoughts. Duff had been against it at first for all the right reasons but Tom had worn him down with the argument for justice.

"What else can I do Duff?" he had asked.

He remembered too, the long conversation on this very rock the night he asked Duffy to help him decide about the job in the first place. Tom knew then that part of him had wanted Duffy to talk him out of it and Duffy had tried. The other half of Tom knew he could do nothing else. He would lose the land that was rightly his and put the lives of both Meg and the children at risk if he didn't take the position.

Sitting on his stone chair, in the silent night, he could hear Duffy ask him,

"How will ye feel, Tom, when ye have t'be the one to tell some bedraggled mother that a bailiff was on his way to smash her house down while her husband was out to sea?"

He could never do that! Not after standing in his granda's yard and watching his da and his uncle carry his own mother out to the bog so she could cry out her labor pains as her da's house burned down behind her. Not after watching his granda's tortured body cut down from the whipping post and buried in a stolen coffin on a thick, black, moonless night. Not after carrying Maureen Dougherty back from the brink of the Clydagh River with her dead, purple baby in her hand.

He had to take the job but not if he had to dance with the devil. If he had to walk on the rim of the precipice he wanted the God of justice at his side. If he had to be Lord Lucan's agent, he would take on the responsibility of protector to his tenants as well. They never needed to know. They would never question the rents being paid. None of them even had the education or worldliness to recognize that their meager harvests of fish or grain would not measure up to the demand of one such as Mr. Gilchrist.

Lord Lucan was no different from any other landlord. He could be fair, at times benevolent, but he had his life and his cruel ways and there was no drunken Irish fisherman alive who would be allowed to change even the number of grapes in his fruit bowl. Mr. Gilchrist would see to that. This he had told Tom and every other man assembled for his periodic visits. Every man on the island knew that the landed class sported their own brand of fairness and their kindness always smelled of iron.

According to Mr. Gilchrist, Lord Lucan was a simple man with simple rules. If the rents weren't met, evictions would follow. The tenants had always known this and did their best to make the rents. They had lived for generations on Achill with very few troubles with Lord Lucan or any other prior landlord. Most of them had never seen the man or set foot in the city of Castlebar where he lived. His undertaker came every season for the rents and until Tom Phalen came, the protestant vicar handed the money over to the man.

Dooley Creahan had told Tom once that it wasn't until he came and on his heels, Mr. Gilchrist of Dublin St., Newport, that anyone had even mentioned the need for an agent to oversee the collection of rents. Old Rev. Trent had done just fine until then but Gilchrist was a snake and refused to deal directly with him. No sir, he would do business with Mr. Thomas Phalen and Mr. Phalen only. From the start there were rumors that they were partners out to bilk the honest Doeega villagers out of their tiny plots of land.

When Tom heard this he almost slugged Dooley. His friend had wrestled his arm to the table and told him not to punish the messenger fer speakin' the truth. As seasons passed Tom heard less and less of this kind of talk and worked hard to establish himself as an honest businessman with a willingness to work hard. After the first few years, if he had made few friends, at least all but the most fractious of the lads grudgingly accepted him.

There were times when he had shared some of his years as a stable hand with the men around a pint but despite their polite listening they never gave him what he longed for. Even the ones whose trust he thought he had earned, Finn Kelly and Jamie Grady, Dooley Creahan whose wife was Meg's first paid help, hired years ago to wetnurse Mary Clare when Meg had become ill, had now begun to look away from him. Even Pete Sweeney, who had come to Doeega after Tom and had no reason to mistrust him, kept his distance after Gilchrist's announcement.

Tom had deceived them all for years, allowing them to believe that they, the husbands and fathers of their families, were responsible for providing for the life of their wives and children. He had silently robbed them of their rights in a way no landlord could.

Tom Phalen, in trying to be fair and equal had turned them into shamefaced shadows of men. They were betrayed, stripped of their pride and their manhood, not by the wrecking ball of a tyrant but by the kiss of a friend. Would it not have been better to see them starve, to stand back and let them be evicted with their own pins beneath them, than to silently saw their legs off inch by inch?

He tapped his pipe on the rock and picked up his silent fiddle. He needed to go to bed. He knew there were no answers to his questions. He had had enough philosophy for one night. What he wanted now was a good sleep in the arms of the woman he loved. He climbed in next to Meg and pulled her close. He thought he knew what he was doing when he took the agent position. He saw his family prosper and his children thrive. Now he wondered how it had all fallen apart so quickly.

What Tom could not know as he held his wife in his arms and pondered their future, was that Mr. Robert Gilchrist of Dublin St. Newport, had just arrived at the Castlebar Arms Hotel. He would need to be well rested for the trip to GlynMor Castle to settle with His Lordship, Jeffrey Wynn, Earl of Canfield. He had kept his end of a bargain made years ago and he was on his way to collect his fee.

Chapter Eight

On a late December morning, 1847, Meg stood up from the bastible where she stirred a thin gruel made from American corn and a handful of crushed walnuts, and wiped her hand across her brow. A fleeting memory of a stew she had made from Dooley Creahan's old cow made her stomach contract. Now, more than a year later, facing another hard and hungry Christmas, Meg could hardly remember how stew tasted. The beef Tom had brought into this kitchen that evening was the last red meat they had had.

Still bending, she set the kettle to boil and swung the big metal crane over the fire. She stood and stuck her hand into the oven that was warming next to the hearth. This morning she would bake more of the flat bread that had fed her family for all of the summer and into the fall. There was no shortening and no leavening so for months she had taken the American corn meal distributed by Rev. Nangle's missionaries, added water and a little of the precious wild honey from a beehive Tom had found nestled in the eaves of the chicken house and made a flat paste of it, baking it in the oven as a sort of bread. Mrs. Trent had explained to the women of Doeega that the American Indians had fed their families on these flat corn patties through many a winter and encouraged them to learn how to make them from the donated meal. At first her family hated the tasteless pancakes but with the honey mixed in, they ate them without complaint. Deciding the oven was hot enough she plopped a few of the patties on a tray and slid them in to bake.

Straightening up sent dull aches from her lower back down both legs and she knew she was again with child. That was the first sign with every baby since Mary Clare. All of her pregnancies had been marked by the typical signs to a greater or lesser degree but Mary Clare had chosen to sit painfully against her lower back for nine months. Now, as soon as she began carrying, her back began to throb. The thought of another baby overwhelmed Meg. After Martha was born over a year ago Meg had really thought her family was complete. Now, here she was almost forty years old and with child again. She hardly knew how to tell Tom.

She looked out the little kitchen window at the strand shimmering silver in the early morning light. How could the world look so normal when every day brought only another round of hunger and death? The potato crop had failed yet again, the cows were long gone and now even Meg and her children were faced with starvation. Tom and she had weathered the first two years of the hunger fairly well by selling her jewelry. Thank God for Duffy and his connections to young George, 3rd. Marquis de Sligo. Lord Sligo had bought Meg's precious diamond necklace and earrings to give as a wedding gift to his bride the spring after the first crop failure. They had lived through the whole spring and summer on that money. Tom had been able to keep the dairy and even subsidize the mid-year rents for 1846.

The chill winds of December whistled down the chimney, sending billows of turf smoke into the little kitchen. Meg took the thin corn tortillas out of the oven and stacked them on an ironstone platter. How she wished she was baking a dark rich fruit cake for Christmas dinner. She remembered the deep purple aroma of plum pudding steaming on the windowsill and the rich gamey giblets stewing for Christmas gravy. Her mind wandered to the day Maureen taught her how to make the traditional Irish stuffing for the roast goose. Maureen told her the secrets to the savory, moist stuffing. First you had to use mashed potatoes as a base for the mixture and mix it all up with the other ingredients. All with your hands, mind you, no spoon, and gobs of butter, first for frying the bread, onions and celery then just because it tasted better that way. When Meg had questioned the addition at the end of a single piece of stale bread dipped in boiling water and rung out before being shredded and mashed into the potato mixture, she simply got a shrug from Maureen. There were some mysteries we needn't solve, she had been told. Meg had never known anything about cooking a goose and Maureen's laughter echoed in her mind as she remembered how funny the maid thought it was that she had eaten this very dressing every Christmas of her life from the experienced hand of Biddy Carrey. Now Meg would have given anything for any kind of stuffing for any kind of bird to grace her Christmas table.

She shook off her reverie and watched the silver light change to gold as the sun spread like honey across the sand. She sighed at the dawn of a new day. How was it they ever looked forward to their mornings? They were so hungry, all of them. She could not believe she was pregnant again. She and Tom had had so little energy for that part of their life. Could it have been on Michealmas?

She remembered how withdrawn Tom had been as the traditional feast of the harvest approached. The praties, as the locals called them, had failed for two years now, so there was no pratie harvest for most of the village. Tom, like so many others, had decided not to plant any potatoes in the spring of '47. They had hoped to avoid spreading the blight to the other crops and the scheme had worked for the most part. Meg's other vegetables had done well but Meg knew the turnips and carrots, cabbages and parsnips were all that they had to subsist on for months. Beans and onions had also been plentiful and the fruit and nut trees had borne well but those foods would never fill a hungry belly like the starchy potatoes that were the staple of their diet.

Meg knew Tom was filled with second thoughts about his decision not to plant potatoes. He, like the others, knew having nothing planted meant no hope of having any harvest and the men who made this decision knew they gambled with their families' lives. But when the few farmers who had planted reaped another rotten harvest, the men simply shook their heads.

"What choice did we have?" they asked each other as they clustered on the roadside to beg a day's work digging ditches.

"See, Paddy, all that fer nothin' and now the stink o'yer yard t'boot."

Thank God the fish had been plentiful and most of the fishermen had been able to make the second half of the rent. Tom had gone in September to deposit the money on Mr. Gilchrist's massive oak desk. He, himself, had taken up a scythe and helped with the corn harvest when neither Peter Feeney nor his wife could manage it. Both Peter and his mother were gravely ill. It was all they could do to get up every day and go to the store. Were there any business to manage, they would not have been able to do it.

In return for Tom's favor, Maryellen Feeney had tearfully given him Peter's old best suit in the hope that it might bring him luck with the undertaker. Suren' Peter wouldn't need it fer burial. When that terrible day came, he would be tossed in a grave with the likes o'them tatie hawkers and fishwives from down below the Shannon Road. He was, God bless his gentle soul, a man of business, a purveyor of nice things in his day. Suren' he was glad t'see Tom's use of it. It was too big for Peter anyway and Tom had shrunken enough to wear it well.

When Tom had left for Newport with the mail boat he could feel the eyes of every villager watching him. They burned through Peter Feeney's jacket and seared Tom's back, each pair blazing with the clear and desperate look of a man on his way to the gallows. As the little curragh headed out toward Clare Island, Meg along with everyone else watched as Tom leaned over the hull and vomited his meager breakfast into the sea.

Once again, Tom had found himself standing alone in the drafty anteroom of Mr. Gilchrist's office. He bore a note from Rev. Nangle declaring Tom's continued leadership of the community and his personal reliance on Tom and Meg for assistance in his soup distribution. It gagged Tom to have a Church of Ireland preacher as his advocate but where Meg was concerned, the note was really true. She had been a great help to Rev. Nangle and had brought many a bucket of soup home after the day's distribution. It was the soup and the American corn that had kept them alive and him able to help Maryellen Feeney in the first place. Between him harvesting the Feeney's field and Denny and him working in the ditches, Tom prayed that Gilchrist would let them stay at least till spring.

As it turned out, Gilchrist wasn't even there. He had been called away on business and his assistant simply took the money and counted it. Once he was satisfied that the right amount was there he handed Tom the receipt and dismissed him through the back door.

When Tom came around the walkway that led to Dublin St., he came upon the English gardener who had mistaken him for the cook's lover so many years ago. It was clear to Tom that the gardener wasn't feeling the pinch of the hunger. His plate was full of food bought with the sweat and blisters of the poor sods who planted it, harvested it and shipped it away from their own families so he could eat white bread in Mr. Gilchrist's kitchen.

The man didn't recognize Tom and scowled at him when he tried to make conversation. Tom later told Meg that the gardener was shocked when he told him who he was. Seeing how tired and hungry Tom looked, he immediately invited him in for a bit of refreshment. He introduced himself as Alexander Briggs and said he hailed from just north of Liverpool. The two had struck up an odd little friendship over the years and with the boss away, the gardener felt quite comfortable entertaining the big man from Doeega.

When Tom told Meg about the first taste of white bread he had had in two years, he had a twinkle in his eye that made her wonder what he was up to. When he pulled a huge loaf of white bread out of his sack and along with it a dozen eggs, a wheel of cheese and two big sausages, she gasped. The cook whose lover he was supposed to have been was out for the afternoon and Tom's friend had slipped a few things to him when the maids weren't looking. Tom was delighted at the effect the humble feast had on Meg and the smell of real food frying in the big iron pannie brought all the children from their play.

The Phalens had been subsisting on watery vegetable broth and flat corn tortillas for months. Who could eat when the air reeked of rotten potatoes and people were dying in the streets of every village in Ireland? Meg knew they were among the lucky ones but even so, she had lost a great deal of weight and Tom's big frame looked more gaunt and sparse than ever. They both routinely sacrificed part of their meager portions for the children and in their bed at night massaged each other's bellies to ease the terrible spasms of hunger.

But not that night. The afternoon Tom Phalen came home from Newport with the good news that all the tenants were secure in their homes, the whole family feasted on eggs scrambled with a bit of sausage and thin slices of toasted white bread topped with creamy, melted English Stilton cheese. Meg wanted more than anything to cook it all up and really celebrate but she knew the food was too rich and would serve them all better the next day when they'd only be hungry again. The cheese would feed them for a month if she was careful with it. That night they all went to bed with full stomachs and Tom and Meg made sweet, tender love for the first time in months.

The next day when Tom went into the village to make his report, he was pleased to be able to tell the men crowded into McCoys that they had dodged the wrecking ball for another season. They were all relieved that they would be left alone for the winter but they still had to get through the spring when nothing was there to be harvested. Tom could only hope along with the others that Gilchrist would accept the rent for the whole year next fall when the crops were in again. He had told Meg that he had his suspicions that Mr. Gilchrist wrote his own rules and that a direct appeal to Lord Lucan would result in a very different answer. When he faced the townspeople, he kept these thoughts to himself.

Well, thought Meg on this cold December morning, that was then. She stirred the gruel, lumpy and gray, wishing she had a bit of salt in the salt cellar. The cheese had lasted a month but that was a long time ago. The hunger that was so easily relieved had returned with a vengeance.

Last night after tenderly kneading Tom's hollow abdomen, Meg lay in the dark contemplating how much an act of love it was to try to ease each other's pain. The passion of their early years had fallen away even as the flesh from their bones had wasted but the love they had for each other's tired, emaciated bodies seemed only dearer to them. Where they had burned with desire for the firm flesh and soft hair of their younger, healthier selves, they now wanted only to bring comfort to bony ribs and balding heads. Both of them had lost clumps of their thick wavy hair and bore scabs and open sores from lack of nutrition. Meg was glad she had sold her looking glass with the second set of jewelry. She knew what Tom looked like and could only imagine the sorry ugliness of her own starved face.

She had awakened before dawn as she did almost every morning, her stomach seized by deep, burning spasms of hunger. Remembering the usual nausea of early pregnancy, Meg marveled that any baby could grow where there was no nourishment. She worried about this baby. She wished the pain in her belly was the old, familiar unpleasantness. Instead, the swirling queasiness of her usual early months had been replaced by the deep hollow emptiness of true hunger.

As she sat waiting for the children to get up she hugged herself hard trying to relieve the burning pangs. She drank water drawn last night from the well but it didn't satisfy her belly. It never did. They had taken to filling a pot every evening in anticipation of the night hunger and Meg arose almost nightly now trying in vain to fill the deep pit of her stomach with the cool clear draft. She wanted to cry with frustration as she downed cup after cup of the water, feeling not full but bloated knowing that within minutes the liquid would run through her and she would be left grinding her fist into her belly as the cramping began again.

The children hardly played anymore. During the warm summer and autumn, they had enjoyed their usual games and had dutifully done their chores but since the winter had set in and the cold winds started to come down off the mountains they had no energy, drifting through their chores and spending their daylight hours listlessly doing their figures or writing their letters. They were actually more obedient than ever and Meg worried that they were losing their usual feisty energy.

Rose, at twelve, should have been flowering into the full roundness of adolescence but was thin and flat-chested. Her cycles had not begun and Meg wondered if they might have if she had good hearty food to eat. Mary Clare, who had never been strong, hardly looked her ten years. She had virtually stopped growing and had also lost some of her wavy auburn hair. Denny was always the sturdiest of her babies and despite his thinness still maintained a look of ability if not strength. He worked hard digging ditches with Tom and the other men and boys of Doeega but where his body seemed to be weathering the hunger better than the others, he was surly and rarely spoke. Meg knew he snuck off at night to town and feared his association with some of the more rebellious boys who hung around Feeney's store. Sometimes when she looked at his hard face and set jaw it was unbelievable that he was only eleven years old. He seemed driven by anger that bordered on hate, fueled by his own hunger pains in the night. She shivered at the sight of him, a black shadow crossing her heart every time she heard the kitchen door latch click in the night. She knew she would someday lose him to the Blackthorn Brotherhood and her heart broke every time she thought of his hateful words about the English.

Meg pulled out the crisp flat breads and set another batch to bake. In a small pot she stirred a tiny portion of dried raspberries in water to add to the porridge. Her daily challenge was to ration out the little bit of meal she had and add some of the nutrients from their garden. She did fairly well making the food at least palatable by adding honey and fruit to it. It was just that there were so many growing mouths to feed and there was so little food to last them until spring.

She had been appalled when Mr. Gilchrist had returned at All Hallows Eve to demand a portion of the fruit and vegetables she had preserved for the winter. Someone in the village had complained against them that they had hoarded these things unfairly and Mr. Gilchrist had demanded them to be turned over to him as part payment against the rent for the second half of the year, claiming his assistant had made an error in the math. Thank God no one knew about the honey or the dried fruit hanging from the eaves in the loft. At least they had that to help them survive.

Taking the last of the flat cakes from the oven, Meg heard rustling from the loft and knew her little ones would soon be climbing down the ladder looking for something to eat. Like all mothers facing this great hunger, Meg was consumed by the driving force of her children's empty bellies. She worried so about her little girls and her babies, Francis and Martha. Somehow the girls seemed to be growing but their hair was thin and lank and their bellies had the bloated look of the other village children. Francis had never been a big eater and like Denny seemed to be weathering the endless broth and gruel and flat, dry bread fairly well. As for Martha, Meg still nursed her as much as she could and she seemed content to eat mashed turnip or thin porridge the rest of the time. Poor little thing had no idea what good food really was.

The one Meg worried about the most was Thomas. At seven, he was very small and coughed constantly. He had never recovered from the pneumonia he had suffered after his escapade on the mountain after Danny Kinneally's funeral and during the last two winters had taken ill with coughing and wheezing that gripped him for weeks. Only the warm spring sun seemed to help him but he was weak and tired all the time.

Now he lay in a feverish, fretful sleep on the settle bed next to the hearth. He had come in yesterday complaining of a headache and Meg had jumped at the burning red cheeks and glazed eyes that looked at her. He had resisted her hugs and just lay down on the cool flagstone floor where he promptly fell asleep. She had opened up the settle and put him there, bunking Gracie and Ellen with Rose and Mary Clare in the addition Tom had put on the east end of the house years ago. Francis she put in the loft with Denny and Martha she kept with Tom and her in their room. Thomas had slept deeply into the evening. As his fever climbed, he wrestled in his dreams, swiping at imaginary foes as she crooned soothing lullabies in a vain attempt to comfort him. Exhausted, Meg finally settled him down about midnight.

Thomas was her favorite, her gentle dreamer. She often looked at him as he lay on his back in the yard holding a creature toward the sun, examining it in different light, studying the fine hairs of a caterpillar or the curled, ordered chambers of a nautilus shell. Tom had often said he thought Thomas would have been a druid had he been born in ancient times. He had a sixth sense about things and Meg had caught him more than once deep in contemplation and marveled at the faraway look he would give when she disturbed him. Sometimes she thought he had the makings of a saint or at least a priest of the church. Meg looked over at the settle and saw that he slept deeply, his breathing shallow and raspy but slower and less labored than the night before.

Meg had kept her promise to God and studied a great deal toward becoming a Catholic. Fr. O'Boyle had come personally to instruct her in the Scriptures and the traditions of the faith. Had she had any real formation in her own Anglican faith, Meg would have recognized the many similarities between the two. She often shook her head at the deep hatred one group of faithful had for the other when they were all begun by the same Jewish savior whose love for them all drove him to give his life on Calvary. Fr. O'Boyle was pleased with Meg's interest and very impressed at her insights into the deep spiritual truths that had stumped even the great theologians. He gave her a book of the writings of St. Teresa of Avila as a gift when she completed the first year of learning and only time and the terrible fate of starvation stood between her and the final sacraments of initiation in the church. The last months had been so occupied with mere survival that neither Meg nor Fr. O'Boyle had given her formation much thought.

Sitting down on a creepie, Meg stirred her pots and pulled the crane around to stop the kettle from boiling dry. Again, her back seized up and she grunted in pain until the aching muscles relaxed. When did she conceive this child? Her cycles had been sporadic since the second year of the hunger and she had had only one since she had Martha. She still nursed but admittedly her milk was poor at best so the last thing she thought was that she could conceive at all. It must have been on Michaelmas. That night they had actually eaten and she and Tom had felt up to lovemaking.

They had killed most of the chickens last year but they still needed eggs and so the two skinniest hens and the rooster had been spared. Meg had even allowed them in the house at night to keep them from being stolen for someone else's table. Meg had learned many ways to fix eggs and her family had survived the terrible summer and fall because of them. Years ago, Maureen had shown Meg how to preserve eggs by snatching them hot from under the hens and rolling them in her buttered hands, then either burying them underground or placing them deep in the booley.

Meg had done this when they still had cows, but they hadn't had butter since last spring. While the hens were still laying, Meg had preserved a good number of eggs by boiling them and pickling them in sour apple juice. But they had eaten the last of those by the middle of September.

Then on Michaelmas morning Meg woke to find the hens dead. The poor creatures had simply starved like so many others in the village. They had eaten the skinny hens for supper and traded the rooster for a piece of gingham and some thread from Peter Feeney.

The chickens were dry and stringy but no one complained. Everyone sat around the table sucking on the bones. No one spoke of it but they all knew that there would be no more eggs and soon they too would have to beg in the streets.

That night she and Tom went to bed on full stomachs for the first time since he had brought the feast from Gilchrist's kitchen. They had made tired, gentle love that night. Meg's cycles had all but stopped so she had no way to tell when she conceived. One thing she did know though, was that she and Tom were so weak they hardly came together at all so God must really want this baby to be born. Meg's eyes filled with tears at the thought of another baby. She was so exhausted from the hunger and so weak from nursing Martha that she could not imagine doing it all again. But she and Tom had always enjoyed the marriage act. She had always felt so cherished in his arms and he was such a tender lover.

The night they ate the chickens was the last time they had made love. Neither of them had had the strength to do it since. She remembered how good it felt to caress each other without pain, to gently arouse in each other sensations long deadened by hunger. He had reached for her and she was happy to go to him. They made love silently, both feeling their way as if for the first time. He felt so different in her arms, so thin around the shoulders and arms. She remembered wondering how she felt to him. Her breasts were almost flat and she could see her ribs when she dressed herself. That same day when she had pulled Francis onto her lap he had yelped when her sharp hipbone dug into his skinny rear end.

People were getting desperate. There were food riots all over and the Church of Ireland had begun serving long lines of hungry people soup and bread. The only way to get the food was to renounce the papist faith and embrace Protestantism. Meg thought this was despicable and felt sorry for the Catholics who had been forced to betray their church or watch their children die. They stood in line filled with shame, many of them nearly naked. They waited in their rags for a crust of bread and a cup of soup while other stronger villagers called out

"Soupers! Where's yer pope now?"

Protestants and Catholics alike mocked and shoved the soupers. People who had danced at their weddings and shared a pipe at their hearths now reviled them as traitors, guilty of apostasy and surely on their way to hell for a mug of broth. The next week, half-dead and feeling the pain of their own bare cupboards, many of those jeering joined the ranks of the damned so they might live to see another day.

So far Meg had been able to beg or steal enough to keep them alive. She had had only a few lace pieces and her old seal coat to sell this season and that brought only a barrel of oats and a few sacks of Indian cornmeal from America. Meg had squirreled away the last of that for Christmas dinner and once it was gone they would have to join the long line of soupers again down at St. Mary's. Meg knew that the missionaries from Slievemore fed her family without question because she was Church of Ireland and somewhere in the recesses of her mind Meg wondered if she could stay Protestant long enough to stay alive and still keep her promise to God later when this hunger had passed and she didn't need the Church of Ireland to feed her and her family.

She had made dresses for the girls and shirts for Tom and the boys from the gingham she got for the rooster. She knew Peter Feeney had given her far more than the skinny fellow was worth but she took the cloth and the thread gratefully, knowing that they would at least be able to cover themselves with the clothes. She was astounded at the level of degradation into which her fellow villagers had sunk. Many of them had no clothes at all and those who had wore rags unfit for wiping up the floor.

During the summer, desperate women were seen stripping off their skirts and taking the shirts and trousers right off the backs of their sons to trade to tinkers or gypsies for a little food. Now that the cold winds of winter blew, these same half-naked bodies were now being found frozen in the ditches and hedgerows along the road. Meg had prayed many a grateful Ave as she worked her needle and thread to make the few garments for her family to wear on Christmas morning and who knew how long after. Meg looked around her as she waited for Peter to cut the cloth for her. Never had a purchase seemed so frivolous to her. She almost stopped Peter with the sheers in his hand as she took in her surroundings.

The day she traded the rooster for the bolt of checkered cloth, she was astonished at the sight of the empty shelves in the store. The little post office grocery was simply empty, its stock cleaned out by the hungry villagers months ago. Rows of shelves stacked from floor to ceiling behind the counter, once filled with sacks of grain and jars of honey, bolts of cloth and rows of brogues shipped in from the east coast shoe factories now stood gray and empty. There were no barrels of pickled cucumbers and eggs, no sacks of flour or pans of dried smelts and kippers. No bacon hung from the big meat hook.

The milk tins that Tom used to fill daily from their own farm stood in a dusty pyramid in the corner. Jars that used to hold sweet yellow man and dulse for the children to suck on as they strolled home from the hedge school now held American cornmeal at a premium price. Even the hungriest villagers hesitated to try the strange yellow meal. No one really knew how to use it. They had no flour, no eggs, no butter or oil, no yeast or leaven of any kind. There were no dried currants or sultanas, no nuts or seeds to add to the meal. The meal and worse, the unground corn itself was useless without any way to prepare it. Some villagers had taken it and boiled it with water to form a thin gruel. As tasteless and gritty as it was, this mealy broth was all that kept some families from starving to death.

But even that came with a price. Peter Feeney had extended credit to everyone in the village for so long he hardly remembered who owed him what. Meg watched him as he cut the cloth for her. His hand shook like a he had the palsy. The sinews of his forearm were so prominent she wondered if he had any flesh on his arms at all. His eyes were rheumy and clouded as he turned to her with her parcel and dragged the half-dead rooster across the counter as payment.

When Mary Feeney came out of the back room to take the rooster Meg started to say hello. Then she saw the woman who had delivered her children and had been her friend for over ten years. Mary's eyes were completely clouded over and Meg could tell she did not see her. Peter placed the rooster in her skinny hands and she immediately snapped its neck. Feeling her way to the end of the counter she sat down on the tall stool that always stood near the ledger where she and Peter kept their figures. Meg began to realize that Mary was blind as she watched her pluck the feathers from the dead bird with rote precision. Peter tried to thank Meg for the business but his voice, once so strong and clear came out like the croak of a frog.

"Me mam's not too well, as ye can see."

Meg had to lean close to understand the rasped message. As she drew her face close to his, she could smell the foul stench of bad teeth and see clearly the yellow cast on his skin. It had been weeks since she had come to the store. There was no money. There were no provisions. There was no social life in the village. Even the prospect of receiving mail held no allure for the hungry people of Doeega.

Meg turned to go. A man entered as she stopped to check her empty post box. In the dim light of the store, Meg knew he was a stranger. There were so many strangers now. People wandered in every direction from every county and townland looking for something to eat. She wanted to scream at the strange man that there was nothing on this island for him! She wanted to push him away, to send him back home. He had no business being here taking the food, what little there was, from the mouths of people like her.

While hunger caused the greatest pain, fever caused the greatest fear. The poor wretches were dying in the ditches and being buried as soon as possible but the fever continued to spread. It was the fever that took Peter and his mother not a week after Meg had been in their empty store. Thomas had a fever now that had her up this morning staring out at the dawn creeping from the east like a thief.

Meg shuddered at the image. Why would she think the dawn crept like a thief? They had nothing left to steal. Meg again heard rustling, this time from the settlebed where Thomas lay roasting beneath a light layer of old sheeting. He was so restless, picking at his covers and tossing his curly, dark head from side to side. She had slept on the flagstones to be close to him in the night and bent once again to moisten his mouth.

Meg felt in her apron pocket for her rosary. Tom had given her the prayer beads for Christmas the year the blight first came. She knew he wanted her to convert to his faith and she had been studying with Fr. O'Boyle all that summer. They had talked about her being received into St. Dymphna's at Easter Mass.

Then the hunger came and her whole life became a frantic effort to keep her little household alive. The conversion was forgotten and when he presented her with the beautiful Connemara marble beads, she was overwhelmed. He had picked them up in Newport on his last visit to Mr. Gilchrist's and had hidden them away for when she was received into the church. That Christmas, he had changed his mind and decided to give them to her early. She had cherished them ever since despite not knowing how to pray them. Eventually, she would get around to becoming Catholic and then she would learn which bead was for what prayer.

Meanwhile she carried them with her at all times. She took them out and ran her fingers gently over the smooth green marble beads. Her thumb rested on the tiny figure of Jesus, rough against the polished wooden cross. Looking at the tiny

Christ, Meg let her tears flow. The corpus blurred and the cross became wet and smoother still.

Kneeling beside Thomas she wept. Her tears fell on his bedclothes, on his hair, on his hot rosy cheek. Meg's tears moistened the little face whose eyes were too dry to shed tears of their own. She brushed a salty drop from his temple as it found its crooked path toward his little silken ear. Her finger rested on his cheekbone, so hot beneath his waxy, translucent skin.

How plump he had been! Her little lad just out of babyhood now as thin and gaunt as an old man. She wept for Thomas, for fear that he would die, for his patient suffering eyes that looked to her for one more bite when there was none. She wept for Martha who wailed for milk when her breasts were shriveled and dry. Her tears fell for the baby she carried now who would suck the life out of her in its fight to survive. She couldn't be pregnant. Who would take care of her other children if having this baby killed her?

Meg knelt, fingering the beads, weeping her silent Aves on them. Crushing them until pain shot through her palm, she wept. She rested her head on Thomas's chest and sobbed great wracking gulps and groans that failed to wake him. Her tears soaking through his tunic failed to stir him. The heat from his body made her perspire, sweat mingling with her tears until she could not tell them apart. Still she clutched the beads. The little crucifix dug into her palm and burned where the Christ assaulted her flesh, digging and pressing his imprint on her skin.

Meg knew Thomas would die. As well as she knew he would be born, she knew he was leaving her. He was so thin when he should have been so chubby. His legs were like sticks beneath the sheet but his knees looked huge and swollen. She let the rosary drop onto the mattress and ran her throbbing hand over his bulging tummy. How was it that the hungrier her children got, the greater the size of their bellies? At first when Meg saw this she was encouraged that maybe they wouldn't waste away after all. But soon enough she saw other children, the Gleason boys, Dooley Creahan's oldest girl, the grandson of Lizzie

Ballard lying dead by the side of the road, their bellies bulging beneath their ragged clothes. And then Lizzie herself by the side of the road, her mouth pulled back over teeth stained green; her parched lips blistered in a permanent sneer that spoke its last lie to the clouds as she clutched wads of grassy sod in her fists.

Meg wept for Christmas coming. For the times she had placed a fattened goose on their table and passed steaming bowls of buttery colcannon and hearty vegetables, potato bread and sweet pudding. For the ruffled dresses and pressed shirts hanging ready for early Mass and the trinkets Tom presented to each of them with that merry twinkle in his eye. She wept for that twinkle that had turned to slate. How Meg longed to see Tom's real eyes again! He had so long ago retreated into himself that she hardly knew him. His eyes were veiled with shame and sorrow and his clear, blue gaze reflected the flat, gray hopelessness of death.

Meg gazed down at Thomas. This child was without a doubt her angel. This boy was so like his father that had his name not been Thomas she would have called him that anyway. He couldn't die. In a few short days he would have to read the Christmas story before the fire just as his older brother and sisters had before him. Tom had held him on his knee and taught the words from the bible brought all the way from Clydagh Glyn. Big Thomas and little Thomas sharing one normal thing amidst this terrible insanity around them.

Meg suddenly felt like the greatest of fools. There was no Christmas this year. There was no hope. She rubbed her thumb over the sore spot on her palm and studied the imprint of the crucified. How odd, that it was so clearly there, that she could make out the deeper indentation of the knees bent in agony, the tiny hands outstretched in death. She grabbed the rosary again. Oh, Mary, Mother of God, save us! Save my babies! Save our love! Save Christmas!

Even as she begged for the tender mercy of her heavenly mother, Meg knew this gentle woman could not save Thomas. Her tears washed over the little Christ as she searched her son's face for signs of awakening where there were none. What right did she have to ask this anyway? Who was she Meg Phalen, Lady Meg, if you please, to ask for this miracle when the wails of mothers all across Ireland went unheeded. Whose God would hear her? Would the God of judgment that scolded his people into heaven from her childhood pulpit hear her? He would only sniff in indignation that she had so many children in the first place. Would it be the God of mystery that Fr. O'Boyle kept referring to even as his face grew thinner and his skin more sallow every Sunday? Where was Jesus in this whole thing? He fed five thousand with only a few fish and a little bread! Where were their loaves and fishes?

Oh, Mary, mother of God, if you couldn't save your baby boy, what of mine? She looked again at the indentation on her palm. It was fading into a pale pink smudge. Meg's tears had dried and her face felt taut and hollow. She gazed at Thomas and he opened his eyes.

"Thomas!" Meg whispered leaning over so he could see her face.

Without answering he looked right at her. His black curls were damp on his temple where Meg's tears had fallen and the roots of his dark lashes showed clearly through the papery skin of his eyelids. His eyes ever on her face, he probed her soul. Meg felt her tears threatening again as she recognized that look. She had seen it in Tom's eyes countless times as he reached for her in love. It was a look that bared her soul to God and left her heart naked and unashamed.

She lifted his hand and kissed his sweet little fingers one by one. With his other hand Thomas reached up and ran his thumb along her cheekbone tracing her chin just the way he had when she nursed him as an infant. His cracked lips formed a silent kiss and his hand dropped from her cheek. She searched his eyes and saw in their depths the sweetest forgiveness she would ever know. Then he was gone. Just like that, no more.

Meg knelt there stunned. Slowly, as though for the first time, she felt the hair on her neck. The floor beneath her knees became so hard that she had to shift and finally stand up. Gently she gathered up her little man and sat on the hearthstone. Facing the flickering flames he looked like he was simply staring into the fire as he had so many other mornings.

Thomas was always her early riser. He had mastered a way to slip out of the bed from the bottom to avoid crawling over his brother and silently creep down to join her as she sipped her tea by the fire. If she was nursing one of the babies, he would somehow insinuate himself under her bosom on the other side even if he just rested his head on her knee. Thomas was the only one of hers that did that and Meg had cherished him all the more for it.

He had never recovered from the pneumonia he had after the episode of Danny Kinneally's funeral. He had been sick throughout the winter and in the spring when he began to gather strength, the whole village breathed a sigh of relief. But his lungs had remained weak. When he ran he quickly became winded and simple activities often made him gasp and wheeze. Gone was the robust, rambunctious little scamp who had teased and played tricks on everyone. In his stead, came a thin, pale boy who grew slowly and developed a fondness for reading and fishing. Ever since that fateful November day, Thomas had preferred to sit at Meg's side and card wool or clean vegetables while the other children ran shrieking by or frolicked in the foamy sea.

Now, sitting by the hearth in the early dawn, Meg and her little boy parted from each other. Her womb ached. Her breasts throbbed and tingled. In some strange apologetic way, as if the child within her knew and received the death of the brother it would never know, a great, groaning goodbye reached out from within her womb. Meg knew then that this child within her must live. Even if Meg had to give her own life to bring this child into the world, it must live for in this moment so wretched and bereft, this child had somehow connected its life with Thomas in a mystical bond that only God Himself understood.

Meg sat dry-eyed and numb, willing the lingering spirit of her sweet boy to enter into the babe within her. In a lesson greater than any text Fr. O'Boyle could have assigned her, Meg experienced at that moment an exchange of spirit, a deluge of grace so fierce in its gentleness, so overpowering in its silence that her baptism was complete. No one would ever know how the eternal being of God had revealed himself to her before her hearth for she could barely witness to it. She would never be able to express the mystery of what had just happened to her.

She had heard women speak of "thin places" where the spirit world and the temporal world met but Meg knew this was even more than that. This was not merely a meeting but a union of some kind.

In a great epiphany of blinding light, Meg realized with simple clarity the mystery of the crucifixion and the resurrection. The death of her beloved Thomas and the dawn of life in her womb brought her to a realization of the continuum of life and she simply, unaffectedly understood the incarnation of Christ.

Life and death were connected in a way that she had never fathomed. With the guilelessness of fresh faith, Meg knew the strange aching warmth within her womb was born of light shining in the deep darkness where her baby nestled. If she looked up from Thomas's still face she knew she would see angels but she was content to gaze upon his tender lips drawn upward in the least shadow of a smile. The little form of Jesus on her palm throbbed anew as she caressed his still, silent mouth. Tenderly Meg took her thumb and closed his eyelids, brushing his feathery lashes one last time. The moment was gone, the gracious epiphany passed. Meg's mind went empty as she sat rocking Thomas gently.

Meg sat alone with Thomas until the light in the window began to shine on his face. His weight in her lap numbed her legs until they were heavy and cold. Together they sat and sat until the turf fire receded into ashes and threatened to go cold. Meg had never let the fire go cold in her house. She knew this would bring bad luck.

Bad luck! Somehow this struck her as funny and she began to laugh. She threw her head back and shook with silent abandon as waves of laughter overcame her. Bad luck! How much worse could it get? She bared her teeth and imagined she looked like Lizzie Ballard grimacing at the sky. Her eyes dry in their sockets she looked again at Thomas's face fully expecting him to turn his head and smile. Still he lay silent in her arms.

Meg was relieved that his fever was gone. She felt his forehead and kissed his curly head as she made plans to set him down and resurrect the fire for breakfast. She found she could not move him. She found that no matter how she tried to persuade herself to raise him off her lap she could not lift him.

"Tom?" Meg spoke her husband's name but no sound came out.

"Tom?"

That was better but still not loud enough. Thomas was getting very heavy now and Meg was growing frightened at the numbness in her legs. With the fire down she was becoming chilled. She really needed to put him down.

"Tom?"

Now he must be able to hear her. She noted herself that there was a hint of panic in her voice but it was still too soft to bring him. What was wrong with her? Why did she want Tom? She knew that if he came he would take Thomas from her. Yes, that was why she called him but that was also why she didn't call him loud enough. She couldn't let him hear her. She couldn't let him take her baby from her lap.

She needed to want him for something else. The fire. Yes, she could call Tom to restart the fire. He would understand that she couldn't do it with Thomas so heavy in her lap. Of course, he'd understand. Tom was her best friend and he would know what to say and what to do next. Fix the fire. Get the kettle started. Boil water for the usual thin gruel that satisfied no one's hunger but was all they had. Crush the mint leaves for tea.

"Tom! Tom!"

Now she was screaming. Surely he would hear her now.

"Tom!" she wailed and he came running from his sleep. Around the corner of the bedroom door he came, banging into the lintel and almost falling over a creepie.

"Tom!"

Her voice screeched his name and he was there, wakened from the depths of a dream, so stunned that he never noticed Thomas not moving.

"What, what, Meg? What are ye screamin' about fer all the saints?"

"Oh, Tom, the fire's gone out. Just look at that. I've let the fire go out. Can you imagine?"

He just stood there staring at the two of them on the hearthstone bench. What was she talking about?

Meg looked up at him expectantly as his eyes took in the sight. Slowly he saw. Slowly he slid to his knees next to his wife and son.

Meg reached out and ran her hand down the back of his head. As though she had never noticed, she saw how gray his curls were on the nape of his neck. She would have to mention it to him later.

Now she just listened as he whispered over and over,

"Sweet Mother of God, no."

Didn't Tom know it was no use? Didn't he know she had tried all that already? Meg nodded knowingly at the graying head in her lap and knew he'd understand sooner or later. She understood perfectly. Of course Sweet Mother of God could do nothing. Hadn't she stood at the foot of the cross, helpless to save her own son? How could she save theirs? Meg would have to think about that later too. Now, she was really cold and wanted Tom to build her a fire in the hearth. Her cries had brought the children down from the loft and she needed to feed them their breakfast.

Chapter Nine

Lady Beverly leaned back into the worn Morocco cushion of the hired Jenny Lind buggy. Lord above, this had been a tedious trip! It would feel so good to finally arrive at Robert's and kick off these awful leather boots and get out of these heavy traveling clothes. She looked across the narrow aisle at Reina. Massive in her black wool cape and full bombazine skirt, Reina filled a whole seat meant for two or three passengers.

Beverly smiled to herself. Reina had enjoyed herself in Dublin. She and her mistress had shopped and primped and behaved like two schoolgirls. The night of the ball Reina had waited up for her and together they greeted the dawn as Beverly regaled Reina with all the details of the court of Dublin Castle.

Robert had been invited to the closing ceremonies surrounding the tenth anniversary year of Queen Victoria's coronation. He had asked Beverly to accompany him and she had jumped at the chance. She and Reina had spent days scouring the shops of Dublin for just the right reticule and the perfect pair of dancing slippers.

Beverly sighed. How different her life was since Jeffrey's accident. Once she had begun to expand her horizons a bit,

Beverly had come alive, traveling and trading horses at fairs and country manors across Ireland. Of course, Jeffrey had cut off her money as soon as he found out but she didn't need her money, now his money by law. She had simply packed her bags and gone to Robert's. She knew he would take care of her. Ever since, her life had been one round of parties after another. There was the Christmas season filled with gala events and sumptuous banquets, the spring festivals around May Morning and long sunny summers spent along the south of France.

Then there were the hunts. In the fall Robert took her into the highlands of Scotland and into the green fields of Tipperary for fox hunting and horse racing. Life had never been so rich. Beverly had grown plump and prosperous. Robert had sued Jeffrey for a portion of her money and he had been pressured to agree to an allowance as long as she never approached his room again. Beverly was happy to comply and on the rare occasions when she resided at GlynMor Castle, she kept to herself in her wing of the huge house.

She was just as happy to leave Jeffrey to his gambling and cigars. He had chosen to keep the company of such sordid men that she wanted nothing to do with him anyway. She despised his friends but was especially put off by that smarmy little weasel, Gilchrist, Lord Lucan's lackey.

For no particular reason, Beverly had never liked Lucan either. He had once wanted to marry her but she had fancied Jeffrey, a thought that brought a sneer to her lips. She remembered Lucan making some unflattering remark about her to her father and being sent packing the night she refused him. That had been enough for Beverly to snub him and Lady Lucan ever since. Not that they had much to do with each other. But every so often they would be invited to some event for the church or the house of a mutual friend and the Wynns had always had another commitment.

Now, the circle had been completed. Her daughter and that stable hand were living on Lucan's land in Doeega, Achill Island. This information had brought life to Jeffrey's otherwise dull existence. Ever since he had gotten word that Tom Phalen had been made the rental agent for Lord Lucan he had regularly sent Lucan's sleazy undertaker to Achill to watch his progress. Beverly suspected he was not happy that Tom was doing so well and wouldn't have been surprised if he plotted with Gilchrist to bring Tom down.

Beverly had her own spies to report on her daughter's family. She had heavily financed the missionary work of the Rev. Edward Nangle when he set up the Church of of Ireland missionary settlement at Slievemore on the northern coast of Achill back in 1831. Then in 1835, right before Meg announced her intention to marry Tom Phalen, Beverly had helped finance the purchase of a printing press for the reverend to start a formal newspaper. Once Meg's folly turned her household upside down and then after Jeffrey had his accident, Beverly lost touch with Rev. Nangle.

It wasn't until a doctor named Browne had written to her and Jeffrey of that shipwreck years ago that they even knew where the two of them ended up. Beverly was both shocked and amused that they had taken Maureen Dougherty with them. What good would she be? She wasn't even a good maid when she was at GlynMor. Of course, Jeffrey had no use for her after his fall. From the reports from Rev. Nangle, Tom spent any of his manly energy making babies with Meg. Good heavens, what did they have now, seven or eight?

The last time she had a letter from Rev. Nangle had been last year. Beverly had followed the failure of the potato crops carefully and Rev. Nangle's newsletter last Christmas had been filled with stories of whole families being wiped out and of the good and noble efforts of the missionaries in feeding the wretched heathens in exchange for their baptism.

Beverly thought him most clever to bring them into the church this way and she and Robert had both generously supported his work. His letter had been very grim, though. She really hoped he wouldn't be so descriptive in his Christmas letter this year. She thought it in poor taste to burden the eyes and senses of good Christians so close to Christmas with such depressing descriptions and illustrations. After all, Christmas was supposed to be a time of fun and gaity.

This was why she and Reina stayed away from GlynMor Castle most of the year and did not expect to return until after the season. She and Robert had worked out a very satisfactory schedule of horse breeding and trading that fit so very nicely into their social life.

She did return home in the spring for mating and Robert always came with her. He brought the mares, as he had for years and together they bred some of the finest horseflesh in Ireland. Let the others brag throughout Tipperary about their horses, Beverly knew she and Robert were responsible for populating the west of Ireland with the fastest and strongest horses, never mind the most beautiful.

For now though, Beverly and Reina would be focusing on the whirlwind social season of Christmas. For them it had already started in Dublin. Robert had invited her to be his companion at a number of parties to celebrate their young queen. It was hard to believe she had been on the throne ten years! Of course, she had been married to her cousin Albert for eight of those years and had a whole passel of children with him. They were supposedly madly in love. Beverly shrugged. If the racing little feet in the halls of Buckingham Palace were any testimony to love, they would have twenty children by the time they were through!

Beverly had not been to Dublin since Meg was a little girl and she had thrilled at the prospect of mingling with high society again. She and Reina had had a wonderful time. Robert had given her unlimited spending money and had even accompanied her on some of her shopping trips. She felt like a princess as he waved his hand across whole counters filled with the softest lambskin gloves and colorful dyed stockings instructing the shop girls to wrap up a pair of each color for the lady. Reina had enjoyed Sir Robert's extravagance too as Beverly passed on to her some of her finery to make room for the new things.

Together they had played and eaten sweets and cavorted around like girls and Robert had gleefully indulged them. The masses of starving peasants and dying booley dwellers that clogged the roads across county Cork on the way to Robert's seemed no more real than the mannequins and dress forms in the Dublin shops. The roads were clogged with foot traffic as swarms of destitute, starving people wandered in search of food.

Around noon, the coach had stopped in Thurles to switch horses and rest the passengers. Beverly and Reina debarked in the shade of an ancient stone tower alongside a shallow brook. The town was teeming with refugees, displaced from homes that had been demolished in their sight by the infamous Crowbar Brigade. The two women hurried to refresh themselves and get something to eat at The Crown and Crest, an inn with a teashop overlooking the water.

A waiter in crisp livery seated them at a table by a window on the street side. Beverly would have preferred a table by the water but business was brisk and they were fortunate to be seated at all.

Beverly was very distressed at the sight of whole families dragging carts and slidecars filled with tattered belongings and family members too weak to walk. Some of the children stopped at the window gawking at the delicacies on Beverly and Reina's plates. Reina kept her eyes averted and silently ate a bowl of steaming mussel chowder. Beverly could hardly eat despite her hunger. All these people staring at her food! Finally she called the waiter over and he drew the heavy velvet drapes across the window. Regaining her appetite, she slathered butter on sweet oatcakes and sipped steaming amber tea from a hand-painted Belleek teacup.

"Where are they all going? What can possibly be at the end of their journey?" she asked Reina.

"The driver, he say they go to Cobh and then to *D'Estat Unis* or *Anglitaire*, some even to Australia. Anyplace but here, O*ui, Madame*?"

"Indeed. From the looks of them, they will never make it.

Cobh is miles from here! They must be from all over Ireland! If they would only accept their lot in life and stay put! I'm certain their landlords are doing their best to feed them. Why I just read an article in the coach about how many were dismissed for idleness. Someone had left it in the pocket with the reading material. It's an old article from last February but reliable enough I suppose. It was entitled Parliamentary Papers and if I'm not mistaken, of the number of able bodied men given good, honest work in the quarries, only half of them reported for work! The fine men trying to help these workers had no choice but to strike them off. If they're not going to work then why should they expect to be fed? Do they think they'll find someone in America or Australia who will give them food for standing around?"

"And what about the fares for their passage? I realize that many of them have sold everything to take their families away from here but many of them are traveling on donated fares. I know because Robert and I donated generously to the The Irish Relief Association and some of that went for relocation."

Beverly refreshed her cup, spilling tea on the white linen tablecloth in her agitation. Flustered, she put the pot down hard, splashing still more tea on the table.

"See, Reina, how these people distress me? I can hardly bear these swarming masses, the sight of them, the stench!"

Reina was on her feet mopping the spilled tea with her napkin and pouring her mistress a fresh cup of tea.

"*Madame* must not disturb herself, *non, non, non*! You are not to blame for their misery. *S'il vous plait, Madame* should finish her meal and we can leave this upsetting place."

The two women finished their soup and left the inn as soon as they were able. Soon they were back on the road to Killarney.

The landscape was bleak as the carriage bore the two women westward. The day was dreary and gray, typical of December and the coach felt damp and chilly. Beverly hunkered down beneath the smelly fur lap robe provided by the driver and tried unsuccessfully to doze. As the hired coach passed through towns and farms that reeked of death and rot Reina peeked out from behind the velvet curtains drawn against the unpleasantness.

"*Madame, c'est une tragedie*, tsk, tsk," she said quietly at the sights.

At one point, her curiosity peaked; Beverly herself pulled back the drape and looked out. There were no crowds like the one they had left behind in Thurles but there was a steady stream of gray, shivering people staggering aimlessly along the side of the road. She could see a thin, ragged man stumbling after the coach, a child in each arm. Seized by a fit of coughing, he sank to his knees in the ditch as the coach rolled on. Beverly shuddered and forbade Reina from any further pulling back of the curtains.

"Reina, you must restrain yourself. Haven't we been exposed to enough filth and destitition for one day? You were correct to say that Lord Robert and I have been very generous to the cause of saving these wretched people from this terrible situation. And in the spirit of Christmas we will again donate substantially to the relief efforts. But we must never let the plight of these unfortunates distract us from our proper place in this world. But for the grace of God go we, yes, but we are blessed with the grace of God are we not? Let us not ruin that joy by tarnishing our mind's eye with these horrible sights."

Beverly decided to forget the effect of the children ogling her teacakes in the window of The Crown and Crest tearoom.

"*Oui, Madame.*"

"And if it makes you feel better, Reina, we can forego our pudding tonight as a personal sacrifice. Though I don't see how our leaving sweets on my brother's table is going to help those people out there on the road."

"*Oui, Madame.*"

It was almost dusk when the carriage rounded the long drive into Cushing Park, Sir Robert's home along the larger of the Killarney lakes. The high hedges on either side of the drive threw the macadam road into deep shadow and Lady Beverly shivered with the shortening day. Soon they'd be warm and snug in the great library of her brother's house enjoying the crackling fire and comfortable overstuffed chairs.

And the sherry! Robert stocked his wine cellar with the best of European wines but his sherry was made right here on his estate and very fine. Beverly was grateful they had no social engagements scheduled for the next few days. Robert planned to host the vicar and his wife for Christmas Eve dinner and the vicar's mother-in-law, of course. That intolerable old bat could actually be amusing if someone set her off. Beverly smiled to herself. She and Robert would have to come up with something to get a rise out of her.

Boxing Day was the big day in Killarney and Robert and Beverly had for the last several years been right at the center of the charitable distribution of food and goods to the poor of the city. That was why Robert had the Reverend and Mrs. Smythe for dinner on Christmas Eve. Their time together was as much a planning session for St. Stephen's Day as a celebration of the birth of Jesus. This year Beverly did not anticipate it would be as enjoyable as in other years. The poor were poorer since the crop failures and they were just so wretched to look at!

The coach stopped in front of two huge oak doors flanked by great stone pots filled with holly topiaries. In the lowering darkness the topiaries looked like emaciated people and the holly leaves like hands reaching out for food. Beverly shuddered. Enough thinking about the poor! The images of them lining the Dublin streets and the roads west to Killarney had sullied the grand entrance of her brother's beautiful home. The coachman and Lord Robert's footmen helped the women from the Jenny Lind buggy and unloaded their trunks.

Lady Beverly noted with approval the new liveries sported by the two footmen. She had helped Robert select new suits for all his servants and the smart striped waistcoats complemented the hunter green worsted of the jackets. The tailor at Moses and Company, Dame Street, Dublin had highly recommended the use of the striped satin material for the vest and lapels of the waistcoats. To save money, Lord Robert could always have the back of the waistcoats made from a plain drab or black worsted. Beverly was impressed with the ready cut pieces that the clerk, a Mr. Isaacs, had laid out on the counter.

What had he called them? The latest result of the new "system of cutting mathematically?" Well, whatever he called it, the young men looked very smart and tidy in their new livery. Robert could always be counted on to keep up with the latest in fashion even for his servants. Why, he had even insisted on outfitting Reina in new clothing for the holiday season. Knowing how much extra expense would go into dressing the large woman, Beverly had protested but in the end Robert had convinced her that Reina's appearance would be a direct reflection on her and for that reason Beverly had consented. Reina appeared to care little for the reason she had acquired new livery, she was just happy to strut around Dublin all dressed up.

Beverly had sent on many of their new purchases with Robert who had left the two women to await the final fittings on their holiday clothes. Still the trunks and bags, hatboxes and packages took the footmen several trips to unload.

Richard, the butler and Mrs. Hilly, the housekeeper, met Beverly and Reina with the news that Lord Robert had been called away on urgent business two days ago and would not be home until later that evening. Lady Beverly was disappointed but Mrs. Hilly assured her that she would send up a nice tray to tide the two women over until dinner.

Once inside, Lady Beverly and Reina were shown directly to their rooms. Her brother had arrived home from Dublin a few weeks before and had had their other items carefully unpacked by his two best upstairs maids. The two Parisians, Clarisse and Maude were waiting stiffly at the foot of Lady Beverly's four-poster bed where her new finery was laid out for inspection. Reina, while at Lord Robert's, was treated more like a companion to Beverly than a maid and reveled in Maude's assignment to wait on her. She was particularly delighted to be able to speak French with the girls.

Mrs. Hilly was as good as her word. No sooner had Beverly

slipped out of her traveling suit and into her new burgundy velveteen pelisse that a tray arrived. Clarisse had laid a fire in the little marble fireplace and set about hanging dresses in the massive clothespress and stashing away stockings and undergarments in the matching mahogany dresser. Beverly snuggled into her pelisse, grateful for the soft warm ermine that trimmed the collar and cuffs. If there was one thing Beverly knew how to buy, it was comfort. Even while living in misery with Jeffrey, Beverly had always known how to pamper herself with little indulgences. She had always kept herself supplied with good sherry, fine tea, the best of chocolates and especially warm, comfortable clothes for lounging around her room. She never regarded these things as luxuries. For her, as for so many of her class, they were essentials to good living.

Now, her tired body was relieved of the whale-boned bodice and tight kid boots. Clarisse had helped her out of the mauve and gray tweed suit and her outer petticoats. After untying the crescent shaped bustle, Clarisse helped her into the new pelisse taking note of the fine broad fur trimmed lapels. Beverly had bought the coat for outdoor wear after the weather warmed up a bit but tonight it was perfect for the drafty rooms of Cushing Park. Her brother's house was actually less drafty than GlynMor Castle but still required warm dress in the winter. Clarisse set the tray on a small round table next to the fireplace. Beverly sank back into a deep brocade winged chair her feet tucked under a soft chenille lap robe.

Clarisse poured her a glass of sherry and set a plate of cold beef and cheese on the arm of the chair. A small loaf of warm white bread sat steaming on a wooden carving board and Beverly tore off a piece. The yeasty smell of the fresh bread, which she slathered with fresh sweet butter, and the warm sting of the sherry on her tongue made Beverly sigh with contentment. It was so good to be here. There was not a monetary figure, a gift of enough magnificence, or a promise of great enough loyalty to repay her brother for what he had done for her. He had literally saved her life.

Years ago, after Jeffrey's accident Beverly had begun to spread her wings and expand her social life. She spent a great deal of time away from GlynMor, trading horses and attending fairs and parties with old friends and new business partners. She spent that whole first winter in England with her cousin Henry and his wife where she learned to ride the hunt. She had been free with her allowance and spent huge amounts on horses and clothing. The following spring, the party returned to Ireland and on Shrove Tuesday, she and her new companions had enjoyed the hunting of the hare in Waterford so much they decided to stay through Easter and enjoy the May Festival. When she returned home she discovered that Jeffrey had cut off her allowance and with great pleasure announced the end of her freedom.

At first Beverly had been despondent at the thought of corralling her newfound lifestyle. She sank into a deep depression that drove her to consume great quantities of sherry. It was the order placed with her brother Robert's wine steward that saved her in the end. Robert had sent her two cases of sherry at Christmas and when Justin came to him with another order from Beverly in June, he decided to pay her a visit himself. What he found the morning he arrived alarmed him. Beverly didn't even greet him. He had to persuade Reina to take him upstairs and he found his sister well on her way to drunkenness despite the early hour.

That very morning he had her in his Landeau on her way to Cushing Park while he confronted his brother-in-law. In the stable, old Ben was saddling up Bay Rum and readying Beverly's latest purchase, a roan mare named Dublin Belle. These were the only two worth any money and Robert didn't want Jeffrey to sell them out from under Beverly.

Robert had not seen Jeffrey since the accident and he was appalled by his horrendous appearance. Later, he had given Beverly a complete accounting of their confrontation. Robert had told her in no uncertain terms that she was never to see him again. He was appalled that she had ever had to witness the terrible sight of him. His face was a mass of shiny silver scars and he had grown paunchy over the months of inactivity.

Jeffrey who had always been a slight man now had a belly to rival the composite caricature of the well-fed country gentlemen that graced posters and newspapers throughout Ireland. He had allowed his hair to grow long and a pathetic half-beard grew out of the healthy side of his face while sparse wisps hung limp from the unscarred areas of the burned side. His left ear was withered and deformed where it had rested against the pan of hot coals the night of his accident. He wore a patch over his left eye and Robert could tell when he entered that Jeffrey's vision in his good eye was greatly diminished. Jeffrey had always had poor vision but now he looked right through Robert in a haze of cigar smoke. At Jeffrey's insistence, the room was kept dark. The light hurt his eye and he preferred hiding his gross deformities from the few people he permitted to visit him.

Robert had approached him alone, finding him seated at a card table with a young man he recognized as Stiller's nephew Peter. His man George was clearing away chips and cards from the game they had just finished. Stiller stood behind Jeffrey counting his money for him. Robert could see from the large wad of bills that Jeffrey had just won.

Jeffrey, whose senses had become more acute since his fall looked up before Robert even entered the room and demanded,

"Who is it?"

At the same time, Stiller said,

"Lord Cushing, sir."

"Well, well, Robert. Took you long enough to come. Take a good, gawking look and be done with it. Then we can offer you a chair and you can lose some of your massive wealth to me. Too bad you just missed my friend, Mr. Gilchrist, from Newport. You could have lined his pockets and shared the wealth with County Mayo."

Beverly remembered how Robert looked ill when he described Jeffrey. He had smiled in Robert's direction, his mouth drawn up on one side and frozen in a permanent grimace on the other. Lord Robert was not sure Jeffrey could see him so he approached the table.

"I have no time for cards, Jeffrey. I have urgent business to discuss. Can we speak privately?"

Lord Jeffrey had simply laughed.

"I can't even piss privately Robert! Anything you have to say to me you can say right here."

"Really, sir, I prefer to discuss the matter alone."

"Must be about my lovely drunken wife then. Eh, Robert? These gentlemen certainly need not leave for that boring conversation."

"Jeffrey, with due respect, I must object to your treatment of Beverly. She is my sister after all and this castle has been in our family for generations. You have kept her a virtual prisoner here for years and now that she is experiencing her freedom, have ceased to provide her monthly allowance. I find this reprehensible and expect an immediate reversal of this situation."

Robert had trembled with rage. Ordinarily the most even-tempered man, he felt his gorge rise as Jeffrey had squinted at him, his contempt punctuated by a thin stream of drool oozing out of the left corner of his sneering smile.

"Well, Robert, you have a point. Beverly has had a difficult time coping with my accident. She is a brave and charitable woman. In my need she has provided me with many reasons to be grateful. I'm grateful that I no longer see her with both eyes. I am grateful that I can only hear her sniveling voice in one ear. I am most grateful that she has spent so much time out of my home. I suppose I should be grateful she keeps tabs on her bitch daughter and her pig husband. It provides me with hours of amusement imagining him plowing into her every night and Mr. Gilchrist reassures me that she spends most of her time pregnant. Good! She deserves him! I hope he fills her belly with bastards until she topples over dead!"

"So I suppose I should be grateful to Beverly for spawning the she-goat and hiring the baboon who took her out of here.

No loss there. But I will not have my wife draining my bank account playing the grande dame around the Irish countryside. No, sir, I will not. So if the topic of your 'private discussion' is what I think it is, save it. Beverly is probably in the east wing, drunk and undressed. Go have a private discussion with her."

He motioned impatiently for Stiller to wheel him away from the table.

Robert approached the card table. Leaning into Jeffrey's face, he could smell the fetid breath of an opium addict and the stale stench of urine. Jeffrey looked well-kept and clean but his inability to control his bodily functions was vividly apparent close up.

Jeffrey bellowed, "Get him out of here! No one gets this close to me unless I want him to! Damn you Cushing! Get away from me!"

Robert was shocked at Jeffrey's reaction. He could almost sense above the stinking ammonia odor of excrement, the distinctive smell of fear. Beverly had been surprised to hear this. She thought Jeffrey bullied everyone and feared no one.

Robert reminded her that bullies were really very frightened inside. That's why they were bullies. Jeffrey's fear gave Robert the edge over him and so he went on.

"Jeffrey, you have no power over me! Stifle your filthy mouth and listen. I have already removed my sister from this place. As we speak, she is on her way to my home. You will have a difficult time impoverishing her even if you try. I will never allow it. Consider yourself served due notice. You will be hearing from my solicitor."

"Even if you succeed in denying my sister her birthright, I guarantee you I will ruin you. I have enough money to tie you up in legal action for decades. This property was in my family long before you arrived. You will not prevail, I promise you. You will be the one in the workhouse, Jeffrey. Mark my words."

Just as Stiller and George had come around the table to seize him, Robert stood up and with one hand tipped the table over. Cards and poker chips went flying amid curses from Lord

Jeffrey. Lord Cushing turned on his heel and stalked out of the room. It wasn't until he had ridden half-way to Derryhick Lough that he finally calmed down.

Beverly loved to think about Robert standing up to Jeffrey. She had for so many years tolerated his outbursts, his contemptuous sneers, his women and girls. When Jeffrey had beaten Meg that horrible morning that changed their lives forever, Beverly had been truly frightened. She absolutely believed she would be next. That was the reason she had fled like a fugitive when she was sure he could not chase her.

It never occurred to her that he could have tracked her down and dragged her back to GlynMor Castle. She was gone from him and would die before giving up that freedom. She had been so naïve when she had returned home that spring. What had she thought? Of course he would punish her for running away. And then, her dear brother, like a knight in shining armor had come for her. It was still so fresh in her mind Beverly couldn't believe it was more than ten years ago.

Robert had met up with Beverly and Reina in Castlebar. Beverly had been feeling quite ill after her hasty departure and they weren't able to leave for Killarney until the next day. But once they were on their way, Beverly knew she would never have to worry again about money. Robert adored her as she did him. Whatever Jeffrey might do to bring her down, Robert would take care of her. And he had. Nothing she wanted had been denied her. Robert had no one else to spend his money on and she had made her home with him.

Both of them had their own lives and there were months when they were apart. She and Reina had gone abroad several times in the first years but as she aged, Beverly preferred to travel in Ireland. She still loved London and Dublin and did enjoy visiting there with Robert but generally the two women preferred country living to the city. Over the years, Robert had tried to persuade her to go with him to America more than once but she had no desire to set foot on that shore.

No, Beverly was content. Killarney was a lovely town and

Robert had a very nice group of friends. Beverly had made friends with several of the women from St. Michael's Church of Ireland and she and Reina could not have asked for anything. For excitement, there were the horse fairs and races. For private, reflective times she rode the beautiful forests around the famed lakes of Killarney. Robert always arranged to be home when Beverly wanted a traveling companion and together they trouped around paddocks and stables, buying, selling, mating and racing the gorgeous animals that brought them so much pleasure and so very much money.

As she poured herself a second glass of sherry, Beverly wondered what had taken Robert away in such a hurry. Three days before Christmas and in such dismal weather! It must have been important.

Around eight o'clock, Reina came in and announced Robert's return. She advised Beverly that dinner would be served at nine and Lord Robert awaited her in the library.

Clarisse appeared unbidden and Beverly smiled to think how Reina loved being able to summon another servant to care for her mistress. Beverly loved Reina as a friend and was delighted that the faithful maid's load had been lightened since coming to her brother's home.

Beverly had chosen a soft, green heather wool dress for dinner. Fitted with a stylish boned bodice of deep tucks trimmed with ivory rick-rack and tiny dark green velvet bows at the waist, the skirt swept back over Beverly's petticoats to be gathered at the back in a gently flowing train of leaf green velveteen. Beverly hated having to submit to tight corseting after donning more comfortable nightclothes and she was grateful to herself for keeping all of her petticoats and her corset on under her pelisse in anticipation of the call to dinner.

She fastened a dark jade dragon broach at her throat. She had had this piece since her wedding trip and admired the arc of garnets rising from its mouth representing the flames of the dragon's breath. Clarisse swept her hair into a French twist, tightly anchoring the golden curls with matching jade combs carved to look like lotus blossoms. Beverly's hair was streaked with silver but not enough yet to begin using a pomatum to cover it. She dreaded the day when she would have to begin that. It was so hard to find anything in the right color. Maybe a marechal pomatum would work if it weren't too red. She loved her natural golden color but eventually the gray would overtake it and vanity would win out.

The hardest part of redressing after such a pleasant rest was putting her swollen feet back into the tight little shoes she had bought to go with this dress. Dark green silk satin with tiny bows to match those at her waist, they were definitely a vanity purchase. As Clarisse laced the silk ribbons around her ankles, Beverly thought she had been crazy to buy them. She literally hobbled into the library where Robert stood warming himself by the massive marble fireplace surrounded on all four walls with oak bookcases groaning with his extensive collection of books.

"There you are, my dear!"

He greeted her with his customary kiss on the cheek.

"Such as I am," Beverly pecked his stubbly cheek in return.

"Where were you?" she asked him as she sat on a russet velvet settee. Spreading her skirt around her, Beverly looked expectantly at her brother.

"I had to go to Westport. There have been some troublemakers that have come to the attention of some of the landlords and they convened a meeting at Browne's. Sligo sent for me because he wasn't able to attend himself and he and I had been talking about it last month when I sold him that filly from Templemore you decided not to keep. I'm glad I stopped at Westport House anyway. I picked up a little surprise Christmas gift for someone I know."

His eyes twinkled when he said this and Beverly knew it was something for her.

"Troublemakers? Who?" she asked.

"Troublemakers, by the name of John Mitchell, Morris Leyne, a fellow named McManus and one of the McGees though there are so many of them no one is quite sure which one is the culprit.. They've been working around there to reignite some of the members of that splinter group left over from the old Catholic Defenders. You know. The ones that gave our father and his lads so much trouble fifty years ago."

"Fifty years ago! Do you mean to say they're still at it?"

Beverly could not believe these people. Why couldn't they just let it go?

"Yes, they're still at it. Or at it again, I suppose. The fanatics keep the embers burning and eventually another generation of young ones rise to the top and flare up in our faces again. I remember Father talking about them. They were out of Armagh back then. That was around the time we were born. They gave the king a run for his money right around the turn of the century. The United Irishmen joined up with the Catholic Defenders somewhere in the nineties and actually tried to invade Bantry Bay! Now that Victoria is ten years into her reign, I guess they figure it's time she cut her teeth."

He poured himself a glass of whiskey and offered Beverly a sherry.

Beverly took the sherry though she knew she had probably had enough.

"Bantry Bay! What did they think they would accomplish?"

"I'm not sure, but they were foiled by a storm."

Robert sipped his whiskey and chuckled.

"Leave it to the Irish weather to keep the rebels in line. We don't even need an army. Just let them drown on their own shilling. Might even lower our taxes."

Beverly could smell the wonderful aroma of a mutton stew and felt her stomach contract with hunger. Trying to be polite and distract her anxious appetite, she quizzed Robert further.

"So, what of this new group?"

Robert was warming to his subject as he enjoyed the smooth, hot descent of good liquor in his throat.

"Well, no one knows when they plan to strike but most of the lads are convinced that they will. This damned hunger has all the constituents in a dither. And now people are beyond begging. They're starving to death by the thousands. Every day the lords are seeing more and more. There have been food riots and the criminal element is primed for a revolt. Whole towns are on the move. Truly, Beverly, we've never seen, at least in our lifetime so many migrating at once. And the truth is, there is nowhere for them to go. It's the same all over. No potatoes, no rent money and death everywhere."

"Some of the lads are all for eviction, the hard liners, you know. Trevalyan and his bunch publish great records, flowing sheaves of records but nothing seems to be stemming the tide. Workhouses are being built everywhere; women and little girls are digging ditches for heaven's sake and all for what? Six old pennies a day and all they do is dig and fill, dig and fill. None of the work has even a pittance of worth!"

"Surely you're getting yourself all worked up over this, dear Robert. Please calm down. You'll spoil your supper with dyspepsia. Besides, I read a segment of Mr. Trevalyan's Parliamentary Papers that was in the newspaper and it made sense to me. And, after all, he is the Assistant Secretary to the Treasury, so the Crown must think he's doing something right."

"I suppose he's doing what he thinks is enough but I, too, read the Parliamentary Papers back in January when they were first published and I must say, I was greatly distressed to read his theory of Divine Providence. Good Lord, Beverly, if that holds true, there really is no hope for those poor people! The very man who holds the relief measures in his hand believes that God Himself is cleaning house. And he is the self-appointed angel of death to the people starving in the streets!"

"Oh, really now, Robert, you musn't!"

Beverly thought she could do without poor Robert's dramatics tonight. It had been such a long day. But her brother wasn't finished.

Pouring another drink, he continued, "What he's trying to do is justify continued profits on goods that should be flowing in abundance to the mouths of the poor. I say never mind the profits! Let the people eat! And for heaven's sake don't blame

God for them dying!"

He turned to see Beverly staring out the window, her back stiff.

"Forgive me Beverly, I am forgetting myself. You have had a long trip and you must be starving. I am so sorry to burden you with all of this. Let me see what is happening with our supper."

He moved to investigate the delay just as Richard entered the library.

"Ah, Richard, impeccable timing as always."

Robert extended his arm to escort Beverly into the dining room

"My dear?"

Relieved, Beverly gladly took her brother's arm and patted his wrist soothingly. Entering the dining room, she looked around with girlish delight, all thoughts of God, the hungry and Mr. Edward Trevalyan banished.

"Robert! How lovely the mural looks!"

Beverly had not seen the new artwork commissioned for the renovated dining room.

"When was this done?"

"Finished while we danced at Dublin Castle. I rather like it myself though that artist was a penance. I won't be having him back here anytime soon. He practically cried every time I wanted anything changed."

"Well, he certainly knows his trade. The pillars are exquisite and the Tuscan countryside looks as if you could walk right into it. And look at how he did the *trompe l'oeil.* I feel as though I could lean right on that balcony railing. A splendid work, Robert, you should be very pleased."

"Oh, I am. I'm just glad he's off to Waterford to do a cathedral or something that will keep him out of my hair for a while. He was paid handsomely for a job well done and we're even. I'm delighted that you like it so well, my dear. We'll be looking at it for a long time."

Beverly nodded at the offer of a second ladle of steaming

cream of mushroom soup. How good it was to be home. As she savored the rich broth, Robert picked up the thread of his report from his meeting.

"Bear with me, Beverly, I feel I must complete my little report. And now I've got you as a captive audience, spoon in hand."

He smiled at her over his own steaming soup.

"Where was I?"

Anxious to avoid any more talk of the controversial policies of Her Majesty's Treasury Department, Beverly returned to an earlier part of their conversation.

"You were extolling the efforts to fill holes in the roads of Ireland, if I'm not mistaken."

"Yes, and all because of the generosity of the gentlefolk of Ireland. Anything to give the tenants something of their pride. They can't feed themselves so the least we can give them is honest work. Even if it's useless work, as long as they can do it they're kept out of the workhouses."

"I've heard reports of some of the finest acts of charity since Sunday school classes too. Not only Sligo, everyone knows what a gent he is just like his father. But even Blosse Lynch and the Earl of Arran, what's his name? I can't remember. Generous, very generous; grain, oatmeal, Indian meal. That especially from the Knox brothers in Castlerea and Kirkwood and Bourke. I think there was mention of Major Gardiner from Farmhill in that report too. They sent Kirkwood all the way to Liverpool to get it and then Bourke it was, I think, who paid for the transport from the port to the people."

"A lot of the gents are responding well. Some of them, I remember from school but most of the ones reported in the local papers are younger. There was one chap, a fellow by the name of Moore. You remember him. He won a fine purse at the Chester Cup last year with that sweet filly Coranna. Remember? If I recall, you coveted that horse."

"I did no such thing! Why would I covet a horse when I have a stable full of the finest?"

Beverly could hardly keep from sputtering around a mouthful of succulent mushrooms.

Robert smiled and shook his head.

"Yes you did. She was really pretty and then when she won you were in a snit for an hour."

"Robert, surely you exaggerate!"

Robert laughed out loud. He loved to get her goat and Beverly knew she was biting the bait.

"Well, regardless, he's a fine chap and sent his money home to his mother to keep his tenants fed and happy."

Knowing how unusual this gesture was, Robert smiled at Richard's raised eyebrow, as the old butler stooped to remove his soupbowl.

As Richard ladled the hearty mutton stew into deep crocks, Robert generously buttered two biscuits, handing one to Beverly. She took a bite, lapping melted butter off her finger. Giggling at her messiness she tried to be serious. She knew how Robert loved to talk politics.

"So then, why do they suspect a revolt on the horizon if they're all bending over backwards to help the tenants? I mean, even the Irish have some sense of loyalty to men who treat them well."

"Oh, they do. There was one report read from last January where a carrier for George Moore was accosted by a hungry mob that stole his cargo of flour. When they found out who the flour was for, they put it right back on the wagon. Said they'd rather die than meddle with his property. But not all the gents are regarded that way. Some would use any excuse to evict. And as I said, there are so many doing useless labor for so little money that they can't feed themselves on the wages. I mean, Beverly, little girls digging ditches? They've all got one foot in the workhouse!"

As she accepted another helping of the savory meat and vegetables, Beverly had a thought.

"Robert, what do you suppose is happening to Meg and her family? I haven't heard from Rev. Nangle in several months."

"Actually, I was getting to that. The report from Slievemore is pretty dismal. Rev. Nangle has expanded his soup kitchens south and they've been operating one in Doeega for six months. So far, no one has seen Meg or Tom Phalen there. A Rev. Gibbs was at the meeting representing Lord Lucan and he spoke highly of Lucan's efforts to help. Said he matched every hundred pounds donated by the residents of Castlebar with fifty of his own. But that was last year. I don't know how he's doing this year. In any event, there was no mention of Meg or Tom. We met at Browne's Inn. I know Tom is friendly with the innkeeper but I know how you feel about letting on that you're interested in them so I kept my cards close to the vest. I hope that was the right thing to do."

"Oh, I suppose so, Robert. She left on her own and has made her life on her own. She has never made any effort to contact me during prosperity and I don't expect anything from her in poverty either. She's a proud one my dear, so like mother. I do worry though. I'm afraid everyone blames me for how this all turned out but I do care about her, Robert, I really do."

"Of course you do, Beverly! You're her mother after all. You never have to defend yourself with me. I know you have kept an eye on things from a distance. Tell you what. I'll try as a Christmas gift to you, to find out whatever I can over the next few weeks. I have to go back to another meeting after the social season is over. That one will be in Westport again. Maybe I'll take a little trip across the bay. I haven't been in a curragh since university!"

"Robert you are a dear man but Clew Bay in January is no place for a pleasure trip. I'll write to Rev. Nangle myself and inquire. I should send him something as a Christmas offering anyway."

Beverly rose stiffly from her chair. The trip had definitely been long and tiring.

"If you'll excuse me Robert, I promised Reina that I would sacrifice my pudding tonight for the poor wretches we saw on the road from the carriage window on the way here. You can have mine."

"Beverly, you may rest assured it will not go to waste. I happen to know that Mrs. O'Rourke has a fine bread pudding for us. And even some yellowman as an early holiday treat."

"Yellowman? Oh, Robert, you know I have such a weakness for yellowman! Reina too! Have her send some up to my room. I'll forsake my pudding but I never promised to fast all evening now did I?"

As the clock struck eleven, Beverly sucked on the last piece of yellowman, letting the crisp sweet foam candy melt on her tongue. The rough bubbly texture of the sweet caramelized sugar brought her right back to the nursery of her childhood home in London. Her nurse allowed her very few sweets but yellowman was a Christmas favorite and she had even been allowed to watch Cook make it. First she would boil the sugar and thick imported cane syrup with a dollop of sweet cream butter and a measure of sour smelling vinegar. Then Beverly would watch entranced as Cook dropped a spot of the mixture into cold water. In a silent litany of scoops and drops, she would repeat this again and again until the blob hardened to just the right consistency in the water. The next step never failed to thrill Beverly and in later years, Robert. Cook would add a scoop of baking soda to the thick bubbling confection, creating an explosion of foaming sweet liquid that she immediately poured out onto a thick marble slab coated with butter.

Meanwhile she would slather her hands with butter for the "pullin' o'the man" as she put it. Once the bubbling liquid was cooled enough she folded it over and over again on itself, pulling and tugging at it until it stretched and glistened honey gold in the candlelight. Then she would let Beverly and Robert have a piece to stretch and pull between them. This was the only time Cook ever allowed them to help in the kitchen. Squealing with delight they pulled and folded, pulled and folded until the toffee was tough and shimmering gold. Then they reluctantly placed it in a greased tin to cool. Once it was cool, Cook took it out in one piece and cracked it hard with a toffee hammer. The shiny yellowman shattered into dozens of small chunks and with great ceremony Beverly and Robert lined up to receive their favorite Christmas treat.

The yellowman was often served with dulse especially at the Ould Lammas Fair at the end of the summer. Why anyone would combine the two was a mystery to Beverly who had never liked the purple seaweed. She preferred her yellowman in its pure perfection unaccompanied by any other treat except, perhaps, a cup of milky tea. Now, as the last of it melted on her tongue, she thought of a little ditty she had stitched as a sampler when she was about ten years old.

"Did you treat your Mary Ann to dulse and yellowman
at the Ould Lammas Fair at Ballycastle-O?"

Still savoring the sweet taste on her lips, Beverly summoned Reina to get her out of her stays. The older she became the harder it was to be in the stiff boned bodice far into the evening. She kicked off her satin slippers and wiggled her toes. It had been a very long day and her bed awaited her. Tomorrow she and Robert planned to ride early and she needed to get to sleep.

The next few days were crammed with Christmas preparations as greens and garlands were delivered from Castlebar and lush Mexican poinsettias imported by Beverly's mother years ago and nurtured and coddled in the Cushing greenhouses ever since were brought in and set about in the foyer. They were a great source of pride for the gardeners who repotted the tiny bulbous seeds every January and kept them in a painted greenhouse where the sun was filtered and they enjoyed warm tropical conditions in which to grow. Some of the plants were simply pruned and hidden from the sun until the following autumn when they were all brought into the light on Michaelmas to begin the forced blooming. Sometime after All Hallows Eve someone would notice the greenhouse windows filled with rich red blooms and announce the coming of Christmas to the rest of the house.

Robert had continued the family tradition of rewarding the first to see the poinsettias with a gold sovereign. The servants and their families would be tripping over themselves trying to be the one to see the first blooms. It had quickly become such a competition that, years ago, Beverly's father had made a rule that no one could win twice until everyone had won once. Robert had continued that wise practice and the contest had evolved into a favorite game of the children of the Cushing Park staff. This year Tommy Gallagher, the ten year old son of the blacksmith had been the lucky one. He would receive his prize on Christmas Morning when Lord Robert distributed the servants' gifts.

Beverly had never enjoyed Christmas at GlynMor. Jeffrey had always spoiled it by getting drunk and she knew any gifts she received from him had been ordered and purchased by Meg or one of the servants. One year he had said he was buying her a horse but he never did.

Christmas at Cushing Park was a totally different affair. Her brother Robert was a kind, sentimental man who had loved the traditions and trappings of the holiday since he was a little boy.

The tragic death of his wife and child on Christmas Eve so many years ago had clouded his celebration of his favorite holiday for years but eventually he began to enjoy it again and now it was almost a ritual celebration of their memory. He had had their bodies brought here from London to be buried when he made this glorious Eden his permanent home and had built a shrine to them in pure white Italian marble.

There had been a great outcry among the tenants about disturbing the dead and tempting the wrath of the banshee but in the end his lordship did what all the gentry did. He ignored the people and did what he wanted. They consoled themselves with the fact that the dead were English and French, and no self-respecting banshee would be bothered with them.

Early on Christmas Eve, Beverly was coming down the grand curved staircase into the foyer when a great commotion arose outside the front door. The maids were arranging the last of the poinsettias around the entrance to the drawing room and fastening the red velvet ribbon around the garland along the banister. How gorgeous it all looked wound through the wrought iron ballisters and gathered up in bunches festooned with huge velvet bows. Each carved mahogany newel post, the two at the flanged bottom stair and the two at the narrower top step had holly topiaries fastened to them with gold ribbon. Strands of gold and white hand blown beads imported from Russia wound through the branches and draped in swags through the stiff glossy leaves. Atop each newel post there was secured a tall candelabra with long red tapers waiting to be lit for her brother's annual Christmas Eve dinner.

Robert and Beverly had discussed the new practice of bringing a fir tree into the house and decorating it in much the same fashion but they had decided that they preferred the traditional yule log as the centerpiece of their decorations. This was what the commotion was about. The men were bringing in the huge log trimmed from a yew tree last spring and carefully dried to guarantee a bright fire. They were dragging it across the marble floor of the foyer on an old Turkish carpet. The huge branch had been hewn to just the right length and height for the great drawing room fireplace.

Furniture had been shoved against the walls and the rugs in the drawing room had been rolled up to make way for the procession. The floor-to-ceiling bay window, now banked with red poinsettias and hung with sweet pine garland intertwined with white, hothouse roses and mistletoe, gleamed in the sun. Buckets filled with warm water and oil soap waited in the corner ready to wash the parquet floor once all the muddy boots were out of the room. Piles of mistletoe and strings of garland to be hung in the doorway rested on the window seat until the log was in place and the mess cleared away.

The downstairs maids hustled and swept, careful to stay out

of the line of traffic from the front door. Clarisse and Maude had been pressed into service carrying sweet pine boughs and bouquets of red roses upstairs to the guest bedrooms. Mrs. Hilly's two young nieces were assembling huge red and gold bows as fast as their little hands could make them while pages and footmen carted them through the dining room to be hung along the sconces in the corridors with clusters of holly and mistletoe. The whole house was suffused with the aroma of fresh pine and holly berry. The special beeswax candles, made right on the estate from Robert's own beehives and reserved for this special day, stood straight and tall in the sconces awaiting their lighting at dusk.

Mrs. Hilly bustled about in her stiff black taffeta, pointing here, waving there; all the while barking orders and cuffing the ears of any maid who failed to hear her. Richard did the same with the footmen and pages. The place looked to Beverly like a chaotic backstage but in reality everything was under control. The two elder servants had been planning and orchestrating Sir Robert's affairs for two decades and despite the appearance of frenzied activity, they were certain all would be ready on time.

Beverly strolled into the drawing room behind the parade of gardeners dragging the yule log. Robert was leaning against a small bookcase on the far wall, surrounded by chairs and ottomans, rolled rugs and small, carved tables. Lamps lined up along the baseboard polished and gleaming, their wicks trimmed and ready, their prisms throwing rainbows across the leafy inlaid pattern of the floor. Beverly had always admired this floor. It was imported from France, made of light cherry inlaid with a dark cherry pattern of ivy entwined with leafy branches around the perimeter. In the center was a circle of dark cherry vines intertwined with leaves and flowers of pale yellow oak.

In the summer, Robert never covered this floor and Beverly relished sitting in this room in the morning as the sun streamed through the hundreds of small diamond-shaped panes of the enormous floor to ceiling bay window. Each pane was made of beveled glass outlined in lead. The huge triptych was interspersed with gold and purple, green and red stained glass panes depicting the crests of the family who built the house. For the entire first half of the day this glorious window captured the sun and threw spots of color and dapples of bouncing light all over the gleaming wood of the floor. But as much as she loved the high sheen of the floor in the summer, Beverly was grateful for the rich Persian rugs that warmed the room in the winter. The damp Irish winters could chill the great mansion and warm carpets were essential to keeping the big rooms comfortable.

Beverly crossed the room and joined her brother as the great yule log was lifted onto the raised flagstone hearth and rolled with great heaving and grunting into the fireplace. The huge andirons let out a shriek as they slid against the stone floor of the fireplace under the weight of the log. Two young apprentice gardeners were practically trapped inside the fireplace with the log as they positioned the best side facing out. Once they extricated themselves from the fireplace and the broken twigs and pieces of bark were picked up, the boys followed the others from the room leaving a trail of sooty boot prints all the way to the front door.

Immediately the maids swung into action and in no time the floor was washed and dried, the buckets removed and the rugs unrolled. These rugs, each hand loomed by the small skilled hands of little brown slave children in the Tigris Valley were woven from brilliant crimson and gold, lapis and emerald green threads. The patterns of each of the two huge carpets were unique but complimentary and both were trimmed with fine silk fringe that had to be combed daily by the maids to keep it looking tidy and smooth. The rug that would lay where Robert was standing now was designed to depict the story of a royal wedding.

The bride was positioned on the left in an entourage approaching the middle of the scene. Veiled and dressed in flowing robes of lapis and emerald green, she rode in a canopied carrier borne by slaves in gold loincloths. The skin of the Nubian slaves was so finely woven of crimson and black threads it appeared to be shimmering brown and in the right light Beverly could almost detect the sheen of their sweat as they bore their princess to her groom. A bevy of veiled maidens and powerfully built eunuchs with swords drawn accompanied the procession and camels of gold and throngs of guests in saffron and yellow, deep blue and rose paraded in from the four corners of the rug.

The groom, resplendent in robes of lapis with a gold turban on his head rode in from the right side astride a huge horse woven from the same combination of colors as the slaves who bore his bride. Horsemen and the veiled women of the harem along with beautiful slave girls in flowing tunics trailed behind him. The whole scene was framed along the edges of the carpet in a wavy pattern of blues and greens with red and gold water lilies.

The other rug was woven to depict the reception after the wedding. This scene was as brilliant and splendid as the other but the setting was inside the courtyard of the royal house with lapis fountains and intricate grillwork woven in gold. The edge of this carpet was woven of deep purple and gold to look like the arches surrounding the courtyard. At the center was a table of gold laden with a bounty of fruit, nuts and roasted whole lambs and goats. The colors used to weave the fruit were the same rich greens and russets as the other carpet and the roasted animals picked up the varying shades of brown. Behind the table the bride and groom greeted each other as slaves and attendants flanked them in brilliant azure and crimson contrasting with subtle pinks and ivory.

Beverly marveled at how little time it took for the room to be put in order. Only moments ago the place had been a hubbub of pulling and pushing, hollered orders and immediate action. Now, she and Robert smiled at each other in amazement as once again order was restored and furniture returned to its familiar position. Once the last string of garland was hung over the door and the last sprig of mistletoe tucked into its beribboned center, the beehive of activity moved on to the next room and the next strand of greens.

Robert and Beverly followed the bustling workers into the dining room. There the table had been set, as usual, for breakfast. There they could eat and watch the decorating from the comfort of their chairs.

The dining room decorations were similar but even more elaborate than the ones in the drawing room. Every sconce in the dining room had a cluster of fresh hothouse roses in red, yellow and white. These were adorned with full gold velvet bows with streamers trailing to the floor. Gathered at the center of each bow were more Russian beads of brilliant colors and whimsical shapes. Tiny red conch shells and gold pears, elongated egg shapes in bright blue and stars of emerald green glinted in the sunlight. These were fashioned into clusters with long trailing strands running down the front of the gold ribbons. Swags of gold velvet were draped from sconce to sconce and these too were festooned with yards of colorful beads. Beverly knew from other Christmases that in the candlelight these beads would glisten and gleam, dancing in the flickering firelight in a cascade of color to rival the aurora borealis she had once read about.

Beverly was almost too excited to eat but when the kitchen maids brought out the trays of sizzling sausages and bacon, fluffy eggs scrambled with bits of browned onion, oozing with melted cheese, she could not resist. These were followed by delectable sweet scones speckled with sultanas. A huge bowl of fresh whipped butter and a smaller one of raspberry jam were set in front of her along with a sterling silver bowl piled high with whipped cream. These she knew were for the scones. She had learned in Dublin how to properly dress and eat a scone. The young queen of England had made the confections popular as a treat served with tea.

Robert had laughed at Beverly's immediate love for the rich crumbly buns and the even richer toppings she heaped on them. By the time she had decorated a scone she could hardly get her mouth around it providing an endless source of amusement for him. Still, he knew how much she loved them and was kind enough to serve them to her whenever she liked. She would be all right if she could keep from laughing as she tried to be dainty while stuffing her mouth full of sticky jam and melting whipped cream.

Scones were served warm and required a quick and deft hand to eat before all the delicious toppings slid back onto the plate. They both agreed that despite their wonderful flavor, their mother would not have approved of scones for her table because of the difficulty in maintaining any sort of decorum while eating them.

She filled herself with the lovely scones and washed them down with steaming hot coffee. Beverly preferred tea with her supper and at bedtime. In the morning she liked the brisk masculine taste of a good cup of coffee. While Robert enjoyed Kenyan coffee from the mountains of East Africa, she preferred the richer, less winey flavor of South American or Caribbean coffee.

She had once received a gift of coffee from a friend who had visited America's southern city of New Orleans. This had been laced with chickory and she had found it very bracing and delicious. She also enjoyed the thick, rich Turkish coffee she had in London once at that restaurant that served the exotic stuffed grape leaves and odd lamb dishes seasoned with nutmeg and cloves. Robert usually enjoyed Turkish coffee too, as Kenyan was so hard to find.

After breakfast, Robert met with Richard to run through the last details of the evening while Beverly consulted with Mrs. Hilly on the menu and timetable for the meal. Beverly had put together her selections for food and wine long ago and was relieved to see that everything she had asked for was available and being prepared. She had ordered a roasted suckling pig for the main course along with a standing rib roast of beef. For the fish dish she had selected the traditional salmon, poached in parchment and served whole on a bed of spinach and tiny potatoes. There were no potatoes since the crops had been failing but Mrs. Hilly said that Cook had procured tender young parsnips and would serve them fried in butter and arranged round the salmon in a fan of little golden spikes. She assured Beverly it would make a very pretty plate.

Of course, there had to be golden rutabaga, one of Beverly's favorites and plenty of rich pork gravy to pour over it. The soup would be beef consommé as always and there would be a nice blood pudding and plenty of carrots, peas and pearl onions roasted and swimming in pan gravy. There would be hot-sweet curried apple chutney to accompany the pork. Beverly had had this dish years ago when the son of a friend had returned from service in India. She had enjoyed it so much then that she requested it whenever she had pork. Of course, she had accommodated Robert's fondness for the vile root of the horseradish with his beef. She had specifically requested that it be grated fresh the way he liked it.

Beverly had also requested both Spotted Dick, the holiday soda bread filled with whiskey soaked currents, and soft dinner rolls. She was particularly fond of plump buns brushed with egg white on the outside to give them a deep brown crust but as white as goose down on the inside. Robert loved Yorkshire pudding so Mrs. O'Rourke was planning to whip up a batch of that too to go with the beef.

There would be raspberry trifle and dainty sugar cookies for dessert along with huge crystal bowls filled with golden peaches put up last August and apricots in thick sweet nectar. Crates of nuts from as far away as India had arrived yesterday and the youngest maids in the kitchen had been put to work roasting and shelling them for tomorrow's Christmas pastries. Sterling silver bowls, many of them trophies for races won by Beverly and Robert's horses stood on sideboards in the dining room and on tables in the library and drawing room. These were filled with unshelled pecans and walnuts, hazelnuts and rare, odd shaped brazil nuts.

The nuts were for the men to shell as they visited and chatted. Nutcrackers and picks lined up along the back of the sideboard while smaller bowls awaited the shells. Beverly thought it far too much work and really quite unladylike to shell nuts at a party but men seemed to need something to occupy their hands while they talked and if they didn't smoke and have the lighting and snuffing of a sheroot or pipe to keep them busy they seemed to enjoy the absent minded shelling and eating ritual.

Finding everything in order, she moved on to the corridor that led to the kitchen. As soon as the massive swinging door leading to the hall closed behind her the aroma of roasting pork and beef surrounded her. Oh, what a wonderful smell! She caught wafts of curry too and the unmistakable yeasty smell of fresh bread. Beverly had always known the value of a good cook and never more than on this early morning of Christmas Eve, 1847.

Chapter Ten

Reverend and Mrs. Smythe were due to arrive late in the afternoon and supper was to be early so they could all relax before heading to the church for the midnight service. The reverend had spent all day supervising his own Christmas preparations and thoroughly welcomed the respite offered by a hearty meal and good wine. This year he had been breaking in a new organist and had been particularly stressed over some of the man's choices of music. St. Michael's was a very traditional parish and enjoyed very traditional rituals. They had been accustomed to having a string quartet made up of four aging spinster sisters accompany the organ every year at Christmas. Ancient instrumental melodies had been played every year and no one missed singing the words.

This year, the young organist, a very talented fellow by the name of James Holmewood wanted the rafters to ring with song and had spent hours cleaning and polishing the old organ for the occasion. He had tuned it and repaired some of the pipes, polished and buffed the rich rosewood case and reupholstered the bench cushion himself. He had recruited as many of the parishioners as he could to form a choir and they had been rehearsing since October. Rev. Smythe had to admit they sounded splendid and the Lowe sisters, once they got over the disappointment, had actually seemed relieved not to have to play.

He sat now in Robert's library, mulling over his sermon surveying the best assortment of liquor in Killarney and munching on hazelnuts. He popped another hazelnut into the little nutcracker and gave it a squeeze. The nut had not been positioned quite right and it flew across the room pinging off the brass andiron and into the fire.

"Well, well, Mr. Smythe, I had no idea you were such a good aim," Lord Robert chuckled as he took in the older man's consternation.

"You probably could not do that again if you tried."

"Surely, My Lord, you must know that was an accident," he sputtered thoroughly embarrassed.

Robert merely laughed.

"A fortunate accident. I could have been felled like Goliath had it been just a little to the left!"

"Oh, please sir, never the thought!"

The Rev. Paul Smythe was a very old, very stout man with many chins that wiggled and bobbled as he spoke. When he was sermonizing with has characteristic passion, his head seemed to float above his body suspended over a jiggly cushion wrapped in his high white collar and surplice. The bow fixed at his neck only made it worse as it completely concealed any evidence of a neck at all.

Craning to his left to look at Robert now, his chins seemed to drag themselves down as his face strained upward giving him the appearance of an ancient tortoise. His wife Louise was as thin as he was fat and together they made one of the oddest couples Robert had ever seen. Louise was a tall woman, with a long face and neck. She was fond of wearing her hair pulled up on top of her head in a severe bun making her even taller. Feathery bangs were pomaded into little spikes across her forehead in a tidy row.

Her long jaw and equally long ears gave a peculiarly angular look to her head. Standing together, she looked a bit like a fork and he like a spoon, his skinny legs forming the handle, her straight rectangular hairdo forming the tines. They were dressed modestly as became their position and no one could fault them on their refinement. They provided good company while they were present and great company when they were not.

One evening after hearing about their two successful sons, both unmarried, both in the ministry, Beverly swore she was going straight to hell for embarking on hilarious speculation on the creation of those sons. She and Robert had been ill with laughter as she regaled him with images of the two oddly mated partners frolicking in their bed in the consummation of the marital act.

Beverly wasn't sure whether she was glad or disappointed that Louise Smythe's mother; Mrs. Gwyneth Beardsley, had not come. She had taken ill with a cold and sent her regrets. Her acerbic commentary on the meal, the weather, the terrible condition of the world, the inefficiency of Robert's servants and her favorite topic, the benefits of regular bowel cleansing, would not be missed. Beverly did regret, however, the loss of entertaining fodder for post-holiday conversations with her brother. Mrs. Beardsley was certainly good for a story or two over dinner.

"I certainly forgive you your poor aim, my dear Reverend. Perhaps I can help improve it by an offer of a bit of Christmas cheer."

Robert held up a heavy Venetian cut crystal decanter and waved it like a pendulum, swirling the amber potion around gently.

"Some brandy perhaps? Or our very own sherry? I also have the best single-malt Scotch whiskey and an excellent Irish whiskey. Or, on the lighter side a cup of hot rum punch perhaps."

Rev, Smythe cleared his voice nervously. He had a weakness for Robert's sherry but on his vicar's salary he could ill afford good whiskey.

"The Scotch, my boy. Neat."

"There you are, good sir, and the ladies? Sherry or punch?"

Beverly and Louise Smythe had just come from viewing the new dining room mural.

"Punch!" they responded in unison making Louise giggle like a girl.

Her long jet earbobs flitted about her neck like two huge wasps looking for the entrance to their nest. She wore mourning for her long deceased father. Despite the years that had passed since her beloved father had died, Louise still insisted on wearing black. Dr. Smythe had inherited Louise's father's vicarage thirty years ago and Louise and her mother had simply been part of the transaction. The middle-aged minister had found Louise to be a passable specimen for the wife of a minister and if never a beauty, at least she was used to the duties of the role.

Her mother had seemed benign enough and having been the only brother among ten sisters, Rev. Smythe thouight he could get along with any woman. Little did he know that he would inherit his salvation because of the virtues he was forced to practice around Gwyneth Beardsley. Many a night he found himself wishing he could trade places with the Rev. Charles Beardsley, late of St. Michael's Parish.

He had surprised himself when he fathered not one but two handsome sons. He had no delusions about the natural endowments of either his wife or himself but the boys were very striking, somehow reaching back into their ancestry for their looks. Roger, the elder son was nearing thirty and still unmarried but courting a fine young lady from Canterbury where he was stationed.

Rev. Smythe tried hard not to be envious of his son but to preach in the cathedral at Canterbury! The very seat of the church! He himself had angled and lobbied on Roger's behalf for that nugget of gold and had no regrets. But Roger had been a soul mate, the only respite he had from the women in his household and he not only missed him terribly, he was painfully jealous of his good fortune.

Their other son, Griffin, named for Mrs. Beardsley's Welsh father, was another case altogether. He had such papist leanings that he not only worried and angered his father and mother, he made them very nervous. The reverend had encouraged him to follow his older brother into the ministry but often wondered if he had made a grievous mistake. Griffin was seven years younger than Roger and still in seminary but given the letters filled with dire warnings that his parents regularly received from the dean of students at St. Polycarp's, his future in the church was not looking good. Griffin had always been his own person and Rev. Smythe had prodded him toward the ministry at the urging of his wife when Griffin had begun seeing a Catholic girl from the village. The girl's parents, equally alarmed, had packed her off to a convent in Ballyhooley.

Now, with Griffin railing against the crown for what he saw as the systematic genocide of the Irish Catholic population, Rev. Smythe wondered that he hadn't been arrested much less thrown out of the seminary. He patted the latest letter from the dean sitting unopened in the breast pocket of his good black frock coat. He could read it later. Now he was supposed to be enjoying himself.

Robert was over by the huge double doors of the library conferring with Richard. The feast, more sumptuous and plentiful than anything the Smythe's could afford, was something the reverend looked forward to with great pleasure. Lord Robert was one of the parish's largest benefactors and part of his generosity was his benevolent care and feeding of his canon. He knew he was a good preacher but his parish was small and not particularly wealthy. There was Lord Cushing, of course and the new residents of Muckross House and the Spinners of Grace Park but one of the disadvantages of ministering to a few wealthy families was that the majority of the village was populated by their servants who were primarily Catholic.

Killarney was no exception. The beautiful lakes had a few landed families and many poor servant class families. There were fair weather worshippers, those who came in the summer and fall to holiday among the beautiful mountains of Kerry's famous ring, fishing and hunting. Many of these sportsmen brought their families to stay in the inns of the pretty town of Killarney, taking jaunting cart rides into the forests around the lakes, picnicking and gathering wildflowers and beautiful rocks. Some used the Killarney lakes as a stop-over on their way to Dingle or Galway Bay. But most left by Michaelmas and everyone was gone by All Hallow's Eve. Once winter arrived with its rain and bluster, Rev. Smythe was lucky to fill the first few pews of his little stone church. He and Louise had enjoyed Christmas with Robert Cushing ever since the boys were young and now that they were gone he was even more grateful for the company of Robert and his sister.

Lady Beverly was an odd one though, he thought. Louise liked her very much but Louise took people at face value. She was a chatty gossip who loved to entertain Louise with her stories, which Louise guilelessly believed. Paul Smythe saw a very different woman when he looked at Beverly. He saw a woman torn. He knew instinctively that she carried a great secret, one that burdened her greatly. He could see that she wanted to be better than she was and created her persona to suit the character expected of her. He had seen her over the years as light-hearted as a schoolgirl and within minutes as withdrawn as a nun. One knew about Lady Beverly only what she wished to reveal. Sometimes she was very like her brother but Rev. Smythe thought this was because she so obviously admired Robert, not because she was as intrinsically good as he was.

Her Ladyship shifted like sand depending on whom she was with and what topic was being discussed. She was well educated and could converse intelligently about most things and about horses most passionately. She had never mentioned having a family in all the years she had been living at Cushing Park. He found this to be both odd and very revealing. Her name was Lady Wynn yet where was Lord Wynn? Had she any children, she never let on. Discretion dictated no exploration of these mysteries though he had often encouraged Louise to speak of their sons to see if she might be spurred on to say something about her own family.

The only hint of their existence had come very early on when his mother-in-law had blurted out a stupid remark about a painting. Mrs. Beardsley had been gawking around the foyer, marveling at the pale green silk wall coverings and huge family portraits of Lord and Lady Cushing, Robert and Beverly as both children and adults and Beverly as a young woman astride a beautiful mahogany horse with a horseshoe shaped wreath of roses around its neck. Mrs. Beardsley had asked if the young woman was Beverly or her daughter. Lady Beverly had flushed deep crimson and Lord Robert had too quickly affirmed that it was indeed Beverly in the portrait. They had been ushered immediately into the drawing room and the subject never broached again.

Rev. Smythe's mother-in-law had made it a personal crusade for several visits to find out the truth but the reverend had warned her sternly to limit her enquiries within the bounds of the utmost discretion. This dictate, of course, had allowed no probing or delving and therefore resulted in no revelation whatsoever. He had finally put a stop to it altogether. Lord Cushing was the only one of his wealthy parishioners who still invited them out socially and Rev. Smythe knew it was because Mrs. Beardsley had embarrassed both of the other genteel families on the lake.

Richard was calling everyone to dinner. Lady Beverly and Louise had already swept out of the library and Rev. Smythe could hear them chatting gaily in the corridor. He allowed Richard to hold his drink as he pried himself out of the deep plump leather chair. He must remember to sit in a firm chair for the rest of the visit. It was embarrassing to have to pop himself out of the depths of these confounded cushions like some sort of seed in a pod. Rev. Smythe had always been self-conscious about his combined rotundity and spindliness. Now that he was ridden with gouty arthritis he was even more obviously impeded by his girth.

Richard, for his part, saw nothing, as was only fitting and proper. The reverend had no idea how the butler struggled for composure as he rolled and heaved himself to his feet. He joined the party in the dining room, still wheezing from the effort, slopping his scotch across his thumb in his haste. Not wishing to lose a drop, he pretended to cough, bringing his hand to his mouth and licking the precious liquid off.

Lady Beverly was in fine form tonight. She was so proud of the newly finished dining room that she simply glowed. She had good reason to be proud. The mural was exquisite with delicately shaded hillsides and olive trees so real that the fruit looked like it could be plucked. The shadows of the lit candles on the walls only emphasized the realistic shadows painted below fluffy white clouds in the Mediterranean sky. The sconces along the wall had been decorated for the holiday but the gold velvet ribbon and clusters of roses only made the Tuscan backdrop seem more real. The mural lent itself to richness of both color and depth. The hills were subtly shaded in a sea of celadon and delicate lime and yellow-green. The leaves of olive trees were the perfect combination of sage and silver gray that made them look as though they rustled softly in a warm breeze. The tiny farms and outbuildings were of soft coral and pink just like the Umbrian stone of the tiles Robert had brought back from Italy and now had paving his foyer. Sheep dotted the hillsides on the left and tiny rows of grapevines ran up and over the undulating fields on the right.

Beverly was saying that the artist had wanted to wrap the mural around the far wall leading to the foyer but had had to settle for carrying the theme of grapevines across the Corinthian carved fruitwood lintel. Robert was clearly amused at his sister's portrayal of the temperamental man especially given that she had only met him once and the work had been done while she and Reina were away. Once Garvey, the wine steward, had filled the glasses, Robert raised his to toast the gathering.

Beverly had chosen a soft fruity white to go with the pork

and a pungent red to compliment the beef. Her brother raised his glass like a trophy, the deep burgundy catching the candlelight and the expertly cut Waterford crystal throwing a cascade of little red triangles across the white damask cloth.

"May we ever be friends. May we ever be content. May we ever be as blessed as we are this day. May our fortunes be many and our worries few and may this year at its close be the harbinger of even better days to come in the next."

The toast was the same every year. This was the toast Lord Robert's father had reserved for Christmas and he proudly carried on the tradition. Richard brought out the heavy tureen of consommé and a liveried footman ladled it out ceremoniously. Once they all had their portion of the steaming bronze soup, Rev. Smythe bowed his head for the blessing.

"Lord Jesus, as you came to us a mere child, we too approach you with a child's faith. We ask your blessing on our homes, on our work and on our families. We ask you to feed us and care for us well and give us the heart to feed and care for those you deem as lesser men, who share not our faith, who share not our fortune but rely instead on the grace of your divine heart so generously planted within our own human hearts. On this the eve of Christmas may we be mindful of our blessed state O Lord, to have been chosen by you to lead papists and pagans alike to your door. May we be ever graced to know and share the true faith with those who would put mere humans before You. Amen."

"Thank you Reverend Smythe. Very nice indeed."

Robert picked up his spoon, indicating that the others should do likewise and another traditional Christmas Eve feast was launched. Outside a heavy rain had begun but the four people around the table hardly noticed. They simply stuffed themselves with salmon so tender it melted in their mouths, succulent meat and smooth savory gravy and warm rolls lavished with mounds of creamy butter. They munched happily of sweet parsnips and lovely roasted vegetables, hardly missing the traditional roasted potatoes.

Oohs and aahs were traded and compliments conveyed to the kitchen as tray after tray of delights were brought forth and devoured. The suckling pig was magnificent, turned to a perfect bronze crispness on the outside and delicate pinkish white on the inside. When Richard set it before Robert, Beverly's mouth had watered and she brought her napkin delicately to her lips. They all had laughed when Robert made the first cut and clear juice shot across the table nearly soiling Louise's black silk and spattering the front of Richard's white silk Christmas vest. Richard looked so dismayed that Robert actually offered to lend him one of his own for Christmas day. The slicing and passing, chewing and offers of more continued without further mishap while Richard hastened to the kitchen to see to his messy uniform. Few words were spoken while everyone ate.

The golden room glowed in the light of a dozen candles as the sound of sterling silver ticking against fine china, wine pouring musically into crystal glasses and the murmuring of polite conversation drifted across the table. Maids and footmen stood ramrod straight awaiting any gesture or request. The room was suffused in genteel fineness, the huge candelabra on the table dressed as topiaries of green holly layered with oranges and tangerines and topped with pineapples all imported from southern Spain. Refinement filled every corner as these four good Christians celebrated the holiday created for them. They ate well, spoke of refined things and drank heartily, if discreetly of the finest wine money could buy.

The Reverend and Mrs. Smythe knew in their private hearts that they were extremely fortunate to be invited year after year to this lavish table. Nothing they said or did could ever put at risk the privilege of this treat. They were both secretly relieved that neither Louise's mother nor their misguided son Griffin was there to say anything foolish.

Indeed, Robert noted with pleasure how relaxed and congenial his guests seemed this year though he wasn't sure why. He was just content to play the charming host, a role that came naturally to him. He harbored ill feelings toward no man save his brother-in–law but he did harbor a secret. He had arranged for his bank in Dublin to send a large donation to St. Michael's for a bell tower and had commissioned his own blacksmith to begin work on bells.

The little church had never had a bell tower and had relied on a freestanding bell in the front yard to call the faithful to services. The man who had been designated to toll the bell with a huge sledge-hammer had recently died and Robert had felt the time was right to install a proper tower with a proper tinnabulum. His blacksmith was delighted to have been asked and promised a set of bells that would sound over the whole lower lake calling the faithful to God. Robert had been grateful that at least one of his servants wasn't papist.

By the time dessert was brought in it was nine o'clock. The reverend could hardly imagine putting still more food in his mouth but his fleshy pink lips fairly quivered at the sight of the high trifle mounded with whipped cream and peaked with a cluster of raspberries in syrup. The syrup ran down the sides of the cream in pretty red rivulets and the layers of berries and cream, ladyfingers and nuts that peeked out from the crystal bowl made him want to dive into their depths. He grabbed his spoon in eager anticipation but Louise's gentle hand on his wrist reminded him where he was and he deftly set it down unnoticed. The huge bowls of peaches and apricots came next swimming in sweet syrup with whole nutmegs floating among the golden orbs. Another silver bowl of whipped cream followed along with a plate of sugar cookies cut into whimsical shapes and iced with pastel frosting sprinkled with colored sugar.

Of course, each of them had to have a portion of everything and by the time they adjourned to the library to discuss the final preparations for Boxing Day they were all groaning with satisfied discomfort.

They never heard the servant's Christmas prayer nor did they listen for the sound of them satisfying their own bellies with the remains of the day. The kitchen noises were very different from the sounds of their own meal. There were grunts of approval and even some belches as the leftover feast was devoured for a second time by those who had worked to create it. Forks speared tender pork and pieces of luscious beef and fingers were slapped away from the platters of vegetables. Cook threatened to take up her ladle and smack anyone who grabbed rudely. There was plenty for all and they could at least pretend they had manners, now couldn't they. This was greeted by groans of impatient hunger but they listened. Most of them had felt the wrath of the ladle wielding cook and none of them wanted to feel it again.

Richard insisted on a prayer kept mercifully brief and Cook doled out the portions evenly and fairly. She was fair if anything and respected the appetites of the female servants as well as the males. The men were not happy about this as they were used to being the first served and most generously in their own homes. But Mrs. O'Rourke had fed thirteen children of her own from the leftovers in this very kitchen and was not above smacking anybody who thought he deserved more than anybody else.

She also knew that the homes of these hard working people had no Christmas dinner at all in this, the third winter of the hunger. She pretended not to see the fat trimmings and bones being stuffed into pockets and wrapped in kerchiefs from plates and platters. She knew that the only food many of their people would have for the week would be the scraps from their scraps and the baskets laden with gifts of food that lined the wall by the door. Lord Robert had never given a second thought to the kitchen budget and Mrs. O'Rourke had always included plenty of food for the help on her shopping list. At Christmas he pulled out all the stops both in his home and later, on Boxing Day, in the village. No one knew Sir Robert's generosity like Mrs. O'Rourke and no one appreciated working for any master as much as his staff. He was a rare man among many who would just as soon see them all starve.

There were baskets filled with round loaves of bread and colorful jars of jam awaiting distribution on Christmas morning when Lord Robert and Lady Beverly gave out their annual gift to their faithful help. Mrs. O'Rourke had also packed the baskets with small jars of peaches and apricots. In the morning she would add sausages and fresh eggs, a jug of milk, and a brick of butter for each servant's family. Everyone received a small bottle of Lord Robert's own sherry for their Christmas toast and packet of good English tea for their dinner.

The only one who raised an eyebrow at her generosity with her master's money was that Frenchy one, the maid from Clydagh Glyn. Mrs O'Rourke noted with a harrumph that she never refused a second helping nor did she now. Even her mistress, his lordship's sister, lost some of her chilliness on Boxing Day. No one spoke of it but it was no secret that without the food that left Lord Robert's kitchen in a steady trickle, the families of his servants would have died from hunger long ago. Mrs. O'Rourke was deeply grateful and very proud to be the agent of his humble generosity.

While the help had their own Christmas Eve feast, the reverend was expounding on the generous gift Robert had just given him.

"Surely you are too generous, sir!"

He flushed with pinkness to his ears when he opened the envelope with the bank note from Lord Robert.

"Nonsense, my good man, I only want the countryside to ring with the tintinnabulation of St. Michael's new bells. I want everyone to hear them and come to our little church. You are both my pastor and my friend and I wish more people could benefit from your wise words as I have over the years."

Reverend Smythe was visibly moved and Louise was speechless. She approached Robert and, having had more wine than was prudent, stood on her tiptoes and kissed Robert heartily on the cheek. Rev. Smythe turned deeper red and began to stammer some excuse for his wife but Robert rescued the moment by pointing out the mistletoe and bowing gracefully toward Louise.

"You have caught me beneath the mistletoe, dear lady, and I stand a willing victim of your kiss."

Louise Smythe, completely aghast at her own behavior, simply plunked herself down on a brocade settee and contemplated her lap. Beverly turned toward the fireplace to hide her mirth at this unlikely scene and the kindly minister, also having well imbibed, stood behind his mortified wife with his pudgy hand resting gently on her shoulder.

The Smythes left soon after to attend to the last minute details of the midnight service. Robert and Beverly bid them farewell and promised to see them shortly. Together they returned to the library where Richard waited with coffee and tea. Beverly was still chuckling at the Smythe's hasty departure after Louise's impulsive act of gratitude.

"I think she's in love with you, Robert."

Beverly's face was awash with mischief as she took a cup of steaming tea from Richard.

"Oh, please. Spare me from such clandestine treachery!"

Robert stirred his demitasse of thick Turkish coffee and shook his head.

"She is a sad little piece isn't she? One of the oddest-looking women I've ever met but very nice with it all. I imagine she would never have married if old Smythe hadn't come around. How much older than her do you think he is?"

Beverly thought a moment and said, "At least twenty years, maybe twenty-five. She has to be sixty if she's a day and he was at St. Peter's in Ballyvaughan for years before he came to Killarney. He must have been fifty or fifty-five when he married her. They've been married about thirty years and he just had his eighty-fifth birthday in June, remember? So I'd say she's between sixty and sixty-five though she uses so much marachel pomerand and pomade on her hair it's hard to tell from that. But her hands give her away. She has very wrinkled hands and there lies your proof that I'm right. You always did attract older women, Robert."

She threw back her head and laughed.

Robert simply smiled.

"Never you mind about that, big sister."

Beverly wouldn't let it go.

"Oh Robert, you should have asked for permission when we were in Dublin to court Lady Quinn and you know it. It's still not too late, you know."

"Beverly."

"Well it's not!"

She came away from the fireplace her red and green plaid taffeta skirt rustling.

"She really cares for you, Robert and she would bring a great fortune with her!"

"Beverly."

The tone of his voice stopped her teasing. Poor Robert would never get over losing Adelaide and their baby on Christmas Eve all those years ago. Beverly suspected that was why he kept so closely to his Christmas Eve traditions and was so extravagant in his generosity. As much wine as Beverly had consumed, she knew she came very close to crossing a line she must never cross.

"Fine, my darling. Forgive me for even mentioning it. Let's talk about tomorrow."

She swept over to him and impulsively pecked his smooth, freshly shaven cheek.

He smiled again, relaxing at the change of topic.

"Twice caught under the mistletoe."

He sat in his favorite leather chair and put his feet up on the matching hassock.

Beverly spread her pretty skirt around her as she perched on the edge of a richly brocaded chair. She preferred the seating in the library to that of the drawing room. Here Robert had more of the armless chairs that could comfortably accommodate the voluminous skirts and bustles dictated by the current fashion.

"But first you must compliment me on how beautiful I am."

She smiled at him, showing all her teeth like a child.

"Now that is not difficult at all. Stand up and show me your finery so I can give it just due."

Beverly stood up and turned around so her brother could

admire her from all angles. She wore a pretty red and green plaid taffeta dress with a wide, hooped skirt and small pert bustle in the back. The bodice was simply cut of plain green velveteen with short puff sleeves trimmed in plaid piping.

Robert actually thought the dress a little youthful for a woman Beverly's age, though he wisely kept that opinion to himself. He knew she had chosen it over something more suitable for dinner because she didn't want to have to change again for church. The dress had a short capelet of matching plaid taffeta that would make it very suitable for the midnight Christmas service.

Robert knew how needy his sister was for reassurance of her beauty. That bastard she married had all but destroyed her. He smiled in genuine affection as she twirled around so he could admire her.

"You are a lovely sight, my dear."

Beverly curtsied deeply.

"Thank you dear brother. I know you adore me so I can't really believe you. But thank you. Tomorrow I will wear the one you and I picked out together in Dublin."

Robert just shook his head. Comfort was the main requirement for him. He sat with his feet up on a hassock, his fine, short leather boots buffed to a rich chestnut sheen. His forest green evening trousers and dress coat were fashionably cut and made from the softest merino wool money could buy. Nothing he wore constricted or pinched him. Even his high collar was cut to fit him perfectly. Instead of white tie usually required for dinner, he wore one of his Christmas waistcoats sewn exquisitely of elegant deep green and burgundy striped silk. A loosely tied cravat of plain burgundy accented the stiff snow-white collar. He pulled out his father's watch from the pocket of his waistcoat.

"Fashion show over!" he exclaimed as he bounded to his feet. "Time to head to Church."

Richard, ever awaiting his master's next request appeared unbidden at the library door.

"Sir."

"Thank you, Richard."

Stooping slightly in front of a great gilded mirror, he straightened his heavy, caped cashmere overcoat and adjusted his tall beaver hat. Taking a black silk umbrella from Richard's outstretched hand he stood patiently waiting for Beverly.

Her ritual was a bit more complicated.

First Beverly had to change her little green silk shoes. Clarisse brought her boots and knelt before her on the cold tile floor and quickly fastened the last button around Beverly's right ankle. Robert marveled at her speed as she slipped the other soft kid boot up over Beverly's proffered left foot and whipped up the row of hooks and buttons with a silver button-hook. She was a good maid. He was pleased that she took such good care of his sister.

Reina held Beverly's dark green wool pelisse for her. She had a deep crimson velvet one she had hoped to wear tonight but it was pouring rain. Beverly tied the plump satin bow of her dyed beaver hat and ran her fingers over the soft chinchilla trim. Clarisse waited with her matching chinchilla muff as Beverly pulled on a pair of warm rabbit-skin gloves also dyed to match her coat and hat.

Reina shrugged into her own massive black wool pelisse as Maude waited with her black wool bonnet and beaver muff.

Once they were all safely loaded into Lord Robert's new four passenger brougham both Clarisse and Maude raced to their own quarters to change for church. The kitchen staff, mostly Catholic had already left for midnight Mass. Clarisse and Maude knew they would have to find a space in the back of the crowded church to stand. The only one who would be left at home was Richard. He eschewed formal church services for the sweet privacy of the empty manor house. Pouring himself a tidy glass of Sir Robert's best scotch whiskey, he silently wished himself a Merry Christmas and put his own polished brogans on the leather hassock in his master's library. No one would be home for almost two hours and he was lord of the manor now.

Outside, the rain continued to pour down. Clarisse and Maude hurried to St. Clare's along the side of the road. As they rounded the bend into the village, ducking deep within their hooded pelisses, a carriage rumbled by on its way to St. Michael's. The driver, blinded by the rain, never saw the deep puddle that kept the girl's from crossing the road and as he flew by with his charges drove right through it. The girls were drenched from head to toe with black oily water filled with muddy blobs of slush. The beautiful red wool coats they had made themselves from one of Reina's cast-offs were badly stained. They had mud and offal in their hair and on their faces. Clarisse, who had hoped to meet up at Mass with her beau, the stable boy from Muckross House, began to cry. Her friend tried to clean her off a bit with her sleeve and they both raised their faces toward the sky to rinse the mud spatters off their cheeks. Satisfied that they had removed most of the muck, the two girls picked their way across the street and joined the rest of the servant class of Killarney in their celebration of this holy night.

The next few days were packed with good will, good food and the very best of times. Christmas Day was marked by the ceremonial lighting of the Yule Log. All the servants were invited into the decorated drawing room and smartly lined up along the huge bay window. The gift baskets were piled on every table chair and bench. Everyone, even the lowliest footman and scullery maid, was dressed in new livery. Richard and Mrs. Hilly lined up in the doorway with Mrs. O'Rourke and the head groom, driver, blacksmith and gardener. The room simply glowed with Christmas cheer and generosity.

Lord Robert and Lady Beverly stood beaming by the side of the great marble mantel as the assistant head gardener stoked more twigs around the dry kindling that formed the bed for the huge yew branch brought in the day before.

Richard, highest ranking among the servants, cautiously

carried a long smoldering stick from the library fireplace and stooped to touch its sparking orange tip to the twigs. The kindling snapped and crackled as the flames began to dart up and catch the dry bark of the yule log. Once it was fully engaged and there was no danger of it fizzling out, a great cheer led by Lord Robert himself went up from the group of servants. Gifts were distributed and gratefully acknowledged.

There was a collective gasp among the entire staff when the doorbell rang and a surprise delivery arrived. They all ran to the front door amid the squawking and honking of caged foul stacked outside in the cold drizzle of Christmas morning. Even Richard and Mrs. O'Rourke had known nothing of this surprise. Lord Robert had arranged with a local poultry farmer months ago to have delivered, a plump chicken for every underservant and a nice fat goose for higher ranked members of his staff. No one would lack for a real Christmas dinner this year.

Many of the servants had tears in their eyes as they accepted their envelopes from the master. They knew that the money he gave them would probably mean the difference between life and death for their families. Despite the good health and well-nourished appearance of the Cushing House staff, their families were deeply afflicted by the critical potato blight and many of them had lost beloved members to the fever brought on by the great hunger. Every one of the staff knew on that Christmas morning how fortunate they were to work for such a master as Lord Robert Cushing and they demonstrated absolute sincerity in their gratitude. They were all anxious to get back to the work of clearing up breakfast and preparing the early dinner that would afford them the rest of the day free to celebrate Christmas with their own people.

Once the servants had been dispatched to their various posts, Beverly and Robert settled in by the raging fire to open their own gifts. Beverly wore a beautiful eggshell velvet morning coat cut in the 18th century polonaise style. Beverly had always thought this cut very flattering and despite its old fashioned appearance, the Dublin dressmaker had obliged her taste. The gown was trimmed with a deep collar of gold satin that criss-crossed her bosom with wide lapels that ended in an empire waist. The front was cinched with three gold satin frog closures and the wide skirt, gathered high in the back fell in sweeping folds over a bustle. As Beverly turned and stooped to pile Robert's gifts at his feet, her gown shimmered in the firelight like the fur of a sleek white cat. Her hair was simply dressed in a figure eight at the nape of her neck. Gold beads and pearls wound through the plaited chignon and plain teardrop pearl earbobs glinted in the flickering light every time she moved her head.

Beneath the luxurious robe, Beverly was firmly stayed and ready to dress for dinner. The two young maids would have only to help her into her elegant Christmas dress before they were free to go home for their own holiday.

Robert had on a morning coat of deep royal blue velvet and pale butternut breeches clasped below the knee with handsome leather buckles. He had wanted something more subdued than the usual shiny gold clasps and Mr. Moses had been happy to oblige when Robert had visited his Dame St. pantechnethica during his recent Dublin trip. The pantechnethica was the latest addition to the manufacturing of fine menswear. Under this new system, hundreds of tailors willing to work for low wages made it possible to produce made-to-measure suits in less than a day. It was infinitely more efficient than hiring one tailor to spend days sewing a single suit.

Moses & Co. wasn't the only pantechnethica in Ireland. There was John McGee's place in Belfast where Robert once bought a hat but he had never liked traveling so far for a suit. If he was going to travel to shop he wanted to make a pleasure trip of it and take in the theater and court events in Dublin. Robert had always shopped in Dublin and for the last several years had enjoyed the handsome fit and fine fabrics of Moses & Co. He still marveled at the possibility of walking into a tailor shop in the morning with an idea and leaving that very night with a new suit of clothes. Ever since the arrival of the pantechnethica and merchant tailor system, the quick and easy availability of fine menswear had taken the Irish market by storm.

Now, filled with Christmas cheer and brotherly affection Robert beamed in his finery. His slender frame beneath the expertly tailored and padded coat looked full and robust. The soft britches fit his long legs perfectly and the satin of his blue and gold striped waistcoat glinted in the firelight. Beneath the breeches he sported fine merino wool stockings to match and soft suede leather house shoes. His thick salt and pepper hair was swept back from his high brow and worn in loose waves around his high collar giving him a handsome, rakish appearance. His blue eyes danced with pleasure as he watched Beverly stack the huge pile of gifts by his chair.

When she was finished she sat down and waited expectantly for him to do the same. He sat for a moment teasing her into believing he had nothing for her. When he saw the crestfallen look on her face he couldn't be so cruel. He pulled a long satin cord dangling next to his chair. At his signal two footmen entered. The first had a tidy pile of small boxes and bundles that he laid at her feet. The second merely stood at the door. Lady Beverly tried to hide her disappointment at the small number of gifts but before she could say anything, she heard a loud whinny from the front hall. The footman with the help of Darby, Cushing Park's head groom, led a beautiful white filly through the wide drawing room doors.

Beverly shot up from her seat.

"Robert! What have you done?"

She put her hands to her face and stood transfixed by the sight of a horse in the house. It was a few seconds before she realized that the horse was her Christmas gift from her brother.

Robert, meanwhile, sat in his chair and grinned at his sister. The dramatic presentation had had its desired effect. Beverly was such a child! He knew her delight would be magnified if he pulled a stunt like this.

"Well, go over and say hello, Beverly. Her name is Gilded Lily. I've taken to calling her Lil."

"But Robert where did she come from? I've never seen one so pure white."

"Well, she's not totally white. She has a light brown streak, almost blond, up around her right gaskin close to the flank. See? That's the gilded part of the lily."

"Oh, Robert she's too beautiful! Look at those caramel colored eyes and her mane is like corn silk."

Beverly had crossed the room and was petting the docile animal.

"She was sired by that nice caramel colored Arabian you admired last year at the Ballinisloe fair and her dame is the lovely gray from Tipperary that we almost bought a few years ago from that Osborne fellow. Where she got all that white from is a mystery. I would imagine from her dame's side. I think her sire is dark all the way back. At first I thought she was albino but not with the brown eyes. Darby says she's just a fair Irish maiden. Isn't that so Darby?"

The shy groom nodded and held fast to the reins. He could talk a blue streak to his lordship alone but this one from Clydagh Glyn made him nervous. Reminded him of a nun he once had a run in with when he was just a boyeen. Smacked him good, he remembered.

"Well, Robert I don't know what to say! She's breathtaking. Will she be a runner?"

"That remains to be seen. Her sire was a fair runner but her dame was never bred to race. You know me Beverly. I'm more smitten by a pretty face than a fleet set of legs. Now, perhaps we should let Darby take her out to the stable before we have a nervous horse disaster on my fine oriental rug. Thank you, Darby. And Merry Christmas."

"And ye too, M'Lord. M'Lady." He tipped his corduroy cap and led the filly out through the front door.

"Well Robert, I don't know if any of my gifts can compare to that! Thank you so much!"

Robert sat down and picked up the biggest of the parcels at his chair.

"Let's see what we have here."

There was no disguising the shape of the sleek new American made Henry rifle.

"Oh, Big Sister this is a fine looking piece. Wherever did you get an American rifle? Oh! She's a sweetheart!"

He caressed the fine long barrel and fingered the etched gold decoration.

"The same fair where you got Lil. There was a real American cowboy there. You missed his tent because I wanted you to. I took his name while you were buying cattle and had Darby come with me to check out the guns."

"Rifles," he corrected gently. "Guns are different."

"Well, now you know why I took Darby to help me pick it out."

Robert checked the inner workings of the rifle.

"My, it's a breach-loader and carries sixteen shots. Thank you Beverly! It's a beautiful firearm. I remember seeing these when I was in the States the last time but never thought of buying one. This is a great surprise."

They took turns opening their presents. Robert had gotten Beverly lovely scented French perfume and several colorful pairs of Limerick gloves. These were packed cleverly in walnut shells, the main reason for the littleness of Beverly's gift pile. She marveled at how the glove maker was able to pack them so tightly into the tiny shells. There were sweets from London and chocolate candies imported from Greece, delicate hankies and a new ermine muff to go with her red velvet pelisse. There were tickets to a Dublin opera that was bringing its show to Killarney in January and a beautiful pair of diamond and ruby earrings.

She had bought Robert the ammunition to go with his new rifle, some handsome hose and two new waistcoats. There was a new humidor to replace the one his terrier puppy had chewed last Christmas Eve while they were all at midnight services and two large boxes of cigars handmade by the women of Serbia. He too received chocolates filled with cashews and hazelnuts imported from Holland. The last gift to be opened was a large tin of his favorite brand of Kenyan coffee, difficult to get in Killarney. Beverly was thrilled when she found it in Dublin the day before she and Reina left.

Finally, there was just one gift left for Beverly to open. It was a very small box Beverly hoped was jewelry. Robert seemed particularly pleased with this gift, a last minute purchase from Westport. Beverly opened the flat square box and gasped, the color draining from her face.

"Where did you get this Robert?"

"Why, none other than George, the Marquis de Sligo. Why, Beverly what's wrong? Is it broken?"

He leaned forward, alarmed at her sudden pallor.

"No, no, Robert. It's Mother's! She used to wear it when we were little. How did he end up with it?"

"Surely it must be a duplicate. George never even knew Mother!"

"No, it has a small flaw. I stepped on this once when I was a child. I remember, I was angry with her and being very naughty in her room. I took it from her dresser and stomped on it."

"See? The last horse has a small break in the leg."

Robert took the brooch from his sister. It was an unusually large piece designed to be worn on a bulky collar or cape. Lady Cushing had often worn it to clasp a tartan plaid shawl in the colors of her mother's clan. Beverly's grandmother was Scottish of the clan McIntosh and had proudly worn that tartan every year on the anniversary of the death of Robert the Bruce, first king of Scotland. When she died, Beverly's mother continued the tradition.

The brooch was oval, rimmed in gold. The center was made of ivory carved into a tiny scene of four horses pulling a carriage with a fine lady and gentleman waiting to be picked up. There was a house behind them with a perfectly carved portico with two pillars on either side and delicately carved evergreens beneath a bay window on the left. Beverly had admired it from her earliest childhood and had purposely tried to destroy it in a tantrum after being switched for misbehaving. With close scrutiny, the bottom of the last horse's leg could be seen to be missing. Robert returned it with a shrug. Now, Beverly held in her hand the one thing she had longed for when her mother died and had never been able to find among her belongings. Neither one of them could figure out how the Marquis de Sligo came to possess the brooch. It was a lovely piece but held more value to her than to anyone else.

Beverly pinned it to her lapel. Here was a mystery they would need to pursue.

Richard opened the drawing room door and announced dinner in an hour. As brother and sister climbed the curved stairway to change for dinner, they were quiet, both pondering the mysterious brooch.

Chapter Eleven

Spring 1848

They buried Thomas at St. Dymphna's on the 21st of December, the winter solstice, the shortest day of the year. Meg had begged Fr. O'Boyle to let her have him until after Christmas and the kindly Franciscan was hard put to deny her but the law stepped in and demanded he be buried immediately. Meg's mind had snapped when Constable Grady, himself widowed only the previous week, gently informed her that Thomas would be interred in a mass grave with fifty other villagers who had died that night. She barricaded herself and Thomas in the loft pulling the ladder up behind them and threatening to set fire to the straw mattresses if anyone tried to take him from her. It was Fr. O'Boyle himself who persuaded Meg to let him take Thomas by agreeing to a traditional burial in St. Dymphna's with the observance of all the Irish peculiarities, as she put them.

Thus it was that little Thomas Phalen had a funeral when no other villager was afforded the privilege. This went a long way to put their neighbors over the edge, their hunger-fueled resentment spilling over into acrimony toward the whole Phalen family.

Rumor spread that the grand Mrs. Phalen had lost her mind and taken the life of her child. Others claimed that they had the killing fever at the Phalen's and it was only a matter of time before they infected the whole village. The kindest rumors were those that accused Mr. Phalen of abandoning his family after he placed Mrs. Phalen in the Mercy Sisters convent over on Clare Island, her mind completely gone. Like the others, this rumor was gleefully started by Maggie Ballard and once she realized how eager the villagers were to believe her lies, she added that the Phalen children were on their way to the Westport workhouse and would never live to see the light of day again.

On Christmas morning, while Meg lay motionless in her bed, Rose, Denny and Tom tried to fix some semblance of a Christmas breakfast for the younger children. The best they could do was a stack of the thin maize pancakes spread with a bit of honey and crushed walnuts from the tiny reserve Meg had hidden from Gilchrist the day of his sortie through her little brightly painted dresser. The children were thrilled to have a bit of sweet on Christmas and Tom found his eyes misting at their naïve pleasure. Meg joined them for the traditional Christmas prayers, curled up deep in the corner of the settle, wrapped in an old wool shawl.

As the oldest child, Rose started the prayers. In years past, the whole family eagerly awaited Rose's Christmas prayer because it was usually long and filled with whimsical wishes for the New Year. Today, they all bowed their heads and waited for her to start. Finally, her voice heavy with tears, Rose gave them not a happy litany of childish desires but two sad little requests.

"Dear Lord Jesus, keep Thomas warm this day and help Mam and Da feel better. Amen."

Denny, his voice barely audible took up the prayer with a simple "God bless us all."

Mary Clare, usually the most genuinely pious and devout of the children, made a great show of kneeling upright before the fire, folding her hands just so and pulling her shawl over her head like she was in church. Everyone waited, heads bowed while she stammered through a series of ums, and finally blurted out, "Heavenly Father, if we could just have Thomas back fer a wee few days that would be grand. If not let us just see him sometimes in the sky. Amen."

Next it was Thomas's turn and the little turf fire sputtered and smoked in the damp cold draft of the chimney. No one knew how to fill the empty space when Thomas would have read the Christmas story he had been practicing since Michaelmas. Finally, Grace whispered a soft little prayer for more food and Ellen smacked her because that was her prayer and Grace stole it. After that Ellen refused to pray at all.

Francis wouldn't say his prayer out loud, instead burying his face in Meg's lap and mumbling into her skirt a prayer for only God's ears. Meg stroked his fair hair and cupped his soft, plump baby cheek in her hand. When it came time for Tom and Meg to pray, they fell back on the traditional Our Father and Hail Mary that they could recite without baring their heavy hearts before their children.

There were no gifts this sad Christmas morning but Rose had dressed everyone in the new clothes Meg had made from the gingham cloth and together they all marched over the mountain to church. Even Meg had made the trek leaning heavily on Tom as she stumbled up the same path she had taken to bury her little man only days before.

As they made their way up the steep path, Tom noted to Meg how fair the day was. The sky was clear and pale blue as the winter sun shed its white light on them. The day was warm for December and beads of perspiration gathered on his forehead as he helped Meg negotiate the stony trail. None of the villagers, not even the Phalens had shoes anymore. If they had ever had shoes, every pair had been sold or traded for food long ago. Meg's tender feet had never gotten used to walking barefoot and she carefully avoided the sharp pebbles and pieces of shale that dotted the long way over the foothills of Croaghan Mountain.

Just as they rounded the low stone fence that cordoned off the graveyard, Maggie Ballard, who had lost both her husband and mother-in-law to the terrible flux caused by eating grass, turned on Meg and spit in her face. Maggie was not from Achill and had hated Doeega and everyone in the village since Vince Ballard had brought her from Galway five years ago. She and Vince had never had any children and her hate for the village, the island and the people had taken on a bit of madness as she grieved her barrenness. When he died, she had just found out she was carrying a child but only days before her confinement she lost her son. For some reason, Maggie had found an outlet for her venom in Meg Phalen and had spread the rumors that she was hoarding the preserves and nut butter that had brought Mr. Gilchrist to Meg's door.

Now, as Meg and Tom passed the very spot where their own baby lay in the cold damp soil, Maggie Ballard vented her madness in Meg's face, leaving a green trickle of sputum on Meg's cheek.

"Ye're the curse of this island, Miss High and Mighty, Yer Ladyship, ye royal she-divil! Look at ye in yer rags, yer little English brats dressed in the finest clothes around! Look at yer big man all skinny and stooped, holdin' ye up when ye ought t' be layin' face down in the dirt. Who are ye now Yer Ladyship? Who are ye now that yer own are sick and dyin' like the rest of us? Where's yer fine fur coat now? Ye're nothin' but a fraud, nothin' but a rich, disgustin' fake, ye are. Look at ye now, all bent and skinny. Ye'll be next, ye will, and then who will yer fine, dandy husband walk to church with? Oh, he'll find someone fer sure. Maybe even me!"

With this Denny and Rose both charged at Maggie's back and would have taken her down into the dirt if Fr. O'Boyle hadn't seen and heard everything and stepped in. He thrust Maggie Ballard away from the Phalens and bellowed for her to head back down the mountain. He took a threadbare old hanky from the sleeve of his soutane and wiped Meg's cheek.

"Pay her no mind Meg Phalen, she's as mad as a hatter and not long fer this world, may God have mercy on her tormented soul."

Meg, who had withdrawn completely from everything when Thomas died, had not even registered the insults hurled at her.

Tom's pallor was marked with dangerous purple blotches creeping up his cheeks and his hand under her arm had hardened into a fist as he guided her and the children into the church. His other hand he kept tightly clamped on Denny's shoulder. Rose he fixed with a black scowl and she marched furiously straight to the pew. If Meg hadn't registered Maggie's insults, Rose was well aware of their effect on Tom.

Tom sat rigid in the pew, rage threatening to spill over him. Meg could feel the tension in his arm and she gently patted the soft golden hair on his wrist, absently caressing the thin skin on the back of his hand. After so many years being married to this man, Meg instinctively knew what he was thinking. She had watched him with deep concern the last few days despite the numbing burden of her own grief.

Tom had taken the little children's book about the first Christmas and placed it in the makeshift coffin with Thomas the day he was buried. He had sat with the other children and read the story to them as they sat vigil for their brother for the last hour before he and Denny carried the little box over the mountain to St. Dymphna's. Meg remembered how he held the slim volume over Thomas's cold body, unable to let go of it. Finally, after several moments of tense foot shuffling, Rose simply touched her da's fingers and he gently let it slide into the coffin.

Tom was so shocked at Thomas's death he had hardly slept in the nights that followed. They only had Thomas for one day and one night before they had to bury him. Tom and Denny had taken a partition out from between two mangers in the empty byre to make a little wooden box for Thomas to lay in. The icy wind off the Atlantic howled around the stone byre as Tom cut the pieces to fit together. Tom never felt the cold as he burned with shame at the thought that he could sell off his byre board by board to make coffins for the dying of Doeega and then buy food for his own family.

Denny had stood shivering in the thin, worn, corduroy jacket Meg had made from an old pair of pants Tom had found in a house left empty after a family had all died. Tom watched him, a boy on the cusp of manhood, his tall, twelve-year-old body too big for the flimsy jacket, his gangly wrists projecting from the sleeves. He held the last length of wood steady as Tom fitted it between the two short ends. Tom was furious at the sight of Denny's hands, the cracked, dirty fingernails, the boyish knuckles so much bigger than the long, spindly fingers that wrapped tightly around the piece.

He had slammed the hammer down to secure the last nail in the tiny coffin. His son should have big hands like his own, fleshed out and sturdy, clean and groomed. Instead, Denny's hands looked thin and frail like a woman's, the food that should have fed him and made a man out of him non-existent, leaving him instead a little scarecrow of a lad, hardly able to hold a board. Denny had not spoken a word since Tom gathered the children around the hearth and told them of Thomas's death that morning. He had silently stood in the bedroom door watching his mam bathe his brother's body and had torn out the kitchen door when she barricaded herself in the loft where he had slept with Thomas since they were wee laddies. Tom had sent Rose after him but he had refused to come out from behind the booley where he sat pitching stones in the gravel.

Tom's heart broke as Denny picked up the lid and, gently setting it inside the box, lifted his brother's final bed and carried it into the kitchen. He had never understood Denny and until the last year or so, had found him very hard to like. None of the other children, least of all Thomas, had ever been on the receiving end of his switch the way Denny had been. He remembered once having to take Rose to the booley for lying to Fr. O'Boyle and refusing to go to confession but he had only been able to lay the switch on her twice when he had to stop. The horrible image of Meg's beaten body slumped in a chair at GlynMor Castle stopped his arm midair and he never raised a switch to any of his daughters again. To be true, he had never used the switch on Thomas at all.

But Denny had been a different story. He almost relished

the drama of being hauled by the collar to the little stone shed and his pride seemed to swell as he took his licks like a man. Tom firmly believed that hard discipline made a man's character and Denny was no exception. His own da, as gentle as he was, had not hesitated to use the switch on his boys if he thought they deserved it. Tom had been whipped once and when he saw the pain on his father's face when he was finished, never crossed his da again.

Davey was the one who defied his father and Tom remembered hiding in the corner of the kitchen with Paulie whenever Da had taken the rod to his back. In the end, Davey was the one who left, defiant till the last goodbye and Tom saw again the same pain in his father's eyes as he watched his son walk away from the kitchen door. Now, he thought of his da living out his last days in Davey's home, Davey and his wife spooning gruel into his toothless mouth. Whatever the problem had been between them, it was forgiven or forgotten and the last time Tom had seen them both they had shown nothing but kindness for each other.

Tom caught a glimpse of the birch switch over the booley door as Denny ducked beneath it carefully balancing the coffin as he tried to fit his awkward new height beneath the low lintel. He suddenly felt a surge of love for the boy who had been his most difficult child. As he approached young manhood, the boyeen had somehow settled down and found a purpose and direction in his life. Tom knew Denny was involved with the Blackthorn Brotherhood but kept his concerns to himself.

Denny was only twelve and Tom thought that he needed some way to survive this hunger and if the passionate rhetoric and foolish plans of the little band of renegades filled Denny's empty gut then so be it. He felt that Denny had plenty of time to outgrow his fascination with the secret meetings and the dark philosophies of the Brotherhood. Besides, Tom believed that the Brotherhood was right and where he could no longer voice the passions he had left behind when he married the daughter of an earl, he could hardly stop his son from carrying on the fight that his Irish ancestors had died for, now could he?

The thirst for freedom was enough to make even a weak man fight and Tom knew, every time Denny left the booley, hitching his pants up over his bruised backside, that his son was stronger than the last time he took the switch. God, bless him, he thought. If he stayed with the fighting men, he would break his mother's heart. But Tom could no more deny Denny his destiny than he could change his own. A stabbing pain went through his chest at the thought of having lost Thomas and at the very real possibility that he could lose Denny or any of his other children too. God bless them all and may they someday walk free and fat and wear a smile on their faces again.

The darkness of the solstice closed in early that night and he and Meg sat for hours in the settle by the fire, the little coffin resting on two chairs against the opposite wall. When they did sleep they did not rest. Tom had awakened the night of the funeral after dozing fitfully for a few hours. Meg who had not slept at all, had his head in her lap. As she absently curled his hair around her finger, he told her of the dream that had haunted his sleep.

He had found himself caught in swirling blackness filling his hearth with a fog darker than turf smoke. He sat in his wicker hearth chair over by the front door as the amorphous creature reached out with clawlike tendrils inching first toward Rose, then Francis and Denny as he scrambled to gather the others into his lap. The pattern repeated itself over and over as Tom tossed his head back and forth in the chair trying to shake off the dreadful specter. The smoky creature would reach and grab, he would pull a child into his lap with one hand and try to open the door with the other. One by one Tom would reach and gather a child unto himself only to find the door held fast from the outside. Unable to pass any of his children to safety, Tom felt the weight of them piling up on his lap until he could no longer breathe and he had to push them all off and the specter would start again to billow and grasp.

He could not rise from the chair, the weight of his own

body pinning him to the seat. The cries of his babies waiting to be devoured tortured him as he reached and stretched again and again pulling them from the jaws of death only to find he had nowhere for them to go. Each time it was the same. Tom awoke from his nightmare when he heard his own voice cry out "Mother of God, no!"

Then Thomas's face would enter the black cloud and be sucked up the chimney as the weight of his other children kept Tom from reaching him and pulling him back. He never saw Meg in the dream except at the end when Thomas appeared. Then he could see her lap beneath the little curly head as her hands smoothed the dark hair away from his brow. Then Thomas would be gone up the chimney and Meg would be hidden deep in the billows of blackness. When Tom awoke it was to find his own head in Meg's lap and her fingers caressing his own hair.

Now, sitting next to her in the cold stone church on Christmas morning, he felt her hand on his, soothing his rage with her cool, calm touch. He realized how lonely he had been since the day Gilchrist took away his livelihood, trying to strip away his manhood before his wife and children. He had shrunk into himself like a wounded dog and, in that sense, Gilchrist had had his way with him. His friends avoided him but the lads at McCoy's hadn't had a pint together anyhow since the taps went dry six months earlier. Poor McCoy had finally shut his doors and joined the other lads digging ditches while his wife and daughter took to sorting fish for anyone who'd hire them on.

Tom hadn't the energy to try and figure out the lean, sullen men he used to see in the village or at church. He had always been apart from them because of his role as agent for Lord Lucan and it was no different now. What hurt Tom was the limbo he lived in now. He was really more like the other lads than at any time since he and Meg had arrived on Achill but the distance established then still followed him despite his poverty and humiliation. He thought for years that it never mattered to him what the others thought. He had always been his own man and took his pleasure and pride in his beautiful wife and family.

As he sat on the hard wooden pew, Tom knew that had all been a charade. Of course, it mattered to him what the others thought. He was a son of the sod just like them and despite the high birth of his wife, the heroes and legends, the beliefs and superstitions of their people were his too. The great clans of O'Neill, Fitzgerald and Meagher were his too. He had the right to lay claim on the feats of the pirate Queen O'Malley and the holy saint that founded the very church he sat in.

He too was born of the rich black sod and the hard enduring stone of this beautiful mythical land. For hundreds of years his people had walked the green hills and cool valleys of Ireland. The vast sky and billowing white clouds that parted to sprinkle the rain, the rainbows that arced over the lakes and mountains all across this gorgeous land, the crashing surf and ancient grey cliffs sang to him the moaning lullabies that soothed his soul. These belonged to him and he to them. He had as much right to the pride and the fierce kinship to all Ireland as any other man in the village. But the ability to say so, to stand in the village square and bellow for freedom, had been denied him since he left Clydagh Glyn. He had buried for years the pain of that loss.

Tom thought of the night he had stood grinding his knuckles into the pigsty wall behind his father's house. He remembered the smell of the thatch burning the day Lord Bentley's bailiff evicted his family from his granda's house. He felt hot pain sear his chest as he recalled the sound of the damp clay thudding on his mam's coffin after she died only days after giving birth to his brother in a bog. Now the terrible potato failure had happened for still another year and God preserve them, they'd even lost one of their own. Ellen crawled onto his lap and he put his free arm around her. Holding her tiny body against his chest he felt her ribs beneath his hand. Looking down on her thin, fair hair, he was overcome by his own failure. His wife and children were as hungry and ragged as any other Achill family. But even the pride in their survival was denied him. He was not the one. His wife was Church of Ireland. They lived because she was able to get broth for them from Rev. Nangle's missionaries. Deep shame enveloped him and threatened to reignite his rage as he sat with Meg and realized that it was she and not he who kept his children alive. How it hurt him to have failed both her and them. It would have been better if Stiller and George had clubbed him senseless that night on her father's doorstep, freeing her and keeping these innocent children from ever having been born to this terrible fate.

Even today, sitting in their customary pew on Christmas morning, clean and scrubbed, dressed in the new clothes Meg had so painstakenly made, he grieved them. He wanted to reach out and snatch them all to himself like he had in his dream and beg forgiveness for having let them down. His grief over failing them threatened to overpower him.

Tom ached for Meg. He had watched her fade away from him ever since the day when Gilchrist took their cows and thrust his family deep into the hunger along with everyone else in Doeega. Until then he had hoped he could trade his own pride for the security of his family. But he had failed to do that and now with one son lost and the rest of his family in peril he felt more a failure than he had on the front step of GlynMor castle the night Lord Jeffrey locked Meg away from him. It was as if that wretched bastard himself was the smoky creature of his dreams. The evil that visited his sleep endangered his beloved children and took the heart of his wife, evoking the same fury in Tom's heart that he had felt that night so many years ago.

He needed to get them off this island. He needed to get them away from the clutches of Lord Lucan and that vermin undertaker Gilchrist. How he hated himself for allowing himself to be taken in by the promise of a place of his own, a nice living and the endless possibilities that living had offered his sons. It had seemed like a sure thing when he and Meg had discussed it all those years ago. They would do well as dairy farmers and someday Lord Lucan would reward Tom with the land that was rightfully his to begin with. Denny would eventually inherit the land and the others could divide the fields and have little plots of their own to graze livestock and grow tatties. They would have the sea at their doorstep and fishing rights to some of the best shoreline in County Mayo.

He and Meg would sit back and watch their grandchildren grow healthy and fat on the good food and milk from their own cows while their cheeks grew rosy from the clean salt air. He would listen to their laughter as they battled the tide, gathering mussels and dulse for Meg to cook up in a grand pot of cruasach. He would sit by the hearth with a curly haired boy and tell grand tales of Meg and the first clay baked chicken dinner and the time after a late night at McCoy's when he mistakenly dressed in one of her chemises while looking for his nightshirt in the dark. He would tickle them and laugh at their antics and Meg would smack at him with her spoon and shoo them all out the door while she put a fine loaf of soda bread in the oven for tea.

What a fool he was! Tom Phalen, the biggest edjit in all Ireland not only thought he could marry an aristocrat and get away with it but had continued to believe the lie for years afterward. Defeated and exhausted he felt the steam go out of him as he slumped in the pew. From far away, the bells rang and it was time to stand up.

Meg felt Tom's fury leave him and his body relax at the sound of the tinnabulum announcing the beginning of Holy Mass. He stood and took her hand in his as Fr. O'Boyle emerged from the sacristy. Ellen slipped off Tom's lap and stood on the kneeler, her dark eyes barely able to see over the pew in front of her. As the priest intoned the Introit, the rhythmic Latin lulled Meg into mute resignation. Tom gently set her hand on her lap and helped her to her feet. Fr. O'Boyle prayed on. When he began the Confiteor, the ritual prayer of repentance, Meg looked up. How many times had she heard the hard but beautiful words of the humble confession of sinfulness. Her sinfulness. Her fault. Yes, all of this was her fault.

Meg had always grappled with the concept of forgiveness. Fr. O'Boyle had been so gentle about sin, neither pretending it didn't exist nor claiming that Meg was not to be held responsible for her own failings before God. Instead, he was steadfast but gentle in his belief that God's mercy was stronger and more powerful than any sin she could commit. When she had come to him for her first confession, she trembled at his feet, kneeling in fear and sorrow as she poured out her litany of sins.

It seemed a lifetime ago that she and Tom had sat on the strand one night watching a late summer meteor shower and she had asked him about that night in Newport when he had confessed his sins to Fr. Finnegan and walked away a free man. Tom had been so strong as they talked late into that night. She remembered how soft his voice was and the conviction with which he promised her the same joy and liberation if she would only avail herself of the grace he found in that mysterious sacrament. Hadn't he, after all, turned his back on his faith for years before coming full circle again? If God could forgive him certainly he would smile upon Meg.

Tom had taken her hand and kissed her palm to punctuate the sweet name of Jesus every time it passed his lips. She knew without a doubt that Tom loved her truly as she listened to him pour out his heart's desire to see her embrace the faith of his baptism. Knowing this and knowing from Tom's own lips that Jesus loved her far more than he as a man could ever love her should have brought Meg comfort. But she felt even more unworthy as she contemplated the kind of love the Savior had for her.

The day she finally made the long journey over the mountain to kneel at the feet of the kindly Franciscan, Tom walked with her and prayed silently in the back of the church while she submitted to her examination of conscience. When Fr. O'Boyle gestured for her to approach, Meg did so, her head bowed and her heartbeat thundering in her ears. She had always been taught about the wrath of God, the thunder of His fury and the hardness of His justice. When Fr. O'Boyle spoke of God as a loving father, Meg tried hard to imagine how this was supposed to feel. Her only knowledge of father was her own father, cold and distant at best, murderously enraged when Meg sinned with Tom and created a child.

Now, as she heard the beginnings of the Gloria, on this sad and hollow Christmas morning, she remembered how she had wept in this very church, wrapped in Fr. O'Boyle's arms as he heard her first confession of that sin and how his words fell on her head as he prompted her line by line through her act of contrition. When he took her by the shoulders and looked straight into her face absolving her *"In Nomine, Patris et Filii et Spiritus Sancti"*, she had indeed felt cleansed. Her soul had finally been set free.

She and Tom had returned down the mountain with hearts as light as children and for many days Meg had cherished the joy she felt. She knew this freedom of her soul was the thread that tied her to Tom the night he came home with Duffy and she met him on the beach. She knew this freedom made their lovemaking that night an act of unity with God their creator and father. The mystery of those moments were etched in her heart but once the crops failed and her life became one long fight for survival, she never went any further with her formal training in the Church. There were no more long leisurely conversations about God and love and forgiveness. There was just hunger and death and one disappointing season after another. There was only sorrow and loss and familiar faces looking like haggard strangers wearing death masks stained with green around their mouths.

Meg needed only to receive her first Eucharist and be confirmed in the church to be officially accepted but it all seemed so silly now. How could she believe in a God of mercy when those who did died in the street while those who didn't received soup? How could she risk losing all her children to the hunger when she saw so many who loved this church forced to deny it in order to get enough to eat?

Her eyes settled on the crèche, a tradition begun by St. Francis of Assisi, the founder of Fr. O'Boyle's order. He had told her the story of St. Francis and his dramatic conversion from a sinful lothario and drunkard, how he had become so enamored with the crucified Christ that he abandoned his family home and pursued a life of poverty and penance. When she dared ask, her voice a mere whisper, if he had ever gone home again and Fr. O'Boyle shook his head, her heart broke. Meg knew she needed to go home someday. Despite their cool relationship, she missed her mother. Even with the breathtaking beauty of the sea and strand around her house and the happiness she and Tom shared, this famine and especially the loss of her son made her yearn for the familiar things of her past.

Meg knew she had never been accepted in Doeega. She had always been able to content herself with a few friends and her houseful of children, her gardens and the many tasks she had to do every day. Her life had been hard but good. Her days had been full and busy and her children were her pride and joy. She thought again about the night back in 1845 when they knew nothing of famine and heartache. As clearly as the crèche in front of her she could see Tom on the strand, walking toward her, stopping to take her in as she stood frozen in time with nothing but his handsome face in her sights. She flushed with the memory right here in church, of their lovemaking that night and the mystical quality of Martha's conception.

Now that life was over. She had failed at everything. With her few friends dead, she knew no one who really liked her and her family. She had not completed her studies and taken the final steps toward becoming Catholic, she could hardly feed her family or give Tom the comforts of their bed, and worst of all she could not save her sweet Thomas from the ravages of lung fever because she walked right past him on the mountain when he needed her most. She thought with sorrow of his last year, afflicted with a constant, wracking cough, sitting by the hearth weak as a little sparrow. On days when he was too tired to come downstairs, he would watch longingly out the little window in the loft for the other children to come home from begging the evening meal. How could God ever forgive her when she was so clearly guilty? How could God ever want her when she had done everything wrong?

It was easy for Fr. O'Boyle to be kind and hold her head against his rough wool cowl, soothing and coaxing her to believe but she didn't dare believe! She knew the truth! She knew that Andrew Feeney had spoken the truth. Meg was evil from her father's seed and her life was a lie. She had to believe Andrew. After all, he knew the evil that she carried from her father because he carried it too. Denny was right, Andrew was right and she needed to go home and see for herself what had happened to her parents and her home all because she sinned with a lover and ran away from the punishment she really deserved.

What made her think her father should not have whipped her? He should have whipped her more! What made her feel that she deserved better than to be locked up for the rest of her life? Look what her disobedience and willfulness had wrought! Here she was, in a crumbling church on a harsh, windswept island, surrounded by starving people, her own children thin and wasted, her husband stooped and broken and her baby lying cold and still beneath the soil of a church yard she would never be worthy to enter.

Maggie Ballard was right. She was a fraud and a liar. She took food from the Church of Ireland and shelter from the good graces of Lord Lucan and then stood here in a Catholic Church on Christmas morning as brazen as could be. What was she thinking? It was no surprise the other villagers hated her. She played the role of one while living the life of another. How was it she never saw it before? How must Tom feel every time he looked at her and wondered who his wife really was? Fr. O'Boyle couldn't forgive her. He didn't even know her! How could that holy man bless her with membership in his church when she still had one foot in her old church? How could he welcome her into his sacraments when she had the deep secret sin of her own birth on her soul?

The few congregants had sat down for the Offertory prayers and Meg did likewise, grateful for the rest. Fr. O'Boyle recited quietly the private prayers over the bread and wine that prepared them for the consecration into the Body and Blood of Christ. She knew this was a mystery that both drew her to the altar and forced her to stand back. There was so much these people accepted just because the church said it was so, so much they believed without question.

This was such a departure from her old way of thinking that she knew she must accept it on pure faith or decide to reject it altogether. She wanted to believe! More than anything Meg wanted to know the freedom she witnessed on the steep climb up Croagh Patrick all those years ago. Those wretched, broken people had such perseverance and joy. She hadn't thought of that pilgrimage in years but here in this church, on Christmas morning, she could see in her mind's eye clearly the bent back of the mother bearing her unborn child, carrying another and leading two more by the hand. Then the faces of those sons bearing the litter with the shrunken twisted body of their father on it! The purity of their faces was almost more than she could bear to remember. How she ached for that kind of faith to burn in her heart.

How she longed at this very moment for the strength Maureen had drawn from the sacraments for years after the death of her own baby. Why not believe? What did she have to lose by saying yes, Lord, I believe? Would she be lying if she stood before this altar and professed to believe? Was her desire for faith less worthy than the faith of the others around her? Why not believe, indeed? Hadn't Christ died so she would believe? Hadn't Christ brought her to this place in time so she would say yes?

Meg looked around at the few congregants who had actually made it to Christmas Mass. They were all like her, exhausted, ragged and thin. Every family represented had lost someone to the hunger. Elsie McDonough sat alone in the pew across from Meg. Now, there was a woman who had lost everything; ten children and her husband and then a year later her last living son and her parents, all from starvation and fever. Yet there she sat, her lank red hair clean, her gaunt face scrubbed, her eyes ever on the priest as he said the holy ritual prayers. There she sat in a dress of rags with one of her mother's old shawls over her head. How did a person who had lost so much go on? How did a religion become such a source of life for someone who had no life?

Elsie knelt straight as nun on the wooden kneeler never taking her eyes off Fr. O'Boyle as he raised the little host high above his head. The boy serving the altar rang the tiny brass bells as the faithful bowed their heads. Meg turned and looked up at Fr. O'Boyle. He looked the same as always, his fine hands raising the host to the heavens, his thumbs and forefingers joined together on either side of the chalice as he deftly avoided touching anything with them now that he had touched the consecrated host. Every time it was the same. Every time he never wavered from his obedience to the traditions of his church. Every time he invoked, *"Spiritus Sancti"*, the power of the Holy Spirit, his faith in that power brought the Living Christ into the little bit of bread and wine in his hands. How did one get that kind of faith? What was Elsie McDonough thinking as she gazed raptly at the white disk and the humble chalice?

Meg bowed her head in shame. She had no business being in here, kneeling before this sacrament, pretending to believe. The ritual continued, *"Pater Noster…"; "Agnus Dei "… "Miserere nobis."*

Yes, Miserare nobis! Have mercy on us, Lamb of God, you who take away the sins of the world. Yes, the world! That must mean the grand sins of birth and class as well as the little sins of everyday meanness. That must be the perfect prayer for her and her horrid father and her distant, indifferent mother! If there was indeed a sin on her soul for being born into aristocracy then this was the way to be washed pure. If there was a sin in being educated and refined in a world filled with ignorance and poverty than this was her moment of redemption.

Meg's heart cried out in silent prayer, "Lamb of God, take away my sin, you who take away the sins of the world, have mercy on me, Meg Phalen. Not just Meg Phalen, but Lady Meg

Wynn, daughter of Lord Jeffrey and Lady Beverly Wynn! Have mercy on me when those around me would stone me just for living. Mercy on me for having a funeral for my Thomas. Mercy on me for marrying into their life when I could have stayed in my own and never laid eyes on their shame."

This Lamb of God, sacrificed for the sins of the world was calling her to take him into her heart and make a dwelling place for him within her. He wanted her with her wealthy pedigree. Jesus wanted her with all her past indifferences and slights to him and his poor. He wanted her not just now that she was poor herself, full of loss and heartbreak but because he loved her. If she dressed in the silks and laces of her former life He would love her. If she sang from a gilded hymnal and wiped her eyes with a powdered hanky He would love her. But somehow Meg knew intuitively that where and who she was now had somehow made her realize this love in a way she would never have known had she taken a different path in life. She bowed her head and begged for the mercy of the Lamb of God. Finally, as Fr. O'Boyle raised the host and chalice together Meg heard, as though for the first time, the words that changed her heart forever.

She knew this one. This one she knew in Latin, Irish and English. She knelt with her head bowed and struck her breast in contrition along with everyone else in the church.

"O, Lord I am not worthy. Say but the word and my soul shall be healed."

Oh, how she needed to be healed! Meg felt her body like a dead weight in the pew. Fr. O'Boyle had told her that she could receive her first communion any time she was ready since she had already had her first confession. The pull to the altar was overpowering but her legs would not move.

"O, Lord I am not worthy that Thou shouldst enter under my roof; say but the word and my soul shall be healed."

Dear Lord, what should she do? Meg knew that if she didn't go now, if she didn't obey the urges of her heart so filled with longing for this mystery, she would never in truth be able to say

"I believe".

The pews in front of her emptied as one by one, the faithful approached the altar. Tom rose and the older children followed. Still Meg knelt. Tom hardly noticed her as this was the way it had always been. But across the aisle, Elsie McDonough scrambled from her pew and as she entered the aisle behind Tom, looked Meg full in the face. Meg saw in her eyes the same tender forgiveness she had seen in Thomas's eyes right before he died. She gasped at the pure love that penetrated her heart in that gaze. Elsie and she had never known each other well nor had she ever spoken to her about more than the weather. Now in an instant, she beheld in this stranger's eyes all the wrongs she had ever committed, all the failures she had ever had and all the ways she was not worthy to receive her Lord and in the same unblinking gaze she saw the pure and absolute love of her Savior, forgiving, longing and inviting.

"O, Lord I am not worthy…"

Like the good thief hanging next to Jesus, Meg knew that the promise of paradise was for her too. This day she would be with Jesus in this paradise. This day she would be with Thomas in a way that death could never understand.

"O, Lord I am not worthy… say but the word…"

Meg began to rise from her knees and reached out for the carved knob at the end of the pew to steady herself. Elsie took her arm and helped her to her feet.

As she leaned into the pew, she smiled and said, "Meg".

"…Say but the word… Say the word, O Lord… my name, O, Lord and my soul shall be healed.

Meg rose slowly and approached the altar. Fr. O'Boyle raised the consecrated host before her and, tears in his eyes, said,

"Corpus Christi."

Without a moment's hesitation, Meg whispered *"Amen"* and felt her salvation on her tongue.

When the little group left the church, they realized that it had rained while they were praying. The day was too warm for snow but slushy wet sleet had glazed the stones along the path to the village. The whole of Croaghan Mountain gleamed like polished silver as the slick coating caught the morning sun, once again brilliant in the sky. Meg shielded her eyes from the glare of thousands of tiny pebbles sparkling along the rocky path. The branches of the scrubby trees hung to the ground under their heavy icing, tinkling and chiming their own Christmas song as clumps of glittering mush trickled through the branches and landed on the ground.

The members of St. Dymphna's skidded and slid down the mountain, children and adults alike squealing with pleasure at the surprise playground. Bare feet that should have been aching with cold, sloshed and slipped through the melting slush as boys of all ages packed slobbering wet balls to pelt at each other. By the time the villagers arrived at the bottom of the steep path, most of the gushy, wet stuff had melted and the mountain wore a fresh clean look. Invigorated by their impromptu Christmas celebration, people who had climbed the mountain with hungry bellies and heavy hearts called out to each other joyful Christmas greetings. As they returned, one by one to their dank kitchens and the reality of their empty kettles, the joy of that heavenly gift somehow smoothed the jagged edge of their hunger a bit and gentled their voices among them.

Later that night, lying in bed, Tom turned to face Meg. Taking Meg's hand in his he raised it to his lips, "Welcome home, Darlin."

Meg had wondered if he would make note of her receiving Holy Communion but now that he did she was too tired to respond.

She simply took his big rough hand in hers and returned the kiss. With his hand tucked beneath her cheek, they fell asleep without another word.

The days following the Christmas ice storm turned fair. Anyone well enough enjoyed high pale skies dotted with thin wispy clouds. The usual storms and winds of January seemed to have forgotten Achill. Most of the villagers passed the season in a haze of sickness and death, and an eerie silence settled over the village as winter turned to spring. Tom said little about Meg's change of heart on Christmas morning but he seemed to smile more often than before. Despite the deep penetrating sorrow the whole family carried for Thomas, there was a peace in the house that soothed them and made them try hard to be good to each other. Meg grew larger as her pregnancy advanced but that didn't stop her from working alongside Tom, Rose and Denny digging ditches. There were days when she thought her back would break but she could dig harder and longer than Mary Clare so she took on that hard task while Mary Clare minded the younger children.

Mary Clare would walk them two hours every day down to Mundy's Bluff where there was a small inlet. This was a favorite spot for fishermen to bring in the haul of sweet crab so coveted by the London market. Here Mary Clare would line up her brother and sisters and they would beg in the street. Sometimes they would get a crab or two from one of the merchants who came over by curragh from Westport. Sometimes they would be run off the warf by irate fishmongers' wives who were trying to beg for a few throw-backs themselves.

The Phalen children eventually became favorites of one particular merchant, an English gent named Fellowes from Louisburg who, in addition to owning a popular pub in Castlebar, ran a big inn and restaurant along the Louisburg Road. At first shy, they said nothing to the big, burly man. Then one day he brought his grandson with him. The boy was a few years older than Rose and that day she had joined the younger children when there was no digging for her to do. His name was Jimmy Malone and he stood a full head taller than Denny. Jimmy Malone was a fresh, outgoing lad who winked at Rose and made her blush. When she stuck her tongue out at him he only laughed and scooted off to lug a crate of crabs for his grandfather. Mary Clare thought Rose was very unkind to stick out her tongue at Jimmy Malone and told her so on the way home. Even after being rebuffed by her big sister, Jimmy had let Mary Clare beg a sack full of fresh crabs from him and as the girls dragged the heavy sack home between them she asked Rose why she had been so rude.

"Oh, Peaches," she sighed using her nickname for her younger sister. "Boys are just so, I don't know, so full o'the divil, I guess. Suren' I'm not needin' none o'his shenanigans now am I?"

"No, but he seemed to like ye' enough t'give ye a wink, now didn't he?"

"Well, there ye are at that, Peaches! That's exactly the kind o'tauntin' I'm not havin'! Any lad what wants Rose Phalen t'look his way can just keep his winkin' eyes t'himself, and that's the all of it."

Mary Clare dropped the subject when Grace spotted a patroller and they all ducked behind a dune with the sack of crabs. The patrollers were not above hanging children if they thought they'd been poaching or so Maggie Ballard had said one day last month when she stole a fat softshell crab and two nice flounder they had begged from Mr. Fellowes. When they went to bed hungry that night, they decided they were not going to let that happen again. Neither Maggie Ballard nor the mounted patrol would come between them and their dinner again.

In March the men again held a town meeting to decide whether to try planting potatoes or not. They sat around the tables in McCoy's abandoned pub though the spigots had no more stout and the clay pipes filled with sponc offered the only comfort they could find. It was finally decided that they would try a crop if they could get some seed potatoes from Westport.

While the men blew great clouds of smoke around the inside of McCoy's, deciding the fate of their families, the women sat on the low stone wall that marked the edge of the main street and waited. It was odd that the main street of Doeega had no formal name but everyone called it The Shannon Road. No one knew how it got its name as most of the villagers had never been anywhere near Shannon. But no one had disputed the name for a dozen generations.

The women were somber and silent as they sat listlessly along the stone wall. Occasionally one would get up to corral a wandering child or jostle a cranky baby but most of them just sat. Meg looked around her at the faces she had come to know over the years. Kit Grady was ashen, so wasted that her skin drew dangerously thin over her high cheekbones, emphasizing her huge grey eyes in their deep sockets. Poor Kit had the look of death about her and she so recently a mother for the first time.

She balanced a listless toddler on her narrow lap, the child of her sister Millie and young Mark McCoy, while Millie went around inside the pub offering the men cool water in the big heavy glasses that used to hold the rich amber stout they had once so proudly served. At Kit's feet lay a tiny, wizened infant wrapped in rags. Little Mary Grady looked frail and half-starved but by some miracle, Kit did have milk to feed her and when Mary was hungry she let out a nice lusty cry that amazed the other women and brought a proud blush to Kit's sallow cheeks.

Maggie Creahan and her sister-in-law, Polly Maher sat at the far end of the wall. They were deep in conversation with Annie McGrath and her sister Deirdre recently from Slievemore to the north. Meg felt sorry for the two young sisters. They had lost their husbands and all their kin to this awful famine and had fled Slievemore for Doeega following behind the missionaries and their soup toureens. They had relatives in Liverpool who had sent them tickets to the States and if they could only get to England they could get on a ship to America. Meg wished they would be on their way before someone stole their fare. People were so desperate they'd steal communion from a nun.

Peg Sweeney came up to Meg and shifting her baby son on her hip, nodded a hello. Peg was one of the few village women who had befriended Meg and had never wavered even when many of the others had turned away.

"How be ye, dearie?" Peg looked at Meg with soft blue eyes

that were clear and kind in her gaunt face.

"I'm living, barely. How are you Peg?"

"Been better, been worse. Did ye hear about Maggie Ballard?" Peg loved nothing more than a good gossip but Meg hadn't heard anything about Maggie Ballard.

"No, what about her?" Meg shifted Martha to her other knee and stroked Francis's hair as he leaned listlessly against her. The other babies were with Rose back at the house. Meg was so exhausted carrying this baby that she could truly manage only one or two children at a time. She couldn't manage at all without her dear Rose. What a godsend that girl was.

"She took her own life, she did. Found her hangin' in a booley behind O'Fearon's old place out by the hedge school. Young Bernie O'Dowda himself found her and him only ten years old. They said she had been there for days and Jamie Grady so weak with the hunger himself he couldn't cut her down so old Seamus Mulcahy did it. I didn't even know he was still alive. No one goes to the hedge school anymore and he just sort of disappeared. Looks like a goblin but then he always did, a bit, don't ye know?"

Peg chuckled at her clever observation about poor Mr. Mulcahy's skinny physique.

"Anyway there was murmuring that Seamus was always a little sweet on Maggie ever since Vince brought her here, not that anything improper ever took place, mind ye. There's none that can point a finger at a single thing Seamus Mulcahy has ever done. God bless him, his lusts are for the Latin and Greek not for anything that'll send him t'hell, fer sure. Meself, I find him a crashin' bore and way too skinny. But 'tis a shame about Maggie. She didn't have nice way about her but I hate t'think of her roastin' in hell fer takin' her own life, sich as it was, the poor, miserable wretch."

Meg had to smile in spite of herself at Peg's colorful speech. She had always enjoyed Peg so much. A simple plain girl, Peg could never be the friend Maureen had been but her red hair and brown eyes reminded Meg of her old friend gone so long from

Doeega. She shook her head at Peg's disparagement of the skinny populace of Doeega. Peg had been so stout when the famine started that she actually looked healthy now. When everyone began to look haggard and drawn, Peg looked trim. Now that everyone else was gaunt and bony, Peg was simply thin. She would probably outlive them all thanks to the extra layer of fat she started out with. Pete Sweeney, too. He was as round and plump as a Christmas goose the day of his own wedding and Meg remembered the lads speculating on how he and his bride would ever consummate their marriage without bouncing right out of the bed. Now they were average sized while everyone else looked like a good wind would snap them in two.

Pete came out just then and pecked Peg on the back of the head. That was another thing Meg liked about the Sweeneys. They cared little for propriety and decorum and would kiss and tickle each other no matter who looked on and more than once Meg's own children had come running from town to report Mr. Sweeney pinching Mrs. Sweeney and her chasing him with a stick hollering idle threats about turning him out on the street with no supper. Now poor Pete got no supper anyway but not because Peg wouldn't cook him one if she had the food. None of them had any food. They begged for work and lined up for soup, their shame written across their once proud faces. Every Sunday Fr. O'Boyle noted sadly fewer and fewer people in the pews as one by one his faithful took on the sin of apostasy, lining up for a bowl of soup for the price of their eternal soul.

Behind Pete Sweeney the rest of the men filed out of McCoy's. They had decided to plant if they could get the seed potatoes and there were tears of relief from many a wife. There was no hope of any food if they didn't at least try and the men needed to redeem themselves for their disastrous decision to forego planting potatoes last year. By the time they reached their miserable hovels they had talked themselves into the best crop Achill Island would ever remember and fatter bellies than any of them had ever had. They'd plant their tatties and their corn.

They'd give that slimy undertaker his rent and enjoy grand fish suppers and tattie cakes fried in butter.

"Just wait, darlin', until ye see the size of them tubers and taste the pure whiteness of their flesh. They'll put the roses back in yer pretty cheeks fer sure and bring a smile t'yer face again."

"Suren' the pot'l be boilin' over with the likes of 'em, too big even fer the black bastible to hold."

In early May, on a warm, balmy day after weeks of rain, Meg was delivered early of a tiny baby boy she named Patrick Thomas. He was baptized in the kitchen the next day. There was no party, no feast. There were only the family and two guests at the house, Patrick's godparents, Peg Sweeney and by proxy, Duffy McGee. Pete Sweeney was in London trying to find work and Duffy had agreed to stand in as godfather for him. Meg barely survived the delivery. The hunger had not let up and she had grown thinner and weaker as her time neared.

She lay bundled in the settle as Fr. O'Boyle, himself weak and thin as a twig, intoned the sacred blessing over her baby's head. She had always been relieved to observe the custom of 'churching' that prohibited a woman who had just given birth from attending church until she had stopped bleeding. This baptism was different. Hot tears trickled into the thin hair on her temples as she listened to the weak cries of her son. Even the younger children knew their tiny little brother would not be with them long.

Early the next evening Meg was trying to nurse Patrick and suddenly his tired little mouth ceased its struggle to suck and his body became totally still. Meg knew immediately that this sweet baby boy had joined his brother in the arms of the heavenly angels. The communion of their souls that she had witnessed the morning Thomas died was now complete. The little brothers were united in death and her sorrow was accomplished.

She silently wrapped the little body in a ratty blanket that had warmed all of her children and was now the only one she had. Cradling her tiny son, Meg walked slowly outside where Tom was working with Rose on her fiddling. Mary Clare, Gracie, Ellen and Francis were just arriving with their meager gleanings from Mundy's Bluff. Martha toddled around poking the sand with a stick. Denny sat further down the strand pitching stones into the ocean with his friend Michael Creahan.

Meg surveyed the little group. They were all so thin and sickly. Tom looked so much older than his fifty-four years. Skinny legs protruded from short pants and his ragged, sleeveless shirt revealed the wasting of his once powerful arms. The soft blond hair of his forearms glinted in the late afternoon sun and Meg felt a rush cascade through her from her head to her heels.

The sight of Tom's beautiful arms had once been enough to make her weak with desire. This afternoon, Meg's knees went weak at the sight of him but for a totally different reason. The sensation charging through her extremities threatened to drag her down into the very earth beneath the smooth sand while at the same time drawing her inexorably into the unknown future. The rush that flooded her loins and sent shocks through her legs and feet was laden with time spent and time fleeting like the tide.

She felt like she was being thrust into the future by the galloping past, helpless to redirect the course of the thundering waves that pummeled her from behind, shoving her toward the blank horizon even as they consumed her and rooted her where she stood. Her spinning head felt hollow and her tiny baby weighed heavily in her arms threatening to overpower her strength.

The scene before her possessed all she had ever been. Here was everything: her family, her home, her very life. Here was the place she had arrived, standing in this moment. Her mind careened back to another moment on this same strand, her family in front of her, her life about to flee before her with a sigh as soft as her baby's last breath.

But this was not then, this was now. The strand, the ocean,

the vast, changeable sky she had grown to read and understand; this was all she was and all she had. This was her world and her place. She saw this world now in a golden haze, the ones she loved motionless, suspended. Even as she felt the tides of the past ebbing and flowing through her body her skin felt parched and prickly. Even as the pounding surf within her skull had washed away her thoughts, her voice was clear when she called out to Tom.

The baby in her arms held all of her hope and now he was dead. Patrick was dead, Thomas was dead and Meg looked at her family in the thin, horizontal light of the lowering sun and she knew fear as she had never known it. Moment by moment, day by day, the years of her existence pooled in her feet, paralyzing and petrifying her. A primal wail rose up from deep within her throat and Tom whipped around to see Meg standing there.

His name! Over and over Meg cried out the name she loved but he only heard it once.

Carried on the breeze the single anguished syllable of his name jolted him back to the drawing room at GlynMor Castle. Terror gripped him the way Stiller and George had done, so long ago. He looked at Meg, the bundled body of their son in her arms and felt slammed by the power of his need to protect her. There she stood, thin and ragged, barely a phantom of the striking, graceful woman he had been forced to leave in that gilded prison at the end of that horrible day.

Tom thought now, at this moment that his redemption was at hand. He would not leave Meg again, the agonizing sound of his name on her lips. He was her protector. No force on earth would keep him from catching her as she swayed before him in the shimmering warmth of the sun-drenched beach. He was the strong one now. He sprang up from the thinking rock and bolted toward her. Seeing her standing on the windswept strand, her skirt billowing in rags around her knees, her bare feet sunk in the hot dry sand, he was overpowered by love.

He sprang to her side and caught her just as she started to go down. Lifting her in his arms, he felt her weight like a robin's, her thin hair like corn silk blowing across his face. Tom carried Meg into the dim kitchen and sat down with her on the settle. Tom had cradled Meg and Patrick in his arms for several long moments when he heard a stifled sob. Neither of them had noticed the silent children filing into the kitchen. They looked up to see Rose and Mary Clare crying. Denny stood rigid, his jaw working against his feelings. The little ones hid behind their older brother and sisters, frightened into silence by the terrible keening sound of their mam's voice carried across the strand.

Meg motioned for them to come to her and together they huddled by the hearth. One little family bound by love, holding each other against the sweeping tide of events that threatened to tear them apart. One little group, left behind by a life of warmth and plenty, seized by death and flung headlong into despair. Tom and Meg encircled their children, gathering them to their breasts and hugging them to their knees. One by one, they kissed their faces, blessing them and praying over them, pouring upon them the soothing balm of their love.

They had nothing else to give them and the setting sun found them still clutching each other in defiance of the hunger that devoured their hope even as it sucked the life from their marrow.

They buried Patrick the next day, holding a quiet little funeral in the back yard under a budding cherry tree. They had gotten word to Duffy through Mr. Pidgeon and his mail boat and he had rowed over that morning to join them in their prayers. Denny had come back from St. Dymphna's with the news that Fr. O'Boyle was sick with the fever and not expected to live so they had their own funeral without him. They each prayed over the tiny body and Meg let each of the children sprinkle holy water on the little mound of fresh soil. Meg was so weak she needed to lean on both Denny and Duffy while Tom buried the tiny wooden box.

Later as she lay staring at their bedroom ceiling, Tom came in and sat next to her on the bed.

"Meg, darlin' we need t'talk."

He had just seen Duffy off in his curragh after a long walk along the strand. His friend had just broken to him the worst news he had heard since the first crop failed in '45.

"Meg, Duff is plannin' t'leave' Westport. He's finally packin' it in and goin' to America. He says he plans t'work at the inn until the end of the season and head over as a swabbie on one of the coffin ships. He can't take it anymore and his cousin D'Arcy is so thick with the Blackthorn Brotherhood that Duff's afraid he'll take the whole family down with him if he gets caught. There's talk that D'Arcy's involved in gun smuggling and that the brotherhood plans t'take out some o'the landlords. D'Arcy has been in the inn more than once raisin' a stir and carryin' on about the shame of a McGee workin' like a dog fer the likes o'Lord Sligo and his bunch. It seems Lord Sligo has hosted many a meeting with the other landlords at Duffy's place. He's got another one planned in a few weeks."

"Duff got a real scare last month when D'Arcy and his boys barely got away in a curragh before the constable came in with two earls from Dublin lookin' fer a room. It was way too close fer Duffy and I can't say that I blame him. He'd be gone now but he has to see things through till the meeting is over to protect a priest friend who would certainly be caught if Duff suddenly disappeared. D'Arcy hasn't been around for a bit and he really thinks he'd be better off waiting until the landlords are gone and the season slows down. I told him if D'Arcy comes around again both he and the priest may be swabbing the decks."

Meg lay there in stunned silence as she listened to Tom's news. She always knew Duffy was made for better things than tending bar and harvesting oysters but she never thought he'd be forced to leave Ireland. He had made no secret of the shift in the political tide during his latest visits across the bay. She had been shocked that Lord Sligo exacted the same harvest from Duffy as before the hunger, allowing him no extra oysters to eat or sell himself. After all the years of loyal friendship, the young man Duffy had once mentored on the fauna and flora of Achill Island now treated him like any other tenant.

Duffy made excuses for young George which only made Tom slam his fist on the table and storm out of the house. The young Marquis was cowed by the older landlords and their undertakers who thought he was too soft with the tenants. They accused him of playing fast and loose with his loyalty to the crown and last spring when Duffy overheard some shitegob from Castlebar openly upbraid his friend for letting the workers at the inn have more than a fair ration of meat, Duffy knew his luck was about to change.

Shortly after that, Sligo sent Duffy a missive decreeing that all food purchased for the inn must be used for inn patrons and the share of oysters previously enjoyed by the harvesters was now required to offset the rents on their homes. Since that time, Mr. Charles Bertram, the deputy undertaker for Lord Sligo's estate, had taken over the inventory for Browne's Inn. If the number of meals dispensed did not match the number of guests staying at the inn, Duffy was called on the carpet to account for the missing food. It was then that the portions served at Browne's became larger and the leftover scraps became supper for the crew. If Mr. Bertram knew this was taking place, he never let on. If there were no guests at the inn, the crew went to bed hungry and Mr. Bertram counted the unused provisions toward the next day.

Meg rolled over and faced the wall. Life had taken one down turn after another. She and Tom and their family had lost all but their home. First Maureen, then Thomas, now baby Patrick and dear, dear Duffy. She felt the warmth of Tom's body leave her as he silently left Meg to digest this latest news.

Somehow Tom, Meg and the children managed to weather the next few weeks, day after day digging ditches and begging from the fishermen at Mundy's Bluff. If it weren't for the protection of Mr. Fellowes's patronage, the little Phalen children would have been run off the bluff. People were so hungry they did terrible violence to each other and never looked back. Once a girl was found stripped and beaten for her gleanings and the one who robbed her fell only yards away, fainted in the road with the booty still clutched in his hands. Without shame, the first one to pass the grisly sight helped himself to the stolen bundle, leaving the man to die and the child calling after him for help.

The day Mary Clare vomited her meager supper and Gracie blurted out how her sister had been chased and her hair pulled clear out of her head, Tom nearly went mad with fury. Mary Clare had only saved the few fish and clams Mr. Fellowes had given them by tossing them to Gracie while she took the brunt of the beating from the woman who screamed in madness behind her. Tom's eyes went pale with rage when he separated Mary Clare's dark curls to see the bloody bare spot where her beautiful hair had been ripped from her head. His face black as thunder, he roared at the lowering sky over the Minaun Cliffs as he paced up and down the strand waving his arms. The next morning he was off to Westport in a borrowed curragh to see Duffy McGee. When he returned he was taciturn and distant leaving Meg to guess at the nature and result of his visit.

Meg and Tom saw little of Duffy in the weeks following the funeral but they were so busy trying to keep out of the workhouse they hardly realized the passage of time. The second week of June, Francis spotted Duffy's curragh approaching the strand with a second, larger boat in tow. Meg and Tom, returning from the field where the potato crop was green and lush so far, wandered down to the shore to meet him.

Duffy waved from the curragh as he closed in on the shore. He gasped at the sight of his friends waiting on the strand. Meg looked as old as a crone. Her dress hung from her bony shoulders and billowed shapelessly around her emaciated body. She had her dull, stringy hair tied back with a small leather thong but as always it escaped in wisps around her face and ears, her natural curl all but gone. She had deep dark circles around eyes too bright in their hollow sockets. The shadows only emphasized the clear green orbs and the fluttery blond lashes that framed them.

Duffy was astonished at how her beauty had intensified as her body wasted. She was sylphlike and ethereal, a wraith or a fairy creature barely able to withstand the stiff breeze that took her skirt and blew it around. He stood mesmerized as the ragged skirt was lofted on the breeze, baring her long legs to the thigh, while she stood before him unashamed. Meg's open bodice, the buttons stripped off long ago and traded for a little American cornmeal, revealed her flat bony chest and protruding collarbones.

As Duffy tried not to stare at her striking nakedness, he saw that there were huge pieces of her skirt that had been torn away and looking at Tom saw that what had once protected Meg's modesty had been made into short functional pants for him. Turning his gaze from Meg he saw that the girls and Francis too wore short chemises made of everything from Meg's lace curtains to old flour sacks. He saw in the unforgiving noonday sun the dire situation his friends were in. This family was barely hanging on to life. The offer he was bringing them was not a day too soon.

The children were listlessly spooning sand over each other's feet and hardly looked up when Duffy called out to them. Only Francis and the older girls had enough energy to run to the shore and greet their old friend. He saw the hollow cheeks and dark circles on the children's faces too. Gone was the little bit of plumpness they had still had in May when he had come for the christening.

These children were clearly starving. Their bellies bulged beneath their little dresses and Francis's bare, bony behind was wrinkled like an old man's as he stooped to pick up shells and proffered them as a gift for Duffy. When Duffy noted Denny's absence, Meg told him Denny was staying in the village lately with his chum Michael Creahan. He and Michael had been lucky enough to get work with a fisherman who had lost his own sons the same night Thomas died. They didn't get any wages but the man poached a throwback or two out of every haul and they lived on that. The man had given up worrying about the law. He told the lads he would die one way or another so he might as well hang with a full stomach as lie down on the road with an empty one. Meg was frantic that Denny would be caught eating pilfered fish but in truth, she and Tom could hardly feed the little ones much less a growing lad Denny's age.

Meg apologized for having nothing for Duffy to eat but he waved her away with his hand. Stooping over the curragh, he pulled out a bundle that made Meg weep. Duffy had scooped up several portions of leftover stew and bread from a meeting held in the inn the night before and he handed Meg a pot that would feed them all for supper. The sight of the meal buoyed her spirits and she sent Grace and Mary Clare around the house to pick mint for tea. Rose was already in the house putting the kettle to the boil.

Duffy had a proposition for them. The family that had worked at the inn got up last Monday and left for America leaving him all alone to run the place. He had spoken to Mr. Bertram about it and he had reported the news to Lord Sligo. He returned with instructions to find replacements as soon as possible as there was to be a meeting of the County Mayo landlords in a few weeks and then of course, the pilgrims would be coming for Reek Sunday at the end of July. The inn must be cleaned and stocked for guests and meals prepared for the meeting.

His proposal was for Tom and Meg to bring their children over to Westport to help him in the inn. They could live above the guestrooms in the third floor servants quarters left vacant by the other family. It was a poor excuse for a home but he would try to make sure they at least had enough to eat. Over the last few weeks, Mr. Bertram had tired of counting every morsel of food that went out of the kitchen and had grown even more weary of counting every picked over fish spine that came back into it. He had decided that weekly inventory would be sufficient and Duffy breathed a sigh of relief as he tucked into his first real meal in a month. With the meeting coming up Duffy knew that fresh food would be delivered in large quantities and Tom and his family could sleep with full stomachs. It seemed Duff's talk of leaving had come to naught and Tom was beyond grateful for that.

The next afternoon, they packed their few clothes into an old carpetbag and rolled the rest of their belongings into their bedding. Duffy told Tom to leave their mattresses behind. There would be plenty of places to sleep at the inn.

Tom couldn't wait to leave Doeega. He had not been able to meet his spring rent even with the ditch digging and had no plans to go to Newport to report that news. He expected Gilchrist would be on the island in a few weeks and could not bear to watch as he and his bailiffs torched the house.

He was licked, he knew. Gilchrist would make good on the promise he made last year, his mouth full of Mrs.Trent's barm brack. Well, let him burn the place. They would be gone from his jurisdiction and out of his evil reach.

Tom looked longingly at the potatoes he and the other lads had planted. They were coming up full and green. Was he making a mistake? Should he wait and see if they were healthy and good to eat? Another week would tell when the first ones were ready for harvest. He and the others had faithfully planted the first seeds on St. Patrick's feast day, calling upon their patron to bless the harvest. He had watched them blossom in the warm sun and stood in the rain and welcomed the water they thrived on.

If the crop was going to be good this year and he wasn't there to harvest it, Gilchrist would simply give his land and his home away to someone else. Someone else's wife would be watching from the window on the sea. Someone else's children would be running across the strand. They would never be able to return to their home by the sea.

He and Meg hardly spoke as they loaded their few belongings into the borrowed curragh. He hated seeing the cloud of defeat that dogged her steps from the house to the boat. She had said nothing to him about the move. There had been no need. They simply had no choice and they both knew it.

Tom had sent Rose into the village to bring Denny home. Mary Clare herded the younger children down the strand to play out of the way while Duffy and Tom dragged their meager belongings across the beach and piled them into the boat. Meg and Tom's heavy bed threatened to send the whole lot into the bottom of the sea but Meg would not leave it behind no matter what Duffy said. She ended up having to put her cook pots and butter churn in Duffy's curragh with him. Her heart ached over the many things she had to leave behind. Would they ever be back or would some other woman move in and bake in her tin oven and stoke her fire in Meg's beloved hearth?

When Rose returned with Denny his protests could be heard up and down the strand. It was almost dusk and the children were tired and hungry. Meg had saved some soda bread from Duffy's bundle and once everyone was in the curragh she passed it around. They traveled in silence until Achill was out of sight. When they rounded Clare Island, Meg looked up and saw for the last time the foothills of Croghaun Mountain and a startling thought stabbed her head with a piercing pain.

Thomas!

Letting out a primal moan and almost upsetting the boat she tried to crawl to the stern as she lost sight of the foothills. Not until she saw the sun setting over the mountain did it fully hit her that she'd never see Thomas again. She had made her peace with Patrick but there had been no time to say goodbye to her other son.

Desperate to turn back she tried to stand up in the curragh. Duffy fought to right the rocking boat and Tom held Meg down as she cried out to the fading shoreline, wailing for her favorite child, left behind. Tom held her close and let her cry, her thin bony shoulders shaking in his arms. Duffy, at the prow of the little curragh was grateful for the salt spray kicking up from the oars. The tears on his own face would be well camouflaged until they reached port and Meg could leave her sorrow in the sea.

White Dawn Rising

With life hanging in the balance, Meg and Tom enter into the next phase of their journey. Carrying their children with them, and relying on their faith and love and the friendship of their dear friend Duffy McGee, they leave Achill Island. What awaits them is a life of hardship and endless toil, but at least they will have the leavings of the wealthy travelers who dine at Browne's Inn, their new home.

In *White Dawn Rising,* the final book of the *Extraordinary Love Trilogy,* Tom and Meg face even greater challenges than those they had already met. There is evil afoot as powerful forces conspire to destroy them and the long reach of Meg's father seems unavoidable after all.

There is also rebellion brewing as the sons of Ireland once again gather arms. The Phalens are dragged into this subterfuge at the risk of losing their very lives at the hands of both the rebels and the lords who oppress them. Amid the continuing dangers of starvation, and the new threat of political unrest, there is a gentle humorous thread that weaves through their lives at Browne's Inn. Finally, they experience a stability that sustains them long enough to face the final shocking turn of events that can either ruin them forever or finally set them free.

White Dawn Rising is the story of fierce endurance. The swirling events surrounding Meg and Tom stretch their intimate love and private faith beyond the breaking point to force them to embrace their larger world with astonishing consequences.

About the Author

Mary Ellen Feron is the maiden name and pen name of Mary Ellen Zablocki, who lives in Buffalo, New York with her husband, Ed. She has two married sons, Francis and Paul. Her writing is done in her 1911 living room on a roll top desk surrounded by over fifty antique family photos spanning three centuries and two continents.

Ms. Feron began writing in high school and has primarily published essays, poetry and spiritual works. She was first published in 1985 in New Covenant Magazine followed by articles and poetry in Franciscan publications The Cord and Tau USA. Her short story, *"Sweet Gloria"* took second place in The Buffalo News first annual short story contest in 2005. Her most recently published poem, "*Night Psalm*", can be found in Prayers from Franciscan Hearts, by Paula Pearce, SFO (St. Anthony Messenger Press, 2007)

Mary Ellen Feron presents *A Tent for the Sun* as the first novel of a trilogy. Books two and three: *My Tears, My Only Bread* and *White Dawn Rising* will be available in early 2013.

Email the author
maryzablocki@roadrunner.com
Find her on Facebook
http://www.facebook.com/mary.feronzablocki
On the Web
www.maryferonzablocki.com

Non-Fictional Characters Disclaimer

A great deal of research has been done and a great number of books have been written on The Great Irish Potato Famine. Much credit for the extensive detail in *My Tears My Only Bread* must go to Ivor Hamrock who compiled and edited *The Famine in Mayo A Portrait from Contemporary Sources 1845-1850.* Mr. Hamrock gathers together in one book, published by the Mayo County Council in 1998 and reprinted in 2004, articles from multiple sources, mostly newspapers of the time, that were invaluable to the research necessary for this book.. *My Tears My Only Bread*, closely intermingles fictional characters with real people in order to personalize this terrible, devastating event in the shared histories of both Ireland and England. In fairness to the facts, I feel compelled to clarify who was and who was not really there when it happened.

The evil Mr. Robert Gilchrist is a fictional character representing the very worst of class elitism and the terrible bias against the Irish that ruled the English aristocracy in the 19th century. There were men whose behavior toward the Irish during the potato famine was nothing if not reprehensible.

One of the names, still loathed by many an Irishman, is Charles Edward Trevalyan. Charles Trevalyan was the Assistant Secretary to the Treasury under Her Majesty, Queen Victoria in the 1840s.

Under the direction of Her Majesty the Queen, he was responsible for the relief efforts to assist the starving Irish. Mr. Trevalyan was of the unwavering view that the balance of supply and demand must govern the economy of buying and selling regardless of the crying need of the poor for sustenance. Trevalyan's fear that to aid the hungry Irish would bring

England, "the risk of paralyzing all private enterprise" coupled with his strong belief in "laissez-faire" set up a disastrous effect on the Irish. He insisted on free trade.

Mr. Trevalyan is also recorded to have publically reprimanded the British Coast Guard Inspector-General, Sir James Dombrain, for feeding starving Irish paupers he had encountered in the west of Ireland. To Trevalyan's recommendation that the Irish should have formed a relief committee and used Irish funds to finance food for themselves, Sir James replied, "There was no one within many miles who could have contributed one shilling…the people were actually dying"

Worse was the blind eye and deaf ear he turned to the failure of his policies and the cry of the starving. At his order, the food depots distributing Indian corn from North America were closed and shipments were refused under his orders. Meanwhile, food riots broke out as the starving Irish watched helplessly as boatloads of grain pulled away from their ports, destined for foreign markets. Trevalyan's response was to send troops to Ireland with orders to shoot anyone in dissent of his policies.

In his Parliamentary Papers of January 6, 1847, the beginning of the worst year of The Great Famine, Trevalyan rationalized his stance thus: "It is hard upon the poor people that they should be deprived of the consolation of knowing that they are suffering from an affliction of God's providence."

All of the aristocracy, however, was not if the ilk of Mr. Gilchrist or Mr. Trevalyan. Many landlords and clergy were desperate to help the people and local relief efforts were widespread. The fictional character of Lord Robert Cushing represents the more benevolent type, while his sister, Lady Beverly, despite her "Christian" mores cannot extricate herself from the irrational cruelty that plagues her social class with the insidious negative bias toward anyone of a lower social standing.

Examples of real benevolence and strong efforts at social justice are reported in a piece from *The Tyrawly Herald* referenced by Lord Robert in chapter nine.

"That we have some such benefactors in this neighborhood will appear from the following fact: Some short time since, Colonel Kirkwood, Walter J. Bourke, Esq., the Castle, Killala; John Knox, Esq., Castlerea; Major Gardiner, Farmhill; Oliver C. Jackson, Esq., Ballina and Ernest Knox, Esq., Castlerea, privately subscribed the purchase money of a cargo of Indian meal." The Tyrawly Herald, (26-11-1846). As the article later describes, the meal was sold at cost, thus making it affordable for the poor.

Other generous gentry mentioned in a conversation between Lord Robert and Lady Beverly are Sir Robert Blosse Lynch and The Earl of Arran, both credited with liberal generosity to their tenantry. *The Telegraph* (22-7-1846) describes Sir Blosse Lynch as "[a] high-minded young baronet" and *The Mayo Constitution* (23-7-1846) credits The Earl of Arran with purchasing a large quantity of oatmeal for his tenants, "with the most benevolent intention".

By far the most lauded of these generous benefactors found in my research, is George Henry Moore, who is described by a letter to the Editor of the *Freeman*, Ballintubber, Ballyglass, Mayo, June 21st, 1849 thus: "Of all his fine qualities there is none in which he so pre-eminently excels, nor for which he is so much admired, as his great tenderness for the poor."

George Moore's benevolence was so admired by the poor he served that in *My Tears My only Bread,* Lord Robert references a story reported by *The Telegraph* of 13-1-1847. The paper reported an amazing incident whereby a man transporting flour was attacked until the crowd found out that one of the barrels was intended for Mr. George Moore. The crowd immediately dispersed and let the man go about his business unharmed.

While Lord Jeffrey Wynn is fictional, George Bingham, 3rd. Earl of Lucan, is not. He is a factual character reported to have employed the wreckers known as the Crowbar Brigade from 1846-1850, evicting extensively and ruthlessly. Despite a fairly positive representation in *The Mayo Constitution* (15-12-1846) describing Lord Lucan as "noble" after he offered to match every hundred pounds collected by residents of Castlebar with

5o pounds of his own money, an 1881 report in *"Landlords and Tenants in Ireland"*, by Finley Dunn, describes his style as "terse and incisive" and he is quoted as saying that [he] "would not breed paupers to pay priests". The Earl of Lucan's marriage and relationship to Robert Gilchrist are purely fictional.

George Browne, the 3rd. Marquis of Sligo is also a real character of history whose reputation for fairness and generosity is well documented. An excerpt from a report of his generosity is found in *The Telegraph* (22-7-1846): "May his lordship live long to enjoy the comforts of his station, since he has so humanely and so timely come to the aid of those who 'to beg were ashamed and to work were not able.' Oh! If appeals to the charity of our contiguous landlords will be of no avail, let at least this powerful example be not lost upon them."

The Marquis of Sligo, a descendant of the Browne family, lived at Westport House. Browne's Inn, as well as the proprietor, Duffy McGee, is fictional but the building where I place it still stands where the Carrowbeg River flows into Clew Bay at the entrance to the woods that lead to Westport House on the Browne property. The marvelous reputation of the oysters harvested from this melding of fresh and salt water is true.

All of the Roman Catholic priests are fictional and based on the many wonderful priests of my acquaintance. The Church of Ireland minister, Reverend Edward Nangle, did have a mission on the northern side of Achill at Slievemore and did indeed have a printing press. His presence in Dooega is purely fictional as are the characters of Rev. and Mrs. Trent and Rev. and Mrs. Smythe of Killarney.

In America, Mrs. Gertrude Fleming was indeed one of the most prominent residents of historic Johnstown, Pa. Her relationship to its founder, Peter Levergood, was real. Whether she ever had a broken arm set by a Dr. Crawford, is unknown but in this book remains fiction.

Glossary of Terms

ACHILL CURRAGH: (SEE CURRAGH) ACHILL CURRAGHS WERE CONSTRUCTED WITH A SPECIFIC REINFORCEMENT IN THE HULL MADE OF OVERLAPPING RATHER THAN SINGLE RIBS. BECAUSE OF THIS, ACHILL CURRAGHS BOASTED GREATER FLEXIBILITY AND SEA-WORTHINESS DURING STORMY WEATHER

AVES: PRAYER HONORING THE VIRGIN MARY, COMMONLY RECITED USING PRAYER BEADS (ROSARY BEADS)

BANSHEE: A FEMALE SPIRIT WHOSE MOURNFUL WAILS ARE BELIEVED TO FOREWARN A FAMILY OF IMPENDING DEATH

BARM BRACK: A TEA BREAD MADE WITH BARM, A YEAST-LIKE LEAVENING MADE FROM OATMEAL JUICE

BAROUCHE: OPEN, FOUR-PASSENGER, FAIR WEATHER VEHICLE WITH HALF HOOD FOR BAD WEATHER

BASTIBLE: A COOKPOT SIMILAR TO A DUTCH OVEN NAMED FOR THE VILLAGE OF ORIGIN: BARNSTABLE, DEVON

BEESTINGS: HIGHLY VALUED YELLOW-COLORED MILK OF A COW RECENTLY CALVED

BELTANE, (FESTIVAL OF): MAY FESTIVAL FROM ANCIENT GAELIC TIMES, SURROUNDED BY SUPERSTITIONS, CELEBRATE THE SURVIVAL OF THE PEOPLE THROUGH THE HARD WINTER AND EARLY SPRING.

BLACKTHORN BROTHERHOOD: FICTIONAL LOCAL BAND OF REFORMERS

BLATHERSKYTE: ONE WHO IS FULL OF TALES, PRIMARILY UNTRUE

BOG FIR ROPES: VERY STRONG HANDMADE ROPES MADE FROM SHREDDED BOG TIMBER

BOG FIR STICKS: SMALL SCRAPS OF BOG TIMBER USED TO IGNITE FIRES

BOG TIMBER: FOSSIL OAK AND PINE OF THE BOGS, USED BY THE IRISH FOR CONSTRUCTION AFTER THE FORESTS WERE STRIPPED IN THE 1600S.

BOOLEY: SMALL STONE OUTBUILDING THAT DOT THE WESTERN IRISH LANDSCAPE BOOLEYS DATE BACK TO ANCIENT TIMES WHEN THEY WERE OFTEN USED TO HOUSE DRUIDS.

BOXTY: RAW, GRATED POTATOES MIXED WITH MILK, FLOUR AND EGGS AND BAKED ON A GRIDDLE. TRADITIONALLY SERVED ON ALL SAINTS DAY

BOYEEN: LITTLE BOY

BREAD PEEL: A WOODEN PADDLE DESIGNED TO PLACE LOAVES OF BREAD IN THE BACK OF AN OVEN

BRIAN BORU: HIGH KING OF IRELAND IN 1002-1014. POPULARLY BELIEVED TO HAVE OVERTHROWN THE VIKINGS IN THE BATTLE OF CLONTARF IN WHICH HE WAS KILLED

BROGUES (BROGANS): HEAVY SHOES WORN BY PEASANTS FOR WORKING

BROUGHAM: ORIGIN, ENGLAND 1837. ELEGANT, BOXLIKE 2 PASSENGER COACH

BUTTER-COOLER: VENTILATED, DOMED CONTAINER USED TO STORE BUTTER UNDERGROUND DURING HOT WEATHER

BYRE: A COVERED MANGER USED TO TETHER COWS AT NIGHT

CAIONE: FUNERAL DIRGE SUNG AT THE GRAVESIDE

CATHOLIC DEFENDERS: 18TH CENTURY IRISH REVOLUTIONARIES, ORIGINATING IN ARMAGH; JOINED WITH THE UNITED IRISHMEN IN A 1796 FAILED ATTACK AGAINST THE BRITISH AT BANTRY BAY

CEAD MILE FAILTE: AN IRISH GREETING LITERALLY MEANING: "A HUNDRED THOUSAND WELCOMES"

CHAMBERSTICK: A CANDLE AND HOLDER DESIGNED TO BE CARRIED TO BED

CHANGELING: A FEEBLE CHILD OF THE FAIRIES BELIEVED TO BE SWITCHED IN THE NIGHT WITH A HEALTHY NEWBORN; USED TO EXPLAIN DEFORMITIES

CHEROOT: A SLENDER CIGAR FAVORED BY THE UPPER CLASSES

CHUCHULAINN: ANCIENT, MYTHICAL IRISH WARRIOR SAID TO HAVE SLAIN "ONE HUNDRED AND THIRTY KINGS"

CLAGHAN: THE CLUSTER OF DWELLINGS BUILT TO HOUSE MEMBERS OF A CLAN IN A SPECIFIC AREA

CLAN: THE EXTENDED MEMBERS OF A FAMILY

CLARENCE CARRIAGE: A DOUBLE BROUGHAM CARRIAGE, LARGE, ELEGANT, WITH A COLLAPSIBLE HOOD, THE CLARENCE, LIKE THE BROUGHAM WAS DRAWN BY FOUR HORSES

CLYDAGH GLYN: FICTIONAL VALLEY BETWEEN THE CLYDAGH RIVER AND DERRYHICK LOUGH

COMPLINE: MONASTIC PRAYER BEFORE RETIRING

COUNTERPANE: LIGHT BEDSPREAD

CRAITHER: VAR. OF CREATURE, REFERRING TO THE DEVIL

CRANE AND HAKE (CRANE AND POT-HOOK): LONG, HINGED, IRON CRANE DESIGNED TO SWING IN AND OUT OF THE HEARTH; HAKE, A NOTCHED ROD THAT OFFERED VARYING HANGING HEIGHTS

CREEL: LARGE UTILITY BASKET, OFTEN WITH A WOVEN STRAP FOR CARRYING ON THE BACK; ALSO CALLED A PARDOG

CREEPIE: THREE LEGGED HEARTH STOOL, KNOWN FOR BEING UNABLE TO BE TIPPED

CROAGH PATRICK: MOUNTAIN WHERE ST. PATRICK IS SAID TO HAVE PRAYED AND FASTED FOR THE CONVERSION OF IRELAND

CROAGHAUN: ANCIENT QUARTZITE MOUNTAINS FORMING MUCH OF THE WESTERN SECTION OF ACHILL ISLAND

CROWBAR BRIGADE: HIRED BY LOCAL BAILIFFS TO TEAR DOWN THE HOMES OF THE EVICTED, THIS MIGRATING BAND OF THUGS WAS MUCH FEARED BY THE POOR IRISH TENANTS

CRUASACH: A DISH MADE UP OF LIMPITS AND VARIOUS SEAWEEDS, COMMONLY FOUND IN FISHING VILLAGES OF THE WEST COAST

CURRAGH: LOW, WIDE FISHING BOAT; RIBBED AND COVERED IN HIDE

DASH CHURN: HAND OPERATED BARREL AND PLUNGER STYLE CHURN

DONNEGAL LONG HOUSE: USUALLY STONE HOUSE WITH A SLOPING FLOOR (FOR EASIER CLEANING) USED TO HOUSE ANIMALS WITH THE FAMILY IN THE WINTER

DRESSER: COMMONLY KNOWN NOW AS A HUTCH; THE MOST IMPORTANT FURNITURE IN THE NINETEENTH CENTURY IRISH KITCHEN

DEMESNE: FROM "DOMAIN", THE LAND OWNED BY THE VERY WEALTHY

DEVIL: CURSE WORD COMMONLY USED INSTEAD OF DAMN

DRUID: A PAGAN PRIEST OF THE ANCIENT CELTIC TRADITION; CONVERTED BY ST. PATRICK TO BECOME THE FIRST BISHOPS OF IRELAND

DULSE: ONE OF SEVERAL KINDS OF SEAWEED HARVESTED FOR HUMAN CONSUMPTION; OTHERS INCLUDE CARRAGEEN, SLOKE, LAVER AND DULAMEN

EAR LOCKS: LONG CURLS OR THIN BRAIDS WORN IN FRONT OF THE EARS LOOSELY LOOPED; SOMETIMES FASTENED AT THE BACK OF THE HEAD.

EEL SPEAR: ANCIENT FLAT TINED, PRONGED SPEAR USED TO IMPALE EELS

FAERIES (FAIRIES): INVISIBLE CREATURES BELIEVED TO HAVE THE POWER TO INFLUENCE DAILY LIFE FOR GOOD OR ILL

FALLING LEAF TABLE: HINGED TABLE, HUNG ON A WALL, UNDER A WINDOW. HUNG FLAT WHEN NOT OPENED FOR MEALS

FARL: ONE QUARTER OF A ROUND, FLAT BREAD BAKED ON A HOT STONE

FARL TOASTERS: WROUGHT IRON RACKS OF VARYING SHAPE USED TO TOAST A SINGLE FARL

FOOD ARK (ALSO MEAL ARK): SINGLE OR DOUBLE COMPARTMENT. USED TO STORE FLOUR AND GRAIN MEAL

GAOL (JAIL): PRISON

GALWAY HEARTH: WITH TWO STONE BENCHES BUILT IN ON EITHER SIDE OF THE FIRE

GARROTE: STRANGLE; NOOSE-LIKE

GROVES KITCHENER STOVE: ONE OF THE EARLIEST CLOSED RANGES KNOWN FOR ITS VERSATILITY

HALF-DOOR: HORIZONTALLY SPLIT DOOR ALLOWING BOTH FRESH AIR AND PRIVACY

HANSOM CAB: A CLASSIC, 2 PASSENGER CAB WITH THE DRIVER'S SEAT HIGH IN THE BACK

HARNEN STAND: WROUGHT IRON STAND FOR TOASTING (HARDENING) A ROUND, FLAT LOAF OF BREAD

HAY BOGEY: HORSE OR DONKEY DRAWN CART USED TO DRAG HAY INTO STORAGE

HAYCOCKS: MOUNDS OF HAY PURPOSELY SHAPED TO WITHSTAND REGIONAL WEATHER

HEDGE SCHOOL: SECRET OUTDOOR SCHOOLS CONDUCTED IN DEFIANCE OF ENGLISH LAW, USUALLY BENEATH THE SHELTER OF HIGH ROADSIDE HEDGES

HEDGEMASTER: HIGHLY REVERED TEACHER, OFTEN RISKING HIS LIFE TO TRADITIONALLY EDUCATE IRISH CHILDREN

HOB-KETTLE: MADE OF CAST IRON OR COPPER, DESIGNED WITH POURING SPOUT

HOOKER: FISHING BOAT

HUNDRED-EYE-LAMP: PRIMITIVE, HANDLED LANTERN WITH HOLES PIERCED ALL OVER TO SHED LIGHT

JENNY LIND: SMALL HARD TOPPED BUGGY COMMONLY USED AS A CAB TO TRANSPORT 1 OR 2; NAMED FOR THE BELOVED SWEDISH SINGER

KEEPING ROOM: SMALL, MULTI-PURPOSE ROOM OFF THE KITCHEN. OFTEN USED TO GIVE BIRTH

KOHL: TRADITIONALLY USED IN THE MIDDLE EAST, EYE PAINT MADE OF SOOT OR ASH

LANDEAU: FOUR WHEELED, SPLIT HOODED CARRIAGE WITH TWO SEATS ACROSS FROM EACH OTHER, DRAWN BY TWO HORSES

LIMPITS: SMALL PLENTIFUL FISH REPUTED TO GIVE GREAT STRENGTH WHEN EATEN

LIMBO: ACCORDING TO ROMAN CATHOLIC TRADITION, PLACE WHERE UNBAPTIZED BABIES WERE ONCE BELIEVED TO GO WHEN THEY DIED

LUCIFER: NAMED FOR THE DEVIL, WOODEN MATCH REPUTED TO LIGHT WHEREVER IT WAS STRUCK

LUMPERS: LUMPY, WATERY, POOR QUALITY POTATOES

MACINTOSH: RAINCOAT

MALARKEY: LOOSE TALK

MAY MORNING: THE FIRST OF MAY; SURROUNDED WITH FOLKLORE AND SUPERSTITION

MEAT-SAFE: WOODEN BOX WITH WIRE-MESH DOOR TO KEEP FLIES OFF OF MEAT AND OTHER PERISHABLES

MICHAELMAS: SEPTEMBER 29, TRADITIONALLY THE FEAST CELEBRATED AROUND THE SLAUGHTER OF THE “BARROW PIG” THE LARGEST OF THE HERD. IT WAS COMMON TO HAVE A GOOSE ON MICHAELMAS FEAST

MOBCAP: SMALL, LACY BONNET WORN AT HOME, OFTEN TO BED

MORGAN LE FAY: POWERFUL SORCERESS OF THE KING ARTHUR LEGEND, AN ADVERSARY OF THE ROUND TABLE DUE TO HER ADULTERY WITH ONE OF THE KNIGHTS

MORNING ROBE: HOUSECOAT, USUALLY WORN BY UPPER CLASS WOMEN DURING MORNING DOMESTIC ROUTINE

MORUADH: A LEGLESS FIN-TAILED WATER NYMPH; A MERMAID

MOSES CRADLE: HOODED, BASKET-WOVEN CRADLE

MUSHA: EXPLETIVE DISMISSING SOMETHING AS NONSENSE

OATCAKE: FLAT HARD CAKES MADE OF OATS, WATER AND BUTTER, AND BAKED AND DRIED

OLLAV: TITLE OF HONOR GIVEN TO A TEACHER

OMETHON: FOOL

PACKAGE BOAT: MAIL BOAT

PALAVER: LOOSE TALK

PANNIE: CAST IRON FRY PAN

PANTECHNETHICA: FORM OF ASSEMBLY LINE MANUFACTURING DESIGNED TO PROVIDE TAILOR MADE GARMENTS IN ONE DAY

PAROXYSM: SEIZURE OF VIOLENT COUGHING

PATTONS: RAISED, OPEN PLATFORM SHOES OFTEN MADE OF IRON AND LEATHER THAT STRAPPED ONTO THE FOOT, ELEVATING THE WALKER ABOVE SLUSH AND MUD

PELISSE: FULL-CUT WOMAN'S ROBE DESIGNED FOR LEISURE WEAR OR IN HEAVIER FABRICS, AS A LIGHT COAT

PHAETON: SPORTY FOUR WHEELED CARRIAGE DRAWN BY ONE OR TWO HORSES, REPUTED TO BE VERY FAST. DRIVEN BY THE OWNER, FAVORED BY PHYSICIANS AND WOMEN

PISEOGS: LOCAL SUPERSTITIONS

POKER OVEN: DEEP BREAD OVEN REQUIRING THE USE OF A POKER TO PLACE AND RETRIEVE LOAVES

POLL COW: A RED COW REPUTED TO PRODUCE EXCEPTIONALLY GOOD MILK AND CREAM

POMATUM: A SETTING LOTION VERY SIMILAR TO MODERN HAIR GEL; MARACHEL POMATUM WAS POMATUM CONTAINING DYE, USUALLY MADE FROM HENNA

POOKA: AN ANIMAL SPIRIT WHOSE UPPER HALF WAS OF A MALE HUMAN AND WHOSE LOWER HALF WAS OF A STEED; THE POOKA IS SAID TO COME AROUND THE FIRST DAY OF NOVEMBER

POTATO BASKET: FLAT ROUND BASKET WITH A WELL IN THE CENTER FOR SALT; USED TO SERVE POTATOES AT THE TABLE

POTEEN: HOMEMADE LIQUOR; MOONSHINE, HOOCH

PRATIES: REGIONAL COLLOQUIALISM FOR POTATOES

QUAY: HARBOR, DOCKSIDE

RACING FOR THE BOTTLE: A WEDDING CUSTOM WHEREBY THE SINGLE MEN FROM BOTH SIDES RACE ON HORSEBACK FROM THE ALEHOUSE TO THE BRIDE'S HOUSE. THE FIRST TO ARRIVE WINS THE BOTTLE WHICH IS FIRST GIVEN TO THE GROOM AND THEN PASSED AROUND THE WHOLE GROUP

REEK SUNDAY: THE LAST SUNDAY IN JULY WHEN PILGRIMS COME FROM ALL OVER IRELAND TO CLIMB CROAGH PATRICK IN HONOR OF THEIR PATRON SAINT.

RETICULE: SMALL PURSE

ST. BRIGET'S CROSS: A TALISMAN MADE FROM RUSHES BELIEVED TO PROTECT A HOUSEHOLD FROM EVIL SPIRITS. ST. BRIGET, WHO WAS A COWHERD, IS AS BELOVED IN IRELAND AS ST. PATRICK. HER FEAST FALLS IN THE SPRING AND IS SURROUNDED WITH SUPERSTITIONS REGARDING LIVESTOCK

ST. DYMPHNA: LEGENDARY SAINT, THE DAUGHTER OF A 7TH. CENTURY IRISH KING, EXILED TO ACHILL FOR REFUSING TO MARRY HIM AFTER HER MOTHER DIED, SHE BUILT THE CHURCH THAT BEARS HER NAME. SHE WAS FORCED TO FLEE TO GEEL, BELGIUM WHERE SHE WAS EVENTUALLY MARTYRED. SHE IS REVERED BY CATHOLICS FOR HER INTERCESSION FOR EMOTIONAL AND MENTAL DISORDERS.

SCULLERY: SMALL AREA ADJACENT TO THE KITCHEN OF WEALTHY HOMES USED EXCLUSIVELY FOR WASHING DISHES

SETTLE BED: WOODEN BENCH BY DAY; OPENED UP TO BECOME A BED AT NIGHT

SHITE: EUPHEMISTIC PRONUNCIATION OF A COMMON EXPLETIVE

SHITEGOB: A MOUTHFUL OF THE ABOVE MENTIONED EXPLETIVE OR ONE WHO SPOUTS SUCH MATTER

SLANE: NARROW SHOVEL USED TO HARVEST TURF

SLIDE-CAR: HORSE OR PONY PULLED CART MADE OF TWO WOODEN POLES CONNECTED BY WOODEN RUNNERS FORMING A PLATFORM FOR BUNDLES

SLIP-BOTTOM CREEL (SLIP-CREEL): BASKET WITH A BOTTOM THAT OPENED FOR DUMPING THE LOAD

SLOKE: A VARIETY OF SEAWEED

SOOT-HOUSE: SMALL HUTS MADE OF SOD AND STONE DESIGNED TO BURN TURF ALL WINTER TO FORM ASH FOR FERTILIZING THE SPRING POTATO CROP

SOUTANE: (FR.) PRIEST'S BLACK CASSOCK

SPALPEEN: MIGRANT WORKERS WHO FOLLOWED THE HARVEST OR HIRED ON TO HERD LIVESTOCK. OFTEN USED AS A DEROGATORY TERM BY THE UPPER CLASSES TO DESCRIBE A YOUNG MAN OF QUESTIONABLE CHARACTER

SPANCEL: ROPE USED TO TIE THE LEGS OF COWS FOR SAFE MILKING

SPONC: POOR MAN'S TOBACCO MADE OF HERBS AND GRASSES

STONE: WEIGHT OR MASS EQUAL TO 14 POUNDS?

STORM LANTERN: CLOSED GLOBED LAMP FOR OUTDOOR USE

STRAW BOBBINS: PEGS USED TO SECURE THATCH ON THE ROOF

SULTANA: DRIED FRUIT COMPARABLE TO A RAISIN

SWISS COTTAGE: FANCIFULLY DESIGNED COTTAGE USED BY THE VERY WEALTHY AS A SUMMER RETREAT. THESE RETREATS WERE FOUND IN IRELAND AS WELL AS CONTINENTAL EUROPE

TATTIES: REGIONAL COLLOQUIALISM FOR POTATOES; SOMETIMES POTATO CAKES

TATTIE-HOKERS: DEROGATORY TERM FOR MIGRANT POTATO PICKERS

TENANTRY: TENANTS

TESTER BED: DESIGNED WITH CANOPY BUT NO SIDES, LOW ENOUGH TO BE COMMONLY USED IN A LOFT

TIN OVEN: A BASIC BOX OVEN MADE OF TIN THAT WAS SET IN THE FRONT OF AN OPEN HEARTH

TINNIE: TIN MILK CAN

TOWNLAND: AREA OF AROUND 325 ACRES OR ½ SQUARE MILE WITH ABOUT 50 INHABITANTS. THE SIZE OF A TOWNLAND IS BASED ON THE FERTILITY OF THE LAND RATHER THAN ACTUAL ACREAGE AND A TOWNLAND NAME IS A LEGAL TITLE CHANGEABLE ONLY BY AN ACT OF PARLIAMENT

TRUCKLE BED: A RAISED BED OFTEN USED IN AREAS OF FLOODING. COMMONLY WHEELED UNDER A CONVENTIONAL BED FOR STORAGE

TURF: FUEL DUG FROM THE BOGS OF IRELAND. CALLED PEAT IN THE NORTHERN COUNTIES

TURF-CREEL: A BASKET USED FOR CARRYING TURF, OFTEN WITH A SLIP BOTTOM FOR EASE OF UNLOADING

TURF-CUTTER: ONE OF THE LOWEST CLASSES OF IRISH PEASANTRY, TURF-CUTTERS LIVED IN THE BOGS THEY HARVESTED, CARVING CAVES IN THE WALLS OF THE BOGS AND LIVING BELOW GROUND

UNDERTAKER: AN ADMINISTRATIVE ASSISTANT TO WEALTHY LANDED GENTRY. AN OVERSEER OF AFFAIRS

WATTLE AND DAUB: BUILDING MATERIALS MOST COMMON IN THE MIDLANDS. WALLS WERE OUTLINED WITH WATTLE, (INTERLACED RODS AND TWIGS) AND COATED WITH DAUB (MUDDY CLAY)

WORKHOUSE: A POORHOUSE WHERE PAUPERS WERE TO BE HOUSED AND FED UNDER THE POOR LAW ACT OF 1838

YELLOW MAN: A HONEYCOMBED, STICKY TOFFEE, SERVED HARD AND BROKEN INTO CHUNKS WITH A HAMMER; POSSIBLY THE ORIGIN OF THE CHOCOLATE COVERED TREAT CALLED SPONGE CANDY